HER SECRET

The Promise Me Series, Book 5

By

Tara Fox Hall

Published by
Melange Books, LLC
White Bear Lake, MN 55110
www.melange-books.com

Cover Art by Caroline Andrus

Her Secret
Tara Fox Hall

In a desperate effort to halt her transformation to vampire, and stop her longing for the sultry Devlin, Sarelle willingly takes a drug to kill her desire, even as Danial prepares for the introduction of their son Theoron at a Vampire Gathering on New Year's Eve. Faced with Theo's betrayal at the eleventh hour, Sarelle must either trust in Danial to save her, or join forces with Devlin, revealing her secret desire for him.

Dedicated to everyone reading this who have never before had a book dedicated to them. This one's for you.

Chapter One

"Get moving!" I said anxiously over my shoulder. "We have to hurry today."

My white German Shepherd, Ghost, looked over at me, then buried his head back in the high grass, searching eagerly for mice with Darkness, my black German Shepherd. I walked off without him, striding fast. My feet tangled in the tall pasture, slowing my passage and making me curse. Darkness bounded up beside me before I'd gone ten strides. Ghost followed, eager not to be left behind.

It was a beautiful October day, about fifty degrees or so. Despite the dark sky, the winter sun was out, its weak warmth barely registering. Yet I closed my eyes and basked in it anyway, thinking sadly of Danial. He would never feel the sun on his skin again.

Danial was vampire. I'd met him a little more than three years ago. From the moment he'd entered my world, everything had changed.

We'd had our ups and downs, especially when I'd chosen his best friend Theo over him. But when Theo was taken right after we'd become engaged and my world had collapsed, it was Danial who'd seen me through, and helped me raise Theo's daughter, Elle. We'd also had a child of our own, a son named Theoron. Despite we weren't together now, I still wore Danial's fang marks on one side of my throat, and the choker he'd given me with his symbol of the golden fox head around my neck, its twin ruby eyes twinkling. Most of my reasoning was security. I'd been hunted by one vampire or another the last few years. Manir, the vampire who'd attacked Danial's home a month ago in an effort to kidnap Theoron and me, was still at large.

Manir wasn't what had me upset today. I was worried about seeing Danial and spending the night with him, wondering how my husband Theo was going to take it.

1

Theo had survived his overseas capture and torture, which had lasted more than a year. I'd discovered him living in Wyoming six months ago in a tumultuous relationship with a werecougar, one of his own species. We'd married soon after, and he'd returned to New York with me, going back into business with Danial. But what had seemed so simple had quickly become a mess of epic proportions.

Elle had a hard time accepting Theo's return. Danial was her dad as far as she was concerned, and she didn't want another. Theo and she had grown closer in the months that he'd been back, but she still favored Danial.

Theoron had remained with Danial when Theo and I moved back into my old house. I could hold my son now, and he no longer tried to bite me for my blood, but he was still aging much quicker than a human child, faster even than Elle was as a werecougar. He was the only dhamphir known to exist. Vampires were sterile by nature. Though a potion existed that had been formulated to let male ones become fertile, it almost never resulted in a pregnancy, and had never before worked well enough to produce a child. Because of Danial's success with me, many vampires were now very interested in our baby and me.

One of those was Devlin, Danial's brother. When he'd saved me from an evil gangster a month ago, sustaining wounds I'd given him blood to heal, he'd turned on me, seducing me with the threat of force. Sometime in that day we'd spent in pleasure, he'd fallen in love, or so he swore. He was in South America now, waiting for me to join him wearing the choker he'd sent me. But I wasn't going, even though the thought of him still weakened me with desire.

Aside from the fact it was morally wrong, I couldn't risk it. I'd developed symptoms of turning in the last month, either from the years with Danial, the intense lovemaking with Devlin, or some mix of the two. What that meant was I'd become afflicted with wantonness as soon as I was around a vampire, my body's only thought on how to finish the turning process. Worse, any vampire capable of turning me was also drawn to me in this state. A week ago that had become apparent, when uncontrollable desire struck Danial and I, compelling us not only to have sex but exchange blood.

Afraid, we'd consulted Terian, Danial's half-demon sorcerer. He'd suggested weekly sessions for me with Danial, and round the clock guards, so I'd not be able to find any unscrupulous vampires to bed or give my blood to. Danial himself would sate my desires with sex while making sure not to exchange any blood or bodily fluids with me. Supposedly, I'd change back fully to human when enough time had passed, though the actual time span wasn't known for certain.

Theo wasn't happy about this at all, but I'd told him I was going ahead with it. Tonight he was going to give me his answer on whether he was going to stay with me, or wanted a separation. I wasn't worried, upsetting as that option was to me. Danial had already asked me to stay with him if Theo left. We'd gotten through something similar years ago when I was pregnant, and I had faith in him…

I put my foot squarely in a mud puddle. Swearing under my breath, I yelled again for the dogs. "Hurry up, guys!" They bounded up beside me, and then passed by, trotting alertly down the woodland path. I followed them, trying to let the peacefulness of my surroundings calm me down.

The forest was serenely beautiful. The last leaves had fallen in a huge rainstorm last night, and the cloudy sky could be seen through their bare branches. Instantly the blue reminded me of Theo's eyes. I let out a sigh.

Asking my husband for permission to bed his best friend made me ashamed, no matter the reason was logical. But what worried me most was that this crisis I was going through would drive Theo back into the arms of Aspen, the woman I'd found him with in Wyoming. My only relief was in knowing that the other woman he loved named Tasha was already the wife of someone else, and with the way he'd left things with Aspen, she was unlikely to ever take him back.

Ghost came running up. He was carrying a soggy mouse nest in his mouth. "Drop it," I said and kept walking. He promptly did, then picked it up again when he thought I wasn't looking. I smiled, despite myself, then the smile dropped from my face. I was home.

Resolute, I crossed the yard and walked up the steps. Theo was there waiting for me, his expression serious. "Can you come inside?" he said.

"Sure," I said uneasily, and followed him in. I gave the dogs each a Cheweez, and then sat beside him on the couch, tense as a spring.

"Sarelle—" Theo began.

He was using my whole name, not my nickname. This was probably going to be bad. I steeled myself.

"I thought a lot about this, and I don't want to share you. When we first got together, I told you I only had one condition, that you be only with me." He took a breath and let it out. "But I understand this isn't you wanting him, not the real you, anyway. This is something you don't have any control over. Most of all, I get that unless I say yes, it's going to be the end of us."

I wanted to sigh with relief, but didn't dare say anything yet.

"You'd go back to Danial if I said I couldn't handle this, wouldn't you?"

"Yes," I said uneasily. "I can't stop what's happening to me. He's the only vampire I know I can trust."

"Strange you don't include Devlin in that, since he saved you," Theo replied, curious. "But then I still don't really trust him either, no matter how good he's acted lately."

"I don't trust him," I said, carefully keeping my voice very neutral. "Besides, he's in another country." Thank God.

Theo nodded. "I'll take care of the dogs while you're gone Saturday nights." He reached out and grabbed my hand. "But I have some conditions, Sar, that I want you to abide by."

I nodded. "Go on."

"The vampire virus evolved with the side effect you're going through now to ensure humans who are partly turned don't stay that way, that they become full vampires. I know Danial agreed not to take your blood, or have unprotected sex. But if his resolve fails, I want you to tell me immediately. I don't want you to become vampire, or get any closer to turning."

"Neither do I. What else?"

"I want you to go to Dr. Camlyn at least every other week to keep track of the virus in your system. If it increases at all, you two are to stop seeing each other. And when you are fully back to human, I want you to stop spending Saturday nights with him."

I nodded again. "That's the plan, and he knows that, too."

Theo squeezed my hand. "If you become pregnant with our child, Sar, I won't let you go to him like this, no matter if you're still partly turned. I don't care if it's safe or not."

Birthing Theoron had hurt me inside, but being partly turned, I was healing slowly with the help of the vampire virus. It was my dearest hope that the virus wouldn't finish the process before I'd gone back to human, because I'd decided I didn't want any more children, no matter that Theo did. "I'm on the pill," I said quickly. "Besides, Dr. Camlyn told me it's not possible yet."

"I know that," Theo said, nodding. "But there's always a possibility."

There wasn't, but I nodded anyway. "Anything else?"

"Yes," Theo said. "I don't want you being intimate with him at his house when I'm around. You can stay over on the Fridays that you work for the night, or on Saturday nights, and have one of the other bodyguards drive you back the following morning. Also, I need to know how often you're going to be gone. I don't know what you've planned with Danial, if you're going once every two weeks, or once a week. I care more that you're honest, so don't say it'll be less if you're going to need more."

"Once a week?" I offered. "Then as the virus ebbs in my blood, most likely less. I don't know, honestly. We aren't even sure this will work. Terian was very vague when he suggested this."

Theo nodded. "I get that. The last thing, and the most important, is that I don't want you coming back to me smelling of sex with him. Shower and change into clothes that you haven't been wearing for him. Can you do that for me?"

Agreeing to the last made me feel like what I was doing was dirty. That made me angry for a moment, then the anger was replaced by despair. This situation was repugnant, and it would soil me in a way I couldn't wash off. But the worst thing was I had no choice. "Yes."

"I can smell you're sad," Theo said, pulling me into his arms. "I'm sorry that you have to go through this at all." He kissed me affectionately, and then pulled back to look in my eyes. "I feel I should warn you that I'm going to go a little crazy this first time you leave. The night's going to be hell, stuck here alone while you're there with him in bed..." Theo stopped, the jealously already thick in his voice, and then started again. "Please forgive me for what I'm going to say."

I waited, but he didn't speak. "Um, you were saying?"

"That I'm going to say things I probably shouldn't. I want you to know now that I won't mean them. I'll try not to say them in the first place. But if something slips out, just ignore it."

Was he going to call me 'vampire's whore' or something like that? I didn't want to ask. "I'll try."

"I'm going to call Danial now and tell him these same conditions," Theo said. "If he agrees to them, I'll bring you the phone to arrange tonight."

I nodded, despair flooding me again.

Theo went in the other room. I watched some TV, trying not to think about what he was saying to Danial. About ten minutes later, Theo came in and wordlessly handed me the phone. Then he went to the door, and called Ghost. Ghost didn't need a second invitation; he bounded to the door. Theo quickly let him out, then turned to me, his eyes anguished.

"I'm going for a walk, Sar."

I opened my mouth to say something, but he left before I could, slamming the door behind him. I closed my eyes, tears threatening and took a few deep breaths. Then I put the phone to my ear. "I'm here," I said, trying to sound normal.

"I know he's upset," Danial said gently. "Are you okay?"

"Yes. But this isn't easy."

"No, it isn't," Danial said, and sighed. "You and I already talked about Saturday nights, which Theo confirmed. Most weeks that will be fine for me. I cleared out all of them for this coming month."

"What's your plan for how to handle Elle? Theoron is so young he's likely not to notice."

"She's going to spend Saturday nights with the foxes at the

werecompound. Cia will be watching over Theoron at night, as she has been. Terian will be on guard duty."

"When do you want me to come…um, arrive?" I blushed, cringing at my choice of words.

"Arrive before dusk," Danial answered, amused. "About three or so. You need to get some sleep, Sar. This first time will likely be the worst, and I'm not sure what's going to happen. I think it's best if we leave plenty of time."

"Okay," I said, trying to sound brave. "I'll be there."

"I'll see you then," Danial said. "A client has been waiting on hold to talk to me now for a good fifteen minutes. I've got to get back to him before he hangs up."

"I'll see you tomorrow, then. Good-bye."

"I love you, Sar. Good-bye for now," Danial said tenderly, then hung up.

Hanging up the phone, I decided impulsively to take a bath. Theo would be gone at least an hour in his mood. I needed to make the most of my time alone, not sit here feeling sorry for myself. Besides, it would give me a chance to sing, something I did too seldom lately.

As I ran the water, I hummed a few songs, then began "Think of Me" as I sank contentedly into the warm water. Darkness lay beside the tub, her eyes watching me intently.

"He improved my voice a lot," I told her with a sigh when I'd finished. "Why did he have to be such a bastard?"

Darkness didn't answer, her eyes still locked on me. I lay back in the water, suddenly disgruntled despite all the happy bubbles all around me. As much as I wanted to stop thinking about how I'd acted with Devlin and all that he'd made me feel, the merest thought of him always brought my memories back in living, vivid color. Then all I wanted was to be back there with him as he sang to me and loved me with his masterful touch. I wanted to see him again, see those golden eyes of his that I loved so much…

I shifted uneasily. Guilt lay heavily on me as it usually did in these stolen moments. Anger welled up at the unfairness; right now, I was just a woman who'd enjoyed a man and wanted to remember him. I pushed the remorse away defiantly, letting my memories flood in.

Devlin's eyes had been filled with fire and lust, no matter how many times we'd coupled, their radiance undimmed. But they had been most beautiful at the night's end, when he'd declared his love for me so passionately. I closed my eyes, remembering his kisses, the brush of his fangs over my skin, the whisper of his words as he quoted me poetry, the feel of his body in mine, caressing me so skillfully…

I let out a long wistful sigh. Then I got out of the tub and went to the bathroom mirror, and pulled out a small vial. Settling back in the tub, I inhaled deeply, shivering in pleasure.

I'd never attributed any particular scent to Devlin. In the time I'd spent with him, I'd either been too nervous, scared, pissed off, or in the case of our interlude, overwhelmed with the many other wonderful things I was experiencing to notice one. But when I'd been in the midst of a craft fair with Elle and my mother two days ago, I'd known the singular scent instantly.

It had taken the better part of a half hour to search though the table of scented candles and essential oils where the smell was coming from. Part of that was my instinct to first try scents I considered sexy, like musk, sandalwood, leather, and even Danial's particular scent, which was like spicy nutmeg and cedar. It wasn't until I'd given up on the candles and reached the more unlikely named oils that I found what I was looking for: Myrtlewood.

I'd held the vial in my hands, knowing it was a mistake to buy it. I wanted to so badly, desperately. So I had taken one last smell, then reluctantly put it back. Later that day, as we were leaving, my mother had surprised me with the vial as a present.

"I could see you liked it," she said with a smile, handing me the package. "I know they're overpriced, but it's only money."

"Thanks," I said, grabbing the bag in my eagerness. "You shouldn't have."

The clock chimed in the other room. Reluctantly, I conceded it was past time for bed. I put the vial back, pulled the bathtub's plug, and put on pajamas. Then I stoked the fire, loading on enough logs to last until morning. The nights were cold now, with winter almost here.

When I let out Darkness, my large black cat, Cavity, was waiting on the stoop.

"What are you doing out there?" I asked him. "Theo must have let you out by accident. Get in here."

Cavity didn't need a second invitation. He dashed inside and curled up near the wood stove next to a sprawled out and sleeping Jess, my black and white cat of the same age.

I let in Darkness and then turned off the lights, leaving one on for Theo out of affection rather than need. He had an animal's night vision, and could see in the dark as well as our pets could. I smiled, thinking of the evening we'd first met, when he'd been wearing sunglasses at night. Sure, he was impulsive, and quick to anger. Yet he was also very easy to love.

As I lay in bed waiting to sleep, I thought back over how we'd first been drawn together years ago. A shared, magically-induced dream had started it, the catalyst a kiss. Still, we'd remained apart, not knowing we'd each shared the dream. After Danial and I had split months later, and he'd moved on to an old rival of mine, Terian had admitted dosing me with a spell that made a shared dream possible. When I'd called Theo to tell him what had happened to us, he'd come to me. It was that same, shared dream Terian had recreated last Spring that had called Theo back to me, causing him to split up with Aspen. We'd married that same morning.

I smiled again, thinking of those few days I'd spent with him out West. They had been uncomplicated, just him and me, sun and sex with the mountains all around us. I wanted to be back there now. But perhaps the reason those days had been so good was that they hadn't lasted long. They had taken on a golden quality for me, as the dreams we'd shared did.

I looked over at the dresser. The cougar Theo had carved for me was there, in front of it the carving he had done of me naked, my hair falling down around my body to cover me. Though they'd been carved years apart, I always thought of them as a two-piece sculpture, The Woman and The Cougar. Strange, I never remembered to tell him that...

As I eased into sleep, Theo came in. But he didn't speak and neither did I.

* * * *

The next morning passed quickly. I slept late, then spent much of the remaining time making chili. As soon as I began chopping up the meat, Theo appeared.

"Chili?" he said, scenting the air. "Texas Red?"

"Of course," I said, giving him a smile. "I wanted to make you something for dinner later. Do you want breakfast?" Glancing at the clock, I amended, "or lunch?"

"I'll wait for dinner," he replied. "I'm not that hungry."

This was a first. I looked at him questioningly.

"I had a few pounds of meat last night," he said, looking guilty.

I knew what that meant. I took a slow burn, but tried to control my anger. "Theo, we've been over this," I said, angry and anxious. "You know it's not safe for you to change here, at least not outside the barn. All you need are some assholes jacking deer to see you, and they'll put a few rounds in you just from sheer excitement."

Theo opened his mouth, but I held up my hand. "I know, I know, they won't kill you. But they'll tell all their friends that they saw you. There will be a mass of hunters here then, shooting at everything—"

"I know," Theo said patiently. "I didn't change outside. I helped Ghost to catch a few rabbits, and then we went into the barn and ate them together. I changed inside the barn, Sar."

Though grossed out by the idea of consuming a whole raw rabbit, much less a few, I kept a straight face. Theo needed raw meat as part of his diet to be healthy, being were. Elle was the same way. Still, there was no getting around my jumping the gun. "I'm sorry for accusing you."

I moved meat around so I could brown more of it. "I'm just worried and nervous—"

"It's okay," Theo said, hugging me. "I know how anxious you are. I'm the same way."

I leaned against his strong body, and tried to relax.

"Sar, is there enough meat here?" he added, measuring the piles with his eyes.

"It's six pounds worth, what the recipe calls for," I said patiently. "You want more?"

"I think you should add more," he said, giving me hopeful teasing eyes.

I raised an eyebrow at him very slightly. "How much more?"

"Say another two pounds?" he replied, an optimistic smile on his face.

I laughed, and then got out more meat. "Fine, you chop it up."

"Sure. Hand me that knife."

In a half hour, the meat was all browned, and the chili was simmering nicely. Glancing at the clock, I saw it was after eleven. If I left at two, I'd get there a little before three.

I turned to Theo. "I've got about three hours. Do you want to watch a movie?"

"Sure. Let's watch *V for Vendetta*."

I resisted the urge to groan. Theo knew that movie by heart now, even quoting some of the lines to me when we watched it together. Still, he was making an effort. "Sure."

As we watched, I contemplated the similarities between V and Theo. They both had scars from torture, and like V, Theo always was armed with both weapons and a plan. But the most comparable thing was their aptitude for revenge.

There was so much about my life and his that would have been different, if not for his being taken from me for those years. We'd have been married for over two years, not just six months. I wouldn't have had Theoron with Danial. Subsequently, vampires wouldn't be hunting me, thinking I was the answer to a question that had plagued them for ages...

I shuddered at that, and dropped the whole mental conversation, and got myself back into the movie. "I wish I had her strength, her fortitude," I said, referring to the heroine.

"You do," Theo said lovingly, with a touch of pride. "You never give in, either."

I felt a momentary stab of guilt, thinking how I'd given in to Devlin. "What do you like about this movie best?" I said quickly.

Theo took a moment before answering. "That V holds the course," he said finally. "He never gives up, though it takes him many years. And also the idea that ideals and revenge are worth dying for."

I'd thought that might be it. I was sorry I'd asked. "I think it's sad. She could've been with him, if only he'd worn armor. He'd planned everything else out so well, he should have found a way for a happy ending."

"He wanted to die, Sar. He'd had enough." There was a note of finality in Theo's voice. "Sometimes there can't be a happy ending."

The stove beeped. Glad of the interruption, I got up and added cornmeal to the chili. "This should be done in another half hour."

"Good, I'm hungry," he replied, his eyes on the screen.

Not wanting any more grim talk, I didn't reply. I'd just finished and sat back down with Theo when Terian suddenly appeared out of thin air, scaring the hell out of us. I recoiled and let out a scream; Theo was already moving, putting his body in front of mine to shield me. He grabbed for his gun, but he wasn't wearing one.

"Sorry!" Terian said with a wicked smile.

"Jesus, Terian!" Theo shouted at him, rattled. "Just because you can teleport doesn't mean you shouldn't call first to tell us you're coming! What the fuck are you doing here?"

"I'm here for Sar," Terian said, with an apologetic look. "Danial said this was the safest way. No worries about her getting in an accident on the way, or anyone trying to grab her."

I narrowed my eyes. Danial had sent Terian to teleport me so he'd have me for those two extra hours I wouldn't be traveling.

"That's bull. He just wants her with him that much longer," Theo growled.

"Hey, I just follow orders, same as you," Terian said mildly. Then he looked at me.

"And this is safer, really. If this is going to be a regular thing on Saturdays, anyone looking to take Sar would know her trips by truck to and from Danial's house would be the best time to grab her."

"You're right," I said, nodding. "We can do it this way from now on."

"I'm just sorry I didn't fry that vampire when I reduced his home to ashes weeks ago," Terian replied. "But no one's seen him since the attack a month ago. Danial's put out a contract on his life, but we've had no takers. Nothing's surfaced about his whereabouts."

"I'm going to collect on that bounty," Theo said evilly. "Soon as he raises his head out of the dirt."

"Sar, are you ready?" Terian asked bluntly.

"I can leave here at two or so, but not before," I said firmly. "Theo and I were just going to eat a late lunch, and then walk the dogs. Danial told me to get there at three."

"Why don't you stay for lunch, Terian?" Theo said, flashing a satisfied smile. "Sar made a ton."

"Sure," Terian said, dialing his phone. "Brace yourselves, though. Danial's not going to be pleased. He was ready for Sar about five minutes ago."

Uneasy at his wording, I got up, and began dishing out the food as Terian called Danial. He hung up shortly after, his expression irritated. "He said to be there as soon as we could."

"Three is fine," Theo said, handing Terian his plate. "Take your time and have seconds."

"Since you're both hungry, I'll save time and walk the dogs," I said quietly to Theo. I left the room and began putting on my jacket.

"Wear your vest, if you're going out alone," Theo reminded me. "And don't go far."

"I won't," I replied neutrally, then grabbed my bulletproof vest. Grimacing at its added weight, I strapped it on, then put my jacket on over it. "Come on, guys."

Ghost and Darkness surged out the open door, running down the stairs. I walked after them, my mind burning through question after question.

What if this situation eventually broke Theo and me up? He was already jealous. How would he act if I needed Danial more than once a week? Worse, what if I asked Danial to bite me again? Would he have enough self-control not to, no matter what I said or did? Unlike Devlin, I knew which of Danial's buttons to push to make him angry enough to lose his reason.

No matter how this played out, one thing was certain: The Lust would change the current dynamics. Danial and I had been adjusting to our new platonic relationship like a divorced couple who shared a child. With intimacy every week, we were sure to grow closer again. He was already expecting me to come when he called, as he had when we'd been together. He loved me, and he'd lost me twice now to Theo. When the time came to stop seeing each other, it was unlikely he'd let me go without a fight, which could only end with me breaking his heart again.

Using him like this wasn't fair. But what else could we do? I kicked at a rock, and kept walking. I came to the end of the field and kept walking into the forest, the dogs at my heels. Who cared what time it was? I wasn't ready to leave yet, so everyone was just going to have to wait.

Minutes passed. The bright sun, the dogs' exuberance, and light singing of the birds slowly wore down my anger, replacing it with calm. As I walked back through the forest towards home, I admitted I was looking forward to seeing Danial tonight. It might not be possible, but I hoped to have some time to talk with him before the stupid Lust raised its ugly head...

I looked up just in time to see Cavity coming to meet us, his bulky frame walking slowly down the trail from the barn. Ghost raised his head and suddenly charged him, Darkness following. Cavity froze, then bolted.

"Stop that!" I yelled. I took a step forward, and a gunshot rang out.

Not surprising, it was hunting season now. There were bears around, and they had become so numerous that a season had opened on them. Some other hunting seasons, like coyote or rabbit, lasted year round. Yet the gun hadn't sounded like a shotgun.

Terian appeared beside me, his gun out. "We heard the shot inside. Theo said it was a rifle not far west. You see anyone?"

"No. It's those New Jersey people," I said with a sigh. "They are getting ready for deer season. You know they opened the county north of us for rifles this year. There are going to be yahoos out there with 30 aught 6's terrorizing everything—"

I took a step toward him, and another rifle shot cracked in the air. Suddenly, something hit me with enough force to knock me off my feet.

Chapter Two

I lay on the ground disgruntled for a moment, then pushed up with my arms. "What the hell?"

"Sar!" Theo ran up to me and went to his knees beside me, pulling my top half into his arms as he checked me over for injuries. "Are you okay?"

Ghost and Darkness were barking, and circling, still protective despite their fear of gunshots. Terian stood over us, gun in hand, scanning the tree line.

"You're fine," Theo said, his words rough with emotion. He poked my side gently. "But it was very close."

I looked over my shoulder to where he was prodding me. A slug was there embedded in my bulletproof vest, shining in the sunlight. The bullet had just caught the vest and missed the elastic strap. It the bullet had been lower, it would have missed the vest altogether.

I sagged in Theo's arms, hugging him. "I didn't see anybody—"

"Track them down," Theo growled.

Terian disappeared

I couldn't get past the bullet gleaming there in the sun. "Thanks," I said weakly. "If you hadn't reminded me, I'd have a hole in me."

"You're going to be sore later," Theo cautioned, helping me up. "Come on, let's get you inside."

We were almost back to the house when Terian appeared, blackness oozing out of him like oily fumes. His eyes shone redly, his anger so powerful that the colored contacts he wore were unable to conceal his demonic nature. "It was a hunter," he grated out. "He didn't know he was so close to the farm, or that she was walking here."

"Did you kill him?" Theo asked, as if it was a given.

"Of course not," Terian said, making a sound of frustration. The blackness surrounding him ebbed, and then disappeared as if it had never been. "You can't kill someone for an accident, even if they deserve it."

Theo looked over at him steadily. "Did you make sure he won't have any more accidents like this one?"

"I put the fear of ages into him. I told him that he'd narrowly missed shooting me. I told him that we hunted here, and if we caught him here again, he would probably be mistaken for a deer. He won't be hunting here again, and neither will his buddies."

I took a deep breath. "Look, I'm pissed off, too, Theo. But he's right. We can't just have people disappearing close to our property. Country people are understanding, but there are limits, like killing trespassers."

"I get it," Theo said, irritated. "I just don't like it. Let's go in, the dogs are still unsettled."

Once we were back inside, I gave each dog a Cheweez and they settled down to chewing.

"It's quarter to three," Terian said hesitantly. "We should go if we're going."

It wasn't going to get any easier. I nodded, then went and got my overnight bag. It contained toiletries, extra clothes to come home in, my explosive bullets gun, and a brick of ammo. I wasn't going anywhere overnight without my gun again, after what had happened to me before.

I came back and hugged Theo. "I'll see you tomorrow."

"Go, Sar," he said, steady. Then he kissed me. It was not a soft good-bye kiss, but a deep and lasting kiss, as if he would possess me one last time, right here in front of Terian. "I'll see you tomorrow morning." He turned from me, and walked into the other room.

Terian took my hand. In an instant, we were standing in Danial's front yard.

I was already trying hard not to think of Theo alone back at the house, probably going crazy. "How do you do that?" I asked Terian, falsely cheerful. "It's amazing."

He grinned. "It's easy," he said, as I followed him to the door. "It was hard to learn, I admit, but once you get the hang of it, it's simple."

"Can you teach me?"

"I can't," he said softly. "You have to be part demon or faerie for this to work for you. This spell won't work otherwise."

"Oh."

"Besides, I know you don't really want to learn," he added. "You're just nervous and upset. Try to relax. Danial knows what to do. I'll be right outside, watching over you both."

I took off my shoes. To my surprise, he was taking off his, too.

"I thought you were leaving?"

"It's less work for Mary. I'm heading out after I tell Danial what happened."

"I can tell him."

"It doesn't matter that you're okay, or that it wasn't an attack. You were shot. Danial will expect that I report it to him." Terian moved off into the house. I followed.

Danial met us in the great room. "Someone shot Sar?" he said, enraged.

After Terian explained what had happened, Danial calmed down visibly. "You handled it well, Terian," he said finally, his rage replaced by quiet approval. "Please leave us."

Terian nodded. With a last glance at me, he left.

I stared at Danial silently. I'd had a child with this man, made love with him countless times, and worked side by side with him for the last two years. Yet I couldn't think of one single thing to say.

He gave me a soft tender look. "Come," he said, taking my hand. "I'd like you to see Theoron before Cia puts him down for his nap." We passed Elle's room. "She's already gone," Danial added. "I didn't want to risk her presence until I saw how much control you had tonight."

"That was wise of you," I said softly. Despite Elle's acceptance of Theo, she likely hoped Danial and I would reconcile. "We should come up with something, in case she does see me here with you."

We came to Theoron's room. Cia was there, just taking back an empty stained glass from Theoron. Theoron saw me. "Mommy!" he shrieked.

I went and took him from Cia, hugging him. "How old are we today?"

"Daddy!" Theoron shrieked right in my ear. I winced a little.

"Still young, but getting bigger every day," Cia replied to me.

"Say 'Cia'," I said to Theoron. "Cia."

"C-ah," he said, saying it phonetically.

Cia laughed, and took him back from me. "I'll put him to sleep," she said, giving us a smile. "Say goodnight, Theo."

"Night!" Theoron said with glee. Danial and I both hugged and kissed him, then left quietly.

"Will she be here the whole time?" I whispered hesitantly as Danial and I walked back into the great room.

"Yes, but she'll stay in there with him, and we'll be in my bedroom, unless your urge to be loved decides on another location."

I resisted the urge to grimace, or tell him it wasn't love. "Why did you want me to come so early?" I asked Danial curiously. "It won't be dark for another hour yet."

Danial pulled me close to him. I was suddenly conscious that he was wearing a robe and nothing else. "Who said we would be going outside until dark, Sar?" he said, every syllable pure seduction.

I groaned as his lips brushed my face, then came the slight prick of his fangs. Like being encompassed by a tidal wave, I lost myself.

"Please," I panted, grasping at him. "Please, I need you Danial—"

"And I, you," he replied gutturally. He sucked gently at my neck. I let out a wanton cry, then pushed back from him. Breathing hard, I shoved down my jeans, stripping them off and throwing them aside. Danial was on me instantly, pushing me back to the couch, pulling off my panties and spreading my legs. With a grunt he slid inside and began moving rapidly, his mouth latched to my throat sucking gently.

I writhed beneath him, moaning and jerking. His hands reached up under my shirt, cupping my breasts beneath my bra. In the midst of pleasure, there suddenly came the pressure of his fangs, then absolute joy as I felt them penetrate me. I pushed up with a jerk, sliding them further in, my orgasm breaking over me as I screamed out my release. Danial jaws worked at my throat, his moans muffled as his movements quickened. Abruptly he came, his fangs coming free as he gave a shout of pure pleasure. Danial pumped his hips a few more times weakly, then let out a contented sigh.

Damn it, we'd done exactly what we shouldn't have. I swallowed hard and began to shake under him.

"Shh, Darling," Danial said softly in my ear. "Things are not as they seem. I wore protection."

I gave him a look of amazement. "How did you manage that?"

He smiled sexily. "Supernatural speed and forethought. I had one in my pocket ready."

I went limp with relief. "But I felt your fangs."

"I didn't drink; I only bit and contracted my jaws lightly. You have only four shallow scratches. They'll likely heal within the hour." He grimaced. "But I wasn't prepared for you to impale yourself on my fangs. I'll have to watch that next time." He withdrew and pulled off the condom. "Come in here and finish undressing."

I grabbed my discarded clothes and my bag and followed him into his bedroom, where he disposed of the condom. "Thank you for handling me so well," I said, slipping out of my clothes. "And thank you for getting me a robe."

"You're welcome on both counts," Danial replied as he sat down on his bed. "The question is did it work?"

"We won't know for at least a few hours," I said, sitting down beside him. "And that's good, because I need to ask you something serious."

Danial's expression changed to one of mild alarm. "What is it?"

"I need to store something in your safe," I said quietly. "Will you let me?"

"What is it?" he said curiously. "I know you have a safe of your own."

I removed the manila envelope I'd brought with me from my bag, and handed it to him. "This."

"It's marked Brennan," he said. "What's inside?"

"Something I don't want to lose, something I need to keep safe."

"In other words, you don't want to tell me." He turned to the far wall, and held his hand over it. Magically, the faint outline of a door appeared.

"I could never figure out how you did that, no matter how many times I watched."

"Magic, of course," Danial said, entering the combination. He opened the door and tucked the envelope inside. "A spell of concealment on an already well-camouflaged compartment." He shut the door and took his hand away. The outline of the safe faded into smooth and unbroken wall.

Danial led me over to his bedroom's small anteroom. The fire within his wood stove was burning cheerily, the warmth relaxing.

"Sit down with me."

I sat down in front of him obediently. When he sat down behind me, I tucked myself into the hollow created by his shoulder and neck, leaning back into his arms.

"I've missed you," he said softly. "We sat here many nights like this, you and I."

Danial had built this room for me. We'd enjoyed it often in the year and a half I'd lived with him. It closely resembled the central room at my house, his wood stove the same model that I had at my home. I'd missed this too, but admitting that would lead to more confessions. "It's good to be here with you, too."

"Now that we're relaxed, what is inside the envelope?" Danial said pointedly. His arms tightened over me. "It's clearly something you didn't want Theo to find. Marking it with the name of your first husband wasn't safe enough. You had to bring it here."

My relaxed mood vanished in an instant. "Poetry from Devlin," I admitted. "It was in the box with the boots. Theo's going to be alone in the house tonight, and he knows the safe's combination. I couldn't risk him finding it by some freak accident."

I didn't mention the gold choker with Devlin's emblem of the grizzly bear that was also in the envelope. If Danial discovered that, he would not just be furious, he'd surely destroy it.

"Who was the poet?" Danial asked.

"There was a book of poetry and some he'd written himself. I burned the book, but I couldn't bear to destroy his words to me. No one ever wrote me poetry before."

Danial was as tense as a board behind me. "Did he ask you to come to him?"

"Yes," I said softly.

"Then he gave you a way to get in touch with him," Danial replied. "Have you contacted him yet?"

"No," I said honestly. "And I'm not going to."

"Sar, I know how much you liked being with him," Danial said jealously. "Don't tell me you're not going to go back for seconds now you've tasted all that he is."

I pulled away angrily and stood. "Don't presume that you know what I feel for him. Even if it was more than physical with us, which it isn't, I can't trust him. Dev wouldn't restrain himself like you just did, no matter how important it was to my welfare."

"Darling," Danial said sarcastically. "I know exactly what you feel. It's in your voice like syrup when you speak of him."

"If I was going to go with him, I'd have gone when he asked me that night," I said angrily. "I'm old enough to know that men don't always mean the words 'I love you' even when they say them repeatedly."

Danial's mouth dropped open. "He said that to you? When? During sex?"

I blushed, casting him a reprimanding look. "He said it many times."

"What did you *do* to him?" Danial said in wonder, looking at me as if he'd never seen me before.

I blushed deep red, thinking about Devlin's ardent cries of love as we'd sated ourselves in the front seat of his Hummer. "Nothing, um…abnormal."

Danial gently drew me down again and hugged me. "You should have told me this. It explains everything."

"Devlin said a lot of things that day, and I'd be surprised if half of them were true," I said bitterly. "But that's my fault. I asked him to lie to me, to tell him he cared for me as part of my fantasy. Don't put too much stock in spoken words."

"He may have lied as part of your fantasy, though I'd be surprised even at that," Danial said slowly. "Dev is always very careful and deliberate about the words he says, even when he seems flippant. In any case, he would never have lied after the sex was done. What would be the point? He'd have just told you goodbye and left."

"There was weirdness," I said conspiratorially. "He gave me lines about wanting to change, and others about how he didn't regret anything and could only be who he was. He said he was sorry for what happened, and then said he wasn't. He was utterly satisfied to leave me covered in his scent after our goodbye sex, and then called me later from the road to tell me how to cover it up."

"Sounds like he was an emotional wreck," Danial said with a faint smile. "Or a man in love."

I looked over my shoulder in exasperation. "Please."

"You sound confused, too, to have been forced into intimacy and then to be grabbing a quickie in his front seat before he left," Danial added, his smile widening. "Perhaps you suffer from the same malaise."

"Perhaps you do," I said sarcastically. "You're jealous one moment and then amused the next."

"I'm jealous slightly," Danial amended. "I'm much more intrigued that you aren't swooning over my brother. Understand, all the women he took from me over the years were nothing to him, though I loved them all. You not only remain immune to his charms, you found a way into his heart past all his defenses. This is bittersweet moment for me, one I'd never expected. I'd enjoy it more thoroughly, except that he and I have made up. There's an element of pity I've got to allow him now."

"How nice for you," I said coolly.

"Stop your sarcasm," Danial whispered, kissing my earlobe. "I mean no disrespect to you, Sweetheart. You know you're the only woman I love."

"That's not hard to believe, seeing as I killed your last lover."

Danial took a sharp intake of breath and drew back slightly.

"I'm sorry I said that," I whispered, cringing inside.

"Let's not speak of it," he said sadly.

My hackles rose instantly. "Yes, we will speak of it," I hissed angrily. "Don't you dare be sad about—"

Don't say her name.

"—her. She caused all of that shit with Devlin and everything that happened before that with Al. I still have nightmares about being whipped—"

"Shh," Danial said, hugging me tightly. "Please, Sar. I know you're hurting. But I'm hurting, too, can you understand that?"

"I'm sorry," I said, turning in his arms to hug him tightly. "I'm not sorry for anything else I did, except for hurting you."

"You didn't," Danial replied consolingly. "Please, let's not waste these hours speaking of suffering. I've missed you too much for that." He moved my robe off my shoulder, then kissed my naked skin gently, his fangs again pricking me.

I took my next breath by inches, my lips parting, my body trembling.

"Devlin's in love with you," he whispered in my ear. "Tell me that doesn't make a difference to you." He slid his fangs down my neck, gently pressing.

As I leaned hard into him, he sensed it and moved slightly back, his fangs pricking but not penetrating. "Answer me," he said seductively. "Don't you want him anymore? Was the one day enough to sate your desire?"

"I wanted him before," I groaned, arching into him. "I want him more now. But I don't love him."

Danial was running his fangs over my skin ardently now, his breaths coming fast. What I was saying was arousing him.

"What do you wish he would do to you?" Danial asked. "Tell me." His hand slipped beneath my robe and rubbed my clit gently. I shuddered and let out a moan.

Danial slid his finger into me, then gripped possessively. I let out a whimper of longing. His fangs pressed again against my shoulder, then suddenly broke the skin.

Images flooded my brain in a burst. I moved quickly, trying to turn my body towards him, my only thought to have him. My searching lips met his and I kissed him, bearing down hard. At once, I tasted blood. Danial pushed me back to the floor, his hands on my wrists as his mouth sought mine, his tongue eagerly licking me.

I tore my wrists from his grasp and reached down, slipping my hands beneath his robe to stroke his stiffening penis. Danial let out a grunt, then rolled onto his back, his hands already busy opening another packet. I moved eagerly to straddle him before he could put it on, but he was quicker. I pushed down onto his shaft just as he finished, his movements forceful as he drove upwards, baring his fangs in a wide snarl of pleasure. The moment I saw them, I bared my throat and leaned forward.

Danial grabbed a fistful of my hair, and pulled my head back. "No, you don't," he said cruelly, thrusting deeply and slowly into me. "Do you want me or my fangs?"

"I want it all," I said wantonly, lust dripping from every deliberate word. "All of you."

"Then please me," Danial said lustfully, going still.

The commanding tone made me shiver. I began to rock rhythmically on him, bringing groans from us both. Then I bit my bottom lip hard, and kissed him.

Danial went crazy, his mouth locked to mine, his tongue delving into me, licking eagerly as he bucked under me. His mouth fastened on my cut lip, and he began to suck hard in time with our rapidly speeding thrusts. With a scream, I orgasmed, writhing against Danial. He began jerking, his moans soft and muffled as he continued to suck. Then he went limp under me, and his mouth released me. We lay gasping in each other's arms.

Danial gently moved out from under me, took off the condom, and threw it away. Then he hugged me close, as our breathing slowly calmed.

I was exhausted as if I'd run a few miles, my body covered in sweat. Within moments, I was asleep.

When I came to, I was in Danial's bed, facing him. One hand was woven in his hair, my other on the back of his neck. His were at my waist, holding me gently. I stirred, shifting my body, and he opened his eyes.

"Are you okay?" Danial asked. "Was I too rough with you?"

"I'm fine," I assured him. "All I felt was pleasure."

"As much as I'd love to cuddle here with you, it's close to eight by now," he said. "Let's shower, and then get you something to eat."

I was supremely happy and the last thing I wanted to do was move. With a reluctant sigh, I pushed back the covers. "Lead on."

When we'd finished showering, I wound my damp hair up and we both got dressed. I followed his lead, unsure of what he had planned for dinner. Yet when we emerged from the bathroom, he promptly plopped down again on the edge of the bed, giving me a satisfied smile.

"What are you doing?" I said softly.

"Watching you," he said contentedly.

"What are we doing?" I amended, flashing him a smile back.

"You mean now that we've had sex twice already?" he said with a dazzling smile. "We're going to find you some food next, unless you pull me back into service. I'm not about to protest. I love that right now my body is somehow immune to the normal laws of physics. "

I cracked a smile, and sat down next to him. "Be serious. I'm worried about you."

He was surprised, his brow knitting up. "About me? Why?"

"I don't want my condition to keep you from finding a lover of your own."

"Don't worry," he sighed, running his fingers through his damp hair. "I'm not about to take another lover even if we stop getting together Saturdays."

"Why not? And don't tell me it's because you love me."

"A lot of reasons," Danial said, meeting my eyes. "Your certain jealousy would complicate our relationship. Also, I really don't care that much about sex without love. But mostly because I can't risk Theoron's life on another bad judgment. When he is eight or nine and old enough to protect himself—"

"Danial, that is almost a decade away. Be reasonable."

"Sar, I wasn't with anyone when you met me, and I hadn't been for a long time. I can stand to be alone for a while. My sex drive is not as strong as my brother's, as you've seen."

"Forget sex. I don't want you to be lonely."

Danial took my hand, caressing it in his cool one. "I'm not lonely. I have you in my life, and the child you gave me, not to mention Elle. Besides, who knows how long it will take, to get you back to normal? I'm going to enjoy you while I can—"

Danial abruptly stopped, holding completely still. "Shit."

Danial almost never swore. "What is it?" I said, alarmed.

"Do you like horses?" Danial asked, hastily slipping on a shirt.

"Yes?" I said uncertainly. "Why?"

He gave me a quick smile, and then led me out of the bedroom to the front door. Someone was knocking. Danial opened the door.

A cheerful man stood there, dressed in denim. Strands of hay clung to his flannel shirt, and his shoes were covered with muck. The scent of horses, hay and saddle oil permeated the air.

These were all good smells to me. I inhaled deeply, giving him a tentative smile.

"How you doing, Racklan?" the man said, giving him a broad smile.

"Fine, Chuck," Danial said, giving him a broad smile in return.

They shook hands. "I've brought Poe tonight, as you asked," Chuck said, eying Danial's clothing. "You going to ride in those?"

"My apologies," Danial said graciously. "I quite forgot I'd asked you to come. Let me present my friend, Sar."

Chuck looked me over thoroughly, appreciation in his eyes. He nodded to me politely. "Ma'am."

"Hello," I said. "My name is Sar. It's good to meet you, Chuck."

"This your lady, Racklan?" Chuck said, switching his eyes to Danial.

Danial never missed a beat. "Yes, she's my lady," he said, prideful. "Would you please take her outside to meet Poe? I'll change and be out shortly."

Chuck nodded, moving aside so I could step out the door. A huge blue dually—an oversized truck with extra back tires made for pulling heavy loads—waited in Danial's driveway, a horse trailer hooked to the back. Chuck went into the trailer, and slowly backed out a beautiful gelding. He was easily eighteen hands tall, very large boned, and glossy black, his coat clean and shiny. Chuck tied Poe to a post, then rummaged around in the back of the truck. Soon he was back with a western saddle, blankets, and a single bit western bridle.

"Danial usually does this," Chuck explained. "But I need to be home in a few hours for my last round of the barn, so I'll help him out, just this once."

Danial must be paying him good money to get him out here. Chuck had most likely been up since dawn, and probably had done more today than I had all week. He likely had more jobs waiting for him at home besides settling his horse Poe in his stall for the night. "I can do it," I said.

Chuck looked at me in surprise.

I took the bridle from him. "Does he mind if the halter is left on? Will he stand for me?"

"Yes, you can take it off. He'll stand still without being tied."

I slipped the halter off Poe slowly, moving confidently. He didn't know me, and I didn't want to startle him. I took the bit in my left hand, and put my finger in Poe's mouth, in the corner, finding the gap between his jaws. I opened his mouth gently, slipping the bit between his teeth, and he accepted it nicely. I slid the bridle over his ears, and made sure the strap was the right length, not too tight and not too loose. Tying the reins loosely to the post, I handed Chuck the halter. "Does he need two blankets?"

"Yes," Chuck said. "He's sensitive, and he'll ride better that way."

I nodded, and put the blankets on, folding them once, putting one back a little farther than the other. Chuck settled the saddle on his withers, as Poe was too tall for me to do it without messing up the blankets. Quickly, I gathered up the girth strap, and leaned into Poe's side. When I felt him draw in breath, I cinched it tight, buckling the saddle on. I tried to move the saddle a few times, as Poe breathed in and out, and it stayed put.

It had been two decades, yet I'd still remembered a lot from my riding lessons. "Can I get on him?" I asked Chuck.

"When I saw you standing there with Danial, from the looks of you, I'd have said no. But it's clear to me you know what you're doing, Miss." Chuck gave me a broad smile. "Go ahead."

I untied the reins. Putting them over the saddle horn, I grasped it with my left hand, and put my left foot in the stirrup. Then I pulled myself up, swinging my right leg up and over. Poe was taller than any horse I'd ever ridden. Yet the saddle's feel under me was familiar.

Chuck checked the stirrups, then shortened them both. "You're all set."

"Does he have a soft mouth?" I asked "Is he easily scared?'

"Nope to both," Chuck said. "Just stay out of the forest. I don't want him tripping over a tree root and throwing you."

I grinned. "Okay." I turned Poe and we began to walk down the drive.

It felt so good to be on horseback again. I tightened my legs into Poe's sides and suddenly he was galloping, stretching out his neck to run. I crouched over his neck, trying to move with him and not bounce, the night air sweeping through my air and lungs invigoratingly.

In ten seconds, we had reached the driveway, and were barreling down it. I eased back on the reins. Poe dropped into a trot and then a fast walk. He was certainly eager to run. In spite of how eager I was for that too, I turned Poe around, and tightened my legs around him again, not wanting to deprive Danial.

Poe and I galloped back down the driveway, tearing across the lawn. We slowed abruptly, coming to a stop in front of Danial and Chuck.

"She's quite a horsewoman, your lady is," Chuck said, giving me a smile.

"So it would seem," Danial said, giving me a considering look. He turned to Chuck. "Next time you come, can you bring a horse for her?"

"Sure thing," Chuck said. "I have another who will suit her just fine."

"Go ahead, Sar," Danial said, giving me a smile. "Ride him a little more. I'm enjoying watching you."

"Are you sure? You were supposed to ride tonight."

"I will, in a while," Danial said. "I want to watch you for now."

"Take him down the driveway," Chuck reminded. "The woods aren't safe to gallop in at night, but the driveway won't have any trips or holes."

I didn't need any more urging. I wheeled Poe around, and we were galloping again in a flash. It took us only a few minutes to reach the road. Turning him, we raced back down it, the speed leaving me breathless and excited.

"You've been wonderful," I said, patting his neck. "Come, let's walk around the yard a bit. Your sides are heaving."

After about thirty minutes of pleasant meandering around the front yard, Poe and I were familiar with each other, and he was no longer breathing hard. Slowly I walked him back to Danial.

"Done?' he said, as he came over to help me dismount.

"Yes," I said, giving both he and Chuck a brilliant smile. "It's been a long time since I rode. But it was fantastic. Thank you." I handed Danial the reins.

Danial gave me one of his soft looks. "You're welcome." He quickly lengthened the stirrups and swung up into the saddle. He looked so good sitting there, as if he belonged on horseback. At four hundred plus, he probably felt more at home there than behind the wheel of a truck.

Danial smiled down at me, then turned Poe with a deft touch on the reins. They ghosted away over the grass, trotting toward the driveway.

"Danial, he really likes to ride," Chuck mentioned, watching then disappear into the night.

I didn't reply, too upset that I'd never known of Danial's love of riding. But Danial hadn't ever mentioned it to me, not in the years we had been together. This couldn't have been an interest he'd developed in the last few months, not with his skill. Why hadn't he shared it with me?

Danial was soon back. Effortlessly, he began elegantly cantering around the yard. It was obvious he was an excellent equestrian. Poe went beautifully for him, seeming to move as an extension of Danial. I watched raptly, enchanted.

A half hour later, Danial rode back to us and dismounted.

"Walk with me," he said to me. "I need to cool down Poe before he goes home."

When we were out of earshot, Danial said softly, "I never knew you could ride."

"I never knew that you enjoyed it as much as I can see you do," I answered. "You never said anything about it, not in all the time we were together."

Danial smiled and took my hand as we walked. "We had other things to think about then. We didn't pay enough attention to one another the first time we were together, or share enough of ourselves. The second time, there was Elle to raise and we were trying to have Theoron." He stopped walking and turned to me. "I am not going to miss this third chance. In the time we have, these Saturdays, I'm going to do with you all the things I never made time for before."

I squeezed his hand, then gave him a soft look of my own. "Good."

As we continued to walk, Poe's breathing quieted. When he was cool, Danial took off Poe's bridle, blanket, and saddle, and gave him a quick rubdown. Chuck covered him with a blanket, then loaded him into the trailer.

"Next week?" Chuck asked, his hand on the truck's door.

"Yes," Danial answered. "And please bring an additional horse."

"You got it. Goodnight."

As they drove off into the night, Danial took my hand and led me back inside. "Are you hungry?"

"Yes," I said expectantly. He wouldn't have offered if he hadn't had something in mind.

"Good." Danial led me into the kitchen with a smile. "This was just delivered via fox."

"Pizza!" I said joyfully. "This just gets better and better."

Danial laughed. "I hope you still say that after the pizza."

"We'll see." Laughing, I carried the pizza and a soda into the great room, quickly demolishing most of it.

After I'd eaten, I lay back on the couch, relaxed and happy.

"Are you tired?" Danial asked. "Your eyes are fluttering."

"No," I whispered to Danial, stretching slightly. "I'm not…"

* * * *

I woke nude lying before the wood stove. I sat up, a little confused. "Danial?"

Danial walked in, his naked skin bathed in shining light. God, he had never looked so gorgeous. I checked my bottom lip to make sure I wasn't drooling.

Danial held some kind of remote up, and pushed a button.

I blinked in surprise. "Don't tell me you put a TV in here—"

The first strains of the Righteous Brothers "Unchained Melody" rose from the room's corners, enveloping me in longing, making my heart pound. Danial walked toward me with intent, his eyes locked on mine. I backed away submissively. When he was close enough, he grasped my naked arms, and began kissing me.

I hugged him, luxuriating in the sensations. My lust for him was rising, but it wasn't the uncontrollable lust that we'd silenced earlier. This was the lust mixed with love that I always had for him, the desire that was never truly silent, never truly gone.

"Are you still mine?" he said softly, looking into my eyes. He kissed me with passion, then he moved lower to my neck, pricking me gently as he had before with his fangs. "Do you want to be?" he whispered.

"Yes," I whispered back. "And it's me answering this time."

Danial bit me again gently. I tensed up, but the lust didn't uncurl within me. Danial applied more pressure, and I felt one fang slide in just slightly. I shivered, waiting for the lust to rear up, but nothing happened.

I went weak with relief. "It's gone."

"Good." Danial smiled, and then reached over, pushing some buttons on his remote again. The song began to play over, and he began to kiss me gently, then more passionately, our crescendo building along with the music as the song repeated again and again. There was none of the franticness of the lust, or the pure physical rush. Instead, we luxuriated in each other, slowly building up to an emotional climax that completely satisfied us in a way the purely physical one had not.

After, we lay in each other's arms, spent. "I loved that," Danial said contentedly. "I wanted us to make love at least once without The Lust."

So had I, but voicing that felt like the betrayal it was. I sighed and pressed myself closer to him. "Thank you for being safe. I know you hate wearing them—"

"No more talking," he whispered. "Sleep, my darling, and have hope. Things will be better tomorrow."

Chapter Three

I opened my eyes. I was warm and everything was absolutely wonderful. I shifted slightly stretching in contentment. Cool arms reached around me to pull me close.

"Good morning," Danial whispered softly, kissing me.

I tensed immediately, and swallowed hard. "Good morning."

"It doesn't sound as if it's good for you," Danial said, concerned. "What is it?"

I'm a complete and utter slut for waking up with you so happy while Theo's home by himself going crazy. I swallowed again, and brushed back tears. "Nothing."

Danial kissed my cheek, then hugged me. "Don't cry, please. I understand. Just stay here a moment with me. I want to hold you for as long as I can before you have to leave."

I blinked rapidly, then shook my head. "No, I've got to go. We did what we set out to, at least for now."

"Did we?" Danial nuzzled my neck softly. "We're two for one in favor of lust over love." His hands moved down, pulling my hips back against his. "Let's make it even."

"Stop," I said halfheartedly. "You know this is wrong."

"What I know is that you want me, Sar," he said teasingly. "Just as much as you ever did. Last night you were happy to be loved."

"Last night was then," I protested.

"You exude satisfaction and happiness now because of how good our last time was. I'm only offering more of the same love while we have the opportunity—"

He moved his hips slowly, flexing his erection against my buttocks. He kissed my neck, and reached his hands up from my waist to cover my breasts, squeezing gently. I drew in a long shuddering breath. The moment my mouth opened he was kissing me, his tongue slipping inside to taste me.

I wanted him all right, and the lust was all my own. I moved against him, pushing backward and spreading my legs deftly. The tip of him penetrated my vagina slightly. Danial let out a groan, then gripped my hips as he pushed, sliding a little further inside. "Ah, God, Sar…you're so warm…"

The Lust hit me like a freight train in the space of a second. I shoved back hard against him, driving him inside me to the hilt. Danial let out a cry, his body thrusting involuntarily as his back arched.

The feel of his bare skin slipping into me was almost more than I could stand. I began to move my hips back and forth, stroking him. He felt so good inside me! I moved faster, straining.

Danial grasped my hips and weakly tried to stop me, but he had no will to stop. He was groaning with each movement of my body, his body jerking involuntarily as he fought not to continue. "Stop, please!" he gasped. "Sar, I'm close!"

"I know," I purred seductively. "I want you to come, Danial. I want to hear you scream for me."

"No." He grabbed my hips and tried to pry me off him. I resisted, sliding on him as fast and tightly as I could. He began to shake with the effort of holding back. "Stop," he groaned. "Stop."

"No," I purred, and moved faster. "Let go."

Danial's back arched as he came, his fangs bared in a primal scream. This was the moment I'd been waiting for. I reached back and yanked his head forward, straining up with my neck. His fangs connected, slicing deep.

The effect was instantaneous: Danial's arms contracted like a vise, his hips pistoning frantically as he finished coming. Even better, his fangs were buried in me, sucking steadily, his soft sighs muffled. Suddenly, he bit down hard.

I let out a scream of pleasure, jerking back against him, another orgasm bursting over me. Danial continued to move. His penis was still stiff within me, but his thrusts were languid now, in time to his long pulls as he drank me down. I lolled in his arms, pleasure radiating through me.

Danial withdrew abruptly, pushing away from me. "God Damn it!"

As he lay near me, shaking in frustration, I came back to myself. Quickly I dashed for the bathroom where I threw up the pizza, and what felt like everything I had ever eaten. I stumbled to the shower, turned it on, and got in, sobbing, rinsing my mouth out and trying to wash away what I had done.

Danial entered the shower. I tried to turn away from him, but he grabbed me, holding me tightly under the water as he looked over my neck. "Hold still." He relaxed his grip. "You're not bleeding. The bite's scabbed over."

His words terrified me. "I'm sorry," I said tearfully, my tone uneven.

"Please, I'm sorry."

Danial held me close to him, and hugged me gently. "I'm sorry. It's my fault, not yours."

We held each other for a moment, and then separated, quickly cleaning ourselves under the showerheads. Danial emerged after me, and we began to dry off.

"I should've known better," Danial grumbled. "I spoke to Devlin about this last night. He said I had to have control of myself utterly because you would not have any."

I didn't know if I wanted Danial talking to Devlin about me like this. But that was irrelevant, as Danial and I needed his advice. "He must have a lot of experience with this."

"Yes," Danial assented. "He's been making vampires for over two hundred years."

I wanted to know if Devlin had asked about me, but this was the worst possible time to ask. Besides, it was better if I didn't talk to him anyway. "Did he have any other pointers?"

"Yes: don't provoke any encounters, which I blew this morning."

"Don't be sorry, Danial," I sighed. "You did just what you were supposed to."

"Either way, it doesn't matter. This isn't working. I think we should get a second opinion from Dr. Camlyn. As much as I want to be intimate with you, I'm not going to risk your life."

"I agree, Danial. I'll call him later today."

"No, I'll call him now." He kissed me on my forehead and left the room.

I brushed my teeth and dressed, taking time to condition my hair. My mind was spinning. I tried hard to get a grip on my situation.

All those nights that I'd imagined would be Danial's and mine were gone now. Our big plan hadn't worked, and I was right back where I started, minus a few vials of blood. *Please, God, let Stephen have some wonder drug up his sleeve…*

I sighed, and grabbed my cell phone out of my purse. Theo answered just as the machine picked up.

"Damn it." He clicked off the recording. "Sorry. Are you coming home soon?"

"No. Can you meet us at Dr. Camlyn's?"

"What did he do?" Theo growled angrily.

I lost it and began crying.

"Sar, why are you crying?" Theo said worriedly. "What happened?"

Damn it, get ahold of yourself, woman. "I'm okay," I managed. "We both are. But it's not working. Danial suggested Dr. Camlyn as a last resort."

"Sar," Danial said from behind me, "We have an appointment today in a half hour. Stephen said he'll fit us in. Terian will teleport us. Tell Theo to leave now to meet us there."

"Danial, it's day," I retorted. "You can't go out in the day."

"I can risk a slight burn for some kind of resolution to this," he replied, dialing Terian. "Tell him."

"What's he saying?" Theo asked loudly. "When are you leaving?"

"Shortly. Can you meet us there in thirty?"

"Yes, or close to it. I'll be there." Theo hung up.

Danial hung up his phone. "Terian will be a few minutes. Also, just as a warning, Stephen said he wants to check you internally."

"Joy," I said, grimacing of the day beginning with a visit to the dreaded stirrups. "While we're all gone, who's going to stay here with the kids?"

"Terian will return immediately," Danial replied. "Janice is with Theoron now, and Elle is with Aran and Aran Jr., helping the former to babysit. They'll be okay. It's you I'm worried about."

"I'm sorry this didn't work out the way…the way we were both hoping it would."

"There's no reason it still can't," Danial said, hugging me. "Providing Stephen has a solution, I'd like you to come Saturdays and spend time with me. Purely platonic, just as friends. We can ride and have dinner, and spend some time with the kids, if you'd prefer them to chaperone. Terian can bring you home afterwards."

"I'd like that," I said softly. "But I have to run it past Theo."

"Undoubtedly," Danial sighed, releasing me. "Come, we'd better get moving."

Ten minutes later, Dr. Camlyn ushered us into Exam Room One. Danial spent the next ten telling him the events of the past week.

"Is there anything you can recommend?" Danial concluded. "This is not like The Lust we experienced before. If it were, I could master it."

Dr. Camlyn drew some of my blood. "First, let's look at how much damage we're talking about. I'll be right back." He left.

"Theo's not going to be happy we started without him," I whispered.

"This concerns you and me directly," Danial replied coolly. "That being the case, we have every right to be informed first."

Dr. Camlyn popped his head in. "Sar, the levels of vampire virus in your blood are consistent with how they were last time. If you'll get undressed, I'll check you internally next." He closed the door.

Grumbling, I shed my clothes and climbed onto the table.

"It will be over with shortly, darling," Danial consoled, taking my hand.

"That's my spot," Theo growled from the doorway. He came inside and over to me, yet Danial didn't move to retreat, just watched him come.

"Knock it off," I growled from the table. "I'm stressed enough already."

Dr. Camlyn came in. "Hello, Theo. I'm just about to check Sar internally—"

"Do you want to wait outside?" Theo said pointedly to Danial.

"No, but you can," Danial replied smoothly. He brought my hand that he was still grasping into both of his, clasping it.

Theo watched him for a few moments, his eyes swimming from blue to yellow. He came to my opposite side and clasped my other hand. Dr. Camlyn watched them uneasily, then began the examination. I shifted, uncomfortable as the minutes passed.

"It will be over soon," Danial repeated, stroking my hand.

"It is over," Dr. Camlyn said, withdrawing his camera-like electronic device. "Let me compare these pictures with the ones I took a month ago. I'll be right back." He went to leave again.

"Doctor," Theo said quickly. "While you're here, can you take some of my blood too?"

"Are you ill?" Dr. Camlyn asked.

"No," Theo said deliberately, his eyes on Danial. "I want a blood test, to make sure my blood's compatible with Sar's."

"We should be able to run that, too. Let me take a sample." Dr. Camlyn quickly took a sample of Theo's blood. "I'll be right back." He went out.

I turned to Danial. "Can you go out for just a moment? I need to discuss something with Theo."

Danial caught my irritation and nodded. "Of course. Call if you need me." He left.

"Why do you need a blood test?" I asked when he'd gone. "Especially right now?"

"Because I don't have to share you after all," Theo replied, satisfied. "But before we even talk about kids, I want to make sure it's completely safe for you. Dr. Camlyn said once that he thought what happened to Tawny might have been because of Rh factors in her blood and mine."

"We don't know that I'll ever heal enough to even make it possible."

"You have the same levels of virus you had before," Theo countered. "Danial's slip might be just enough to let us become parents."

Had he let me get together with Danial because he'd been hoping this would happen? Resentment filled me, mixed with anger. "Theo, I think we should go for marriage counseling."

31

"What?" he said, shooting me a startled look. "Why?"

"Well, let's see," I said sarcastically. "You were apart from me for a few years, were with another woman you wanted to marry, and then another you were living with—"

"I didn't live with Aspen," he interjected.

"It was close enough, yet you married me without telling her first."

"You told Danial after the fact, too—"

My volume ratcheted up a few notches. "Meanwhile, I had a baby with another man, and raised your child with him. We've both been nearly killed at least six times since we've gotten back together. We both still work for my ex, who I had sex with earlier today. You think we might have some issues we need to discuss?"

"Sar, I wasn't saying that we didn't have a lot going on—"

"I'm not sure I want more children, ever," I said emphatically. "No matter if I'm capable or not."

Theo's eyes stared at me, but he didn't speak.

"Will you go with me, or not?"

"Yes," Theo said flatly. "We'll make an appointment sometime today, once I find out some names."

Dr. Camlyn came in, and gave Theo a smile. "Good news! Your blood is compatible."

"How is she inside?" Theo asked.

"Doctor, tell Danial to come back in before you answer," I said quickly.

"Sar, as I told Danial earlier on the phone, please feel free to address me as Stephen. We've been through enough in the last few years to warrant a bit of familiarity." Stephen opened the door. "Danial, please come in."

Danial entered and took up his position at my side, flashing me a grateful smile as he took my hand.

"That's a little harder to answer, Theo," Stephen said. "Sar's blood was always a little unusual. I have some early records of when she and Danial were first together. Back then, her blood shows little change." He shook his head, and smiled ruefully. "I should've checked Sar's blood virus levels as soon as Danial and she got back together, as soon as he began trying to get her pregnant. But everyone, including me, believed that even if Sar got pregnant, that it would end as it had for everyone who had tried it, with the baby aborting."

"Thankfully, that didn't happen," Danial said stiffly.

"I apologize for my assumption," Stephen replied. "If I'd checked her virus levels then, I'd have a better reference point now. The day I verified she was pregnant, her levels were off the scale. Some of that was probably the baby's doing, because of its nature. Though her blood had dangerous concentrations of the virus all through her pregnancy, they fluctuated and she remained unturned. It was only after Sar had the baby that I began to fear for her. Instead of the level of virus in her system plummeting, as I expected it to, it rose a little. It was already above the turning threshold, well above. That's when I told Danial to stop exchanging body fluids with her." Stephen paused. "Given all of that, Sar's current levels aren't bad. She's lower than she was after giving birth, much lower. You're slowly going back to normal."

I let out a sigh of relief. Danial and Theo began talking at once.

"If she's not exposed any more, when will she be back to human?" Theo asked.

"What can you prescribe to help both Sar and I fight our urges?" Danial asked.

Stephen gave me an encouraging smile. "At the rate the virus levels are dropping, you'll be back to normal by New Year's, Sar. You're mostly healed up inside. I'd guess by then you could try getting pregnant." He turned to Danial. "I checked into several options. As you know there are a few drugs on the market that combat turning—"

"Most just give the blood a foul taste while increasing the body's ability to manufacture new blood," Danial said with a grimace. "Those are similar to the blood replenishing packets Sar used before. Mostly hunters use them as a last desperate effort."

"I didn't mean those," Stephen quickly assured him. "I meant something to combat the desire to be bitten. This would work psychotropically, not just physically."

I didn't like the sound of that. "What will it do? And why didn't you mention this before, back when The Lust first presented itself?"

"We couldn't use it before because you were pregnant. The drug will take away your desire to be with a vampire and let you control yourself until the virus leaves your system. *But*," he added, "It's a trade off. You'll feel differently while on it, and it may affect your personality."

"What do you mean?" Theo and Danial said together.

"Sar will lose her desire," Stephen said simply. "Medically, you can't suppress one biological urge, and not suppress another of the same kind. She'll act a lot less driven and passionate about all of her needs and desires."

His explanation scared and repelled me. I'd never wanted to be anyone other than who I was. "Isn't there anything else less severe?"

"Not really," Stephen replied. "Humans who are turning can be very unpredictable, going to enormous lengths to complete the process. They can become violent, or sometimes even harm themselves in an effort to attract a vampire to finish the job."

"What other options are there?" Danial asked.

"There isn't much else. You can either turn her, or Sar goes into solitary confinement for the next two months. Any vampire will be attracted to her in this state, and she will be attracted to them. It won't take long for one to take advantage."

One already had. "Do it," I said softly. "I can't live like I've been living."

Stephen nodded, and left the room.

"Sarelle, are you sure?" Danial said, concerned. "This is what you want?"

I didn't want to be on drugs. What I wanted was to have Theo and Danial both, and maybe Devlin, too. Alas, life regrettably wasn't fantasy. "It's the only line of attack left."

"Say this does work for her," Danial said slowly to Stephen. "What do you have that will work on me? I can't risk taking anything that might compromise my reasoning or reaction time—"

"You should be fine without drugs," Stephen replied. "The one Sar is being prescribed will alter her behavior enough so she won't provoke any encounters. From what you've told me, your actions with her weren't outside a normal vampire's desire for sex and blood. You never sought her out for either from sheer physical need or desire, something I'm surprised at. But you also showed remarkable restraint under The Lust, so it may be either a testament to your strength of will, or that you're so new at making vampires."

"You're sure?" Theo stated. "I don't want to risk him being around her if you aren't."

"We're going to find out. Dose me," I said bitterly. "I have to do something, and this is the only option I can live with."

"I understand why you feel that way, Sar," Danial said. "But I'm hesitant to—"

"It's her body," Theo growled. "So it's her decision, not yours."

"Yes, I know," Danial said. He let go of my hand. "Take the next few days off, both of you. Theo, please call me in twenty-four hours to let me know how she is."

"Will do," Theo said. "Or she will, if she feels well enough."

"Goodbye, Sar," Danial said softly, then left.

Dismayed, I got dressed quickly. When we emerged, Danial was gone. Theo and I picked up the prescription, paid the bill, and then headed to the pharmacy at Alan's Creek.

The pills were small and yellow. The instructions said to take one every day with food. Shrugging, I popped one, and then Theo and I got an early lunch at the Chinese place in Alan's Creek. Theo asked a few times during the meal if

I was feeling okay.

"I don't feel any different. Do I look different?"

"Kind of sad," Theo replied. "But that might be because you're usually smiling, and you aren't now."

"I hadn't noticed," I said slowly.

"We can get through this," Theo said, taking my hand in his. "By Christmas you'll be your old self."

I nodded but didn't reply.

"Do you want dessert? We can stop at the bakery down the street."

"No. Let's go home."

* * * *

After we'd arrived home, and Theo had gone to walk the dogs, I showered again and then brushed out my hair. It was long now, almost to my hips. Irritated, I made a mental note to get it cut. While I was at it, I should get the highlights touched up, too...

"Ready for a dinner?" Theo said from behind me.

"That was fast," I said, cracking a smile.

"What do you mean?" he said curiously. "We've been gone an hour."

I was about to correct him when I caught sight of the clock. He was right, an hour had passed. "I lost track of time."

"It's from all the traveling yesterday and today," Theo said, kissing my cheek. "Next week will be simpler."

"I'm going to Danial again next Saturday," I said. I meant the words to come out flat and bold, but for some reason they were not only hesitant, they were almost pleading.

"Why?" Theo growled.

"Because I want to spend time with him. It won't be anything but friendly—"

"No," Theo said curtly. "You aren't going."

I felt a sudden sense of helplessness and despair, then anger surged up, drowning that out. "The hell I'm not. Now that I can control myself, I want to spend more time with him and with the kids—"

"This has got nothing to do with the kids," Theo growled. "So don't pretend it does."

"We aren't going to fuck," I said nastily. "And that's all you're concerned about, right?"

Theo stared at me aghast, his eyes flashing from blue to yellow. "I don't want you rediscovering your desire for him," he growled. "You're my wife."

Don't remind me. "I'm not spending the night. I'll go for dinner, and some

35

conversation. Most likely Theoron will be there, and probably Elle, too. You made a big deal about me not spending enough time with Theoron a month ago. Now you're telling me I can't?"

"If the kids are going to be there, I've got no problem with it," Theo said, his eyes fading back to blue. "I just wish you'd asked me instead of springing this on me."

"I'm sorry I didn't," I said haltingly. "But I feel confident that the drug will work, and I want to feel normal again. That means spending time with the kids. Danial also has taken up riding, something I liked years ago—"

"He did that sometimes out West," Theo said, nodding. "He's always liked horses. It was something I couldn't share with him. They get very nervous around me."

"Then Elle will probably have trouble, too." I let out a sigh. "But I'm sure he'll want Theoron to learn to ride."

Theo hugged me. "I understand you're going through something, Sar. If you need this, that's okay. This I can handle."

"How was last night?"

"Terrible," Theo said darkly. "I couldn't find enough to keep me busy. I brought over three loads of wood, and took Ghost and Darkness for a long walk until about midnight. They finally refused to walk any further. When we walked today, we went very slowly, as they weren't eager to go. Both dogs have barely moved all day."

I went quickly over to Ghost. Sure enough, his paw pads were tender when I touched them. "You shouldn't have taken them."

"Sar, I didn't know what else to do." His eyes were wild, remembering. "I thought about you and about him and about what you had to be doing and I couldn't stand it! I couldn't sleep or eat." His eyes met mine. "I thought about getting a gun and coming to kill him."

I backed away from him, a look of horror on my face. "What?"

Theo's features were shifting slightly. His eyes changed from blue to yellow and back rapidly, the pupils reforming over and over. "I knew it was wrong! I love him; he's my friend! Still, it kept going through my mind was that if he was dead, you couldn't sleep with him! He did this to you! You never used to be like this! I used to be enough for you! We used to be enough for each other!"

I took a deep breath, and then made myself hug him. "You are enough," I said softly. "What we have is enough." Silently, I hoped to God that it would be.

* * * *

36

I woke up the next morning to the ringing of the phone. "What the hell time is it?" Theo grumbled beside me.

I looked groggily at the clock. "Seven," I said, sighing. "We've overslept. We'll never be at Danial's by eight, not and have time to shower and have breakfast."

The phone continued to ring. Theo crawled over to the end of the bed and swiped it off the dresser. "Yeah," he said grumpily into the receiver. "She's right here."

I took the phone from him. "Danial?"

"No one let me know how you were. It's been twenty four hours."

"I'm okay. I don't feel any different."

Theo picked up the phone in the living room.

"Then can you come today sometime?" Danial asked. "I know I told you to take a few days off, but Elle's been asking for you."

"That's strange," Theo said with a hint of sarcasm. "She never has before."

"She had a nightmare last night," Danial said coldly. "She didn't tell me much, but I gather Sar was hurt in it badly, if not killed. The attacker was a vampire."

"I'm sorry," Theo said quietly. "Is she okay?"

"She's fine. She won't admit it, but I think the vampire in her dream was attacking her, too. I'm guessing this is residue from Manir's attack. She's never mentioned anything prior to this about being afraid of vampires, ever."

"We'll be there in a little while," Theo said darkly. "Do you have any news on Manir's location?"

"I might, if you ask me nicely."

"Look, I deserve that for my earlier comment, but knock off the attitude. We have enough problems without snarling at one another."

"I agree," Danial replied. "Get here as soon as you can."

* * * *

Two hours later, we arrived at Danial's house. Elle ran out to greet us, hurling herself into my arms.

"Mom! Want to go for a walk?"

I hugged her. "Sure, Honey."

Theo came around the truck in a rush and grabbed her. "Can I come, too?" he said, tickling her. She laughed, squirming all over, trying to get away. "Or is this a girls' only outing?"

"No," she said seriously. "You can come. I just thought you had duty tonight, so you had to rest all day."

"Who said that?" Theo asked.

"Brian was talking to Danial."

Theo shot a look to me. "Why don't you go ahead with Mom, Elle? I'll catch up to you."

Elle grabbed my hand and began leading me down the path. With bird guide in hand, she began showing me not only many birds, but also the tracks of many other animals in the moist forest floor.

"You're very smart," I said proudly. "There aren't many kids your age who know as much as you do."

"What do other kids do?" she asked.

Watch TV and play video games. "Waste their time with things that don't matter."

"I wish I had more friends."

"You will," I said quickly. "Aran Jr.'s getting older, and your brother—"

"I want girl friends," Elle said peevishly. "They're boys."

That was impossible right now. Elle had to be closely guarded, as she was an easy way to get to Danial and Theo, not to mention me. "We'll see about you getting those dance lessons you talked about, okay?"

"Yes!" Elle shouted. "Can I really?"

"Maybe," I said mischievously. "If you're good and study hard. Now, what track is that?"

"A deer. A doe by the weight in the press of snow, and young."

"This one?"

"A raccoon," she said, pointing to the small hand print type of trail in the snow.

"And this one?" I said, pointing to a fox track.

She shot me a perfect copy of Theo's long-suffering look. "That's Warren," she said as if it was obvious. "Now what about the lessons?"

"I'll talk to your dad about it, if you'll tell me about this dream you had."

"There was a bad vampire attacking," she said fearfully. "It was you and me alone. You fought, but he...he turned you."

"Are you afraid of that happening to me with Danial?"

"No," Elle said quickly. "But in the dream, when you turned...you came after me."

"That's all movie hype," I said confidently, hoping like hell I was right. "When someone becomes a vampire they aren't suddenly ravening beasts. That's a plot device so that characters can do bad things and then say they had a good reason for that because they weren't in control of themselves."

"How can you know?" Elle said searchingly. "You've never seen anyone turned."

"I've been in a position before when I wasn't in control of myself," I uttered, blushing. "I would not have hurt you, even then. Also, I've heard the story of how Danial and Devlin became vampire and there was no murder or mayhem in it, at least committed by them."

"You're sure?"

"Sure enough to assure you that your dream isn't in danger of coming true. Now let's head back. I'm freezing."

* * * *

When we returned to Danial's house, Theo was waiting for me, his expression stony.

"What is it?"

"Manir has been seen north of here. Danial wants someone to investigate and take him out if he's there."

"Does it have to be you who goes?"

"I want to go, Sar. He was going to take you that night. I owe him for that."

"Will you kill him, Theo?" Elle asked bluntly.

Theo went to a crouch beside her. "Elle, he tried to hurt your mom, and your half-brother. He'll try again, unless someone stops him. The best way to do that is to kill him."

"Please kill him," Elle said seriously. "I don't want him to hurt Mom or me."

He hugged her to him. "He won't be hurting anyone ever again. I'll make sure of that."

So much for his big vow never to leave me alone again. "Should I stay here tonight then? I feel fine, but I haven't seen Danial yet to test out how well, um....I am."

"No." Picking up Elle, he rose to his feet. "Brian is going to take you home, and stay there with you. Should anything happen, anything at all, he has instructions to call Terian and for Terian to teleport you to Danial's home."

"Let me down," Elle said, squirming. "I see some tracks over there that look like bobcat."

Elle ran off. Theo and I walked after her slowly.

"I wish she would let me hold her longer," Theo said regretfully.

"She's not a baby anymore," I said, putting my hand on his shoulder. "But you know she loves you."

"I know. Most of the time that's enough. But I still think about what I missed out on sometimes."

I squeezed his shoulder with my hand, but didn't speak. There was nothing to say.

We walked along, taking our time getting back, and enjoyed perfect autumn scenery. The oak trees alone retained their leaves, their spreading branches white in places from the stubborn patches of snow.

Brian was waiting for me in one of the Expeditions when we returned.

"Let me grab my bag," I said to him.

"Got it already," he answered.

I turned to Theo. "Are you leaving now?"

"Are you?" he said quickly.

My eyes narrowed. "Are you going to give me a hard time if I don't?"

"No," he responded. "But I'd prefer you saw Danial with me present."

I changed topics. "Is anyone going with you?"

"No, I'm going alone. This isn't an assault, Sar. It's an assassination."

No shit. "Be careful," I said, hugging him. "Come back to me when it's done."

"I'll come back to you," he said softly. "Stephen gave me some names. We have an appointment next week with a counselor."

"Good," I said, mustering a smile.

"Get going," Theo said, giving me a quick kiss. "Brian's waiting."

I wanted to see Danial, but maybe it was better to give the meds another day to work. "Bye." I walked over, and got into Brian's truck. "Are you sure you're all set?"

"Yes," Brian said, starting the SUV. "I've got my bags packed, and Demi knows your number for any emergencies."

I hadn't talked to Brian much since the night he'd almost died trying to save me. I felt awkward with a capital A, especially about his poor wife. "How's she doing?"

"Better, now she's living here with me," Brian replied quietly. "Devlin didn't mistreat her, but Demi understood what his plan was and her part in it."

I sat quietly as he drove, trying to think of something to say back and failing.

"Want to listen to music?" Brian said after a few minutes, breaking the silence.

"Sure," I said, relieved.

He turned on the radio. I turned the dial as he drove, finally finding a station that was playing light love songs. The very end of J. Blunt's "You're Beautiful" was playing.

I knew I should turn it off. Instead, like a drug addict that sees another high in sight, my hand moved to the dial and turned it up.

"You like this song?" Brian asked, glancing at me.

I didn't answer him, lost in the music as I sung the end quietly. "—but it's

40

time to face the truth: I will never be with you."

"You have a good voice," Brian said when it ended. "Devlin taught you well."

I didn't reply.

"He'll be happy to know you're missing him."

Chapter Four

I turned to him, gaping. "What?"

"You heard me," Brian said simply. "I meant no offense."

"Then what did you mean?"

"It's been obvious for most of the past two years that he was obsessed with you. It's equally obvious that you're now obsessed with him. I can guess what happened when he rescued you."

I went beet red, pointedly looking away from him as I switched off the stereo. "Don't talk to me anymore about this."

"Okay," Brian said, and fell silent.

We passed the rest of the way home without words, my anger building with every mile. I'd taken the high road: not called Devlin or contacted him. That meant I could long for him all I wanted secretly without judgment from my guards.

When we arrived at my house, I quickly got out and hurried to the door. Brian got there first and blocked me from entering. "I need to check it first. Wait here."

A moment later, he was back. "All set."

I glared at him angrily. "I need to walk the dogs as soon as I've eaten."

"I'll go with you. Let me call in first, and tell them we got here safely." He flipped open his phone and began dialing.

I went about making a sandwich, trying to ignore him. Then I gave a big sigh and let my irritation go. It was too much effort to stay angry, and it wasn't important anyway.

"Do you want a sandwich?" I called to Brian.

"Sure," he called back. "Lots of meat, please."

As I assembled the easy meal of sandwiches, pickles, chips, and sodas, I sang the song's refrain over several times. Turning with the plates, I stopped in mid-note, startled by Brian. He was right behind me, his phone to his ear.

"I almost tripped over you," I chastised.

Brian looked up at me, then back down, nodding. "Yes."

"Tell Danial you'll call him back, or lose your meal."

"I've got to go eat," he said into the receiver. "If anything happens, I'll report it." He closed his phone with a click, then joined me at the table. "Thanks for making this. You didn't have to."

"It's no big deal making two instead of one."

"Look, I can scent your irritation. Please forget what I said earlier. It wasn't my place."

Damn right it wasn't. "I was just surprised."

He nodded, but didn't say anything.

"You don't like Devlin, do you? The hostage-taking aside, of course."

"Like doesn't come into my work relations."

"Okay, why work for him in the first place?"

Brian sighed. "I should have checked into his background better before going to work for him. I was in love with Demi, and I wanted to protect her. He was the biggest name in the U.S. to work for then, the most feared with the best pay. At first, it was great." He ate another bite of sandwich, and then continued. "Demi was safe at his estate, and I was around most of the time, when I wasn't off driving for him. She and I were both happy, pretty much right up until the time he first asked me to apply for a job here, and told me the reason he was asking."

"Is that what you did for him? You were a driver?" He'd shown too much compassion for Erin the night Manir attacked to be a professional bodyguard.

"Pretty much. I didn't have enough experience for anything beyond that." His smile faded. "Devlin wanted me to get some, though," he added grimly.

"Doesn't he have enough other people working for him that are willing to get their hands bloody?" I asked sarcastically.

"He has mostly grizzly weres working for him, because that's his emblem. But he has others, too, and no, they're not afraid to get their hands dirty."

The way he said "others" made me think these weren't humans or weres. "What others?"

Brian looked away. "He has a demon working for him. A full one, not half like Terian. That evil feeling is present all the time around him. And he has a sorceress, too," he continued. "She can be worse than the demon, when she gets her mind to it."

"Worse than a demon how?"

Brian didn't answer, just met my eyes for a moment and dropped them again.

Oiy. "Which is his second in command?" I asked, curious.

"Neither," Brian said, visibly uncomfortable.

"Then who is?"

"I'm not going to talk about him," Brian said flatly. "You can count yourself lucky if you never meet him."

Okay, moving on immediately. "So Demi is okay now?"

"She's settling in. Everyone's been really friendly, which helps. The sorceress, Leri, was the only woman at Devlin's estate, and she wasn't."

"That couldn't be accident, so what's the reason? Does Devlin not trust women as guards?"

"Devlin likes women, but he prefers them in his bed, as you know." I flushed to my toes, and he continued. "It's because of the demon and his witch. Leri's very jealous of other women. Vince, one of the other werebears, once said that Titus put up with Leri only because she was the only woman who would tolerate his evil nature."

I cleared the dishes. "So none stay because they're either scared of him or her?"

"Pretty much, Sarelle."

"Brian, why don't you call me Sar?" I said, loading the dishwasher. "We've fought off attacks and you saved my life. It's odd to hear you keep saying my full name. "

"Devlin said if I ever called you Sar in front of him, he'd have my pelt," Brian replied. "It's habit now."

His tone made the double meaning obvious. "He thinks what happened with Theo and I could happen with you and me?" I said neutrally.

Brian shrugged. "It doesn't matter to him that I'm happily married to Demi, or that we've always treated each other professionally. He said I'd better always think of you as Sarelle, or else."

Had Devlin said that out of defensiveness of Danial, or out of his own jealousy? I'd probably never know. I flipped on the dishwasher, and turned to him. "Ready to walk?"

"Sure."

Ghost and Darkness were a little leery of Brian, keeping their distance from him on the walk, while managing to stay between him and me. Though the woods were beautiful with dazzling fresh snow crystals, I didn't notice, too wrapped up in thoughts of Devlin.

About seven, I dropped exhausted into the nearest armchair. I'd spent hours cleaning and then putting away the many Halloween decorations. Brian was napping in the basement bedroom in preparation for night guard duty.

The phone rang at seven. Instead of Theo, it was my mother-in-law, Brennan's mother, calling from Wyoming.

44

We made polite conversation for a few moments, then she said out of the blue, "We'd like to see you, and Theo, too."

She'd been accepting of my new marriage since her time in therapy, but this was a whole new level. "You're sure?" "We want to see you," she said hesitantly. "He's part of your life now. It's good you have someone again. Maybe next summer?"

Why not go? Theo and I could use a summer vacation, and we could hopefully take Elle with us. "I'll ask him when he gets home from work."

We talked for a while longer, and then I hung up, promising to tell her the moment I made travel plans.

Danial called a few minutes later. "How are you feeling?" he asked immediately.

"I feel fine. Nothing seems different."

"Good," he said, relieved.

"Any word from Theo?"

"No, but there won't be for hours, maybe not until tomorrow evening. It'll take him some time just to get where he's going, and more to discover the best means of getting Manir. Don't worry."

"There's more isn't there? Theo plans on torturing him, doesn't he?"

"Yes. He blames him for you being taken and for what he thinks happened to you later. Manir is going to pay for all of it, for as long as Theo can make it last, anyway."

I didn't comment, both sickened and oddly satisfied.

"Brian is there, watching over you?" Danial continued.

"Yes. Everything has been quiet."

"Good. Get some rest."

"I'm sorry that things didn't work out," I said quickly.

Danial was quiet for so long that I thought maybe we'd gotten disconnected. "Danial?"

"I'm sorry, too," he said sadly. "I'm looking forward to seeing you Saturday."

"Me, too. Goodnight."

"Goodnight, Sar," he said softly. "I love you."

Depressed, I hung up the phone. With irritation, I suddenly remembered I'd forgotten to get the mail. Getting it myself was right out, too. If my life was a novel, this would be the part where I got grabbed by Manir, who had somehow found out where I lived.

I went downstairs and got Brian up.

"Sorry for sleeping so long. I covered for Terian yesterday night and had just got to bed when Theo got me up to come with—"

"Why did Terian need you to cover for him?" I interrupted.

"He said he had a date."

I almost fell over in surprise. "He had a date?"

Brian laughed. "You act like the man's a hermit."

I gave him a look that said that description wasn't far off. "Do you know who it was?"

"No," he said. "But he said he could trust her. I think they've been seeing each other for a while now."

God, let him not have gotten back together with Sundown. She'd broken his heart once already. Suddenly I got shivers: I might have this woman to thank for my life. "Wait, I remember now. He said that night Manir attacked that he had to be somewhere later to be. That's why he couldn't go with Danial and Theo had to go instead. Was it this—?"

"I can't answer that," Brian said politely yet firmly. "I'll go get the mail. You stay here."

I followed him upstairs grumpily. *It was okay to discuss my love life, but not Terian's?*

Brian was back in a few moments. "I'm going to watch from the window here," he said, handing me the mail.

"Thanks," I said civilly. "I'm heading to bed."

I braced myself for some comment about dreams of Devlin as I walked away, but there wasn't one.

* * * *

When I got up at six the next morning, Theo hadn't returned. I put on a robe, and went out to see Brian. He was still in position near the window.

"Good morning," he said politely.

"You can get some sleep if you want. I'm going to stay up."

"Thanks," he said, rising stiffly from his chair. "I'm exhausted."

"I'll let you know if anyone shows up, or if someone calls for you."

"No need for the latter," he called back, heading downstairs. "I have my cell on."

Relieved there would be no awkward discussions this morning, I went about my day. After taking care of the dogs and cats, I showered and set about baking apple pies: one for Brian to take home in thanks, and the other for Theo. I was just removing them from the oven when Theo called.

"I got him, Sar," he murmured, tired but contented.

Twin waves of relief hit me that Theo was okay, and Manir was dead. "Where are you?"

"Right outside," he said. "I'm messy, though. I need you to put some towels down."

I knew what he wanted. "Okay. Bye."

Hastening to the front door, I laid down two layers worth of towels that were usually for wiping the dogs' feet. Then I opened the door. Theo stood there looking as if he had come from a slaughterhouse. There was blood in spatters, splashes and huge patches in his hair, on his face, and even in his eyelashes.

I let him inside, closed the door, then held out my hands. "Give me your clothes."

He took them off and handed them to me, including his sneakers. "You can try washing them, but they might have to be thrown out. Where is Brian?"

"Downstairs sleeping. He just went down about a half hour ago."

He nodded once. "Good. I'm going to shower."

"Is your truck a mess?"

"No, I put down a plastic sheet on the seat before I got in, and wiped my hands off with some wet naps. If the bastard hadn't been in an abandoned house, I'd have washed up before leaving. I don't like you seeing me like this."

"This isn't the first time," I replied, taking his clothes, the towels, and his sneakers into the laundry room. I sprayed the bloodstains liberally with stain remover, then set everything to washing.

A strange mood abruptly came over me; I decided to join Theo in the shower. With all the blood on him, he'd likely welcome a little help getting it off...

Quickly, I shed my clothes and then hurried into the bathroom. "Want some company?"

"You have to ask?"

I slid back the curtain, and got in. Theo turned to me, shampoo still in his hair, and gave me a hungry look. Then he wrapped me in his arms, and kissed me. I ran my hands over the wet skin of his hard shoulders and biceps, then back up his chest, pulling some of the hair. He growled softly, moving his kissed to my neck. I threw my head back, pulling his head down to me tightly. Abruptly, he jerked backward. I was thrown off balance, but steadied myself.

"Sorry, shampoo in the eyes." He washed his face, then got the rest of the shampoo out.

"That's okay," I said teasingly. "I only came in to help you clean off."

"Then help, wife," he replied, smiling enticingly.

"You help first."

"Sure. Come here."

As I shampooed my hair, Theo soaped up my body, caressing me as he rubbed my skin gently. After I rinsed off, I put conditioner on, then rubbed some into his hair, too. Theo began to soap me up again.

"Hey, you got me clean already—" I began.

"I missed a few spots." He gave a wide smile. "That means I have to start all over."

I laughed, then leaned into his hands, loving the feel of them sliding over my body. We stood together in the spray of the shower for some time, rinsing off and kissing.

The water changed rapidly to cool, then cold.

"Out of time," Theo said, pulling back the curtain. "But that's fine with me." He put me over his shoulder with a growl and carried me into the bedroom.

Kissing me hungrily, he lay me down on the bed, then moved one of my legs up to the side. He shifted, then penetrated me all at once. I let out a gasp. Theo covered my mouth with his, licking me, deepening the kiss as he slipped his tongue in to taste me.

He began to move gently. I responded eagerly. He groaned, and begin to move faster, stroking and touching me. The heaviness between us built up swiftly, and I let out a cry, pulling him closer, eager for climax. He began to shake, then came roaring, holding my body tightly against his, possessing me utterly.

Languidly he rolled over on his back, and began to move, holding my hips. I let my head fall back, my hair falling down my back to pool on his thighs. He shivered from the cold sensation and I let out another cry, as he shifted his hips under me, stroking faster. I lasted a minute, and then succumbed, my muscles clenching and releasing as I screamed out his name:

"Theo!"

He growled contentedly, and bit me gently on my throat. He began thrusting as hard and as fast as he could. With a loud roar, he pushed my hips down on his, arching his back, thrusting up into me as he came. When he stopped moving, I eased off him, panting heavily. He hugged me gently as our breathing slowly quieted.

"I love you, Sar," he said contentedly.

"I love you, too," I said, kissing him lingeringly. "And I'm glad you're home safe. I made you some pie."

"My little pie maker," he said affectionately. "I'm looking forward to tasting them. But just stay here with me for a while."

I fell asleep quickly, lulled by the heat of his body and the easy exhaustion of great sex. A few hours later, we awoke.

"Go let Brian know he can leave," Theo murmured. "Now that Al and Manir are toast, you won't need to be under guard all the time. But I still want you to be careful. No taking chances, okay?"

I nodded, and pulled on a robe. "I'll be back."

Brian was groggy, but glad to be on his way. He got up immediately, and began to pack.

"Thanks for waking me," he said as he left. "And thanks for the pie, too. I didn't expect you to make one for me."

"Don't read more into it than politeness," I said edgily. "I often make them for Danial's foxes. Now that you're part of his organization, I wanted to make you feel appreciated."

I said my words deliberately, mostly out of annoyance over his words in our conversation the day before. But Brian didn't take the bait.

"Of course," he said politely. "I'm very happy you're pleased with my effort. Take care and have a good night."

I closed the door with a smile, my annoyance evaporating. Quickly locking it, I went back to bed.

* * * *

Theo shook me awake. "Sar, it's after noon. Are you okay?"

"Sure," I yawned. "I'm just taking advantage of you being home."

"Kidding aside, you seem to be sleeping a lot," he said worriedly.

"It's a side effect of the pills," I said, yawning again. "It says so on the bottle."

"We'll get you off them as soon as we can," he said, touching my face gently. "I promise." He got up and went into the bathroom.

I looked at the closed door oddly. Why had he said that? Did he feel like it was his fault I had to take them? Was I just reading more into it that he'd meant?

Theo came out. "Come on, throw a robe on. I want to taste that pie."

I followed him to the kitchen where he proceeded to eat half the pie out of the plate.

"Wait to eat the rest until after dinner," I said sternly, taking it from him.

He made a face. "What are you making?"

"Grill us some hamburgers?"

"Sure, as soon as I run down and fill the grill's propane tank."

Close to an hour later, as we were relishing the charred meat, Theo said, "What to know how it went?"

Part of me did, and part of me didn't. "Do you want to tell me?"

"Yes," he said simply.

It was either to reassure me, or because he was proud. "Okay, but understand I don't want an actual blow by blow, especially sitting here eating, okay?"

"Understood." He paused. "Manir was in hiding east of us, near Boston. I left on a private plane. I found his location, scoped out the defenses, and then went to work. He had about twenty bears with him, but they were on their own, as he was still sleeping for the day. I had on my body armor, and I mowed them down quickly, before they could mount a real defense."

"I found Manir in the innermost room, still sleeping in a sparkling clean coffin. I knocked on the cover, and he told me to lift the lid. He screamed when he saw it was me."

Theo's pleasure in his remembrance was scaring me, but I didn't speak.

"I spent the next few hours teaching him what it means to fuck with someone I love," Theo said harshly. "When I was done, he was just barely alive. I took his head then, and doused the body with gasoline. I burned it and the warehouse, making sure to sprinkle all the dead flash with a spell of Terian's to make the bodies decompose as fast as possible. There's nothing left of Manir now except a little muck, like moist dirt, and his severed head."

I put my half-eaten hamburger down. *He'd kept the head? Ew…*

Theo saw my disgust. "It wasn't a personal trophy. Danial wanted a photo of the head, with me holding it, bloody. I'll burn it tomorrow, probably."

"Why'd he want the photo?"

"For you. He's already sent it to all of the vampires in America, and the other vampire big shots in the rest of the world. He needed to make an example of Manir, so no one tried again to take you or Theoron." Theo took my hand, and squeezed it hard. "Reality is that if someone wants you bad enough, and has enough men to waste getting you, they'll get you eventually. We needed to make them believe that the cost would be too high."

"I'm grateful he's dead." *More like vastly relieved.*

"I wanted you to know that I paid him back with interest for what he did. He can't ever hurt you again." Theo paused. "What I did to him let me release some of the rage that I've been carrying around inside."

"It wasn't your fault—"

"I know that, but I still needed to make someone pay. Now I can let it go, you can feel safer, and we can get on with our lives."

If only it were that easy. Still, my heart was eased knowing another person who would like to hurt me was dead. "Thank you. I feel like I can breathe again. It'll be nice to go for a walk outside and not be afraid."

He kissed my forehead lightly. "I'll always protect you, Sar. Always."

* * * *

The next morning, I staggered groggily out to take care of the pets. While the Ghost and Darkness were doing their business outside, I checked the laundry. Most of the bloodstains had come out, but faint marks remained. I doused the marks again with stain remover and then put them in for another cycle. As I let the dogs in, the pile of mail from last night lying on my day planner caught my eye.

No use putting it off. I began to go through the stack. I recycled some junk mail and put some bills aside for Theo, and then came across a card. There was no return address. The postage was airmail.

I only knew one person who was living in another country. My blood went cold. Checking quickly to make sure I was alone, I tore open the envelope. The card inside showed a single rose on the cover with a background of black. With shaking hands, I opened it to reveal one cryptic sentence:

Do you remember me the way I remember you?

There was no signature, but I didn't need one. This had been sent by Devlin. The rose pictured was a fire and ice rose, both red and white on each beautiful petal. One of his roses, the ones he'd always given me. The kind I'd looked for in florist shops, but been unable to find. I'd learned by asking that they had to be specially ordered. Those times he'd brought them to me, he'd not just stopped at a drugstore or even a florist's to get them. He'd ordered them ahead of time, and had to go pick them up. Desire for him hit me then like a fist to the gut.

Though I felt weak with longing, I fought off the feeling. The pills helped, keeping me rational. Before I could change my mind, I took the card and envelope, and threw them into the wood stove, where they were shortly reduced to ashes. When there was no trace of it left, I poured myself a glass of wine. I drank about half of it fast, wishing it would hurry and take effect. Then I downed the rest and washed out the glass. It was barely nine, and Theo would know something had happened if he caught me drinking this early.

* * * *

That afternoon after working on email, I spent some time with Elle. She was adamantly trying to get me to take her side against Danial regarding an imminent sleepover.

"Dad's worried something will happen, but it won't."

"Theo also has reservations," I said firmly. "I know you are lonely for friends your own age. But you spending the night away from home is dangerous. You know I don't mean just in you getting kidnapped—"

She looked at me imploringly. "Mom," she said, drawing the word out, "I know! I won't change in front of anyone!"

"Not purposely," I said, hugging her to soften my words. "But what if you get angry? Scared?"

She looked at me like I was an idiot. "I said I wouldn't do it!"

I must have looked at my own mother like that once. This was my punishment. "Elle, how about you ask this girl—"

"Violet," she supplied with a little arrogance.

"Why don't you ask Violet if she would like to come here to spend the night some weekend?"

"It's not the same!" she wailed.

I put my foot down. "I know it's not the same. But it's the best offer you are going to get. And even that isn't going to be easy."

She looked at me resentfully.

"You know normal people don't live like this," I continued. "They don't have bodyguards, or a vampire for a dad, or—"

"You're normal," she said, hugging me hard.

That might have been the first time I'd ever been called normal. But with that basis for comparison, it was true. "Do you want me to ask Theo and Danial about having Violet come here to spend the night, or not?"

"Please," she answered.

"Okay. Before I do that, I need to meet her."

* * * *

Enjoying my newfound freedom from guards, I took Elle to her dance lesson that afternoon. Violet was a shy, polite girl with brown eyes and brown hair. Next to Elle, she looked plain, but she seemed very nice. The only trouble was she not only looked nine as Elle did, she really was nine years old. Was that old enough for her to be suspicious of how abnormal Elle's home life was?

As the class was ending, a woman close to my own age came up to me, an older version of Violet. "Hi, I'm Cathy, Violet's mother. Our girls seem to be becoming fast friends."

"Yes," I said, watching Elle and the other girls practicing.

"You must have married young and had Elle when you were about twenty or so, like I was when I had Violet. It was a challenge being that young and raising a child, wasn't it?"

I didn't know what to say. There was way, way too much to explain. I just smiled and nodded.

"Elle looks like you, but she must get those eyes from her father."

"She does," I replied, watching Elle as she moved across the floor. I opened my mouth to ask her about Violet spending the night, and then my eyes fastened on Theo's form in the dance studio doorway.

Instead of his usual loose clothes, he had on a tight blue T-shirt the color

52

of his eyes, and tight jeans. His clothes stretched across his muscular body like a second skin. His hair, usually messy, was carefully styled. In short, my usually good-looking husband was breathtaking.

"What are you doing here?" I said, giving him a smile.

"Coming to meet Elle's friend," he replied. "I thought we could go for dinner afterwards."

Cathy was staring at him in equal parts amazement and interest.

"This is Violet's mom. Theo, meet Cathy. Cathy, this is Elle's father, Theo."

Cathy gave him her hand to shake. Instead, he kissed it. "Good to meet you," he said, giving her one of his winning smiles.

She gave him a warm smile back, blushing. I barely stopped myself from rolling my eyes.

"Hi," the dance instructor said, coming over to Theo. "Can I help you?"

Theo introduced himself and then kissed her hand, too.

Watching her blush, I became annoyed. We weren't here to be cute, we were here for Elle, who was watching the spectacle with the other girls and looking as irritated as I was.

"Theo, are you going to let Elle come to Violet's sleepover?" Cathy asked.

"We have plans that night as a family," I said smoothly. "But we'd love to have Violet come and spend the night with Elle and us, if she'd like to."

"Sure," Cathy said, her eyes still on Theo. "I'm sure she'd like that."

"Are you coming to Elle's recital?" the dance instructor said to Theo, hopeful.

"Yes," I said smoothly. "Elle's adoptive father will be there as well." I didn't want to leave Danial's name out of everything, especially as she was sure to point him out as her Dad at the recital and he'd already arranged to come.

The two women looked over at me a little strangely. Theo was glaring at me like I'd rained on his parade.

"Theo was a POW for some years," I said seriously, spinning the story I'd worked out on the way here. "I thought he was dead, and Elle was raised by Danial and I. She thinks of him as her Dad. I'm telling you this so you'll understand why Elle will refer to Danial as her Dad. I didn't want anyone to be shocked, or make her feel as if she isn't normal, for having two dads."

Cathy was first to recover. "I understand completely," she said, putting her hand on my arm. "It's terrible to lose someone, and not know if they are coming back to you alive, or if they are dead."

I nodded to her, as the dance instructor echoed her remarks. Theo's stormy expression had left his face.

"Are you going to let us continue?" Elle said, glaring up at Theo from the dance floor. "You're early."

"She's right," the dance instructor said quickly, flustered. She called the class back to attention and they began practicing again.

I exchanged numbers with Cathy. I gave her my cell, leaving it ambiguous whether Elle lived with us, or with Danial.

When the class ended, Elle came over to us. "Was I good?" she asked, giving me a hug.

"You were spectacular," I said, hugging her back.

Theo picked her up. "You were good," he said, prideful.

Elle beamed.

I followed Theo and Elle back to Danial's in my truck. By the time we got back, it was dark. As we slowly walked to the front door, Elle was still talking excitedly about Violet, and how much fun they would both have when she came to stay the night, and how many things she wanted to do. The first thing we heard as we opened the front door was the clash of swords, and yelling.

Chapter Five

Theo drew his gun and ran into the great room, Elle and I hot on his heels. Entering the dining room, he stopped, then holstered his gun.

"I thought there was trouble," he said grumpily. "You're just practicing."

Terian and Danial were sword fighting in the cleared space of the great room. Instead of common rapiers, they were fighting with broadswords.

Terian swung down and Danial blocked him easily. Terian thrust, and Danial knocked it away, deflecting the blade. Terian paused. Danial just waited, his knees bent, his sword held easily in his hand. His hair was held back tightly in a short ponytail, as Terian's was. Both of them had on leggings, soft boots and swordsman's shirts.

Terian circled and Danial circled with him. Though Terian clearly had been practicing, he didn't have anywhere near the skill Danial had. Terian tried several times to strike Danial, but Danial parried his sword easily, deflecting the blade each time. Then Danial went on the offensive, and within a few seconds had Terian's sword away from him. Terian grimaced, and put up his hands.

"You win."

Danial put both blades aside, and went to Terian. "It takes a lot of practice," he said with a smile. "It will get easier."

"I know," Terian said. "I just wish I was making more progress."

"You are," Danial said reassuringly. "You just started this week. You've only had two lessons."

"Tomorrow, then?"

Danial nodded. "Same time."

"I'm going to go shower," Terian said. "If anyone needs me, I'll be out in the woods after, patrolling." He shot us a smile, then left.

"How's he really doing?" Theo said conspiratorially, crossing to Danial.

"Better than you did, when I first taught you," Danial said with a grin.

"Hey, I bet I still can beat you," Theo challenged.

Danial just gave him a cool glance and then tossed him Terian's sword, bending his knees and assuming his former stance. Theo assumed the same stance, and began circling Danial.

I stayed where I was, worried this was more than playing.

Theo ran at Danial suddenly, and they hacked at one another, grunting and crying out as they fought. They moved almost too fast for me to follow them. The swords rang off one another again and again. Theo was swinging with force, but his movements were graceful as Danial's were. They moved as if dancing.

Then suddenly, it was over. Danial moved fast, spinning and hitting Theo's hilt and Theo dropped the blade, shaking his hand. Danial kicked it away, and then he held his sword on Theo.

"You win," Theo said, putting up his hands.

Elle and I gave Danial a round of applause. Danial inclined his head in a gesture of appreciation as he picked up Theo's sword and his, and took them into the cellar.

"Elle, go get out of your clothes and into pajamas," Theo said. "Take a nice shower, and we'll all be in to tuck you in shortly."

"I want to stay up—"

"Now, Elle," I said, giving her my don't-push-it look. "Or Violet is not coming to stay overnight."

She went without another word.

"I'm tired," I said, crossing to Theo. "Let's make this fast."

"We will."

Danial came upstairs, and directly over to me. "Are you sure you are okay?" he said softly, touching my hand with his. "You are having no ill effects from the drugs?"

"No. I'm just tired."

"Hold still, then." He kissed me softly, then deepened the kiss, sliding his tongue into my mouth, holding my face in his hands.

I kissed him back for a full minute, our bodies pressed together. Danial was stiff by the time he drew back, his eyes dark with desire. He waited a moment, his lips inches from mine.

I didn't cross that small space to kiss him again. While I'd enjoyed the kiss a lot, there was no lust rising rampant through me, as there had been last time. The desire that had always flavored our embraces was gone.

Danial searched my eyes, then stepped back. "It is working," he said despondently. "You feel no longing for me at all anymore."

I stepped forward and put my hand to his face. "I still love you as much as ever," I said softly. "Don't sound so sad."

"It's hard not to be," he said a sigh. "But I'm very happy, too. You have control and so do I."

"It's a relief," Theo said, pleased.

"What is this about Violet coming to stay?" Danial said neutrally, changing the subject.

"We can't have Elle leaving, even for a night," I said patiently. "It's not safe to have her sleeping at a place with no guards. The easy solution is to have Violet come to stay instead. If you're agreeable, she can spend that night with Theo and I."

"How do you think that will be easy, Sar?" Danial said edgily.

"Danial, Elle needs friends. She is alone most of the time. I don't want her being so lonely she decides to start changing at night and not telling us again."

He gave me a considering look. "You are right. But how are you going to explain guards? The foxes must come with you, even if it's only one night. And where will she stay?"

"I still have her old bed all set up in what used to be my sewing room. It's a mess now in there, but I can fix it like it was. It's okay if Violet and her mother know where I live."

"That's okay with me," Danial said finally. "But I'm not budging on the guards. Brian will come and spend the night with you. Warren and one of the other foxes will stay outside and watch the house to make sure nothing happens."

Theo was nodding "This will work, Danial. If all goes well, Elle will be able to do this again. Sar's right, she needs friends."

Danial smiled then. "I agree. Go ahead and set it up."

* * * *

Later that night, as Theo and I were driving home, he said, "You were right to say what you did."

I flushed, as I'd been thinking about Devlin, wondering if Danial had talked to him lately, or if he'd return for Danial's Hallows party. "What's that?"

"I was upset when you brought up Danial at the dance studio. But I understand why you did it, and it was the right thing to do." He reached over and grasped my hand in his. "I'm sorry I got upset."

"It's okay," I said, giving him a smile. "By the way, I've been meaning to ask: what happened to the Hallows party? Danial always has one, but no one has mentioned anything yet. If he waits too much longer, it'll have to be a Thanksgiving party."

There was a long pause. "Danial isn't going to have one this year," Theo said finally.

"Why? It's tradition. Danial enjoys the pomp and circumstance, and besides—"

"Because we've had almost every vampire of note and also some non-vampires of power send entreaties to attend the party this year, Sar. Everyone wants to see Theoron. They also all want to see you."

SHIT with capital S, H, I, and T. "What's Danial going to do?"

"Danial is delaying for now. He and I are worried that the drug won't be enough if you're around that many vampires. The non-vampires he can ignore, period, no problem."

"Non-vampires?" I squeaked.

Theo caught the look on my face, and squeezed my hand. "Powerful sorcerers, weres, fairies, with a few others mixed in. There were under twenty requests total from all of those. There have been over a thousand messages from vampires all over the globe."

My heart was beating rapidly. "What's he been telling them?"

"Just that Theoron requires your undivided attention. He thinks he can delay until spring, more than long enough for you to recover."

At my first party with Danial, I'd been a nervous wreck. How much worse would a party with every vampire who was anyone be, knowing they all were coming to see my son and me?

"Do we have to see them?" I asked shakily.

"Danial and I are waiting to see if Manir's death has the ripple effect we're hoping it will before we make any plans." Theo squeezed my hand again tightly. "Don't worry. I'll tell you if I think you need to worry, you know that."

I squeezed his hand back. "I know that."

* * * *

Theo shook me awake when we got home. "Are you okay?"

"Much better," I replied, yawning. "Do you want some dinner?"

"I want you to rest. I'll fix you some soup. I can eat some chicken."

I didn't have much appetite, but I ate the soup he warmed up for me. After I was finished, I took the dishes to the sink. Theo was eating in the other room, the crunching of chicken bones just audible over the TV.

"I'm going to bed," I called.

The crunching stopped. "I'll be in shortly," he replied. "I'm going to be in cougar form, as an FYI."

I put the cats and dogs to bed, and then crawled into bed myself. Theo came in just as I was falling asleep. A few moments later, the bed groaned under his weight as he leapt onto the bed.

58

I looked sleepily into his light yellow eyes. "Don't get any ideas."

Theo rolled his large eyes, then batted me lightly with his paw. He curled up in a circle next to me, and began to purr. I stroked his head, then his flattened nose and his small ears. He grinned happily, purring louder.

We'd never done this in the old days. But since his return from being taken, some nights Theo slept with me in cougar form. Despite my earlier crack, he'd never acted as more than a pet, a companion who wanted platonic love and affection. That would've been fine, but I suspected that he wasn't doing it to experience a new intimacy with me. He'd done this with Tasha, and he missed her deeply.

He'd slept like this with her, curling himself around her body...

I pushed aside my hurt. This was good for us to share, no matter the reason. Theo spent so much time in cougar form now that he had total recall of everything that he did while he was a cougar. Moreover, he had complete control, so much that the cats and dogs would tolerate his animal form, even if they were still leery.

"Goodnight, Theo." I shut off the light, and we lay together in bed, his purr still rumbling low in the darkness.

* * * *

The next morning, I went into work early with Theo. Right after we arrived at Danial's, he left to patrol the grounds, and I went up to Danial's office. There was a note waiting from Danial, asking me to handle the email first.

I booted his computer, and began looking through the company email of Solutions, Inc. There were over thirty valid emails, but that was usual for a week's time.

Danial did consulting to large companies, fixing them structurally to increase profitability and make them more efficient. Yet he was better known for his excellent work in the line of finding-out-what-the-hell-had-happened-when-something-went-wrong. The majority of the email was of that type: high tech detective work.

Also per usual, some of those potential clients wanted more than just their mysterious problem resolved: they wanted the instigator taken out, too. There were also a few carefully worded emails looking for revenge and justice outside the courts: hit requests.

There was a time not long ago when Danial handled those kinds of cases, too. But killing for hire had gotten Danial more than a few death threats. One had led to an attempt on my life not long after we'd met. Danial had given up that business soon after.

Those needed to be forwarded onto Devlin, the new handler of deserved revenge, with a question mark and a number. Then I would reply to the person and tell them that we couldn't help them. Devlin would either contact them directly, or not. What worried me wasn't the potential deaths these emails represented, it was that I had to contact Devlin this morning. It would be the first contact we'd had since the night we'd said goodbye...

Maybe it could be put off. How would Dev handle these anyway, if he was in Rio? Wait, Brian had said he had a demon, Titus. He must know teleportation, as Terian did. Devlin could be anywhere instantly.

What if Devlin teleported here when I was working? That simultaneously worried and exhilarated me. Abruptly, that all changed to worry visualizing the night Devlin arrived at my back door. If he'd teleported then to my house, he could certainly do it again. What if he showed up some night Theo wasn't home?

Desire welled up within me. I rummaged in my purse quickly, and popped another yellow pill. I'd been taking them at lunch, but from now on, I'd take them at breakfast.

The phone rang. Relieved to see it was Theo, I answered. "Hi."

"So how's the email going?"

"A few seem good. I printed those out and left them on Danial's desk. There's also one hate mail."

"Put it in the possible suspects file. Oh, and can you move some of those to the Possible Enemies Drawer? Anything over six months can go there."

"Will do."

"Anything for Devlin?"

I swallowed quickly. "Yes. I'm...I've sent them on to him. I also had a few junk e-mails I deleted."

"Fine. I'm actually calling about Elle. She wants to know if the sleepover's been finalized."

"Not yet. I'll call Cathy shortly."

"I'll tell her. See you about five. Love you."

"Love you." I hung up.

I called Cathy right away and set up a sleep over for the following Friday. She said that would be fine, and I gave her directions to my house. I could tell she wanted to ask if Theo was my husband and what the deal was with Danial, but she was too polite. Amused, I didn't volunteer the information.

Taking stock one more time to make sure I'd done everything, I realized there were no praising emails for Solutions, Inc., as Danial sometimes received. Suddenly inspired, I took a blank sheet of paper and wrote on it in big letters "YOU DO A GREAT JOB AND YOU ARE LOVED :)," then set it where he'd left me his note.

As I went to shut down the computer, a new email arrived. Devlin had replied to one of my emails with just two words in caps: MISS ME?

"Hell, yes," I said longingly before thinking. Flushing quickly, I deleted the email and switched off the computer.

* * * *

After lunch, I relayed the sleepover news to Theo, then went in to see my son bearing some ice cream for a treat. Terian was already in the room, holding him.

"Mommy!" Theoron shrieked.

"Hi," I said happily back, handing Terian the dish of ice cream.

He took it, and started feeding Theoron. "Now don't bite at it. Lick instead."

Theoron was used to blood, being half vampire. He'd adapted to most foods, knowing that solid food required biting and chewing, and liquids could be drunk. But ice cream was kind of in-between.

"Keep your fangs retracted," I encouraged. "You don't need them."

His alone were retractable, like the ones seen in movies. I was happy about that, despite the difficulty Theoron was having with food now. Danial, Devlin, and all other vampires had fangs that were always present. Danial had said once that it had taken him a few months to learn how to speak clearly again, and that he sometimes cut himself on his fangs while speaking. Theoron wouldn't have that problem, once he mastered retracting his upper and lower fangs.

"Trying," Theoron said crossly, managing to retract three of his four fangs.

"Go ahead and drink the rest," I said, offering him the bowl. "It's pretty melted. Then it's to bed with you."

Theoron finished the ice cream quickly, then yawned, all his fangs again out. Terian put him back in his crib, and I gave Theoron a quick kiss. We left him sleeping a few moments later.

Terian and I walked together out to the great room.

"He's managing well," Terian said happily. "He'll probably be able to retract all of them at will by the end of this week."

"That's good," I replied casually. "How was your hot date?"

Terian started, stared at me, and then walked directly into the wall. I cracked up laughing.

"You did that on purpose, Sar," he said, giving me an irritated look.

I gave him an innocent one back. "Are you going to give me her name or not?"

"Brian said something," Terian muttered. "He's the only one I told."

"Hey, I just care if you're happy," I assured him. "Tell me about her."

"Fine. But let's go out in the sun, okay? It's not snowing."

"It's okay by me if you don't mind the mud."

Terian and I went to the mudroom. Sitting down on the stone bench, we pulled on our boots. Terian locked the door behind us, then checked his gun before slipping in into his shoulder holster. We walked over to the edge of the woods in the direction of the werecompound.

"Tell me everything," I said eagerly. "How did you meet?"

"I went to a festival one weekend," Terian said hesitantly. "She was there. I caught sight of her a few times. Although I noticed her, she didn't talk to me."

"Festival?"

"A kind of gala for people like me...well, people who are interested in sorcery, or who practice it."

"Real witches?" I said skeptically.

"About half and half," Terian admitted. "Some pretenders were there, but that's normal. I wasn't looking for friends, anyway, but for local ingredients. Buying online is fine, but it's safer to see what you're paying for before you've paid for it."

"Don't tell me you've ordered eye of newt online and gotten eye of gecko?" I teased.

"In another second I'm not going to tell you anything more," Terian said, frowning at me.

"Sorry, I'll stop. Tell, please. Did you ask her for her number?"

"No," Terian said proudly. "She gave it to me without me asking."

Was this another stripper? "Where?" I managed. "In the parking lot?"

"When everyone went and got pumpkins," Terian said. "Right after your condition presented itself. You and Theo didn't go, remember?"

"I remember. Danial told me about it that Saturday I stayed over."

Danial, Elle, and Theoron had gone with Terian, Cia, Aran, Aran Jr., Janice, and Ivan to a local pumpkin farm, leaving the rest of the foxes behind to watch the estate. They'd had a great time. Elle had picked out a huge pumpkin, and even Danial with all his strength had to have Terian help him lift it into the Expedition. Later that night, they'd set to carving in the great room. When everyone was done, Danial had set them all up together on a table, and taken a picture, which he'd shown me.

Terian had carved the classic face, with triangles for eyes, then used magic to make the pumpkin grow horns. Elle had treated the pumpkin as a canvas, carving the headless horseman. Danial had helped Theoron make a bat. Cia had made a cat silhouette, and Janice and Ivan had seen the competition and also carved classic faces, though Janice had made her face look distinctly fox-like.

Ivan's for some reason had huge bushy eyebrows.

I'd been dismayed about missing that night, and Danial had seen it. With a soft smile, he'd produced another large pumpkin. On it had been carved a fox walking through the snow, leaving footprints behind it, looking over its shoulder.

"You gave it my eyes." They weren't green, and there was nothing else to say they were mine, yet somehow I knew they were.

"That gave me the most problems," he admitted.

"I didn't know you had so much talent," I said, awed. "But now I understand why you encouraged Elle so much—"

"Sar!" Terian said loudly, breaking into my memories. "Are you listening?"

"Sorry," I said, flushing. "Danial never mentioned you met anyone that night."

"He didn't see her. I noticed her, and smiled at her. She returned the smile and came over. We talked about Halloween, and costumes, and then she gave me her number, and said she wanted to see more of me."

"Did she, now?" I grinned widely. "What has she seen so far?"

"You're bad, even when The Lust doesn't have hold of you," Terian said, shaking his head. He stopped walking and turned to me. "We've kissed a little, that's all. But I like her a lot. Maybe it's because she's the first supernatural girl I've been with."

I gaped. "What?"

"Somewhere in her family line there was something other than human. What that was, she hasn't said."

A woman who wasn't fully human would likely find it easier to accept Terian's half-demon nature. I hugged him, relieved. "I'm very happy for you," I said emphatically. "What's her name?"

"Valarie," he said, drawing it out to roll over his tongue.

"When are you seeing her again?"

"This weekend," he sighed. "The problem is waiting until then." He began to walk again.

I followed him down the path, into the werecompound to his lab.

Terian took off his gun, and hung the rig on the door, along with his jacket. "So what is it you're after today, besides gossip?"

"What?" I said, hanging my jacket beside his.

"You followed me all this way for a reason other than my dating life, Sar," he said, giving me a knowing look.

"Two reasons," I admitted. "First, can I get you to give me a box this size that is invisible, or make this one invisible?" I held out a wooden box to him that was three inches on a side.

"For what reason?" he asked suspiciously.

"To keep a choker in," I said vaguely, hoping he'd think I meant Danial's. "I don't want to keep it in my jewelry chest with my other jewelry."

"I can't make it completely invisible," he said slowly, turning the box to examine it. "But I can make it respond to you the way Danial's safe is in his room responds to him. No one will be able to see it but you, except when you open and close it."

"That will be fine." What a relief.

"Leave the box here. It will take me a day or so to do it. What's number two?"

"You said the second potion I drank would end my dream of Theo, make it fade until it was just a normal dream. But he was alive, not dead, and the dream got renewed. What exactly does that mean?"

"I'm not sure," Terian said with a shrug. "That is what the translation of the spell said, that the dream would be renewed."

"Give me your opinion, then."

"I'm guessing that it means that you and he are bound, much as you were the first time."

"Bound how?" I asked. "I can have normal dreams of him now, Terian. That seems to be the only thing that's different. What does it mean for us that we shared the dream again?"

"It's very rare, to have the dream once, Sar. It's rarer still to have it twice."

"That's wonderful, but what does that *mean*?' I asked, frustrated.

"What is it you really want to know? You're upset."

"I thought the dreaming together signified soul mates or something to that effect. If that's true, why did Theo fall in love with someone else?"

"That women you found him with was probably just sex, you know how weres are—"

"I'm not talking about Aspen. Theo loved a girl he met overseas, Terian. He said he loved her as much as me, but that wasn't true; he loved her more. He was planning to come back here, break things off with me if I was still waiting, and then go back and marry her. He admitted as much to me."

Terian said nothing, but a little blackness curled out of him before he clamped down on it. "If he loved her so much, what happened so that he ended up with that other girl out west?" he asked, his tone sulfurous.

"She married someone else at her father's wishes. She told Theo not to come back." I paused. "I need to know if what we had was true love, how could he toss aside what we had so easily?"

"He shouldn't have been able to," Terian said finally. "I know that isn't what you wanted to hear, but that's my only answer."

"He was frozen in cougar form for a while by a sorcerer. Could that have been the reason?"

"No."

"He was apart from me for more than a year, He was badly hurt—"

Terian crossed the room to hold me in his arms. "Sar, stop looking for a reason. Whatever the reason really was, it doesn't matter now. Theo's married to you."

"It does matter," I said, wiping my filling eyes and drawing back from him. "Theo isn't the man he was when he left, and I'm not the woman I was then, no matter how I've tried to be. He doesn't like who I became while he was gone, Terian."

"Sar, he loves you."

"No," I said, resigned. "I think he loves who I was."

"People change over time," Terian said consolingly. "You're much more mature than you were before. That's a good thing."

"That's just it. Theo was the single most important thing in my world years ago, but he's not anymore; Theoron is. Danial's also become much more important to me—"

"I'm sure Theo understands that," Terian assured. "He didn't love this other woman more back then because of how different you are now."

"It's good he and I are going to counseling," I muttered, wiping at my eyes. "I'm constantly upset over this and can't seem to get past it. I know it's irrational, it's not like I was waiting here alone, for God's sake—"

Terian's phone rang. He looked at the caller ID, then smiled widely. "It's Valerie. Can you give me a minute?"

"Sure," I said, going outside the room to collect myself.

I waited there a few awkward moments. As I went to leave, Terian came out.

"Sar, want to go with me to the Alan's Creek Park? Valerie wants to meet me for a walk near the river in a few minutes."

Despite I was dying to have a look at this mystery woman, I tried to take the high road. "No, you should go without me. She's not going to want another woman along on your date—"

"You're married, so she shouldn't care. And it's not a date, just a quick stroll on my break. C'mon, I want you to meet her."

Well, enough of the high road. "Sure. Let me call Brian and tell him where I'm going."

"He still has you call in every hour?" Terian said, raising his eyebrows.

"I'm used to it now," I replied, giving him a smile to soften my defensive

65

tone. "Besides, someone needs to know we're leaving the grounds."

After alerting Brian via cell, Terian grabbed my hand, and instantly, we were standing at the park gates, near some trees.

"Aren't you worried about someone seeing us teleport in?" I asked, peering around for possible gawkers.

"People just think they didn't see you walk up to the spot you appear at, not aware that they couldn't have." Terian let go of my hand. "Valarie is already here, somewhere by the pavilions." He strode off.

I followed, looking uneasily upward at the dark clouds. "That's smart. It didn't look this overcast back at Danial's."

A crack of thunder sounded directly above me, then drops hit my hands and arms.

I stopped and looked at Terian, bewildered. "Wait, it was supposed to be clear today. I watched the Weather Channel—"

Terian grabbed my hand again. We were suddenly standing beneath a pavilion. Lightning cut the sky with a flash, and instantly rain poured down

"So much for your walk," I said as he released my hand. "Do you want to call her back and say we headed home? We'll never find her in this downpour."

"She's not answering," Terian replied, phone to his ear.

The rain was coming down in sheets now, soaking everything, and the wind was coming up. A few cars drove past us towards the park exit, their wipers beating furiously.

"She probably just left—"

"No," Terian said slowly. "That's her."

A woman was coming toward us in the rain. She was pretty, with long brown hair. She also wasn't wet at all.

"You have to ask her how she does that," I whispered, awed.

"I've been trying to reach you, Valarie," Terian said, walking towards her. "Why'd you turn your phone off—?"

She smiled at him, and then raised her hand and hit him with a lightning bolt drawn from the sky. Terian was thrown back on the ground, the bloody hole in his chest smoking.

I let out a scream, and ran to his side. His eyes were open, unseeing. His wound was healing. The woman was advancing cautiously, eyes on me.

My adrenaline spiking, I tried to grab Terian's gun, but it was beneath him. Wedging my arm under him, I felt for the gun, trying to get it out of his back holster.

Terian groaned.

"Wake up!" I shouted in his ear.

He blinked his eyes, then with another groan, pushed himself into a sitting position, raising his hands. He began to murmur words.

"No," the woman said in a commanding tone, raising her hands. Terian's murmur was cut off instantly.

"Who the hell are you?" I said hatefully, still trying to unclasp the goddamn gun.

"I go by Leri," the woman said, her long brown hair blowing in the gale around us. "But my full name is Alerian." She turned hateful. "I'm your mother, Terian."

Chapter Six

Terian and I gaped at Leri, incredulous.

She glared back, then screeched, "Why did you have to show up here, now of all times?"

Terian found his voice. "My brother, Keriam, told me my mother was dead. She died giving birth to me."

"I knew Danial had a half demon working for him, one who was good with potions, and some of the other darker arts," Leri ranted bitterly. "When I heard you mastered teleportation in a few months, I knew you had to be mine."

"You're his mother?" I said disbelievingly. "Are you part demon?"

"She's not," Terian groaned. "I'd have felt it. Why not attack me when we met? Why wait until now?"

She cast a glance at me. "I couldn't handle this in front of Danial. He knows who I am and he's smart enough to figure out the reason. You were supposed to come alone. What kind of dolt brings someone with him to a makeout session?"

"You kissed your own son?" I said, grimacing.

Leri ignored me, looking down at Terian with disdain. "Idiot," she said harshly. "I left you with Keriam all those years ago, altering his memories to cover my trail. He was not your brother at all, he was just a college kid I found who I bespelled to take you in. His name wasn't even Keriam, that is just what I made him believe—"

"Whose son am I?" Terian said angrily, his eyes red. "What demon fathered me?"

"You are Titus's son. He knew I didn't want children, but he wanted a son, badly. So he experimented with a few potions without telling me." She laughed ruefully. "He's a master spell caster."

Terian's father was the demon who worked for Devlin. But Brian had said of the two, Leri was the more dangerous...

"When I found out I was pregnant, I hid it from him with illusions. Everything I tried to rid myself of you failed. I decided to birth you, and then kill you—"

My fury overwhelmed my fear. "This wasn't his fault, you bitch! Why kill him? And why come here now? Terian's been here for years."

Her eyes flicked to me, and then back to Terian. "I expected him to stay in the Midwest, where Titus almost never goes. As Danial found out two years ago, Terian is hard to kill. It was easier to give him another life apart from mine, far away from me. But now you've returned and it's only a matter of time before Titus discovers your real identity."

"I want nothing from you or from him, either," Terian said coldly. "I'm not here to make you answer for your sins."

"It doesn't matter," Leri replied, raising her hands. "I have to erase your existence. If Titus learns of you, he'll know what I did. He's forgiven me many things, but he won't forgive this. I'm not losing him, we've just reconciled after fighting for the last two months."

Lighting arced down from the sky to collect in her hands. I pulled the gun from beneath Terian with a desperate cry, and rolled away from him as Leri threw the lightning into him.

Terian arched his back, screaming, as his chest reopened, the smell of burning flesh filled the air. He collapsed back on the ground, his eyes blank, smoke curling up from him.

As Leri gathered more lightning, I took aim at her and fired, empting the clip of explosive bullets. Her body jerked as the bullets hit her, but she didn't fall, the points of impact bulging, then slowly receding. The lightning in her hands flashed, then disappeared.

"Sar," she said evilly, gasping in pain. "Stop firing or I'll do more than erase your memories of this when it's done. I'll teleport you to Tennessee and give you to the state ruler there, after reactivating your condition—"

I threw the gun at her. "Fuck you and don't call me Sar!"

She evaded the gun, but the swift movement ripped her bulging skin, blood gushing out along with shrapnel. She let out a gasp, and clutched at her gaping skin, murmuring words.

Terian struggled again to a sitting position, hissing in pain, his chest bleeding badly. Leri threw more lightning she'd gathered, but Terian blocked it, a glass sphere forming out of the air to encircle the energy. In a blurred movement, Terian seized and threw the sphere at her, the lightning crackling inside. It hit Leri in the throat, the sphere shattering. Leri convulsed, electrified, then toppled backward without a sound. With a moan, Terian lost consciousness, collapsing back to the muddy ground.

I leapt to my feet, panicked. Terian's phone was a mess of fried plastic. There was no one around. The storm continued around us, raging, the wind howling now. There was zero visibility outside the pavilion.

I kneeled beside Terian. He was breathing was labored. The huge hole in his chest was still bleeding, and not healing. When I tried to put pressure on the wound, I let out a yelp, rubbing my hands vigorously. Damn it, his blood was steaming hot, and so was he.

"Wake up," I said hysterically, shaking Terian. "I can't deal with this alone, I need your help. God, why couldn't we be back at Danial's house—!"

In an instant, Terian and I were in Danial's living room, staring in shock at Aran. Aran let out a surprised yell.

"Danial!" I screamed. "Danial!"

Danial was through his office door and at my side in moments, already dialing Theo. "Hurry, Terian's hurt."

"He needs food!" I yelled hysterically. "We need meat!"

Aran ran into the kitchen and came back with some raw meat. He tried to drip some blood in Terian's mouth, but he was unresponsive. The smell of sulfur from his torn flesh was noxious, sickening me.

"Terian!" I yelled, shaking him again.

Theo slammed open the front door, and then he was kneeling beside us, his expression worried. He shot a glance at Danial, and then offered his wrist. Danial nodded once, and took Theo's wrist, biting down hard with his fangs, and tearing it open. Blood spurted out, and Theo put his wrist into Terian's mouth, using his other hand to hold up Terian's head so he didn't choke. A few seconds passed, and then Terian bit down on Theo's wrist, drinking greedily. Theo grimaced in pain, but made no sound.

Terian's chest wound closed in a few minutes, until his chest was unbroken flesh through the bloody hole in his shirt. Terian opened his eyes, looking with surprise at us all gathered around him. He pulled his mouth from Theo's arm, leaving a ragged wound. "Thanks."

Theo hissed with pain, and leaned back from Terian, cradling his arm. "You're welcome. Now what the hell happened? I didn't even know you'd gone anywhere."

"How did we get back?" Terian said, looking curiously at me.

I shrugged. "I thought you teleported us."

"It wasn't me who got us back."

"Well, it wasn't me," I said defensively. "I can't teleport."

"It had to be you," Terian said slowly, looking at me as if I were something dangerous.

Danial rose to his feet. "Stay put, both of you." He went into the bathroom to wash the wereblood out of his mouth. Theo followed him to clean off the blood on him, his wound already healed.

As I got up to wash the blood off me too, Terian grabbed my arm. "Sar, there's demon blood in you. I don't know why I didn't scent it, but—"

"Terian, just rest," I said calmly. "You almost died. We can talk about this later."

He got to his feet, swaying a little. "No. We have to know what happened, how you did it—" He staggered.

When I reached to steady him, I noticed the bloodstains still on my hands. "Maybe this did it?" I said, showing him. "I tried to stop your bleeding. Your blood was burning hot."

He grabbed my hand and pulled me into the kitchen. His blood came off easily with warm water and soap, leaving my hands clean. "You're okay, you aren't burned."

Something was off about that. It should be harder for me to get off Terian's blood...

"You have the same scent you've always had," Terian said, confused. "Maybe you're part something else? Other supernatural races can learn teleportation, with a lot of hard work—"

"I haven't done any work," I replied flatly. "I tell you it wasn't me."

"Demon blood can penetrate human skin, given enough time," Terian said slowly. "It's a powerful mutagen. But we got it off you, and there wasn't very much on your hands—"

"Not today," I said, my face whitening. "But there was a lot years ago, when you fought Danial."

Terian looked at me, aghast. "What?"

"I gathered up your weapons after the fight. I carried them inside, and washed them off. The blade and stake cleaned off fine, but your blood wouldn't wash off my hands. I scrubbed my hands almost raw getting it off." Suddenly, I had a headache, the pain at the edges of my mind reaching like tendrils inside my skull to influence my thoughts. I rubbed my temples.

"You rubbed it into your skin," Terian said heavily. "Why did you have to go out and get the weapons? Why couldn't you leave them there?"

"I was protecting you," I retorted. "Theo and Danial wanted to kill you then, remember?"

Theo came in to the kitchen, Danial on his heels. "Sar, what happened?"

"Devlin's sorceress, Leri, attacked us. She said she was Terian's mother. Titus is his father."

Danial's mouth dropped open, but he quickly recovered. "I'll call him," he said. "If he tells Titus about Terian, Leri will give up her attacks." He left the room.

As I resisted the urge to grab the nearest phone to listen in, Theo said, "How were you able to get back?"

"Sar has been infected with demon blood," Terian said, resigned. "She got exposed to mine that night Danial and I fought, years ago. She gathered up our weapons—"

"How was I to know there was something to fear?" I interrupted angrily. "As I recall, you didn't say anything that night about it. Danial had Terian's blood all over him and he wasn't upset—"

"Danial is vampire—" Terian began.

"That's not news," Danial said as he came in, his phone pressed to his ear. "What's the matter?"

"Sar got my blood on her that night you and I fought. Did you know that?" Terian said.

Danial went still. "Shit."

"What is the *matter* with all of you?" I yelled. "Tell me what is so bad about getting a little demon blood on your skin if you're human!"

Danial handed me the phone. "Devlin said he'd be glad to tell you, Sar."

SHIT. I couldn't refuse the phone, or Theo and Terian would know that something was not right. I looked at it like a live electric wire that was sparking and ready to electrocute me. Gingerly, I reached out and took it. "Hello?"

"Sar," Devlin's voice rolled out of the phone like music. "I've missed you."

I shut my eyes so no one could see the desire that was forming in them, however weakly, and then walked into the other room with the phone, trying to find my own voice.

"Shall I sing to you, my lover?" Devlin purred. "I would do other things, but you are not in reach—"

"Just tell me what you have to tell me about the demon blood," I whispered.

"But lover, I miss you," he purred teasingly, lust threaded through every word. "Give me just a few kind words. Say you'll—"

I heard the kitchen extension pick up. "Devlin, what's the deal?" Theo asked. "I know demon blood can corrupt, but Sar's not any different than she used to be when I first met her."

Devlin had stopped speaking the instant he'd heard Theo pick up. In his normal voice, he said, "It can corrupt, but that's pure demon blood, like Titus's. Half demon blood would be much less potent, Theo. I don't think you need to worry, especially if it's been years since exposure."

Danial picked up another extension. "You're sure there's no danger?"

"It possibly could change her, but that would have happened years ago," Devlin said. "It wouldn't suddenly manifest itself now."

"But what if the small re-exposure to my blood today altered her further?" said Terian, talking on another extension.

"Has she tried to teleport again and succeeded?" Devlin asked. "That would seem the best course of action to try first, before having hysterics."

"Dev's right," Danial said. "You don't know that you didn't just do it, Terian, when you were badly injured. We'll have Sar try again in the great room shortly. Thanks, Dev."

"Yes, thanks for your help, Dev...lin," I said quickly and hung up.

A few moments later, I stood in the middle of the great room, Terian, Theo, and Danial watching.

"What do I do?" I asked Terian.

"You need to want to go somewhere, Sar. When you think about it, picture the place in your mind. You can say words to focus yourself, but what matters is your concentration."

I concentrated, and tried to put myself out on the lawn. Nothing happened.

"Where are you trying to go?" Terian asked, after a minute.

"Just to the front lawn," I said. "But nothing's happening."

"Try again," he encouraged. "That shouldn't be difficult at all."

I tried again. Nothing happened. "I think it had to be you."

"Maybe you're right," Terian said, shrugging. "I did want to escape, and I was thinking that I had to get you out of there, had to get us back here somehow. Maybe I did do it."

"Try once more, Sar," Danial interrupted.

I concentrated with all my might for several minutes. Nothing happened, other than my headache getting worse. "I give up," I said irritably.

"Terian must have done it," Theo said, coming to stand beside me. "If Sar could do it, take both of them across that great a distance, she would have no problem taking herself a few feet."

"Yes," Danial agreed. "Sar, why don't you go home early today with Theo? It's already been a harrowing day, and you've got blood all over your clothes. Terian, you take the rest of the day, too. I've only got one conference call to take later tonight. The foxes can handle security."

"Thanks," Terian said, and vanished.

"It can't be easy to be him," I said sadly. "That Leri is a world class bitch."

"She is," Danial agreed. "Devlin said he would talk to Titus about what happened. He hadn't known about any of this either. Apparently, Titus and Leri have been staying at his home in Hayden for the past few months to take care of the place and work out some problems. Dev gave them until the end of the year."

"Those two are always fighting," Theo scoffed. "It's a wonder they find the time to work at all."

"This might be a good thing, odd as that probably sounds to you both," Danial said. "Terian had no family and now he does. I know how I feel about my brother, despite his actions." Danial caught my eye pointedly, then looked away.

"Maybe you're right," Theo said, shrugging. "Maybe he can connect with his father, have someone to be close to. Titus's reputation is not bad, all things considered."

But would Terian want to? His human mother had been terrible, could his demon father be any better?

"Let's go," Theo said, touching my arm. "Or those stains are never going to come out."

"He's right," I said, grimacing. "Danial, can I put these in your washer now and borrow some clothes to drive home in?"

Danial nodded to me. "If you want to undress in the bathroom, I'll give Theo some clothes to bring you."

A few moments later, I was dressed in a simple dark blue cotton dress from one of Danial's trunks, and my dirty clothes were washing. "Thanks," I said, hugging him. "I'll bring it back tomorrow."

"No rush," he murmured, hugging me back. "You look lovely. You're sure you're really okay? You aren't hurt?"

"Yes, but I'd like to know if Dev is going to take care of Leri. She mentioned erasing my memories like it was nothing. I don't want to have her coming back for another try."

"I'll find out," he said, then darted in for a quick kiss.

"What are you doing?" I said, trying to frown and not smile.

Danial gave me a satisfied smile. "Stealing a kiss, of course." He helped me put on my coat and shoes. "Watch your words, Sar. Devlin, not Dev."

Flustered, I nodded, then quickly went outside to the truck where Theo was waiting.

* * * *

Later that night, I reclined in front of the merrily burning woodstove, dressed in layers of polar fleece. Theo brought me a cup of hot chocolate with steam wafting from it, then sat down beside me.

"Thanks. You know, you're the perfect husband," I said, leaning into him.

"I know," he said, prideful. He gave me a quick kiss, then slipped his hands under my shirt. "I know a way you can be the perfect wife."

I smiled back at him. "I'm already a pretty good wife."

He stopped, startled. "I know you're a good wife, Sar," he said awkwardly. "Better than I deserve—"

A slap of guilt hit me. I pushed it down. "Hey, I—"

"—and I think you're wonderful." He slid his hand under my bra, cupping my breasts. "Are you too tired?"

I put my cup on the floor before I dropped it, my body shaking slightly under his touch, a soft sigh escaping my lips before they met his. "No."

* * * *

That Thanksgiving, per custom, Elle and I went to my parent's home. Theo accompanied us.

My inner turmoil overshadowed this happy event. In the past week, my passionate nature had evaporated, my desire withering to almost nothing. This terrified me, to see Theo and not want him as I always had. I'd never been one to forgo sex, or to fake an orgasm. But Theo's appetites hadn't changed as mine had. Before much longer, I'd likely have to do one or the other.

This pressure made me nervous, especially around my family. I didn't want them to know anything was wrong. Adding to that, Theo, Elle, and I were heading to Danial's after this dinner, to celebrate there. It was a good bet the werecreatures in attendance would all be able to scent how upset I was, and figure out the cause. Even if they couldn't, Danial would before I'd finished my first sentence.

This stress led to me having two glasses of wine before dinner even started. As we enjoyed a wonderful meal, I continued to drink, finishing my third glass just as dinner ended. I was laughing, having a great time and not thinking of anything but that.

How drunk I was quickly became apparent after a game of Ping-Pong with my stepfather. No matter how I lunged, the ball was never where it was supposed to be. When my stepfather bounced a ball off my forehead, I conceded defeat. Handing off the paddle to Elle, I sat down on the couch, out of breath and dizzy.

"Theo, here's your pie," my mother said, handing him a plate. "Sar, you want some?"

"No," I said, smiling weakly. "I've had enough."

"Thanks, Mom," Theo said, giving her a smile. As she walked off happily, he turned serious. "What's wrong?"

"Mom," Elle said. "Should we bring some home for Theoron? He didn't—"

I blanched. "No," I said sharply, praying if she were overheard they'd

75

think she meant Theopolis.

"Elle, go help your grandmother in the kitchen," Theo said kindly. "Remember what we all talked about."

Elle nodded angrily, then left.

Theo turned back to me. "We should go. She's not going to keep quiet for long in that mood."

"You're right. We should go," I replied, standing up.

Though my parents protested, we were soon on the way to Danial's house. I sagged back into the seat with relief.

"What's wrong with you?" Elle asked, worried. "You're upset."

I hadn't wanted to tell her, but suddenly that added strain was too much. "Elle, I'm going through something right now," I said, turning in my seat to look at her. "I should be okay in another month, but right now I'm stressed out."

"What's wrong with you?" Elle repeated, concerned.

"I was with Danial for so long," I said finally. "He was turning me, though he didn't mean to. I've been acting oddly because my body wants to keep turning, and I'm fighting it."

"Will you get better?" Elle said, tears forming in her eyes.

"Yes," I said, reaching back to clasp her hand. "I'm going to be fine, Elle. It's just taking me a while to go back to how I was when you first came to live with me."

She held my hand tight. "You promise you'll be okay?"

"Yes," I said, putting all the hope I had into that one word. "I'll be fine."

She sat back, satisfied. I did the same, quickly falling asleep. When I awoke, we were at Danial's home.

Elle promptly got out and ran up the stairs. "Dad!"

Danial was there, waiting for her with open arms. He steeled himself at the last moment, catching her as she leapt into his arms.

The sight of him filled me with sudden hunger.

"Did you have a good time?" Danial asked Elle, smoothing some hair out of her eyes. "We should trim your bangs later."

"Mom and I are going next week to get them cut, and her hair, too."

Danial's rich dark eyes fastened on me, his stare caressing. "How are you, Sar?"

I needed him. I wanted him. I had to get him closer…

"She's fine," Theo said gruffly, stepping between us. "Go ahead in. We'll be in shortly."

"Danial," I called softly, knowing he'd hear the invitation. "Come to me."

Danial began walking towards me, but Theo shoved him hard, knocking

76

him back a step. "Don't go to her," he growled. "She's had too much alcohol."

Danial looked for a moment as if he'd go through Theo, then relaxed. He turned to Elle, who was staring at us, her blue eyes wide and scared. "Go inside. We'll be in shortly."

As Elle ran inside the house, Danial began walking toward me again.

Theo pulled his gun, and pointed it at Danial's heart. "Stop."

"If I make a move to bite her, go ahead and shoot," Danial said disgustedly, then took my hand, helping me out. "What is it?"

I clasped him around the neck, pressing my body to his, the coolness of him both soothing and exciting. I rubbed my lips gently down his throat, kissing gently.

Danial sighed, then gently pried me off him. "What happened to the drugs, Theo?"

"She's on them," Theo replied gruffly. "The alcohol must be overriding their effects."

My hands were too cold, and I couldn't get them to work. I leaned into Danial. "Please," I whispered. "I need you."

"And I need you," Danial said, kissing me chastely. "The real you, sweetheart." He stepped back, letting Theo come between us. "Take her for a brief walk, then come in. But don't let her get too cold."

"She's my wife," Theo growled. "I don't need you to tell me how to take care of her."

Danial didn't reply or look back. The front door shut behind him with a soft click.

"C'mon," Theo said, putting his arm around me. "Let's get you sobered up."

Fifteen minutes in the brisk November air had me back to myself, albeit highly embarrassed. "I'm sorry, Theo. I should've watched how many drinks I was having."

"Don't worry about it," he said, forcing a smile. "You're under a lot of stress."

"I'm okay now. Let's get back to the others."

We walked up the porch steps. As we reached for the door, Elle opened it. Danial was there, behind her.

"Told you I'd heard them coming back," Elle said proudly.

"So you did," Danial said approvingly. "Your hearing is near my own now." His eyes met mine. "Please come in, both of you."

"Are you going to act weird again?" Elle asked me point blank.

"I'll try not to," I replied, blushing.

"Dad said you're on drugs," Elle continued. "But when you drink too much they don't work."

"Elle!" Theo roared. "Enough."

"It's true!" she said, shooting him a look. "You told me to always tell the truth."

"What Theo meant, Elle," Danial interrupted, making her look at him, "Is not to lie. It is something else entirely to tell secrets that do no good to be told."

"I'm sorry," she said, looking at him mournfully.

"It is not to me you should apologize," Danial said, turning her to face us.

"I'm sorry," she said, running to give me a hug.

I hugged her back. "We forgive you. Just keep this to yourself, Elle. It isn't polite conversation."

"I'm sure Dad didn't do it on purpose," Elle added. "He doesn't like to see you like this—"

"Elle," I said grimly. "Go to your room. I'll be in to see you in a minute."

"I'll take you there, and we'll wait for Mom together," Danial amended, his eyes meeting mine. He offered her his hand. "Come."

Theo grabbed my arm as I went to follow. "You sure you're okay now?"

"I'll be fine. If you want, stand outside the door."

"I will."

Theo followed me through the great room, giving friendly greetings to everyone. Brian was standing with a woman that must be Demi, but she wouldn't look at me when I smiled at her, though he nodded to me. Saddened, I went on to Elle's room, where she and Danial waited. Theo took up a position outside the door as I went inside.

"Elle," I said, sitting down on her bed beside her, "You're right. Danial didn't change me on purpose. But that's not the issue. The reason we don't talk about it is that it hurts him to think about what I'm going through. Talking about it doesn't change what's happened to me, or make me get better any faster."

"So I shouldn't mention it?" she said.

"Right," I said, hugging her. "You have a right to ask us about it, and we shouldn't have tried to keep it from you. But when you have questions, ask Danial or I in private, okay?"

"Then I have a question," Elle said angrily. "Why doesn't Theoron get to go with us to Grandma's? If Theo can call your mother Mom, and I can call you Mom, why isn't Theoron able to call your mother Grandma? She's his grandma."

"He can, Elle," Danial answered. "Sar's mother is his grandmother."

"You told me not to mention him at all to Grandma and Grandpa. I want to know why he wasn't there with us, and why we can't tell them about him."

"Several reasons," Danial replied seriously. "First and foremost, Theoron is in danger constantly. He never leaves the grounds of our home, Elle. Even then, I am afraid for him all the time." Danial paused. "Secondly, Sarelle's mother doesn't know that we had a child together," he added softly, his eyes flicking to mine, then back to hers. "To complicate that, Theoron is half vampire. You can hide that you're werecougar, but he cannot hide his nature well, not yet. When Sar is confident that Theoron will be old enough to hide it, as you are, she'll take him with you on your holiday visits." He looked at me wistfully. "And then perhaps I will go as well."

Danial's longing was both obvious—and more painful to hear— tentative. He was unsure I would want him to come with us. Guilt flooded me.

I caressed his hand lightly. "You're welcome to accompany us, when that time comes."

Danial squeezed my hand, relieved and happy. "I'm glad of that, Sweetheart."

"But if Sar accepts you and Theoron," Elle continued, "why wouldn't her parents? They're human like she is."

Danial gave me an affectionate look. "Sarelle is unique. She accepts me as no other woman ever has. She is not the usual human, Elle. Take that for the small warning I mean it as. I don't want you to be disappointed."

"Will Mom really get better?"

"Yes," assured Danial. "She will be fine, in time."

"Good," Elle said. "I'm starving. That turkey smells great." She got up, and raced out of the room.

Danial and I looked at each other, pleased. "I meant what I said," I added softly.

"I know you did," he said, kissing me tenderly on the cheek. "Let's go before Theo comes to see what's keeping you."

Theo met us outside the room, relieved. A few moments later, we were standing in the buffet line in the kitchen loading up our plates. The meal was fabulous, from the savory turkey to the triple fudge cake.

"Cia, this cake is perfect," I complimented. "Theoron loves it so much he's trying to eat my piece, too."

"Its roots are in your teaching, Sar," she replied graciously.

"You surpassed me. All I did for this was help you buy the groceries, and make the pies."

"Though I can't add my personal compliments, I thank you again for all your work cooking, Cia," Danial said pleasantly. "Now that the meal is ending, I must ask you what each of you intends to do for Christmas. The need to retain a workable guard is more important this year than it ever has been."

"Demi and I have family we're going home to," Brian said quickly. "We'll be gone on Christmas Eve and the following day, but I'll be available for duty any of the other days."

Warren and Hans said they would be around. Though they didn't volunteer anything more, I had the feeling neither of them had any family.

"I'll be around, too," Terian added.

As far as I knew, he hadn't yet contacted Titus. Maybe Christmas wasn't the ideal time to visit demons, even if they were your father.

"Janice, Ivan, Cia, I, and Aran Jr. will be spending the holidays here," Aran said. "I think I speak for the rest when I ask why you need us all here when Theo will be with Sarelle at all times, and Terian will be with you and Theoron. The holidays are always slow for Solutions, Inc."

"Not this year," Danial said darkly. "Everyone, I will be gone for the two weeks directly before and after Christmas, including New Year's Eve. Terian will accompany me, but the rest of you will remain here to keep my son and daughter safe."

A few gasps sounded from around me. I barely registered them, in shock. Danial had never missed Christmas since I had come into his life. He would be missing Theoron's first Christmas.

Elle was the first to recover. "Dad, you can't not be here for Christmas!"

"What's happened?" I asked loudly. ""Is this some big case?"

"This is tying up loose ends in preparation for a party, one I'm not going to alone," Danial replied coolly. "There is a Gathering on New Year's Eve. We have been invited; you, Theoron and I."

"What kind of Gathering?" I asked, worried.

"A Vampire Gathering," he said anxiously. "Likely the largest in history."

"What vampires will be there?" I asked fearfully.

He let out a breath. "All of them."

Chapter Seven

Danial, Theo, and I faced each other alone in the great room. Danial was weary, yet Theo wore a pleased expression on his face. When Danial glanced at Theo a second later, the pleased look was quickly replaced by a scowl.

Everyone had cleared out almost immediately after Danial's announcement, Cia leading a reluctant Elle away, Theoron in her arms, the festive plans to group-trim the tree abandoned. We'd been fighting for the last ten minutes.

"I'm not going," I said vehemently, for the third time. "No way."

"Sar, you must go," Danial pleaded. "You are Theoron's mother. These Gatherings are only ever held to recognize great events, maybe once every century. The last was a hundred and five years ago, when Michael became the Ruler of Asia. You will not have to do this every year."

I looked at him stonily. "No."

"I get letters weekly now asking for us to attend parties in our honor. Presents have begun arriving, all manner of toys. Soon they will be daily. Their authors all ask same thing: to see Theoron, either by visiting us here, or by us coming to visit them. Soon there will not be one V.I.V. who has not contacted me."

"V.I.V.?"

"Very Important Vampire," Theo supplied. "I know, the acronym sucks."

I suppressed a smirk.

"I have refused them all, but pretty soon they are just going to start showing up," Danial warned angrily. "You'll not think it humorous then, either of you."

"I don't think it's amusing now," Theo growled.

"Let them come," I said, folding my arms across my chest. "Let them come here to the United States if they're so hell bent on seeing me and Theoron."

"You will not feel safe here when there are twenty vampires in Alan's Creek, and their guards outnumber ours," Danial said darkly. "My home's location is likely not a secret to other Rulers, and they are not above telling secrets in order to gain the first glimpse of our son. Now listen to my proposal."

"I'm listening."

"This is a request in name only," Danial continued impatiently, his eyes tinged red. "We must attend the Gathering, or there will be dire consequences. All of the Rulers—or Lords, as some of them prefer—have signed the letter I received inviting us. Samuel of Europe, Michael of the Far East, Zane of Africa, Perseus of South America, and Ebediah, who oversees Canada, and the Northern territories have all guaranteed your safety, and that of Theoron's—"

"Have they guaranteed yours?" Theo asked pointedly.

Danial didn't answer, but from the look he gave Theo, they had not.

"What if they attack you?" I asked, scared. "They could kill you, Danial."

Danial lost his composure. "Sar, Theo, you know if I refuse, there will be trouble! I have no reason that I can use as an excuse not to go! Sar must be there. Even if they were not asking to see her, I would demand that she go. I will not leave her alone when they know how far I would be from her, unable to protect her. It would be too easy for something to go wrong if the three of us were separated."

Belatedly, I realized he meant Theoron, he, and I, not he, Theo, and I. I cast an odd look Theo, wondering why he wasn't protesting he could protect me. He obviously didn't want me to go, but he wasn't speaking, or even looking at Danial or I.

"Your argument makes sense," I ventured. "But my fears do, too. You know if I attend this Gathering, you'll have to mark me again."

"Yes, I know," Danial replied. "And we'll have to arrange to leave Elle with your parents, Sar. I don't want her involved, especially if things go badly. With her not being blood relation to either of us, she shouldn't be in danger."

"I agree," Theo said slowly. "What I don't understand is why you're going to be gone so long before the actual meeting. Where is the meeting, anyway? When is it?"

"Ebediah's home ground, near Niagara Falls, at eight p.m. on New Year's Eve," Danial said. "A Saturday night, I believe."

"We should be there then by seven to check everything," Theo said, his mind already working. "Is it on holy ground?"

"No. I asked that it not be, and that any teleporting of my employees be allowed. Terian will hold Theoron at all times. If there is any danger, he can teleport him to safety. All other teleportation on the grounds of the meeting site is banned. The other Rulers agreed to this."

"What about Sar?"

"You, Brian, and I will be guarding her, Theo."

"That's not enough," Theo said, dismayed. "We could never fight our way out if something went wrong."

"We could not bring enough people with us to fight our way out in any case," Danial said angrily. "After what happened with Monica and Erin, I hesitate to hire any other new people."

Theo began to pace, growling softly to himself. I sank down on the couch, exhausted.

"We need to make it seem that Sar is still Oathed to me, Theo," Danial said pointedly. "She should be back to normal by Christmas. I'll mark her then on the side of her neck that is empty. With the collar, and the bites, she'll look Oathed."

Theo gave him a skeptical look.

"Theo, Samuel already believes it," Danial persisted. "We only have to get the others to believe it, and we'll be fine. Vampire Law is what holds us together, and keeps order. Younger vampires may not respect this, but the older ones do, and the older ones are in control. They will honor that she is sworn to me."

Theo stopped pacing. "How do you propose to mark her?" he said, his tone black with anger and resignation. "Even if she is back to normal, I don't want you being intimate again."

"You and she can have sex, and as she climaxes, I'll bite her—"

Instantaneously I was turned on, then felt appalled at myself and flushed crimson.

Theo shouted, "I cannot believe you'd propose—!"

What would you have me do?" Danial shouted back. "I'm doing my best to keep us from being attacked here! Stop thinking of your own interests, and start thinking about how to get us to the point where we all leave the Gathering together! An ending where you and I aren't dead! If they suspect she's not Oathed to me, they'll take her!"

"Isn't there some numbing potion I could get from Stephen?" I asked.

"Unlikely," Danial retorted. "He wants me not to bite you, no matter the consequences. And Terian has not made any progress in his efforts to learn healing magic."

Theo let out a breath. "Say we do find a way for you to mark her. What particulars have already been arranged?"

"I am leaving on December 18th for the first of the meetings. I'll call in every day. I want to know the instant your condition improves, Sar."

I nodded.

"Theo, Brian will not be coming with me, so you are to call him in case of emergencies. Terian will be watching over Theoron when you and Sar aren't on the premises. Even then, we'll be stretched thin. I have a lot to do and little time." He paused. "I've not told the others, but I want you both to know that I'm planning to borrow a few of Devlin's guards to watch over me. Despite what I said earlier, Terian will have his hands full and there isn't another way."

Theo snarled "Not that evil—"

"No," Danial said quickly. "Not him. Most likely Vince and Kev."

"Him who?" I asked.

"Can you trust them?" Theo said warily, ignoring me. "They have recent history—"

"I trust Dev," Danial said, cutting him off. "Dev guarantees that they'd do what needs doing. Terian is working on spells of protection to use at the party, researching some rarer ones that might not be discovered. If you think of anything additional we can use to help protect us, either of you, tell me. I want to get us out of this safely, whatever it takes."

Theo nodded. "I'll think on it."

Danial hugged me. "Sar, don't worry," he said softly. "We'll find a way out of this."

"I trust you," I said, then gave him a chaste kiss for reassurance. Danial kissed me back passionately, crushing his body to mine. I intensified the kiss, making myself give him the reassurance he needed, despite my desire was once more absent.

Danial broke the kiss, then let me go, striding upstairs to his office.

"Come on," Theo said, taking my hand. "Let's get home. It's been a long night."

* * * *

The next weeks were a flurry of activity. My day-to-day tasks were at odds with the imminent death situation that we were facing to the point I considered them almost absurd. Still, I knew what normal life like the sleepover meant to Elle, so I kept it together for her.

When Cathy called and said Violet had a cold the morning of the big event, we postponed it until the following Friday. Most appointments were kept, like Elle's and my hair appointment, where we each donated a good chunk to Locks of Love. Though Elle did close to two feet, ending up with a very short do, I did the minimum, telling myself I wanted it to remain longer. Down deep I knew that was a lie; I was remembering someone else, who'd always loved my hair long.

My condition didn't improve; if anything, the only change was that I was more tired now than I had been before. Though I slept well and soundly each night, I took naps in the daytime now, too. I chalked it up to winter malaise, not wanting to admit the real cause was likely a long-term effect of the drug I was taking.

During a brief pause in his hectic schedule, Terian finally gave me my box to keep Devlin's choker in. When he gave it to me, it appeared as if he was giving me thin air. The moment I touched it, the box revealed itself, the point of contact with my hands showing first, and moving across the box's structure, until it was completely revealed.

"Thanks, this will be perfect."

"When you put it down, the box will wink out of sight," Terian cautioned. "Remember where you put it, because it's very easy to lose something that isn't visible until you touch it."

"Makes sense," I replied. "Um, I'm not sure how to ask without prying, so I'll just say it. Have you contacted Titus yet?"

"Not yet," he said, an uneasy look passing across his face. "I'm not sure what to say to him. He's been told I exist, and he hasn't contacted me. Besides, Leri isn't dead."

I nodded. "I know. Danial told me last week when we were riding together. I've been nervous about it ever since."

"She shouldn't come back," Terian assured me. "Titus knows about her attack. Danial said Leri hasn't been staying in Hayden."

"She may still blame you and me. She's got to be grieving for what she lost."

"She had only herself to blame," he said darkly. "Now if you're all set, I need to work."

I left Terian's lab and went directly to Danial. "May I have the envelope back?"

He opened his safe without a word. I reached in and pulled it out under his watchful eyes, praying the contents hadn't shifted enough for any metallic clinking. That night I put the choker in the box along with the note Devlin had written me, asking me to come to him. I was tempted again to call him, but instead closed the box quickly, storing it in a drawer where it winked out of sight.

* * * *

Danial began his intense work schedule closer to the beginning of December in an effort to tie up as much business as he could before the holidays. He worked every night, and most days from his home, reporting to clients what needed to be done, what he'd discovered for them, and completing paperwork for each finished case. In his relieved estimation, he would have nearly every open job closed by Christmas.

I did my best to keep up with the increased workload. It helped that there were no new cases to begin or update. Danial had instructed me to tell all new clients that the business would be closed for the month of January. If they were insistent about waiting, he would let them book an appointment now, but otherwise he recommended they find someone else. To my pride, most clients opted to wait. Before long, February was completely booked.

Along with the rest of us, Devlin was also keeping busy. He kept up an almost constant barrage of romantic emails, replying to each of the cases I forwarded to him with suggestive poetry. On December twelfth, I made the mistake of replying to one of his emails, a quote by F.A. Kemble:

What shall I do with all the days and hours that must be counted ere I see your face?

How shall I charm the interval that lowers between this time and that sweet time of grace?

Oh, how, or by what means, may I contrive to bring the hour that brings you back more near?

How may I teach my drooping hopes to live until the blessed time that thou art here?

I wrote back, Stop sending these. You are not making things easy for me. That reply prompted him to send a new email every day instead of just in response to my emails.

I hadn't known that there were so many poems of unrequited love and longing. Worse, poetry was not all. On the thirteenth of December, a deliveryman came with a dozen fire and ice roses to Danial's home. They were for me, from Devlin.

Sar, I know you enjoy these, so I am sending them to you. Today is my birthday, or as close as I remember. Think of me, and know I wish I were there with you, beside you.

Love, Dev

Danial heard the delivery van leave, and came out of his bedroom. "Flowers? They must be from Devlin for you."

Theo never got me flowers, but I thought it disloyal to say that to Danial. "Yes. He said it's his birthday. When you talk to him, tell him Happy Birthday, and I wish the same."

Curious, Danial read the card. His expression became startled.

"What is it?" I asked, breathing in the scent of roses. "God, they smell wonderful."

"Sar, did you read this?" Danial said, his voice strangled.

"Yes," I said slowly, not understanding. "I thought it was sweet."

Danial looked apoplectic. "Sweet?"

"He said he wished he could be here beside me for his birthday. Why are you upset?"

Danial roared with laughter.

"What is so funny?" I said with narrowed eyes, putting my hands on my hips.

"Take another look at the card, Sar," he said, still choking. "The word written there is not beside, it's inside."

My faced turned red by inches, until combustion seemed a certain fate as I was so hot with embarrassment. "Son of a bitch!"

Danial was still smiling with mirth, already dialing his phone with a purpose. He yelled good-naturedly, "Devlin! Sar got your flowers. What the hell are you thinking, sending that note where anyone could read it?" He paused, listening. "Yes, she liked them. At least while she thought the card said beside."

Faint laughter poured out of the phone in a melodious rich burst.

Furious, I ripped the card off the flowers and stalked into Danial's bedroom, where I tore it into miniscule pieces and put it in Danial's wood stove. Then I lit it, watching it burn until it was nothing but ashes. I did laugh, when I was alone in there, but knew I had to keep it to myself, because Danial was right. Devlin was walking a tightrope here, and there was too much at stake to screw around like he had.

Danial hung up as I came back into the great room. "I told him not to do that again, but I'm not sure how much good it will do. Dev said he was sorry, and that he hoped you liked the flowers."

"You know he's not sorry at all."

"I know," he said, kissing my cheek gently. "But he does love you, Sar. I think he's a little obsessed with you, frankly."

"Why?" I said sarcastically. "Because of my summer blood?"

"Because you are not falling at his feet. You have not told him you loved him."

I gave Danial a skeptical look. "Surely other women must have resisted his advances?"

"None I know of," he said. "He always gets his way."

"Then does he really love me, or that he can't have me?"

"Probably a little of both," Danial said honestly. "It's hard to say. I'm his brother and I don't understand how his mind works."

Theo came in the front door, and saw the flowers. "From Devlin?" he said, smelling them. "He got you some like this before. I remembered, because they were so unusual."

"Yes," I said, blushing faintly. "It's his birthday."

Suddenly, it dawned on me that I'd never celebrated a birthday with either of the men standing before me. Deep shame soaked me to the bone that I had never asked, especially Danial. "By the way, when are your birthdays?"

"Mine is in May," Theo said uncomfortably.

"Mine is in the fall, I think," Danial said distantly. "I have not kept track of it for many years. Do not feel badly about it, as I don't celebrate it. Theo hasn't either for many years."

His tone was reminiscent of someone who'd been used to many birthdays slipping by with not only no presents, but also no remembrance. Saddened but resolute, I got pen and paper from my purse and made a note of both months, and their names. "We will celebrate both from now on," I said gently, yet firmly. "We've seen too much death not to take every chance to celebrate life."

Danial obviously didn't know what to say. Theo just nodded happily. For now, that was a small step in the right direction.

* * * *

That next week, Theo and I had our first therapy appointment with Dr. Clay. It wasn't far from Danial's home, near Camlyn's office. To my relief, the psychologist knew that there were conscious creatures besides humans in the world. To my surprise, the doctor was a woman.

"Good to meet you. My name is Carol Clay. You can just call me Carol. And you are?"

"Theo and Sar," I answered.

"And what do you think you can accomplish in the time we spend together? Theo, you go first."

Theo gave her a blank look. She turned to me, inviting me to speak.

"To start, we need to work on Theo's jealousy and my guilt."

"Please explain, Sar," Carol said soothingly. "What is Theo jealous of, and why are you guilty? Did you have an affair?"

"No," I said, feeling better immediately. "Theo and I were apart for a few years. In that time, I went back to the man I'd been with before him, the man I'd left to be with him. I had a baby with that man, and raised Theo's child by another woman with him."

"Why are you jealous about this man, Theo?" Carol said, still soothingly. "You were not together with Sar at the time she was with him."

"I'm not jealous that she was with him then," Theo said, sounding exasperated already. "I'm jealous because she still wants him and because they had sex a month ago."

Carol looked at me questioningly.

"The other man was a vampire," I said hesitantly. "I was starting to turn when I left him. I'm slowly going back to normal, but my doctor said it will take another few months." I took a breath. "This doctor advised me to be intimate with Danial in the meantime, to try to stave off my seeking out another vampire to complete my transformation."

"That's not a suggestion I've heard of before," Carol replied.

"The idea was he'd not exchange any fluids with me, but spending time with him would make my withdrawal more bearable," I explained. "When we tried it, we ended up giving in, despite our efforts not to. When I got home, Theo admitted that he'd wanted to kill Danial, and was going to leave me if I went to Danial for sex again, even if the plan had worked."

"Theo, why aren't you letting Sar see Danial, especially if her doctor says that that is best? This seems not an affair of the heart, but a medical need."

"Because I don't want my wife fucking anyone but me," Theo growled at her.

I rolled my eyes, but Carol took it in stride. "Theo, there is no need for swearing here, as I'm not trying to antagonize you, just to get you to share what you're feeling. But feel free to use whatever words best describes your feelings."

"Okay," Theo said neutrally.

"Carol," I interjected, "When that plan didn't work, I got some drugs from my doctor that take away my desire. It worked a lot better than being with Danial. Frankly, it was a relief not to continue with the former plan, because I didn't like how I felt afterward."

"How did you feel, Sar?"

"Like I was using him. I felt dirty."

"You love this vampire, don't you?" Carol said.

"Danial is his name," I answered. "Yes, I love him a lot."

"Wait a minute" Carol said, recognition in her eyes. "Your name is Sarelle?"

Sigh. I was a famous celebrity now, after all. "Yes, I was the one who had the dhamphir."

"It's so interesting to finally meet you," she said pleasantly.

Theo shifted in his seat, irritated. "Can we get back to our problems?" he said, trying not to growl.

"Of course," she said smoothly. "Excuse me." She paused, and then spoke again. "Sar, I can understand Theo's jealousy, but not your guilt. You didn't cause this problem. Why are you guilty?"

Clearly, I would need a private session to tell her about Devlin. Nevertheless, I had some other reasons that needed to be spoken. "Because deep down inside, I am angry at Theo."

His head swiveled to me instantly, shocked.

"There was another woman he wanted to marry, and he was going to choose her over me," I said emotionally. "And another one he was living with—"

"I didn't live with Aspen—"

"Theo married me without telling her. She confronted him when we were filing our marriage certificate. And before you ask, yes, I knew they were in a relationship."

"Theo, why didn't you tell Aspen that you were going to marry Sar?"

"I planned to tell her," Theo said, running his hands through his hair. "But you weren't there. After the dream ended, I had to be with Sar." He explained about the dream we'd shared briefly. "I was sure she'd married or Oathed to Danial, and when I found out she was free, I couldn't wait another minute." He muttered something.

"Theo, speak your feelings louder. We are listening."

"I said fat lot of good it did me! Sar still wants Danial."

"Some of that is that they had a previous relationship, and some of that is her medical condition," Carol said gently. "It's normal for her to still feel affection toward him, even desire him. What you have to remember is that Sar is your wife, and she doesn't want to be intimate with this other man. She has stated that clearly several times." She paused. "Now if you will accept that—"

"I'll accept that when she's back to normal," Theo interrupted. "She should be like she used to in another few weeks. But we're not here only to talk about what we've discussed. Sar also endured an assault this past fall. She needs to talk to someone about that, because she hasn't told anyone, and she says she can't tell me."

Carol looked at me "Is this true, Sar?"

I nodded reluctantly.

"Sar, do you feel comfortable discussing what happened to you in front of Theo?"

"No," I said. "But I'll tell you the stark outline, if you want me to. This upsets Theo also, because I...I, um...I enjoyed it."

My admission didn't faze her in the slightest. "Are you embarrassed because you enjoyed it, or because you actively fantasize about forced sex? Sometimes women respond in odd ways to—"

"I'm embarrassed because I should have escaped. The first time was—"

"The first time!" Theo roared. "There was more than one? How many times did he have you?"

"I can't do this," I said in a small voice.

"You can," Carol encouraged. She shot Theo a deathly look. "Theo will be silent."

"The first time he forced me, he hurt me, even though he tried not to. But what hurt the most was I couldn't stop him, that no one was stopping him, and I did everything I could to get him off me and it wasn't enough." I wiped away sudden tears.

Theo grabbed my hand. "I'm so sorry," he whispered. "I should've been there."

"What happened after, Sar?"

I chose my words as carefully as I could. "The second time, he told me he wanted me to enjoy it. I tried my best, but I couldn't hold out, and eventually I came for him." I shot Carol a look. "That's all I'm comfortable saying."

Carol caught my unspoken message, and nodded to me once. "You need a private session, Sar, to discuss your feelings about this. This may be the root of your problem."

No maybes about it. "When?"

She checked her desk planner. "I have a three p.m. appointment free tomorrow, if that's doable."

I nodded. "I'll be here."

"Theo, do you feel better, hearing Sar tell you what happened to her?"

"Yes. I couldn't understand what happened from the little I knew. I was angry because she told me that she enjoyed it. I never blamed her for it happening; I blamed myself, and the men who took her." He paused. "I understand now that what I thought occurred wasn't what really happened."

No, it had been that and an ocean more...

"Sar, do you feel better, now that you've told Theo what happened?"

No, I feel guiltier than ever. "A little," I whispered.

"That's enough for today," Carol said, glancing at the clock. "Sar, I'll see you tomorrow."

Later that night as we lay in bed, Theo whispered, "Sar, I'm sorry. I know what it must have cost you to come back to me after and act like everything was fine."

I didn't reply.

"Did Devlin find you—?" he asked haltingly

"He found me naked on a bed, with five men and Alphonse around us, watching," I said coldly. "He killed them all."

"They're dead, all of them," Theo soothed, his arms tightening around me.

"You came through it, and you're going to be okay. I'm going to be here to make sure you're okay. If you need anything, just tell me."

"I didn't want you to know," I said softly. "But it's a relief to talk about it."

"We'll keep going back, Sar. As many times as it takes."

I hugged him tight, and didn't reply.

* * * *

"Good afternoon, Sar."

"Carol, is everything I say to you confidential?"

"Yes. Now what did you not feel comfortable telling me yesterday?"

"You're sure this is confidential?"

"Yes. Not only can I not tell Theo, I can't tell anyone, or I risk losing my license. The exception would be if you'd harmed someone, or planned to hurt someone, including yourself."

I shifted uncomfortably. "I need you to know that there is more to the story."

"Go on," she encouraged. "Tell me about this encounter. What was this man's name?"

Oddly, I didn't want to tell her Devlin's name. "I'd rather not give you his name just yet."

"That's fine. Please go on."

"The man who I enjoyed...um, was with was also the man who rescued me that night from my abductors. He was badly injured doing so. He was also a vampire, and I gave him my blood to heal, though I knew it was wrong."

"Why did you think it was wrong?"

"I wanted him secretly. He had saved me before, and I had wondered what being with him would be like. We'd had sexual chemistry from our first meeting, really. He'd come on to me in the past, and I'd fantasized about what would happen if I said yes."

"Fantasizing doesn't mean that you weren't forced. You refused—"

"No, I gave in," I amended. "I gave him permission."

"Did you feel you had a choice, really?" she asked.

"Not at the time. But when I look back at what happened, I think I wanted him to take me just the way he did. I'm a resourceful woman, and I could've escaped, but I didn't."

"This second-guessing and recrimination is common in rape cases," Carol said neutrally. "What happened wasn't your fault."

I looked away from her earnest gaze. "There's more to the story."

"Please continue."

"I left out a lot of things that Theo can't ever know."

"Such as?'

"That the man who made love to me that day was the best lover I've ever had in my life and most likely the best one I'll ever have."

Carol's eyes went wide with shock. "Why do you say that?" she said carefully.

"He was not afraid to say or do anything that might make the experience better, deeper, more fulfilling for me. He quoted poetry and sang to me as he touched and kissed me. He understood that by speaking to me, he could intensify everything I was feeling with my body. He used not only his body to love me, but his mind."

Carol's face had gone slack, enthralled. Oddly proud of Devlin's skill, I continued. "Needless to say, the experience was amazing. Though I can't feel much desire on these drugs, the thought of him still gets my heart racing."

"Do you know where this man is now?" she asked throatily. "Are you in contact with him?"

Did she want to contact him herself? "Yes. He sends me poetry via e-mail. He sent me cards and some flowers. He wants me to come to him. I haven't responded."

"Given what you've just said, why haven't you?"

"Because I can't trust him. I'm not sure that this other vampire doesn't just see me as a conquest. Also, I love Theo, and I don't want to hurt him. Add to that I'm worried about turning. I'm not sure this other vampire wouldn't turn me, if he decided he wanted to. "

"You mentioned yesterday that you were intimate with him more than once, yet what you've described seems to have lasted several hours," Carol said leadingly.

"Yes. It lasted most of a day."

"And each time, you enjoyed what was happening?" Carol said, her face carefully neutral.

"Yes, very much. The last several times, I was the one who initiated it. Again, I'm wondering now if that was because I was turning. It was out of character for me to do and say the things I did. I remember thinking that at the time."

"You said yesterday that you didn't want to be intimate with Danial, only Theo. But from what you've just said, I understand that when it comes to this other man, you'd rather be with him than Theo; that you would be, if you felt you could trust him."

"That's exactly the way I feel," I retorted. "Which is why I know most, if not all, of my feelings for this other vampire have to stem from my closeness to turning, not from my real feelings, all his prowess aside."

"Sar, it isn't professional to say this. But I will say it to you, one woman to another. You are right to keep this encounter secret. Your husband is a jealous and possessive man, and he could not handle this information, not and continue to be your husband. If you truly want to remain in your marriage, do as you have been: do not contact or see this other vampire again, and keep everything that you've told me today to yourself." Carol paused. "Have you confided in anyone else?"

"I told Danial about what happened, all of it. He agreed not to say anything. The problem isn't knowing what to do, it's constantly feeling like a bitch because I'm keeping this secret from Theo. I'm not a good liar; I never wanted to be. But I don't want this vampire dead, or to have him kill my husband, either."

"I have heard of Theopolis O'Connor," Carol replied. "His reputation has grown this past summer, when he moved into the upper ranking."

My eyes widened, surprised she knew about Theo at all, much less his rank. "What do you mean?"

"He is in the top three, after killing Manir's bodyguard," Carol stated. "That is what I've heard from others in his field, at least."

Theo hadn't told me he'd changed his ranking. It had been fifth, last I'd heard. "Is he second or third? Who did you hear this from?"

"Another client involved in the same business who is unranked. There's some confusion over the number two spot. For a long time the second was believed to be something like a hermit. He'd kept to himself for many years, and no one had seen him. It's just come to light that he's dead. There's confusion over just when he died."

Why was she going into so much detail? "So Theo is three, but he will be two, if this person is declared legally dead?"

"Yes," Carol said, nodding. "You can be relieved, really. Contrary to logic, your husband is statistically less likely to get challenged in his new spot. For many years the top three have stayed pretty much the same. It's unusual in a history of violent men to have a long stretch in a top position, but that's what's happened for several decades now."

She was really into this. How weird. "Thanks for that info."

"It must seem odd to you I know about the ranking," Carol said, smiling. "You'd be surprised how many men in that profession need my services. But I'm getting off topic." She paused, then reached out and touched my hand. "You need to let go of your guilt. What happened that day was not your fault, and you need to let it go. Forget what happened to you. Forgive the man who did this to you, and get on with your life."

"I forgave him the day he did it, and told him so," I said with a rakish smile. "But I wouldn't forget it for the world. But you're right, I should let it go."

A few moments passed in silence. "Tell me, why does the woman Theo was with bother you so much?" Carol said finally. "You were with another man at the time yourself."

"Because I refused to Oath to Danial. It bothers me Theo could have just called and told me to move on. I'd have been pissed off, but I could've built a new life with Danial. Instead he let me hang in limbo." I relayed a brief summary of Theo's capture and torture to finding me with Danial and going west alone.

Carol listened attentively, then said, "Love is not the same for everyone. Theo went through hell. He may have turned to her because he lost faith, lost hope."

"He should have had hope!" I said angrily. "He told you about the dreams we shared. That makes us special!"

"You feel betrayed that you held out and he did not."

"Yes. Also, I always used to think Theo was a standup guy. Though I wouldn't tell him, I'm ashamed of the way he handled Aspen, as satisfied as I was at the time to see it. It was cruel of him to treat her like he did."

"You see a parallel between his cruelness to you with this other woman, and his cruelness to Aspen later on with you?"

"Yes," I admitted.

"Do you have regrets over marrying Theo and not staying with Danial? You sound as if you do."

"Yes," I said, flushing slightly.

"But you told me yesterday you don't want to be with Danial anymore, only Theo."

"I don't know what I feel, or who I am anymore," I said, frustrated. "When I knew Theo and we first were together, nothing could touch us. Now things are different. I'm not sure if it's me or him or my being close to turning. All I do know is that I hate feeling this way."

"That's enough for today," she said cheerfully. "Come back next week. Until you begin to come to terms with how you feel, you should come for both the joint sessions with Theo and alone. Will this time and day of the week be a problem?"

"No. Thank you," I said, getting to my feet.

My phone rang as I was driving out of the parking lot.

"Hello?"

"We have a problem," Theo said angrily.

Chapter Eight

"What is it?" I said, trying to drive and fit my cell phone earpiece in my ear so I didn't get a ticket for talking and driving.

"Elle didn't invite only Violet, she invited three other girls, too."

If this was the biggest problem we had to deal with, this sleepover was going to be a piece of cake. "Then we'll have them sleep on sleeping bags on her floor, and one in bed with her. There should be enough room. If there's not we can buy an air mattress."

"What if she changes in the night?" he said worriedly. "What if she purrs?"

"Then we'll handle it," I said calmly. "I'm heading to the store now to pick up chips and other snacks. Do you want anything?"

"Maybe some doughnuts," he said hopefully.

I laughed. "I'll get two dozen, so there's some left for the girls."

"How was your appointment?" he asked.

"Fine," I said evasively. "She asked questions and I answered them. I made us an appointment for next week, but she wants to see me alone, too."

"Good. That will be the 20th, right?"

There was something unfamiliar in his tone. I pulled into the store parking lot and checked my pocket calendar in my purse. "Yes, December 20th, three p.m. It's a Monday."

"That's fine. I'll be here if any of the girls come early. 'Bye, Sar. I'll see you tonight." He hung up.

I looked at the phone oddly. Theo hadn't told me he loved me. He always said he loved me every time we said good-bye. Didn't he?

He was probably just stressed over the girls coming. It was nothing.

* * * *

Violet was the first girl to arrive. Cathy walked her up to our door.

"Come in!" I said loudly, giving them a welcoming smile. Cathy and Violet gave me one back, and entered, petting the dogs a little nervously.

"They sure are big," Violet said, apprehensive.

Both dogs stood tall enough to almost look her in the eyes.

"They won't hurt you." I handed her a rawhide stick. "Give each of them one of these."

She gave one to Darkness, who took it from her gently. Ghost took the other from her hand a little less gently. When she saw they weren't going to hurt her, Violet smiled, relaxing.

Elle came bounding out. "Hi, Violet! Come see my bedroom!"

With some help from Terian, we'd moved a lot of her things from Danial's house here for the night. My old sewing room had been completely transformed.

That whole ordeal had led to a fight with Theo, who'd wanted to outfit her room here to make it a duplicate of her bedroom at Danial's. Though money wasn't an issue, I'd refused. Though I'd given Theo other reasons, the real one was that Danial had enough on his mind now; he didn't need to worry that Elle might come live with us. It was easy to see that was what Theo was hoping for.

Theo had been angry, of course. He'd asked me directly if I didn't want Elle around. It had been all I could do not to tell him Elle was better off with Danial, who was a much better father.

"Sar?" Cathy said loudly.

Shit, she'd asked me something. "Sorry?"

"I said I love what you've done with the house. All the blues and greens are soothing."

That's because I live with a killer, and he needs to relax. "I like to decorate, especially painting. Did the directions work out okay? I'm not very good, I'm afraid."

"Elle emailed us some from MapQuest."

"Dad did them," Elle called from the other room.

Saved by the vampire computer whiz yet again.

Theo joined us. "Hi. Thanks for bringing Violet. Elle's really been looking forward to this."

"What do you do again?" Cathy asked, giving him a radiant smile.

"Security," Theo said, preening.

"Is it dangerous?" Cathy asked, her eyes wide.

"Only when I have to defend myself," Theo said, giving her a serious smile back. "Then, my life is usually on the line. You've seen TV series about agents where every twenty-four hours is packed with action. Let me tell you, I really have days like that."

I stifled a snort, biting my lip.

More cars drove up the driveway. Soon, Fiona, Diana, and Mary had joined Elle and Violet in her bedroom. There were now three other mothers with Cathy in a semicircle around Theo, as he related the daring tale of being in the bar parking lot that night in Wyoming, and fighting off five men. They were hanging on every word. "Oohs" and "Ahhs" filled the room.

I left them sighing, and went in to tell the girls that dinner would be ready shortly. The moment I opened the door, it was evident we already had another problem.

Elle still wore the fox head necklace Danial had given her at the Hallow's party years ago. To my knowledge, she had not removed it since that night. Either the necklace had lengthened as she grew, or Danial had gotten her a new chain for it. Either way, Elle had never taken it off herself or tried to, until now.

"It won't come off!" Elle yelled in desperation. She pulled with all her might at her choker. "I don't know what's wrong?"

I went to it quickly, fumbling at the hidden clasps. It hesitated, but finally unclasped, when I put all my willpower and concentration to it.

I handed it to her. "It's off. What's the matter?"

Elle grabbed the necklace and quickly tried to fasten it about Violet's neck, but the ends wouldn't close. "Mom, you broke it!"

Shit. "It's not broken, Elle—

"Can I wear it?" Violet said eagerly. "Just for a while?"

"I want to try it on, too!" another girl said.

"Me first!"

"Everyone can try it on briefly," I said firmly. "Then it goes back on Elle. Violet, you're first."

I put it on and took it off for each girl, and it resisted me every time. I'd just gotten it fastened back around Elle's neck when Mary spied my choker. "You have one, too?"

"Can we look at it, please?" they all said in unison.

I sat on the bed as they all clustered around me, touching the pendant. Self-conscious, I was relieved I'd put makeup on my scar from Danial in preparation for meeting the mothers. This close, it couldn't look like anything other than a bite mark.

"Did you get this from Elle's dad?" Fiona asked.

"Yes," I said, smiling. "When we were first dating."

"What does he look like?" one of them asked. "Like Theo?"

"Elle, you must have a sketch of the two of us?" I said, turning to her.

Elle brought out one of her sketchbooks and showed them one of the drawings she had done of Danial and I. There was an instant collective clamor.

"He's so handsome!"

"Does he really look like that? He's so sexy!"

"Guys, he's my Dad!" Elle said sarcastically. "Don't be gross."

"Is he coming to the dance recital tomorrow?" Fiona asked. "Do we get to meet him?"

I'd be missing my ride with Danial tomorrow night, as we'd be at the recital. But I'd been tired this week anyway. There had been so much to do, and the party tonight had weighed on my mind, as the party on New Year's did also. Maybe it was better to give the riding a rest anyway. The snow at Danial's was deep off the driveway.

"Yes," Elle said, "Dad is coming."

I realized abruptly that I'd been in here about ten minutes already. "Dinner is ready, girls. Come on, before it gets cold."

As I led them out, we went past their mothers, who were still being regaled by Theo.

"Mom," Diana said pointedly. "Dad's going to be home soon. Aren't you going out to dinner tonight?"

Diana's mom turned beet red. Then all the mothers began making apologies. Within a few moments, they'd all left.

"Having fun?" I said, giving Theo a knowing look.

"I don't know what you mean," Theo said loftily, then winked.

Happily, the rest of the night went smoothly. When it was bedtime, I shooed the girls into Elle's room, and drew her aside. "There's a reason you can't get off the choker, or put it on yourself, Elle," I whispered.

"Why?"

"No one can make you take it off. Any supernatural being you come into contact with can easily recognize that you are under Danial's protection, as I am."

"They wouldn't hurt us?"

"We wouldn't be a snack or dead."

Elle flinched at my words. "You can take yours off, though. What if someone made you take it off?"

"I'll soon have another mark on the other side on my throat to match the one I have now. Even if someone got the collar off me somehow, those marks say something just by themselves, Elle."

She nodded. "Marny noticed your bite under the makeup. I told her it was an old scar from an animal."

"That's okay," I said, hugging her. "She can think that. Danial won't be offended."

"I'm having a lot of fun," Elle said gratefully. "Thank you."

"Good. If anything happens tonight, come and get me. It's okay, even if the door is closed."

She nodded, and went back inside her bedroom. I went into the living room, where Theo was surfing channels.

I flopped down beside him. "I'm ready for bed now."

"I'm sorry, but there are five girls in the house, so I can't help you."

I pinched him. He began tickling me, fending off my struggles to get free. "Stop!" I pleaded.

Theo backed off, reclining back. "Are they having fun? They seem to be."

"Yes. Are you still hungry? There are some chicken fingers left over."

"Not anymore there's not," Theo replied.

"Did you eat the donuts too?"

"Just three."

There was a commotion from the other room suddenly. I got up and went into Elle's room, where they girls were giggling and shrieking.

"It's time for bed," I said sternly. "No more noise, okay?"

"Okay," they all chimed.

Way too cooperative. They must have flashlights ready for when I left. I shut the door, hearing the muted giggling began again. Walking into the bedroom, I discovered a huge cougar curled up waiting for me.

"Theo!" I chastised. "What do you think you're doing?"

He purred, kneading his claws on the comforter.

"We have strangers in the house, and we need to act as normal as possible, which even on a good day is hard to accomplish."

Theo purred deeper, and flipped over lightly on his back.

I crawled in bed. "Suit yourself. It's on you if one of the girls comes in here and sees you."

* * * *

Elle woke us up the next morning at seven. Theo was still cougar, and we were just lucky she told her friends that all of them coming to surprise us wasn't a good idea.

After plying the girls with donuts, I got them all dressed. They played for a short time outside, and soon after, the first mother arrived to pick her daughter up.

When we'd scheduled the sleepover, I'd expected a long, drawn out, low-key morning, like the ones I experienced in my own youth. But times had changed, and all of the girls had other planned events they had to attend, so they had to get up early. From the mothers' harried explanations, this was the norm. I smiled and sighed with relief, glad Elle's schedule wasn't so hectic.

By the time the last girl was packed off, I was exhausted. I went back to bed, and Theo got up, then helped Elle pack her overnight bags and some of the things she was taking back to Danial's. When I woke up, Terian had already come and picked up Elle.

I felt somehow cheated, but there wasn't time to pity myself. Elle's recital was in a few hours.

After showering and walking the dogs, we dressed hurriedly and drove to the recital hall. We made it in plenty of time, yet Danial had still beaten us there. He was holding court much as Theo had before, several mothers clustered around him.

As we came closer, Danial looked up and saw us. He motioned Theo and me down to him, where he had saved us some second row seats.

"Hey," I said, sitting down next to him. "You're early."

"I didn't want to be late," he said pointedly. "Someone had to save the best seats."

I clasped his hand. "Thanks."

He gave my cheek a gentle kiss. "If so many eyes weren't watching us, I would give you a more preferable kiss, Sar," he teased.

"Knock it off," Theo growled, sitting down on my other side.

"Later," I said to Danial, patting his hand.

Then the curtain went up, and the recital begun.

If you have ever been to a dance recital, they are all much the same. The first few numbers are wonderful, the cute outfits darling. By the tenth number, and the end of the second hour, if you are waiting to see your child, you are beginning to wonder if the torture will ever end.

Finally, our waiting paid off, and Elle came onstage. She was beautiful in her red tutu, her hair gathered sharply up under a sequined band to show her graceful neck. Her moments were feline in their grace, and she was easily the best student in her class. It was there in the lines of her form, and her delicate movements, that one day she would be as sultry and beautiful as her mother, Tawny, had been.

All too soon, she was done and taking a bow as we and the rest of the audience clapped.

After one more routine, the show was over. As all the girls came out to take a bow, Danial produced roses for each of us. We brought them up to the stage together, and handed them to Elle. After a few pictures, Danial lifted her down.

Elle hugged us all, but she talked to Danial the most, asking if he saw her about ten times.

"Yes. You were wonderful, and I am very, very proud of you."

Theo and I echoed Danial's sentiments.

"Go say goodbye to your friends," Danial told Elle. "We must be going."

As Elle raced off, Danial began dialing his phone.

"Are you heading home?" I asked.

"Brian is coming to pick us up," Danial said, giving my hand a quick kiss. "He's waiting around the block. I gather you're not coming home with us?"

"No," I said tiredly. "I'm worn out. Next Saturday?"

"That will be the last before the party," Danial said neutrally. "Yes, I'll plan for it. Riding?"

"No, it's been too cold lately. Let's stay in and rent a movie or something."

"I'll read to you," Danial said, nodding. "Be there at dark." His attention shifted, and he began speaking to Brian.

"I thought you were going to go," Theo whispered, his arms going around my waist. "I'm glad you didn't. But I don't mind if you want to, really."

I did a double take. "You sound like you want me to go."

"No," Theo said, uncomfortably. "I just expected you to. You've gone every Saturday until now."

The more he talked, the odder I was feeling. "The turning is almost reversed, Theo. Aren't you happy about that?"

"Of course," Theo said soothingly. "You know, Elle was great. She's got real talent."

"She may decide to be a dancer."

"I'd rather she used her brain than her body. I need to use both to do my job and eventually, I won't be able to do it anymore. Professional dancers can only dance until they are what, thirty? Then they have to teach, or do something else."

"Theo, that's a long way off. But that reminds me, why didn't you mention you'd become second?"

"Who told you I was second?" Theo said, his eyes narrowing. "Danial?"

"No, he didn't. Are you?"

"No, I'm third. They're still working out the details of the second's demise."

"You never said anything," I said angrily. "Last I knew you were fifth."

"There was an accidental death, or at least, that's the way it's being written up," Theo said wickedly. "But yes, the other was murder, cut and dried. Well, actually, quartered and disemboweled,"

"You know, I think I will go with Danial," I said angrily. I stalked off, just managing to catch the Expedition before it left.

"Mom's coming," Elle said, grabbing hold of the steering wheel. "Wait, Brian."

"You changed your mind?" Danial said as he opened the back door, a pleased expression on his face.

"Yes," I said, climbing in beside him. "Theo needs some time to himself."

Danial gave me an odd look, then nodded, clasping my hand in his. "Then we'll make good use of the time. Come, let's go out to dinner to celebrate Elle's triumph."

"Yes!" Elle shouted. "Pizza!"

"Sounds good," I said, leaning into Danial's shoulder. "We can bring home some dessert for Theoron."

* * * *

"Theo, tell us again why you didn't tell Aspen about Sar before you married her?"

"We've been over this already!" Theo said, exasperated. "I wanted to marry her right then and there. I didn't know where Aspen was at that moment and I didn't care."

"But you were intimate with her, Theo. Don't you feel you should have told her?"

"That doesn't mean I loved her," Theo said simply. "I like sex. I always have. When Aspen came and offered herself to me, I accepted. I wanted her. I never promised her anything."

"Isn't it true though that you asked her to move in with you?" Carol said.

"Yes," Theo said, agitated now. "I wanted her around, because I liked to be with her. Why do we have to talk about her every time we come here? I haven't seen her since the night I told her I didn't ever want to see her again. Why is she even an issue we have to discuss?"

"You were falling in love with her," I spoke up, giving him a glance. "I want to know how you could treat her how you did, and then cry over her afterwards."

Theo's eyes were yellow as he answered. "She wasn't you. After that dream, it was like the years we were apart disappeared. If I hadn't found you in that hotel, I'd have gone back East. I knew I'd find you with Danial. I knew you'd go back to him. You've never been able to stay away from him for very long since you met him."

"That's not true," I said loudly.

"Theo, we were talking of Aspen, not Sar. Did you love her?"

"I liked her. I liked having sex with her. She was werecougar like me, and I'd never been with a female of my own kind. There was animal attraction between us, and it was most of our relationship, as it had been with Tawny, my first lover. I thought in that last month with her that maybe I could come to love her, in time. Most of it was loneliness. I didn't want to hurt her, in any case, and I know I did." He paused. "There isn't anything more to say about her."

"What did you feel for this other woman, Tasha?" Carol asked.

"I loved her," Theo said, his eyes on the floor.

"More than me," I needled. "Be honest."

Carol shot me a warning glance, and then looked back at Theo. "Why did you love her, Theo? Was it because she nursed you back to health?"

Theo didn't answer immediately. He let out a long breath, and finally said, "I don't know that it was any one thing. I was grateful to her for helping me. For being kind to me, for letting me out of the cage I'd been in. For letting me sleep with her inside where it was warm—"

I'd known that's what had prompted all his cougar snuggling with me. Damn her.

"—and for her gentle touch where before I'd had only pain." Theo paused again.

I wanted to be anywhere but there. Hearing this ripped my heart out all over again. Angrily, I asked myself why it bothered me so much. If I couldn't let it go, why the hell was I staying with Theo? I was almost well, and Danial would welcome me back with open arms...

"I felt affection for her, and sexual desire. I hadn't been with anyone in over a year. Sometime after we first had sex, I realized I was in love with her. When she asked me to spend my life with her, I didn't hesitate."

"Why didn't you think about Sar?" Carol asked. "You say you knew she'd go back to Danial. Why not call her and sever the ties completely? And what about Elle? Weren't you worried about your daughter?"

Theo's eyes were yellow again. "I was tired of pain. I was tired of being hurt, of fighting, of killing people. I wanted some peace. I looked at the life I would lead with Tasha, and it seemed a good one. I'd sent Danial back to take care of Sar and Elle. I knew he'd take care of them if he made it back to the hotel, and I expected that he had. He didn't get to be four hundred plus without having a strong will to live. What was the point of calling after a year had passed? If they hadn't made it, I didn't want to know. If they had and were happy together, I didn't want to know that, either."

I stared at him, aghast, trying to find some words to say.

"I understand you went through a horrible ordeal," Carol said neutrally. "I can understand you not wanting to find out on top of that Sar and Elle were dead. But you say you expected them to be alive and well. If the situation had been reversed, can you honestly say you'd understand if Sar was alive and well in another country, and she let you believe she was dead?"

There was silence for a full minute.

"There is nothing I can say that makes sense," Theo said finally. "I should have thought of her and Elle, and I didn't. Some part of me knew I'd find her with Danial, but that wasn't the reason I agreed to stay with Tasha. I feel ashamed of how I acted, looking at it from that perspective. I feel even more ashamed about Elle. Even if I couldn't face Sar and Danial, I should have come back for her, to let her know I was alive."

"Sar, do you feel better, knowing that Theo feels regret over his actions?"

What I felt was that I was going to kill one of them if I didn't get out of this room. "Yes."

"Theo, do you feel better for telling Sar what you told her?"

"Yes," he said simply. "I'm sorry if I hurt you by anything I did. I never meant to."

I took his hand, a sense of peace suddenly filling me. "Thank you."

"Really then, I don't see what other issues there are to work out, at least immediately," Carol said happily. "Enjoy the holiday, and call me in the new year, if you run into problems."

"Are you sure?" I asked her. "That's it?"

"For now at least," she said, standing up and shaking my hands. "You can always call if there's a problem you can't work out on your own. Remember, some conflict is normal."

Theo and I thanked her, and we left. As we drove home, I tried to examine my feelings. With Theo's apology, I'd finally let go of the hurt I'd been harboring for so long...

"You know I love you, right?" Theo said, glancing at me.

"I know it," I replied, giving him a smile.

"Still love me?" he said, glancing over again.

"Always," I said, taking his hand. "By the way, we need to take Elle sledding this week. She's been asking us to."

"How about Thursday then?"

"Okay." I turned to him in the seat, having suddenly remembered my relatives' invitation. "Would you be interested in seeing my former in-laws out west?"

He glanced at me quickly, his expression strange. "Why would they want to see me? I'm the replacement you got for their dead son."

"Nice, Theo," I replied with a grimace. "They want to see me, and they know we're married. We could have a second honeymoon, sort of, maybe next summer. Elle could come, and we could show her some of the sites we spent time at in Wyoming. What do you think?"

I expected Theo to be excited, but he didn't reply right away.

"You don't want to go," I said, crestfallen.

"I feel a little odd about it, that's all," he said finally. "Let me think about it, okay?"

"Sure," I said, settling back in the seat. "Take your time. There's no rush."

Chapter Nine

As the last week before Christmas passed, one thing became crystal clear: my desire had gone completely.

I'd noticed it waning all through the fall, as my body slowly went back to normal. But on December twenty-second, I looked at the world around me, and it no longer interested me at all. I'd tried my best to make it seem as if everything was the same for so long, even as I ceased to care less and less. But my absence of feeling had intensified to the point now where I couldn't pretend anymore. Some of that was that I was tired of pretending. The rest was that I no longer had anything left to pretend with.

I couldn't seem to reach my emotions. I didn't care about watching the latest episodes of the series I followed, or even trying to follow them, so I stopped recording them, deleting the saved episodes I'd stopped watching weeks before. At first, I'd been the loving wife that Theo expected, welcoming his advances like always, even though my heart wasn't in it. Before long, Theo had felt in my kisses that I didn't mean them, and stopped trying to initiate anything. I had once laughed at jokes Terian told and gossiped with Cia, but now I avoided them both, and my family, too. I'd used to love walking with Elle, identifying tracks together in the last non-frigid days of the year. Now, I just nodded to her, the thought of the snow-engulfed woods too daunting for me to set foot outside. That might have been a problem, except my appetite for food had also greatly diminished.

The only thing I really wanted to do anymore was sleep. Those last days before Christmas, I admitted it had to be more than lack of desire that was causing me to act this way; I had to be depressed. Even if it was only due to the lack of daylight as Theo surmised, I had to get some help. This was not good for me, or the people around me.

Dr. Camlyn was less help than I expected. "This is normal for the winter," he said with a shrug. "Especially for what you're going through. Desire is a large part of a person's being. Things will get better, Sar. The virus is almost out of your system. Only a few more weeks, and then you can go off the pills."

"I'm not taking them anymore," I told him in what passed for my normal voice these days.

"How long has it been since you went off them?" he said, concerned.

"Just yesterday," I said, giving him a halfhearted smile. "Danial is gone all this week, and most likely for next week too, traveling. Even if I go to work, no one will be there who will tempt me. By the time he comes back, I should be better."

"Sar, that's fine. But you shouldn't go off them completely cold turkey. Take one every other day, at least for this week, and then stop taking them."

I nodded, but told myself I wasn't going to do what he suggested. I'd had enough of popping pills.

No one would know. I'd come by myself today, as Theo had been working out and I hadn't wanted to bother him. I'd told Terian where I'd be. He said he would have his phone on, to call if anything happened and he would "whisk me away." I managed a small smile at the memory.

"Sar, everything will be okay." He put his hand on my shoulder. "We're almost there."

I nodded.

"Come back in a month. I expect to pronounce you fully better by then. You've healed most of your internal scarring." He smiled encouragingly. "Babies are in your future, if you want them."

I managed a faint smile. "Thanks."

He left the room, the door shutting softly. I got dressed, paid my co-pay at the window, and went out to Theo's older truck I'd driven today.

As I was driving back, I decided not to return to Danial's right away. I went instead to a local park I'd not visited in a long time. It was the one I'd come to with Danial more than three years ago.

I parked at the top, near the office, as I didn't want another police officer to come and yell at me for parking in the wrong area. The day was clear and cold, the roads cleared. Everything was sparkling in the sun. The trees were barren things, branches black against the pale blue sky.

I called Terian and let him know where I was. "I'm going for a short walk."

"Are you all right?"

I said "yes," though we both knew I was lying. "I'll call you if there's anything out of the ordinary."

"Okay. I can teleport there if you need me—"

I hung up on him.

I was worn out, as I'd been feeling lately, but not cold. I'd dressed in four layers of polar fleece, as a precaution. I walked along the plowed road slowly for a long time, looking into the snowy woods. Was this what I wanted, to feel nothing? To want nothing?

Maybe it would have been okay, if I didn't remember that there had been a time when I'd wanted things badly. Wanted Danial, since the first time I'd seen him. Wanted his love, his touch, his heart. Wanted Theo, wanted a life with him. Gone across the country to find him, to tell him I needed him, loved him. Wanted a child, wanted Danial's child, a life that I'd helped create, and shape. Wanted to watch him grow, wanted to see him become so many things. And in all truth, I had wanted Devlin, just to have him, to know if he did love me as Danial said that he had. To know if he would have really welcomed me, if I'd come to him in Rio.

I felt as though I was so distant from those feelings that all I could see of them were the words.

Love.
Truth.
Hope.
Passion.

I might have been moved to write a poem, but I didn't even feel that badly about what I'd lost, though I knew on some level that I'd lost something vital, a part of myself that had disappeared into the snow that surrounded me.

Sure, Dr. Camlyn was right: I'd get well. I just had to hold on a few more weeks. I told myself I could do it. I'd been cut off from my emotions before, when Brennan died. I just had to keep going toward that light at the end of the tunnel. Darkly, I hoped that the light was the summer sun, not the light of an oncoming train.

I walked to the edges of the lake. It was frozen, as it had been that night Danial and I were here. I stepped on the edges, breaking the ice as I had that night. The ice made the same cracking sound as it had that night, but it stirred none of the satisfaction that it had once.

What was I looking to find, coming here after all this time? Memories? Some kind of sign?

I stood for a while on the shore looking out at the lake. The wind blew and the cry of a crow echoed across the trees. I looked for it, but didn't see it. Everything was still and clean, the snow glistening in the weak sunlight.

With surprise, I looked up to see heavy white clouds were rolling in, obscuring the sun. Snow was coming, and soon. That storm predicted had arrived early.

I began walking quickly back, but the storm caught me before I was even halfway. A light snow began to fall, clinging in small flakes to my hair and jacket. I walked through it and thought that it was rather nice. I wasn't too cold, and the flakes were pretty. In fact, it would be beautiful to go into the woods. All the branches had snow outlines, like a delicate layer of decorative frosting that sparkled in the weak light. There was that poem by Frost, about stopping in the snowy woods. These woods weren't dark; they were comforting, as if the branches would enfold me as a lover would, and the snow would cover me as a blanket, and I would rest beneath the trees…

With a start, I realized I'd begin to wander off the path. My feet were wet to the ankles, the snow coming nearly up to my knees. The plowed road was behind me a good twenty feet.

I went back to it quickly, scared at my odd behavior. What was I thinking, strolling through the woods with an approaching storm so close? I had to get my ass home, because by now Theo would be worried. The snow was coming down harder now, and my gut was telling me I'd better get on the road as fast as I could.

By the time I got to the car, I was sweaty, exhausted, and damp with snow. As I started it up, I called Theo.

He answered on the first ring. "Sar, where are you?" he shouted.

"I'm at the park. I'm heading home—"

"You've been gone all day! Where have you been?"

"Theo," I said, slightly irritated, "I've been here walking. I'll be there in about an hour."

"An hour? Sar—!"

I hung up on him, reserving all of my concentration for the road. Theo called back several, times, but I let it go to voicemail.

It took me more like an hour and a half to get home, the slick, fresh snow already several inches deep in places. When I got home, I parked in the garage next to Theo's truck. Theo opened the door in the next moment.

He hugged me tight. "Sar, I was so worried. Thank God you're okay."

"I'm sorry," I said, hugging him. "I needed to get away, just for a while."

"What did Stephen say?" Theo asked. "Terian said you'd gone to see him. Was it bad news?"

"He said another two weeks, and I should be back to normal," I tried to muster a smile.

"Doesn't that make you happy?" he asked sharply.

"I don't feel much of anything about it, though I know I should be happy."

"How can you not be happy?" he said, with a hint of anger.

Not another fight. We'd been fighting a lot lately, ever since Elle's recital when I'd gone off with Danial. Despite we'd made up since then, there seemed to be some undercurrent making Theo angry. Maybe he'd been angry all along, and just hid it well. We'd both been pretending so long that things were okay it was hard to tell. "I don't know. Why do you have to yell at me when I just got home?"

"I'm sorry," he said, hugging me again. "I'm on edge. I was worried."

"You shouldn't have been," I said, gently slipping out of his grasp. "Let's go inside, I'm freezing." I went past him, and into the house. I petted both dogs, then went into the kitchen. "Do you want something to eat?" I said to him, opening the fridge.

He ran his hands through his hair.

"That's not an answer," I said gently.

"I need to leave next week, Sar."

Just the tone of his voice said loud and clear that there was more than he was making it seem. "Leave?" I repeated, not understanding.

He looked at me steadily. "I need to go to Canada ahead of time to check out everything carefully, make sure that nothing is left to chance."

"I thought when we agreed to go, Samuel and the others guaranteed our safety, at least until we got there. We were all going together," I replied tiredly. "What happened?"

"He did say that, but I'm not sure we can trust him. He never guaranteed Danial's safety," Theo said, his stare still unwavering. "I need to do this."

I looked into his eyes and knew he was lying to me. God, this was one time I was glad for my distant emotions. "When are you leaving?" I said, holding his gaze.

"Monday," he said. "The day after Christmas."

"So you'll be here for Christmas?" I asked.

"Sar," he said softly, coming to put his arms around me "I'll be here for Christmas. Elle asked that, when I told her earlier today. I've waited too long to spend a Christmas with you both to miss one. I wouldn't miss it for anything."

"Good," I said softly, putting my head on his shoulder. "This will be our first Christmas together."

"I know." He kissed my forehead. "Are you hungry?"

"No."

"You should eat," he said worriedly. "Did you eat today?"

"I'll eat later," I said, pulling him close. "I want to be with you now, if you want me."

He groaned, and wrapped his arms around me, hugging me tightly. But he made no move to kiss me.

Something was very wrong. I'd put him off for too many days now for him not to be immediately carrying me off to the bedroom. "What's wrong?

Something is."

"I love you," he said suddenly. "I just want you to know that."

Tears formed in my eyes, and I blinked them back. "I love you, too," I said softly.

He kissed me, and then led me by the hand to the bedroom. The sex was gentle, as he had been with me lately, as if he might break me. There was nothing different in the way he touched me; his caresses were as loving and sincere as they'd always been. After, he held me possessively, kissing me tenderly, whispering that things would get better, that the hell we'd been in for months now was finally ending.

I wanted to believe him, but I was certain some new problem waited in the wings for us. It had been in Theo's eyes when he'd lied to me. Strangely, his secrecy prompted not only my resolution to help him see it through, but also my affection for him. Even if the problem was just his alone now, it was going to be mine eventually. For better or for worse, it was already his and he was the other half of me.

I held him to me that night, and told him softly as he slept that I loved him, that I'd always love him, that if he remembered nothing of this night when he awoke, to remember that. I didn't know if he heard me, but I told myself he did, because thinking that let me sleep finally.

* * * *

In the morning, we didn't speak of his lie as we ate, nor on the ride to work. But it was in my thoughts as I climbed the stairs to Danial's office, and began to sort through emails.

Per usual, my daily dose of Devlin was waiting for me on my e-mail. Today's quote was M. Sangster's Forgiven:

And yet if you came back with arms stretched toward me,
Came back tonight with carefree smiling eyes,
I would forget the wounded heart you gave me,
I would forget the bruises on my soul.
My old time gods would rise again to save me,
My dreams would grow supremely new and whole,
If you came back, with arms stretched out before you,
And told me, dear, that you were glad to come!

I had not responded to his emails for the last week and a half, nor sent him any. That seemed the easiest thing to do. No one would be doing jobs over the holidays. But as I looked at the poem, I grew more and more irritated. I was tired of his e-mails, his poetry, his endless scheming to get me to fall at his feet.

I thought for a moment, and then typed a reply of several lines from Swineburne's poem Garden of Proserpine:

I am tired of tears and laughter,
And men that laugh and weep,
Of what may come hereafter,
For men that sow to reap
I am weary of days and hours
Blown buds of barren flowers
Desires and dreams and powers
And everything but sleep.

I hit send, and watched the e-mail disappear.

I worked a short while longer, then decided that I was too tired to continue. I shut down the computer, then went down and spent some time with Theoron. Taking him into Elle's room, we napped for an hour on her bed. About two, I got up, and put him back into his crib. After a quick lunch of canned soup, I decided to rest on the couch.

Theo came in about four, and woke me up. "Sar, maybe we should take you back to see Dr. Camlyn," he said. "You sleep so much now it worries me."

No way. I'd have to tell him I'd stopped taking the pills, and he'd probably make me take them again. I didn't want to see another little yellow pill in my life. Plus, I'd flushed all of mine down the toilet last night as Theo slept. "Theo, I was just there," I said, giving him a reassuring smile. "He checked me out. I'm fine."

He gave me a dubious look.

"Call him if you want. Most likely, it was the long walk I took yesterday that tired me out. It's been a long time since I walked that far."

"I'm calling him now," Theo said. "I want to hear him say sleeping so much is normal."

I nodded absently. As he made the call, I watched the tree lights twinkle merrily, thinking it was good we'd set it up weeks ago. The ornaments Elle had made were there, and the spiders we had all made that Christmas. Theo had participated, confessing later how much he'd enjoyed the trimming. "It was like that time you and the foxes made that natural tree a few years ago."

"You don't mind we don't have one at our house?"

"I'm just happy to be here, not injured or caged. Everything else is extra."

I'd held him after he said that, saying nothing, because there was nothing to say that could take that old pain away, except years of Christmas trees and knowing he was safe and loved.

Theo came back. "Sar, you were right. Dr. Camlyn told me this was normal. But he said I was to make sure you ate as much as possible. Are you ready to go home?" he said, holding out his hand. "We can stop for Chinese food."

I gave him a smile and took his hand. "Take me home, please."

As we drove home, the scent of hot Chinese food permeating the truck cab, I asked Theo about Danial. "Will he be home for Christmas? He told Elle on the phone yesterday he was going to try."

"Probably not. He's trying his best to get everything in order, so that when we go to the Gathering all his open cases are shut."

"He thinks he might not return, doesn't he?" I said watching his face carefully.

"He expects to have to fight for you," Theo said reluctantly. "He'd be facing vampires twice his age in the worst case scenario. It's rational to expect he might not make it."

"What would happen?" I ventured. "Is there some kind of contingency plan?"

Theo didn't reply, yet his silence spoke volumes. Danial was making final preparations.

I couldn't imagine being without Danial. I couldn't imagine being in his house, having everything still exist here and not have him here to smile at me, to hold Theoron, to be the friend and partner that he'd become to me. Panic grasped me hard and fast. "Theo?"

"We're working on it," he said seriously. "As soon as a plan is finalized, I'll tell you Sar. Trust me."

I sat back in the seat, tired and scared, and didn't reply.

* * * *

The next few days passed quickly.

I received more emails from Devlin, but these were all work related. I responded to them as best I was able, but a couple I had to call Danial to ask him the answers. I was glad of the excuse to call him in any case. He'd been gone now for over two weeks. Even when he called back, I received only messages because I was sleeping. Days when I was up, he was sleeping to prepare for the nights he was putting in. In short, I missed him.

I waited until late in the afternoon, and dialed Danial's cell phone. Brian answered on the first ring.

"Hi, Bri. Is Danial awake?"

"Sar, I'm glad this is you," Brian said, relieved. "You saved me time tracking you down. Danial wanted me to wake him early to talk to you before you were sleeping tonight. Wait just a moment." There were sounds of him opening a door. "Sar," he said.

The door closed. "Sar?" Danial asked hopefully.

"It's good to hear your voice. I wanted to call to make sure you were all right."

"I'm glad you did. I'm worried about you. Theo tells me that you are colder."

That was bizarre. "Stephen didn't tell me that. Neither did Theo. When did he tell you?"

"He said he thought your body seemed cooler to him late last night."

"I haven't been any colder that I was. When I got back from walking yesterday, I was chilled and wet. He's probably referencing that. But I'm not sick, or anything."

"Please eat as much as you can," he said, worried. "It's taking a toll on you, getting the virus from your system."

"Danial, don't blame yourself for this."

"Sar, Theo's right on one point: I'm the one who did this to you."

"I wanted our child. I wanted to be with you. I wouldn't undo it, Danial."

He sighed. "If only things were easier."

"Danial, what is going on with Theo? What prompted his sudden need to go to Canada ahead of us?"

There was silence.

"Danial, tell me."

"Ask me Monday night, Sar," he replied. "I'll tell you then."

By that time, Theo would have left. "Tell me now, Danial," I said, mustering a little anger. "Why is he going early? Did you find something out? Are the other Rulers plotting something?"

"Ask him yourself, Sar. If you ask him point blank and tell him you know he's lying, he'll tell you."

"So you know he's lying, too."

"Yes."

Danial almost never answered with a single word.

"Is this another challenge? Is he trying for the number one spot?"

"No," Danial said darkly. "He knows he wouldn't win. Did you call me to discuss this lie, or for some other reason? This subject is closed, Sar."

Angry as I was, when he said those words it meant no amount of my screaming, pleading, or crying would change his mind. *Stubborn Ass.* "I called you for direction on a few questions Devlin posed."

"Leave them in the inbox. I'll log in tonight and answer him directly.

Anything else?"

"No, other than to be careful, and we hope you're back by Christmas."

"I will not be. In fact, I'd appreciate it if you would arrange to stay over that night. Elle and Theoron need as normal a holiday as possible. They need one loving parent there, at least."

While Danial had alluded before to Theo's lack of devotion to Elle, he'd never before made it an insult. More scary, Terian was with Danial, and if he couldn't teleport home just for the evening, he had to be dealing with something not only tough, but very dangerous. "I'll be there, with Theo or without."

"Good," Danial said, obviously relieved. "I hope to be home a few days after. Please take care of yourself, Sweetheart."

"You, too. Bye."

I sat with the phone in my hands, wondering what to do.

Danial and I had messed up when we met. We should have been friends first, and lovers later, when we knew each other. We should have tried to bend more for each other, to give each other more forgiveness. But against the odds, somehow we had become what we should have been to each other all those years ago, in every way but the physical: a solid team that was there for each other, even when it caused us pain.

As for Theo, there was nothing to do but wait and see where the chips fell.

* * * *

Christmas that year was good, if touched with someberness. Elle, Theo, and I went to my parent's house, and opened presents. Elle loved everything that she got; at least, she acted as if she did. That went for everyone really, from the statue Theo had carved of my mother's favorite cat to the gift certificates I received. More importantly, we enjoyed each other's company, and had a great time.

There was one small glitch: my stepfather got Theo absolutely smashed on scotch. I was surprised at first, then slightly amused. But when I saw just how bad Theo was starting to feel, I'd got him packed into the car, and Elle as well.

Driving to Daniel's through the clear December night, I watched glowing stars twinkling above, and thought to myself even if things weren't great, they were still pretty nice.

After I put Theo to bed in Danial's room, I stayed up with Elle and Theoron for another hour playing a board game Danial had given them for Christmas called Peanut Butter and Jelly. It was an odd game: the point was to make sandwiches before animals ate parts of them. Elle won, as I kept getting no bread and too much peanut butter.

116

I put her and Theoron to bed at nine and then went in to Theo. As I crawled in bed with him, and held him in my arms, he stirred slightly. I kissed him very lightly, meaning to just fall asleep. Instead, he kissed me back, and hugged me.

Amused, I went to give him another kiss. My lips were almost on his when he said "Tasha."

I went rigid against him, holding my breath.

"Tasha," he murmured again. He kissed me, groaning softly.

I gently pried myself out of his arms, and got out of bed. I stood there and watched him move in his sleep, clearly dreaming of her and he having sex. I was about to lean over and wake him when he said, "I told you I loved you. I told you I'd come back. Now we'll be together."

I swallowed back bile. Was this what he and I had looked like caught in the throes of the dream we had shared? Even if I couldn't answer that, I now had the answer of where he was really heading to on Monday. Tonight was the only night this week he had not changed form into a cougar, and that was probably only because of all the alcohol in his system.

I went back out to the great room and sat there for a while, thinking about what to do. Ghost and Darkness, who had been dozing near the couch, came and sat near me, wagging their tails hopefully. I petted them, then hugged them.

"He's leaving me for her," I told them softly. "Do you think you could get used to living here again? Ivan will take you for w-a-l-k-s again."

They stared at me intently. I gave a smile, and then lay down on the couch, stretching out. Seeing no walk or treat was in the offing, both dogs lay back down and went to sleep.

Cia walked in, startling me. "Sorry," she whispered. "Danial asked me to check on Theoron. He had Terian teleport me in. I'll be here the same way to feed Theoron tomorrow morning while you take Theo to the airport." She produced a parcel. "He also wanted me to give this to you, if you were still up...um, by yourself."

With foreboding, I took her offered package. "Thanks, Cia."

"We'll be outside on duty until dawn," she assured. "Goodnight."

"Goodnight."

When she'd left, I opened Danial's present. There was a card with a familiar red velvet box. It showed just a full moon. Inside he had written:

I love you
Not only for who you are
But for who I am when I am with you.
I love you

For ignoring the possibilities
of the fool in me
And for laying firm hold
of the possibilities for good.
I love you
Because you have done
More than any creed
To make me happy.
You have done it
Without a word,
Without a touch,
Without a sign.
You have done it
Just by being yourself
After all
Perhaps that is what
Love means.

Underneath he had written:

This was not written by me, but a man by the name of Roy Croft. I wish I had the skill to write words such as these for you, to sing as my brother does for you, or to be the knight in shining armor that Theo has been for you. But I do not, and so I offer you only this: my unconditional love, now and forever.
Love, Danial

I opened the velvet box. There lay another pair of fox head earrings, identical to the ones I'd given Elle. The ruby eyes winked in the light. These were more than security, symbols to wear when we faced the other vampires of the world. They were a gift from a man to a woman he loved, and that he would continue to love, even if they couldn't be together.

Brushing away tears, I put them on, fighting the sudden desire to call him immediately, and tell him I'd be his again, that I'd found out about Tasha. Bitterly, I told myself not to make things worse.

My love for him aside, what would happen if I went back to Danial? Eventually, no matter how careful we were, I'd turn vampire. The status quo hadn't changed. I'd gone through hell to rid myself of the damned vampire virus. Being with Danial would just infect me all over again. I'd likely find myself taking little yellow pills this time next year.

My eyes flooded with tears at the unfairness of it all. *Damn it, I loved*

Theo, and I'd done all this for him, and now he was leaving me for that fucking teenager.

For a long time I sat mopping at my weeping eyes as I thought about my options. Finally, I decided to confront Theo in the morning. If he was leaving me, I wanted to hear it from him.

* * * *

I awoke early the next morning before it was light. Despite my life was going to hell in a hand basket, Elle didn't need her Christmas morning ruined by finding me sleeping out in the great room.

Theo was still sleeping peacefully in Danial's room. There was no smell of sex, as there had been with our dream. Relieved, I got in bed beside him and moved myself gently into his arms. I breathed in the scent of him, of wide blue skies and earth and pine forest, and prairie grass in the summer sun, and finally fell back asleep.

He awoke at ten. "Good morning," he said softly, kissing me. Then his eyes sprang open. "Shit, what time is it?" he said, rolling away from me to check the clock. "I'll miss my flight."

Without speaking, I got up and quickly put on some clothes. Theo was swearing, as he pulled out clothes and shoved them in his duffel. I left him that way, and went to wake up Elle, but she was already awake.

"Get dressed," I told her, giving her a kiss on her forehead. "We have to drive with Theo to the airport in a few minutes, or he's going to miss his plane."

"I want him to miss it," she pouted. "I want him to stay here with us. It's Christmas morning!"

"I wish he was staying too, honey," I said, hugging her. "But he has to go. He'll come back."

"Promise?" she said, looking up at me.

"Ask him yourself at the gate," I said perversely. "Now put some clothes on."

Theo was at the door by that time. "Hurry up, we have to go!"

We piled in the truck fast. Theo went down the driveway at forty-five mph. Somehow we got the airport in one piece. We parked, then walked with Theo to the private airport hanger section to see him off. Security was tightened for the holiday season, and we couldn't go with him to the private plane, as usually was possible.

"Do you have at least two guns?" I asked him softly, as we hugged good-bye.

"I have three," he answered, kissing me roughly. "And there's another waiting for me with a contact who is going to pick me up at the airport. I won't disappear again."

Elle hugged him. "Are you coming back?" she asked nervously.

"I'll always come back for you, Elle," he said affectionately.

"Promise?" she said, tearful and unsure.

"I promise," he assured her. He picked up his luggage, and turned to me. "Please take care of yourself."

"I love you," I told him, and gave him a hug. "Take care of yourself, too."

"I love you, too," he said easily. Then he scented the air suddenly. "What's the matter? You're upset—"

Above us, a speaker came to life. "Passenger for runway eight; your flight has clearance. Please report to hanger fifteen immediately."

"Passenger for runway eight; your flight has clearance. Please report to hanger fifteen immediately."

"That's me, I have to go," Theo said, irritated. "Damn pilots."

"You'd better go," I said, watching him closely. "She's waiting."

Theo blanched, all the blood draining from his face.

If I'd doubted my suspicions, I didn't now. "Tell her I said hi, and I'm going to take care of Elle," I hissed at him. "Don't worry about us, if that crosses your mind, that is."

"Mom!" Elle gasped

Theo's eyes went yellow. "You don't understand—"

"Save it," I said. "I understand enough." I grabbed Elle's hand and strode away angrily.

"Mom! You made him so angry! Why did you say that?" she wailed. "He looked so sad! Now maybe he won't come back!"

I turned around and hugged her. "Elle, I'm sorry you saw that. What happened just now wasn't your fault. Theo had to go work out some things from when he was gone from us. It may be a while until you see him again. But he told you he'd come back, and that means he will."

"How long will that be?" she said tearfully.

"I can't say. But your dad and I'll be here to take care of you, no matter what."

"You have jealousy in your voice," Elle said accusingly. "He's going to another woman, isn't he?"

"Yes," I said hesitantly. "Honestly, I don't know more than that. But the truth is that even when he does come back, he and I might not be together anymore."

"Are you going to get back with Dad?"

"I don't know," I said awkwardly. "Please, let's go home."

"I want Dad!" she wailed.

"We'll go call him," I affirmed. "I need to talk to him myself."

When we returned to Danial's, a package was waiting for me near the door. It was airmail, postmarked South America. Eyeing it, I said, "Elle, do you want to play, or lie down for a bit? I'll see if I can get your father on the phone."

"I'm going to my room," she said tiredly. "I want to talk to Dad, if you get him."

"Go ahead. I'll come get you if he answers."

Elle went into her room. I dialed Danial, but reached only his voicemail. I left him a message, saying that Elle was upset, there had been a scene at the airport, and I knew why Theo had left.

Theo was gone, maybe for good. Screw it. I hung up the phone, then opened the package. Inside was J. Blunt's album on CD, the one with the song "You're Beautiful" on it.

It hadn't been Danial that Brian had been talking to that day as I sung that song's refrain; it had been Devlin. I held my breath, and opened the card.

Sar, Do one last thing for me: Listen to the fourth track on this CD. Pretend it is me, singing to you, and know I mean the words, all of them. If you still don't want to come to me, I will leave you alone.

Good-bye, my lover.

Dev

I took the CD into Danial's bedroom, and used his state of the art CD player to play the song. It took me a while to get it to work, as my hands acted numb. I had tears of frustration in my eyes before I had the CD player working. As the first strains of the song began, I settled down on the floor by the cold and empty wood stove to listen. I looked at the back of the CD, to find the title of the fourth track. The title was "Good-bye My Lover."

Every word wrenched my heart a little more, and by the fourth line, tears were slipping down my face, one after the other. By the time it was over, I was sobbing, because his longing for me was my longing for him. His pain at not being with me was equal to my pain at not being with him. If he really felt all of that for me, I was crazy not to go to him. I wanted him so badly at that moment, I would have called him if I'd had access to his number and told him I would come to him right now, tonight, and damn everything else.

Wait. Devlin's number had to be in Danial's phone, under one of the speed dial buttons. It wouldn't take long to find. I moved toward the phone, and then suddenly, it rang.

I wasn't sure how to answer, this being the private line and not the business line. "Racklan residence," I said hesitantly.

"Sar, I got your message," Danial said, upset. "What did Elle witness? I need to know before I speak to her."

I took the phone over to Danial's bed and lay down. It was the side Theo hadn't slept on. Danial's pillow still smelled faintly of spices. I lay my head on it and breathed in his scent.

"Sar, answer me," Danial said angrily. "Was this a full blown fight? Were any blows struck?"

"You meant did I hit him?" I asked groggily. "No. I just told him to say hi to her for me, and not to worry about Elle or me, if it crossed his mind. He didn't say anything back."

"That's a relief," Danial sighed. "If you'll take the phone to her, I'd like to talk to her. After I've handled that, I'll answer your questions, if you still want answers."

"I think I have the answers," I said coolly. "I got them in bed last night from Theo's own lips. Hold on."

I took the phone to Elle, and handed it to her. She took it, then closed the door. I went back to Danial's bedroom, stripped off my clothes, and got into bed. Within minutes, I was asleep.

A loud knocking woke me. "Mom, are you in there? Dad wants to talk to you."

Anyone else I'd have told to let Danial call me back when he was done with his business, which was clearly above me on his to-do list. But I couldn't say that to Elle. "Come in, Elle."

She came in and handed me the phone. "He told me to go back to the fox compound with Cia. Is that okay?"

"Of course," I said, nodding. "Don't worry if I'm not here when you get back. I planned on going home for a few days until we head off to that party in Canada."

"I want you to stay," Elle pleaded. "Can't you stay?"

"No," I said gently. "Like Theo, I have a few things to work out on my own. But I will see you before we leave, okay?"

She hugged me. "I love you, Mom."

"I love you, too, Elle. Now go play and have a good time."

She left, and I put the phone to my ear. "Racklan residence."

"You're very funny," Danial said crossly. "Where are you? You aren't sleeping at the desk, are you?"

"I'm in your bed," I said, yawning. "Naked."

There was silence for two seconds, then Danial said, "Don't play, Sar. I'm

122

in no mood."

"I'm sorry," I said in a fake apologetic tone. "I was tired and wanted the comfort."

"You mean you really *are* naked in my bed?"

"Yes," I said naughtily. "I wish you were here with me."

The groan he gave was filled with enough love and lust to strike a cord in me. "You are killing me, Sar, with your words and the images they invoke."

"Seriously, I'm sorry," I replied. "Maybe if you spent more time at home you'd know when naked women are around."

"Sar, you are always welcome in my bed, even if I'm not there to share it with you. Get some rest, and stay as long as you like. I heard Elle ask you to stay. I can have your pets taken care of." He paused. "I'm working as fast as possible. It should only be a few more days, if that."

This wasn't fair to him or good for me, teasing like this. "Thank you for the card," I said seriously. "I loved the poem you picked, and what you wrote after it. As for the earrings, I'm wearing them."

"I meant all of it. Forever."

"I know you did. I feel the same way about you."

There was silence for a few breaths, then Danial said, "What was in the package?"

Cia had made a report, no doubt. "Dev sent me a CD."

"Was it him, or someone else?"

"It was Dev," I said, surprised. "Who else would it be? I don't know anyone else in South America."

"No," Danial said with a snort. "I meant was it him on the CD, or someone else singing?"

"It was an artist we both like."

"Have you called him?"

"No," I said guiltily, thinking I would have if Danial hadn't called. "I don't think that will solve my problems, or make their solution any clearer."

"Do you still want to know, about Theo, that is?" Danial asked abruptly.

"Tell me what you know."

"I got a letter two weeks ago. It was addressed to Theo, care of the company. Theo took it and read it in private. When he came back, he asked me to arrange a flight for him. He wanted to be with you and Elle at Christmas, so he waited to fly out until now."

"Did he say if he was going to come back? He told Elle he would."

"He said he would be there with us on Saturday, no matter what. But I can't say after that."

"What was in the note? Don't tell me you don't know."

Danial let out a breath. "He said that the maid had been forced to lie, that Tasha had not been married. She's been waiting all this time for him to come back. She wanted to know if he still loved her, or if he had decided to stay with you."

I closed my eyes.

"I'm sorry," Danial said gently. "I couldn't tell you, Sar. I knew how much it would hurt you when you found out. I tried to dissuade Theo from going, but he wouldn't change his mind." He paused. "How did you find out?"

"Because last night I kissed him, and when he kissed me back, he called me by her name in his sleep."

"I'm sorry," he said again. "I—"

I couldn't talk about this anymore, not even with him. "What are our chances, on New Year's Eve?" I interrupted harshly.

"Honestly? Less than fifty percent," he said ominously. "But they'll go up from that if you will let me mark you again."

"I'm afraid to have sex with you," I said honestly. "I want you as much as ever, but I'm worried that I'll act like I did before. And I don't feel like I can ask Camlyn for advice. He's not going to want me to be intimate with you after we've worked so hard to get me back to human."

"Sar, this is your life we are trying to protect. And you are still taking those pills, so it's unlikely you'll react wildly." He became seductive. "It will be like it was before, Love. Only we'll have to be a good deal more careful, mainly me. Will you do it?"

I didn't answer, not wanting to admit I was off the pills, or commit to the plan. Danial was interested in more than just marking me. If I were with him again, it would be almost impossible for me not to fall back into a relationship with him afterwards, not with how we felt about each other. I couldn't do that unless I accepted the future of becoming vampire. That meant never feeling the sun again, ever. It meant never eating anything other than blood, ever. I'd have to have donors of my own…

"Think about it," Danial continued. "I'll see you Friday night at the latest. Until then, I'll call you every night at your home. Leave me any messages you like on my voicemail."

I'd made a lot of decisions in my life, some good and some bad. This one would be unalterable once it was done.

"Sar?"

"I'll think on it," I answered. "Be careful."

"I love you."

"I love you, too," I replied. "Goodbye for now."

Chapter Ten

The day after Christmas was a rainy Tuesday morning that dawned grimly. Shortly after dawn, the rain became ice that coated the trees, leaving their branches heavy and drooping with weight. I lay in bed, watching them bend further and further as ice pattered at the windows.

"That's how I feel, like those branches," I told the dogs. "But Aran is coming by this morning. Sure, he isn't talkative, but he's cheerful. Let's make him some cookies, okay?"

At the sound of the word cookie, the dogs leapt up from their beds. Smiling, I threw back the covers and got to work.

A few hours later, I took the last of the cookies out of the oven, being careful not to burn myself. My fingers had been clumsier than usual this morning, despite I'd felt much more like my old self. After using both hands to put each cookie one by one on the cooling rack, I went to sit down for a while. Despite my positive mood, I was worn out from all the emotional upset of the day before.

I went over my list, deciding on what I had time to do next before lunch. Today and tomorrow, I planned to spend at home. Friday, I'd go into Danial's to finish up some last email work. Friday night, Danial would return. By then, I had to make a decision if I was willing to be vampire, or die trying to save my humanity.

That was the real question I needed to answer, not was I willing to have sex with him to let him mark me. Danial hadn't been making preparations all this month because he was overcautious. If he was that worried, I had every reason to think that if I entered that vampire Gathering unmarked—or un-Oathed, for that matter—not only was he not coming home, I wasn't either.

Just what fate waited for me at the other Ruler's hands or their minions I didn't know. Danial and Theo had never elaborated about what they feared exactly, except death and my being taken away against my will. But I could imagine being kept a prisoner while powerful vampires studied my blood, or used it to create a legion of dhamphirs. From my experience, un-Oathed humans were somewhere below werecreatures in most vampires' estimation, close to animals. They would take what they wanted from me and cast me aside when they were done.

What choice was there, really, given that? I had to let Danial mark me. Maybe he was right, with enough care we could find a way to be together without endangering me...

The clock chimed eleven. Worried, I glanced outside, wondering if Aran would call to cancel. He'd said he'd be going by on an errand for Cia, but the sky was dull white now. The impending storm forecasted for noon might begin at any moment.

There was no sign of him.

We were supposed to get a foot or more, something that irritated me. We'd gotten three feet so far this season. With no warm days to melt any of it, the drifts were huge, surrounding the plowed driveway like tall mountains.

I let out a yawn, blinking my eyes. With the completion of the cookies, despite my eagerness earlier, my utmost desire was a long nap under a warm blanket. Grinning, I made a deal with myself that as soon as the snow flew, the couch was where I was headed. Until then, I needed to keep on track. I hurriedly did some light cleaning and laundry. I was just putting the vacuum cleaner away when the clock chimed twelve.

I cast a look outside. Snowflakes had begun to fall. Soon, they were falling fast and furiously, obscuring my view of the barn.

"C'mon, Aran," I said, scanning the drive. "You don't get here shortly, I'm walking down those cookies to the mailbox and you can eat them frozen."

All of a sudden, the snow-dampened roar of a motorcycle was heard in the silence. Aran drove down the driveway, his lone headlight catching the snowflakes in its circular light as they fell. He was dressed in his usual black leather.

"You're crazy," I muttered, throwing cookies into a plastic bag quickly. "Maybe werefoxes don't get as cold as normal humans did, but you still have to be cold in that." I closed the bag, then headed for the front door. "At least it's something between you and the pavement."

Aran pulled up in front of the deck and parked the bike, but didn't turn it off. He faced the house for a moment. As I opened the door, he gestured around him, then pointed to my house.

I opened the door and yelled to him, "Sure, you can stay 'til it stops. I'm glad of the company. Go to the bottom garage, I'll let you in!"

He nodded, the visor of his helmet and his shoulders already covered in snow. He drove on as I shut the front door and ran downstairs. Pressing the button, I raised the overhead door and he drove in.

Shivering in the cold blast from the door, I quickly shut it as he parked his Harley and shut off the engine. He began brushing the snow off himself.

"Why'd you bring the bike today of all days?" I said, giving him a sarcastic smile. "I told you it was going to storm. Now you're stuck here. Cia's not going to be happy."

Aran got off his bike and continued to brush him and it off, melting snow creating puddles on the concrete floor.

"Why don't you give me your coat, and I'll put it near the fire. If you want, we can watch a movie or something. I was planning to head to the couch any—"

Aran unbuckled his helmet and in one smooth motion pulled it off his head. Gold curls and waves fell almost to his shoulders.

This was not Aran.

This was Devlin.

He stepped off the bike, and came toward me. I was lost from the moment I looked into his golden eyes.

The garage remote dropped from my nerveless hand as I moved toward him, shaking slightly. I stretched out my arms to him, winding them around his neck, pulling him down to kiss me. He kissed me lightly, nibbling the edge of my lips with his fangs.

"Miss me?" he said seductively.

I pushed my body tight against his, desire pouring through me. He groaned and clasped me to him, his soft kiss becoming intent and reckless. Suddenly he lifted me, his leather creaking as he carried me into the basement bedroom. He laid me on the bed, kissing my mouth passionately, delving into me with his tongue, then began to kiss his way down my body. I felt the brush of his fangs on my bare skin and shivered, letting out a wild cry.

He drew back suddenly to look at me, his eyes molten. He paused for a second as if he was going to speak, then seemed to reconsider his words. Instead, he kissed me again on my throat and shoulders, pulling down my loose sweater so he could run his fangs over my bare skin.

I tried to unzip his jacket so I could touch him, but my hands couldn't seem to clasp the zipper. Devlin gently pushed my hands back, and unzipped it, throwing it to one side. He had on a black T-shirt underneath and I ran my hands underneath it, into his chest hair. His skin was cool under my hands, and my desire increased tenfold. He shut his eyes at the feel of my hands on his skin, his lips parting slightly in pleasure.

The sight of his fang tips made me sigh in eagerness, my rapid breathing speeding up still more. "Please." I tried to pull him onto me.

Devlin looked down at me through lowered eyelids. "Danial was right," he said seductively. Oddly, there was a sad undercurrent beneath the desire.

"Don't be sad," I murmured eagerly. "I want you. God, I want you so much!"

Devlin pressed his body to me. I felt his shaft hard against my groin, so wonderfully long and ready for me, and instantly forgot everything else. I arched my back, trying to push my body that much closer to him, baring my throat to him.

"Don't worry, Sar," he murmured to me between kisses. "I'll give you what you've been wanting." He bit me gently, not breaking the skin. At once, my lust roared up inside of me as I gasped, writhing beneath him. I hadn't felt The Lust in months, not like this. The pills had kept it at bay, but I'd gone off them...

"Please," I gasped. "Please, Dev, I need you!"

"I know what you need, Sar," he murmured. He held me to the bed with one hand and began to kiss me, running his fangs over my neck. He breathing quickened as he pulled up my shirt, and unclasped my bra, moving it aside as his mouth came down over my breasts, his fangs pressing down slightly as he kissed and sucked at my skin.

It was sweet torture. No matter how I begged and writhed, he seemed to foresee my movements, speedily avoiding my efforts to impale myself on his fangs. Finally, I was near tears with frustration, crying out repeatedly in desperate need.

"No," he said teasingly, drawing his lips from my reddened breast. "I'm not done with the foreplay, Love. You'll have to wait."

"Please, Dev, please," I whispered, looking into his molten eyes. "I'm in agony. I want you inside me. Please, stop teasing me, please!"

He bared his fangs slightly, then kissed me hard. Quickly, he moved back from me and began to peel off his boots and socks. Then he slipped off his pants and pulled his T-shirt over his head. He turned towards me nude, and I feasted my eyes on the body I'd dreamed of for so many nights. The sight of his swollen erection made me scramble for him, but he gently pushed me back to the bed. Slowly, he rolled down my leggings and then my underwear, kissing me as he did it. With shaking fingers, I yanked off my sweater and my bra and threw them aside, then reached for him, beckoning him as I lay back, my heart hammering.

As Devlin lowered his body atop mine, I felt the length of him pressing, seeking entry. My hand darted down to grab hold of him, but he pushed me to the bed, holding me in place beneath him. "I had plans for us, Sar," he murmured in my ear. "But you're worse off than I thought. They'll have to wait."

I didn't know what he was talking about and I didn't care. I was aching for him, my desire back as if it'd never left. Abruptly, he shifted his hips, bearing down and began to penetrate me. "Hold still, Love," he whispered, hissing my ear. "I'll be as gentle as I can."

I shook beneath him, fighting my wanton desire to pump my hips and get him inside faster as he slid into me ever so slowly. My heart was pounding. I was beyond breathing hard, the breath tearing out of me.

Finally, he was mostly inside me, my body encasing him like a tight sheath. He held still then, his eyes closed, savoring being in me, a look of utter satisfaction on his face. Then he began to move, stroking me repeatedly as he had months ago.

"I can't wait," I panted, clasping his buttocks as I strained upward. "Please, don't make me wait."

Devlin let out an eager moan and began thrusting fast within me almost immediately, though he didn't go very deep. It wasn't enough. I wanted all of him. I wrapped my arms around him and tried to pull his hips as close to me as I could.

Devlin resisted, pushing back slightly. "Sar, don't," he said roughly, the need for orgasm heavy in his words. "Your body's not ready for all of mine, I'll hurt you—"

"I can't wait anymore, Dev! Please!" I screamed. "I need you! All of you!"

"Then you shall have me," Devlin growled, baring his fangs and sinking them deep into my neck.

The feeling of utter release after being denied so long brought me spasming, screaming at the top of my lungs. Devlin felt me come, and pushed deep, even as he drank me down. His blissful sighs were muffled, even as he thrust faster. I continued to spasm, continued to come for him, waves of pleasure crashing over me from what his body was doing to mine. I screamed over and over wordlessly, my arms clasped tightly around his head and shoulders as he sucked rhythmically. Dev made a muffled cry, then clutched me to him as tight as he could, driving himself completely into me with abandon as he came. In the next second, he bit deeper, his fangs sliding in completely as he sucked insistently.

The sensation was too much, too good, too big. I blacked out in his arms.

The next thing I knew, I smelled the sharp odor of alcohol. I jerked my head back from it. "Sar," someone said softly. "Wake up, Sar."

I opened my eyes. Devlin was looking down at me, attentive but not worried. He put the alcohol soaked rag to the side and gathered me back into his arms. He was dressed in his T-shirt and pants again, though I was still naked. We were still on the bed downstairs.

"Why are you dressed?" I asked curiously.

He gave me a considering look. "I thought you might want me to leave when you came to," he said simply. "Now that you are back in control."

I burrowed into his arms. "I don't want you to leave."

He sighed, and held me close to him. For a while, we said nothing. Soon enough, my curiosity got the better of me.

"Where is the real Aran, Dev? Is he okay?"

"I had a message left for him that you had decided to put off making cookies until this afternoon, until the storm passes. Brian will come to your home tomorrow to pick them up in his stead."

"Brian is still working for you, isn't he?"

"Of course," Devlin said, kissing my forehead. "He has been watching over you for me much as he did before. Did you think I would go off to another country and leave you unprotected after how I told you I felt about you?"

"I was surprised when you left at all," I murmured, gazing up into his eyes. "Despite what you said."

"I was sure you would tell Theo of what I had done. I appreciate that you didn't, as we agreed."

"I told Danial."

"I know," he said, something unidentifiable in his tone. "Why did you tell him?"

"There was no way not to tell him. He knows me too well. He knew something was up before I'd said one sentence to him."

"And Theo does not know you so well?"

"Not anymore," I replied, pulling back from him. Immediately I was dizzy.

Devlin grabbed hold of me. "Lay back down," he ordered. "I took a lot of your blood. I don't want my bites to reopen."

I went rigid, reaching up to my neck. There were two bites on the left side, and another one on the right. Alarmingly, my right wrist also bore fang marks. With mounting fear, I saw the left did, too. The bites were red, but they had already begun to heal, even though they'd been made less than an hour before.

There was no decision for me to make now. Devlin had made it for me as I slept. I began to sob.

Devlin turned my face up to his. "Sar, stop your crying," he said harshly. "Right now."

I shrank back from him, afraid at his anger. "How could you do this to me—?"

"Hear this, if you hear nothing else I say. You are not close to turning, not remotely. I'll wager that you never were."

I looked at him in shock. "Dr. Camlyn said—"

Devlin talked over me angrily, his eyes red as blood. "I don't care what he said to you, Sar! You might be cooler than a normal human. You might have elevated levels of the vampire virus in your blood, or more lustrous skin, or heal faster, or have brighter eyes. But that doesn't mean you are turning."

"What the hell else could it mean?" I yelled at him.

"Danial told me that your blood was already way past the point it needed to be for you to be a vampire back when you were checked, right after you had Theoron. Right?"

I nodded, still angry. "What does that have to do with anything?"

"Did it ever occur to you, to anyone, that your body had maybe been altered from a different experience? You bore a vampire's child, Sar! For nine months, you carried him in your body! Did none of you think that might have some lasting effects?"

My mouth dropped open in shock. *No, it hadn't.* "How do you know for sure I'm not turning?"

"I've been with many women as they were turning. I turned a fair number of those women myself. Most of them, actually."

Was that pride in his voice? Ick.

"You have been partly turned now for more than a year and a half," Devlin continued. "You would have turned by now if you were going to. When a human is close to turning, a vampire can taste it in their blood. It becomes bitter, as the blood changes from human to vampire blood. Yours still tastes of summer," he added sadly. "Though I can taste the drug you were dosing yourself with faintly."

"If I wasn't turning, why was I so drawn to Danial?" I protested desperately. "The way I acted with you and him…I was out of control."

Devlin shot me a seductive smirk. "I can't speak to your attraction to my brother, but your attraction to me is simple: you love what I can do to you. You can't get enough of me."

Arrogant prick. "You know what I mean, Devlin! When Danial tried to stop, I wouldn't let him. I made him bite me and practically raped him."

Devlin's eyebrows shot up. "You were having consensual sex, at least how he described it. It was more a matter of Danial getting just what he deserved. I told him to watch his step."

I seized on that. "Why did you tell him that?"

Devlin's rich laugh sent shivers through me. "If he had taken you as you wanted him to, you both would have gotten some relief. But Theo wouldn't have liked that, I'm sure."

"Please, say what you mean."

"Your body is telling you what it needs, and has been all along: you need more of the vampire virus in you. Your body has changed from having Theoron. You need what I just gave you."

I trembled in his arms. "To lose most of my blood?"

He held me tighter. "To be bitten and for some of my saliva to get into your bloodstream through the open wounds. That is why you were okay for a month after letting me love you." He rubbed his cheek against mine tenderly. "My other bodily secretions were not going to be enough, not this time."

"So when I was with Danial, trying to stop my urges, all I was doing was torturing myself?" I asked, anguished.

"It would seem so to me," Devlin said, bringing my wrist to his mouth. He kissed it gently. "Remember, don't move. You've reopened these already."

Wait a minute! I pushed him away roughly, then turned on him, livid. "That day we were together! You said you could taste it in my blood! You said I was close to turning!"

"I lied," Devlin said, giving me a defiant look, that same faint smile on his face.

"You complete and utter bastard! All that time I worried, taking those pills, feeling like I wasn't myself! How could you not tell me, tell somebody?"

"You should have come to me as I asked," he replied coolly. "If you had, I'd have told you."

The handsome, seductive son of a bitch had betrayed me. Worse, he'd let me suffer because of his own Goddamn ego.

"You're angry," Devlin said, taking a deep breath. "At me, I'm sure. But what did you expect me to do? You'd not have believed me, if I'd told you. Don't lie and say you would have."

What had I expected of him? To be decent, the gentleman who'd seduced me, the lover who'd made me believe he cared about me. I'd been naïve, believing all of his fabrications when I'd known down deep what he was. The worst thing was I'd known from the start, and still fooled myself, romanticizing him so much I'd fallen in love with what I'd remembered him to be. That romantic loving image was a fantasy. It had always been one.

"You asshole," I shouted bitterly, with tears in my eyes. "You have done nothing but lie to me from the beginning. But the worst was your lie about loving me, because you fucking made me believe you!"

Devlin went utterly still at my words, and then lunged at me, growling. I evaded him, running out of the bedroom and into the garage, quickly slamming the door behind me and locking it.

He hit it with his shoulders. "Sar! Come back here!"

The door held, the frame cracking. Devlin hit it again. This time the frame snapped, and he was instantly through, reaching for me. As he did, I ducked under the opening garage door.

Naked, I ran out into the storm, into the daylight where he couldn't follow.

"Damn you," Devlin growled, glaring at me with red eyes. "Come back in here."

I faced him, shivering, my hair blowing around me, holding one bare foot out of the snow at a time to minimize the freezing cold, and frantically went over my options. If I headed toward the forest, I might freeze to death before reaching a neighbor. But if I could somehow circle around to the barn, I could take shelter in my woodshed. There was plastic sheeting there...

Dev's eyes were pools of fire as he looked out at me, then down at the daylight that was an inch from his body. Then he turned fast from me, going to his motorcycle for his gloves and helmet.

I turned with a gasp to run through the snow as fast as I could. I made it only about fifty feet before he came after me, swearing loudly. In a few more seconds, he tackled me and we both went into the snow.

I screamed at the shock of the cold snow on my bare skin. Devlin grabbed my hands with a furious snarl, and pulled me to my feet. Without a word, he began dragging me back through the snow to the house, my hands in front of me, my wrists clamped together in his left hand.

I shook with cold and fear. Once he got me inside, I'd be at his mercy. I had to escape! I dragged my feet, pulling against him, but he was much stronger than I was.

If I only had a weapon, I could stop him...*wait!*

Before I could reconsider, I reached down to his wrist with my captive hands, and dug my fingers into the gap between his leather jacket cuff and his leather glove. With as much speed as I could, I pulled the cuff of his glove down toward his hand that was holding my wrists together, and exposed his wrist and part of his hand to the weak light of the sun.

The effect was instantaneous. Devlin let out a shriek, and let me go. His wrist was smoking, and he covered it as fast as he could, hissing in pain, as I ran from him. Before I'd gone ten feet, he tackled me again. This time he didn't help me up. We lay there in the snow, his body on top of me, as I shrieked, over and over, writhing.

"Please let me up! Please!"

"You burned me! You are such a bitch, Sar!" Devlin growled down at me through his helmet. "You're lucky I do love you, or I'd stay here with you in the snow until you froze to death."

"Let me up, please!"

"No. You fucking want to kill yourself; we'll just give you a taste of it right here."

"I want to live," I gasped, then began crying. "Please, let me up! Please!"

Devlin held me there, his breathing ragged, smoke still wafting faintly from his injured hand. I struggled, then went limp in the snow, lightheaded again.

"You're bleeding," he said, standing and lifting me in his arms. "Don't struggle."

Devlin carried me into the basement, shutting the garage door behind us. Then he carried me up the cellar stairs, and past the growling and barking dogs. Ignoring them, he set me down by the wood stove, propping me up in the nearby armchair. He lowered my blinds, until the room was in twilight, and turned on the light.

My fire was almost out, but he got it going again with some fire starter and some small logs. When that was done, he took off his helmet and his gloves, then his jacket, his T-shirt, and his pants. He hung everything over the nearby furniture as it all was wet now, or at least semi-wet. He took off his boots, and socks, and put them to the side of the fire to dry. Ghost and Darkness had stopped barking and now watched him uneasily.

Devlin grabbed two blankets from the nearby rack. Laying one on the floor before the stove, he sat on it and threw the other around his shoulders. "Come to me." He beckoned.

I eased myself down beside him and he enfolded me in his arms, wrapping the blanket around us. By this time, warmth had started to flow out of the stove. Devlin started rubbing my arms and legs. Slowly the redness and numbness went away.

"I'm sorry for my language," he said finally. "I lost my temper, because I was worried."

I didn't reply, save for trembling a little.

"Are you warm enough?" he asked. "I can open the dampers more, if you're not."

"How did you know how to start my fire?" I asked hesitantly.

He gave me a look. "That night you found Danial, who do you think loaned him that equipment, Sar? Did you ever see him use it again, or the truck for that matter? I'm surprised you didn't figure that out before now."

Danial had only used that Avalanche truck the first week we'd been dating. I'd assumed he's rented it, and the camping equipment. Danial was a hotel kind of guy. "He said it was his."

"There are more than a few things that he says are his that turn out to be mine, Sar," Devlin said pointedly. He lifted my hair, kissing my neck.

134

"The truck was *yours*? *You* go camping? That's harder to believe than Danial camping."

"Technically, it was my friend Lash's truck and stuff, but—"

"*You* have friends?" I said, giving him raised eyebrows.

"Stop being a bitch, Sar," he said, kissing my half scabbed over wound. Before I had time to react, he'd slid his fangs in. I jerked in his arms, gasping at the rush of pleasure. Devlin held me tightly, his mouth moving on me as he sucked gently. As he did, I watched the wrist that I'd exposed to sunlight heal. New skin formed, and slowly the burn disappeared until it was gone, his wrist and hand healed completely.

I reached back with my right hand. Devlin stiffened against me as if he expected a slap, but didn't stop drinking or release me. Gently, I touched his face with my hand, feeling his stubble growing under my fingers as his body renewed itself with my blood. As I slid my fingers into his hair and caressed him, he trembled slightly. Abruptly, he kissed my wound, holding his mouth over it so that the wound closed.

"It's too deep for that," I sighed.

He took his mouth off my neck. "No, it's not. None of the bites you bear is deeper than my normal love bites, Sar. A little of my blood will heal the others, too. I don't want them reopening again." He gave the healed skin a final kiss, and then moved to the other side of my neck.

"Why did you come to me?" I asked.

He kissed that bite a few times, then said, "To see you. To make love with you, if you would let me."

"Did you think I would refuse?" I said, turning and kissing the side of his neck. "I've wanted that since the moment we parted."

"Then why didn't you come to me in Rio?" he whispered sadly. "I asked you to many times."

"Because I have responsibilities to more than myself. There's Theoron and Elle to consider, not to mention I'm technically still married."

"What do you mean by technically?" Devlin asked, suddenly alert. "Theo is in Canada checking out the Gathering arrangements, isn't he? Are you breaking up? Danial said nothing."

"No, he wouldn't have," I said, irritated. "Theo has another woman, one he loved when he was gone those two years. She wrote him a letter out of the blue, and he's left to see her. I'm guessing a divorce is in the making when he returns."

"I thought you were a little less morally uptight," Devlin said teasingly. "Here I thought it was just you finally coming to your senses."

Just like that, I was angry at him again. He'd trashed my life, with what

135

he'd done to me. "If I'd come to my senses, you'd be on your ass out there in the sun."

Devlin took a sharp intake of breath, his arms loosening. I knew I'd hurt him, but remembered how he'd lied to me and didn't apologize.

"Did you like my gifts?" he said hesitantly. "Danial said he gave them to you."

"Yes. I'm sorry I didn't thank you for them. I should have emailed you a thank you."

"It doesn't matter," he said softly. He got up, and helped me to my feet. "I should go."

"Don't go," I said, reaching out to him, and caressing his cheek with my hand.

He took my hand off him angrily. "What do you want of me, Sar, that you want me not to leave? Speak."

"I want you not to go. Stay with me. I'm alone until Friday night, until Danial returns and we all leave for the meeting in Canada. I'd like to spend that time with you, if you want to spend it with me."

He turned away and began checking his clothes to see if they were dry. "It's not enough."

"What do you want from me?" I said in exasperation. "That day back in the fall, you seduced me just for sex, or so you told me then. After, you told me you loved me and that you were leaving and never coming back. Then you send me presents and ask me to drop my whole life to come to you. You come back to me months later with no warning, and initiate sex again. I don't understand what you're really after. Would you tell me the truth for once in your life?"

He turned to me then, the look in his eyes hitting me like a physical blow. "I want you to be with me, to try to have my child as you had Danial's child, to give me your Oath, to let me give you my love, to share my life."

I gaped at him, my mouth open. If he was telling the truth, I ached for him, because it wasn't going to happen. If he was lying, I hated him for saying that any of that mattered to him when it didn't.

"But it's enough for me, right now, if you just tell me you love me, Sar," Devlin said, looking at me defiantly. "Tell me you love me, and I'll stay."

"I can't."

"Can't or won't?" Devlin said, raising his eyebrows.

"I'm not in love with you," I said, reaching for him.

He eluded me. "Why?" he said indignantly. "I used all of my skill with you that day. I held back nothing of myself, told you everything I was feeling when I was with you, made your every wish a reality. It was likely the best sex of your life. Why aren't you in love with me?"

I thought about saying a lot of things, but decided the truth was best. *That was the whole point here, wasn't it?* "Because I can't trust you."

"You trusted me earlier today," he said, coming closer to stand in front of me. "You came willingly without a thought when you saw it was me."

"I've desired nothing but you for months now." I reached for him again.

Again, Devlin stepped away. "You have an odd way of showing it, Sarelle. Every attempt I made was met with rejection. But the worst was your apathy. I wasn't even worth a moment of your time, much less a thank you."

The use of my full name from him infuriated me. "You want to know how I feel?" I shouted hatefully. "I'll tell you. I hate you for what you've done to me! Do you know how many times I thought of you, wished you were with me? How many times I wanted to call that number you gave me, just to hear your voice? How much I wanted to put on the choker and go to you, even knowing what it would do to everyone I love? I had to finally put it in Danial's safe, so I wouldn't be tempted—"

Devlin's eyes widened "He knows? He said nothing—"

"No, he doesn't know!" I shouted. "I knew he'd destroy it, or that Theo would. I couldn't leave it there, either! I had to ask Terian for a box to hide it in finally—"

"Why not just burn it, like you burned the book I gave you?" he said sarcastically, his eyes molten with anger.

Danial must have told him. It didn't even dent my anger. "Because I couldn't bear to destroy it, or to let anyone else destroy it! I loved it! I hated that I couldn't wear it, that a time would never come when I could!"

"I wanted you to wear it," he said sadly. "If you had only come to me—"

"I drugged myself for another reason besides being able to control myself around Danial, and other vampires. I had to stop thinking of you, dreaming of you, wanting you! I want you more than I have ever wanted anyone in my life. Does that mean anything to you, you son of a bitch?" I put my hands over my face, crying.

Devlin came close and put his arms around me. "Yes," he said softly. "It means something to me, to have heard those words from you, to hear in your voice you mean them. Please don't cry, Love."

"Call me Sar," I sniffled.

"Sar," he said tenderly, then brushed his lips gently down my neck. "Shh, Sar."

I relaxed into him, running my fingers up through his hair. It was shoulder length now, as Danial's was naturally.

"This is the length it always grows back to," he said, kissing the side of my neck. "And I'm not cutting it short for you, so don't ask."

I gave him a grimace. "I never asked anyone to cut their hair for me." I pulled back to look at him, and the words just fell out of my mouth. "I like you just as you are. I just wish you wouldn't lie to me, so I could love you."

Devlin gaped at me, lips parted.

I went crimson. "I'm sorry. I shouldn't—"

"No, you're right," Devlin said, pulling me against him. "There have been enough lies between us, even though some of them were necessary. Ask me, and I'll tell you the truth."

"Anything?"

"Anything."

"Was it really your truck?"

"It is Lash's truck. Yes, I have friends. Sar, but I can count them on one hand, and that includes my brother and Lash."

"Who is he?"

"He is to me what Theo is to Danial, but I've known him much, much longer."

Lash. He was the one Brian was so afraid of. "Was he with you the night you came for me?"

"If he had been, I'd not have lost to Terian and Theo," Devlin said darkly. "He was with me the night I came to save you from Alphonse. He led the main assault on the house, diverting most of the guard's attention so I could rescue you. He is the one who entered the bedroom, who told us to hurry."

"I remember." Lash sounded a lot like Devlin, capable of anything. No wonder they were good buddies. "Can you trust him?"

"Yes," Devlin said. "I trust him and Danial, and that's about it."

"What did you mean when you said that Danial enjoyed wielding power?" I asked next.

"He's gotten more ruthless since coming to power, and becoming a father a second time. Power is hard to resist exercising, in and of itself. That is a good change I approve of. Those under him need reminders that there are lines that are not to be crossed."

That sounded bad but true. "Why did you come back when you told me you wouldn't?"

"First of all, I never told you I wouldn't come back."

"You said you loved me and that you weren't coming back in my lifetime."

"And I meant it, until you said you loved my eyes." Devlin kissed me chastely, moving my head with his so our eyes met. "I knew if you could love part of me, you could come to love me in time. So I told you I'd return."

"Was I in the same truck you were? You said no such thing."

138

"You said you knew poetry," Devlin said. "You don't know 'Love is like a Red, Red Rose'?"

I gave him a blank look. "No."

"The end goes thus, Sar: Fare thee well, my only love; Fare thee well awhile. For I will come again, my love, though it be ten thousand miles."

I'd been so worried about Theo finding out about Devlin I'd not paid enough attention. "I know the poem. I didn't know that is what you were saying."

"I perhaps should have said it more blatantly," Devlin said, nibbling my ear. "But in any case, I made good on my word."

"Why did you come back, really? Because Theo isn't here? For the Gathering?"

"Many reasons. To find out why you didn't come to me. To find out if you cared for me. To be with you again, like we were today." He paused. "But most of all to save you, Sar."

"Save me from what?" I said, alarmed.

"You were dying," Devlin replied.

Chapter Eleven

"What the hell are you talking about?" I said, incredulous.

"Danial told me only two days ago that you weren't getting warmer, you were getting colder. I would have come sooner if I'd known, but he said nothing to me until then—"

"Known what?" I cried.

"That you hadn't been turning at all; your body had changed and if you didn't get more of the vampire virus into your system, you were going to die."

I huddled against him. "That can't be true."

Devlin picked me up, and carried me back into the cellar, speaking softly. "That is why I had to come in the day. I had to get to you in time. Waiting for nightfall might have been too late for you." He helped me under the covers and then got in beside me.

"You've been tired lately," he said sadly, wrapping me in his arms. "Sleeping more, your body cooling down, slowing down, getting ready to shut down. By now if you hadn't been on the drug, you'd have sought out another vampire, if not Danial. Your body was giving you warning signs, but you weren't hearing them."

Fear was coursing through me. I practically tried to crawl inside his chest, wanting to be as close to him as possible.

"Shh," Devlin said, hugging me tightly. "You'll be fine now. Being with me has started your body repairing itself. You should notice a difference by tomorrow."

"Dr. Camlyn said that needing the extra sleep was normal, that I just needed more time to get back to normal."

"Another few days and you would have gone to sleep and not woken up," Devlin said ominously. "You need regular doses of the vampire virus now to live."

I shivered against him. "Why didn't you call and warn me?"

"I should have come to you back in the fall, that first night Danial called asking for advice," Devlin said bitterly. "He said you had both lost control, that you had wanted one another. I thought that he had taken more of your blood and given you some of his, and he was ashamed to say so. The symptoms seemed right to me. Women who are turning act as you did. Then he said after you had been together that it hadn't worked, that you had still been wild, and it was in his voice that he'd had your blood again. When he said you were going to take a drug to stop the wanting, I thought that was probably the only choice. I knew if I came back and tried to be with you then that I might cause you to turn. I didn't want that. So I stayed away."

Anger replaced fear. "Why didn't you call and tell Danial I needed more of the virus?"

"As I'm trying to tell you, I was worried I might be wrong." He took a breath. "I'm sorry I lied to you, and told you that you were turning months ago. It was the best way to get your permission then. As I told you then, I would not have had another chance to be with you." He kissed me lovingly. "Just as I'm not going to miss this one."

"Everything you've said makes sense," I said slowly. "But there is a good deal you're leaving out."

"Such as?"

"Such as camping doesn't usually prepare you to operate a wood stove; it shows you how to make an open fire."

"Starting a fire is the same wherever you do it," Devlin replied, annoyed. "The point I was making is that I don't spend all my time behind a desk or inside comfortable walls. I know the outdoors, and how to handle the normal tools of life, woodstoves included."

"So you're a regular country man in addition to being a dashing singer and lover," I said sarcastically. "I'd never have guessed you were so multi-faceted."

"That is because you're short-sighted," Devlin said loftily.

"Actually, my view is almost always the long term," I retorted. "Which brings me to my next question: have you regained the ability to make vampires?"

"I'm not what I was when we first met," Devlin said slowly. "I know you don't want to be vampire, so I'm not sure what you're really asking, Sar."

"Could you turn me accidentally?"

"No," he assured me. "I'll be able to taste when you get close in your blood. I'll stop sharing myself with you if I sense you turning. It could not happen accidentally, ever."

"Why not?"

"I believe you are resistant to the virus. I'm not sure you can be turned, without a massive infusion of my blood. You've already had enough from me today to turn a normal human woman of your size twice over, yet you taste as sweet as ever." He put his lips to my wrist and kissed it lightly.

"What are you not saying?"

Devlin leaned up on one arm, and I rolled onto my back, looking up at him. "You can still be drained if I take too much, Sar. That will still kill you."

"How do you know all this?" I said in consternation. "You aren't just guessing."

Sadness drowned his eyes again. "Annabelle was like you."

Anna was the woman who'd been Devlin's that Danial had seduced away from him, beginning their long feud. "You loved her a long time ago."

"Yes," he said, old pain in each word. "I loved her very much."

"Tell me about her."

"Anna and I were together for years. She got to a point, and never progressed further than that. No matter how much I was with her, loved her, her body refused to turn. It was then that we thought we might try having a child."

Anna had died in miscarriage. I'd deduced that was because Devlin had not waited for the potion to work completely. "What happened?"

"I knew of the potion. She was afraid, but she wanted to try it. It took us a year of trying before it worked. The day she told me that she was pregnant was the happiest day of my life."

"I'm sorry," I said awkwardly.

"She tasted of spring, Sar," he said, haunted. "It's been two hundred years she has been gone from me, and I can still remember it clearly."

Worried at his sudden encompassing melancholy, I tried to bring him back to the present. "How did you discover she was resistant? Did she behave like I did?"

He took a deep breath and let it out. "After we'd been together a year, her body changed. We didn't know it until I had to be away for a month on business. When I got back, she was as you were earlier today. She slept a lot, her body was cold, and she had difficulty moving. She thought it was depression, from missing me. Yet she went wild when I returned, provoking me to bite her. After I spent that night with her, she began to feel better. In a few days, she was fine again. But I never left her alone again for more than a week after that."

He shook his head as if shaking off the fetters of the past, and took another deep breath, letting it out slowly. He tilted my chin up to look at him. "You'll have to monitor your blood virus levels from now on, and make sure they never drop under a certain threshold. I can help with that, if you permit me to. There is also a benefit, Sar, a substantial one." He kissed me softly, then drew back.

"You won't age as fast, if at all. You won't ever have to die, unless you want to. Yet you won't be vampire, you will still be able to walk in the sun."

I stared at him, aghast.

"You don't seem as pleased by that as I thought you might be," Devlin said, searching my eyes with his own. "Danial said that was the reason you wouldn't give him your Oath: you would not stay young and he would. Now there is no reason for you not to be with him, as you both want to be. In fact, you must be his blood lover again, if you are not with me."

Hearing his words, my life changed again utterly. *I could be with Danial. We could have a life together now. But the flip side was that Theo and I were finished for good.*

"You're distressed," Devlin said curiously. "You can't seriously still be thinking of Theo?"

Theo had wanted me to go back to Danial, had pushed us together at Elle's recital. He'd probably be happy this tied me up as a loose end. *But Elle...she would age and so would my parents...I might live to see them die...maybe Theoron, too...*Panic and fear coursed through me.

"Sar," Devlin murmured. "Breathe."

I took a deep breath and put his supposition out of my mind. I had the here and now. I'd worry about the future when I had to, when we knew for sure he was right.

"And again," he encouraged. "You have many questions, I'm sure. I can give you answers to—"

"Blood lover?" I said disdainfully.

"There's no need to be offended," Devlin said wickedly. "It merely means a lover who agrees to donate blood to a vampire, nothing more."

I rolled my eyes. "All the same, I'd prefer you never refer to me that way, ever."

"If you wish."

"I do have one more question for you, Dev."

"Ask it," he said softly, kissing my neck, his fangs pricking gently.

I took another deep breath. "What were you planning for me that night you came for me?"

He drew back, startled. "You don't want to know."

"You're right, I don't. I need to know. Tell me the truth. Whatever it is, my imagination will do worse. But if I know the truth, I can let it go. And so can you."

Devlin moved away from me, and looked at the wall. "Don't ask me this."

"Tell me, Dev," I said firmly. "Or it will always be something unspoken between us. You and I have that history. We always will. If you'd gotten your way then, really gotten it, I'd have gone home with you. What was waiting for me, besides Lash?"

He sighed. "You know what I'm capable of. Why do you have to ask me this, now?"

"Because you haven't changed, just your feelings for me have. You want me to trust you, tell me this and don't lie."

He stared at me, incredulous. "I don't see how admitting my evil to you helps me gain your trust."

"I need to know I can trust you to tell me the truth. And if there was anything you'd want to lie about, it would be this."

He gave a faint smile. "You're right. But you won't forgive me if I tell you."

I gave him merciless eyes. "Tell me or get on your bike and leave."

He took a deep breath. "I didn't know what I would do if Danial relinquished you. I was so sure he wouldn't that I didn't plan anything for that reason alone. But there were a lot of things that I thought about doing to you." He closed his eyes.

"Such as?"

"I thought about draining you with Danial, as we almost did before Terian and Theo rode to the rescue. Your blood reminded me of Annabelle's blood, even then. I was angry that you were Danial's and not mine. I was breathtaking *and* the most powerful and you still wanted him and not me—"

"Did Annabelle care about your power?"

"I knew her before I was a Ruler. I was more Danial's level, when you first met him. I hadn't any power then, save the power of an ordinary vampire, as compared with a human—"

"Devlin, you are talking around the question. Yes or no?"

"No, she didn't care if I was powerful, so long as I could protect her."

"Why would I be any different?"

He looked away from me, and shrugged.

"Go on."

"Danial refused to share you with me. You didn't want me to have any part of you either." He abruptly cut off, and started again. "Angelica was not the only woman we drained over the centuries," he said, emotionless. "It's a common punishment for Oathbreaking and vampire murdering, and often, it falls to the Ruler of a territory to mete out—"

I'd guessed that after Danial had threatened to do it to Monica. "I know all this. Go to—"

"No," he said sinisterly. "You want to know it all, I'll tell it my way. I was fully prepared to drink you down with him that night, to make sure that he could not have what I had been denied. It wasn't everything I wanted from you, but at least then I'd have gotten part of what I desired. I'd have finished you off that night, if Terian hadn't interfered." He gazed at me and swallowed. "I'm so glad he did, I'd have made the biggest mistake of my life—"

"Say you'd gotten Danial to relinquish me," I replied coolly. "What then?"

"I wanted to bring you to my home and have you every way I could think of. To take you by force if not by seduction, to drink in your fear along with your blood for as long as it lasted, as long as I could draw it out. After I'd possessed you in all ways, I was going to keep you for a while. I loved your hair even then, and wanted it to grow out to the length it had been when I first saw you. By the time it had, I would be ready to sire a child on you, Sar. And I was going to, whether you wanted one or not. No matter how long it took, or what I had to do—"

"I Oathed you. Why have a child with me?"

"I knew you'd gotten pregnant amazingly fast. Your blood was so similar to Anna's. Together, that was enough to make me want to try. You don't look like she did, but that didn't matter. I was determined to mold you into the woman she was. To recreate her, so to speak." His eyes found mine and held. "I'd have destroyed you in the process."

I drew in a long shuddering breath. "Do you still want to do any of that to me?"

"No!" he said vehemently. "I dislike even admitting to thinking it in the past. But you wanted to know, so I was honest."

"I can't be her, ever," I said quietly. "I can only be myself."

"I know that," Devlin said, hurt. "I don't want her back. I want you, Sar."

"You're sure?"

"Until you, the memory of her stood in the path of any living woman. Since we were together, all my fantasies have been of you," he said, reaching out hesitantly to clasp my hand. "Of us happy together, loving each other. I'm sure."

The moment he touched me, my resistance crumbled. I moved closer to him, and hugged him. He looked down at me, surprise still on his face. "If I were standing, I'd get down on my knees and beg your forgiveness," he said seriously, drawing back from me. "Can you ever forgive me?"

I pulled his head down to me and kissed him slowly. "I will if you make love to me again."

Devlin kissed me eagerly, then rolled his body on top of mine, pushing me gently down into the sheets. He spread my legs, moving into position. My desire came roaring back and I writhed under him, again baring my throat. He slowly bore down again with his hips, pushing his erection deeper as I strained upwards to receive him. The feeling of being utterly filled washed over me. At once, Devlin began sliding fast, each stroke determined.

"Bite me," I breathed.

The moment he sank his fangs into me I came for him, arching up into him. Though he didn't drink from me, my climax was as powerful as if he had, each thrust bringing cry after cry from my parted lips.

When I stopped shuddering, Devlin withdrew his fangs, giving my neck gentle kisses. Abruptly, he quickened his movements. With a sudden jerk, he climaxed, his satisfied moans stirring as he clutched me.

"I love hearing you come," I said languidly, as he moved to my side.

"I'm glad to please you," he said tenderly. "I love you." He settled back, moving me so my head rested on his chest, and began to stroke my hair.

"I care for you, too," I replied affectionately, reaching up to stroke his face. It was rough under my hands.

It had been years since I'd felt a man's stubble. Oddly, Theo had never had any that was noticeable, and Danial never grew any, as he hadn't had any when he'd been turned.

Devlin smiled under my hand. "I should shave," he said, irritated. "This gets so old."

"You don't have to. I don't mind. But I do have to get up," I said, turning to him. "Theo and Danial will be calling after dusk, and I have a lot to do before then."

"It's already dark," he said, throwing off the blankets. "I'll come with you."

Naked, we went upstairs. It was close to five, the house dark. After turning on the lights, and getting the fire going strong, I put on some jeans and a sweater.

Devlin checked his clothes. "They're still a little wet."

My dryer wasn't going to be of help. I gave him an apologetic look. "Do you have any others with you?"

"No," he said ruefully. "I planned to be inside when the storm hit."

"Hold on," I said, heading back downstairs. "There are some of Danial's old clothes beneath the guest bed." After locating two pair of jeans and a couple shirts, I went back upstairs and handed them to him. "They should fit you."

"Sure. We're close enough," he said, looking them over. He slipped into a pair of the jeans and one of the shirts, a black one. "Do they look okay? They're a bit long."

He looked to die for, but some of that was his incredible inherent sexiness. *He'd probably be sexy in a garbage bag.*

"Sar?" he said, amused.

"You look great. I have some socks you can borrow," I said quickly, suddenly shy. I went into my bedroom, rummaging through the sock drawer for a pair of Theo's. No sooner had I grabbed one then the whining, boisterous dogs knocked it from my hands in their eagerness to walk.

"Hush!" I said, rounding on them. "I'm moving as fast as I can—"

Right then, it hit me. I did feel better. I had more energy than I'd had in months. My hands were steady, and I wasn't tired, despite I'd been awake all afternoon. Although the bedroom was cold, I wasn't shivering.

Devlin had been right.

Socks forgotten, I ran back to him, and kissed him thoroughly, sliding my tongue into his mouth, pulling him against me forcibly. He kissed me back for a moment, and then drew back. "Do you need more already?" he whispered heatedly.

"I can feel it," I said euphorically, looking at him in wonder. "You were right. You saved me."

"Yes," he agreed happily.

I stepped back from him, then faced him and stretched out my arms to him. "I am glad to come to you."

He tilted his head, giving me a surprised look.

"Your last poem," I explained.

Devlin leaned down and kissed me. "I will be making you very glad to come in a little while, Sar. Now please, I need some socks."

I got the socks, still blushing. As he pulled them on, I looked out the windows. The storm was still howling, and it looked as if I had at least a foot of snow out here. That meant I'd need to plow. I began pulling on my coat, hat, and mittens.

"Where are you going?" Devlin asked. "Outside in this?"

I handed him a heavy jacket that had been Brennan's. It was more of a duster, but it was very good at repelling water. "I need to walk the dogs. I'd like you to come with me."

"Then I'm there," he said jovially. Then he saw my face wasn't smiling. "What is it?"

"I'll need to plow when we get back," I said, making a face. "I'll be a few hours probably."

"Danial hired someone to do that, didn't he?"

"He'll be busy until late morning, easy. I'm not comfortable being snowbound with the current vampire situation, even with your delicious self to keep me company. Are you?"

"If it must be done, I will do it for you," he said with a tone of authority.

"Have you ever driven a tractor on ice?" I asked skeptically. "Can you operate a front end loader?"

He looked dubious, then shrugged. "How hard can it be?"

I laughed before I could stop myself. "If you can shovel the deck off, I can handle the plowing. But I'll need you to move the bike over a little, so I can get the tractor out. You're parked in front of it."

He nodded, then took my hand. "Sure. But let us walk first, together."

I never liked walking in snowstorms, especially when the snow was deep. But with Devlin at my side, I wasn't as worried as usual. It helped we didn't go far. Devlin seemed completely at ease though, throwing snowballs for the dogs to chase. We watched the snow falling, catching the lights of the barn to shine like fire in the air. We held hands for a while as we walked, my mittened hand in his ungloved one.

As I got the mail, I looked over the road. It hadn't been touched, the deep layer of snow pristine. The plows were waiting for the morning, with school not in session over Christmas.

"So much for your plan," he said, leading me back to the house. "Even if you plow the drive, we're still snowed in."

"If I don't do it, I'm going to worry," I explained, dressing in heavy insulated gear. "I know it doesn't make sense—"

"But it's your routine," Devlin finished, nodding as he followed me downstairs. "I understand." He rotated the end of his motorcycle, and walked it out of the way, so the tractor had a clear path. "Plow away."

The tractor worked well, as it always did. I had a little trouble with traction, but not much. The snow was light, not wet and heavy, and my tractor was a John Deere 5310, large enough to push a car in drive in reverse with no problem. I did have to move some drifts, but there wasn't much problem. The tractor went right through them.

I was self-conscious as I plowed, hoping I looked both smooth and skilled, and that I didn't dig up the driveway if Dev was watching. The angle of the bucket was very important. Too much and the earth got dug up. Too little, and a few inches of snow was left covering the driveway that would turn to ice.

When I finally finished scraping the drive, I turned smoothly and headed back into the house. As I shut down the tractor, Devlin came down the stairs. When I stood up to step off the tractor, he lifted me down.

"Thanks," I said. "Come on, I want to get out of these wet clothes."

After hanging my outer clothes next to the wood stove beside his, I went into my bedroom. To my surprise, candles were lit and the Jacuzzi was full and running. I turned to Devlin behind me to see he was already taking off his clothes.

"You read my mind," I said gratefully, slipping off the rest of my clothes.

As I settled down into the heavenly warm water, I watched Devlin step in and sit down. How many nights had I sat here and imagined this? Now he was here, and we were alone...

An unwelcome conscience spoiled my lustful thoughts, as it reminded stridently that this was Theo's domain. Grimacing, I tried to drive it away.

Devlin unexpectedly moved to get out.

"No, stay," I said firmly, stopping him. "You saved my life three times now. I want you here. Don't take my being a little uncomfortable as a rejection."

He nodded, and sank back down into the tub.

"Thank you for doing this," I added. "I was cold."

"You looked cold out there."

"It's okay. I'm warm now."

"You'll be warmer still very soon," he said languidly, handing me a glass of wine.

I took it. He clinked my glass with his own. "To the rest of this week with you," he said. "And what comes after."

"What comes after?" I asked, sipping my wine.

"Whatever we make of it," he answered devilishly, taking a sip of his wine. He put his wine to the side and relaxed back against the jets. I did the same, some of the tightness in my muscles leaving me.

We stayed in there for quite a while, just luxuriating in the warm water, not talking. After a half hour, he beckoned to me. As I settled into his lap, I felt him stiff beneath me. I turned and gave him a look of surprise. Devlin grinned at me, then stood up and took my hand. I opened the drain, then followed him. He led me to my bed, and pushed me down on it, covering my body with his.

I stopped him. "I have to eat something first, Dev. I'm starving."

"That's good, Sar," he said, relieved. "I was worried that you hadn't been hungry all day."

I got up and handed him his jeans.

"I don't have to dress," he said wickedly. "Unless my nakedness distracts you as much as it once did."

I held them out to him. "Attacks, Devlin. Possible attacks."

He put them on as I put on a robe. We walked to the kitchen, hand in hand.

"The desire for food left me with all my other ones," I said seriously, rummaging around in my cupboards. "But I feel it again, thanks to you." I gave him a smile and started heating up some water for pasta. "Want to watch something?"

He gave me a look. "Not likely."

I handed him the remote. "No action movies, I promise. You can pick."

As he sat down to peruse the channels, I went through the mail. Oddly, there was a package for Theo.

I looked at the padded envelope curiously. Who would be sending him a package? This wasn't big enough for a gun, a box of ammo, or even a book. I shrugged, put it aside for him, and looked through the rest. There was a bill, some junk mail, and a few pleas from animal shelters asking for money. Tossing the junk mail, I wrote a quick check for the bill, and paper clipped it to January as a reminder. If we didn't make it back, there was no use paying it. Taking a deep breath, I sorted through the pleas. Though I ended up pitching most, several I put aside to send a few dollars to. Throwing the pasta into the now boiling water, I went over and sat by Devlin.

"Decide on anything?"

Devlin looked at me, then leaned closer. "What's wrong?" he asked. "Your eyes are greener than they were. You're upset."

"I just was reading some pleas for animal related causes," I replied. "It makes me sad, to hear about them eating dogs in Korea, or hurting greyhounds in order to make money from racing them."

"Then why do you read these things? Why purposely feel bad?"

"Because someone has to," I said staunchly. "Someone has to care, in order for the world to change. Someone has to let themselves be moved enough to say that doing this is wrong and that they aren't going to act as if everything is okay. Most days I try to be that someone."

Devlin hugged me close. "I know," he said lovingly. "You're a white knight on a steed, Love."

Embarrassed, I drew back. "I have old episodes of 'Supernatural', if you're interested."

"I know Danial followed that," Devlin said. "But I'm more of a classics man. Come, let's check TCM."

We watched only a little of some black and white movie before my timer sounded. Then I sank happily into pasta joy, eating an entire plateful. Logy with satisfaction, I settled back onto the couch with Dev. Within minutes, I was asleep in his arms.

I woke up to the ringing of the phone. "Want me to get it?" Dev offered.

I shot him a look, got to my feet, and answered the phone. "Hello?"

"Sar?" Danial said anxiously. "How are you weathering the storm?"

"Very well," I said, forcing my tone to be solemn and not gleefully reckless. "I finished plowing and had dinner."

"You sound like your old self," he said happily.

"I felt a lot better today."

"I'm glad. I've been worried about you."

"I'm better," I replied, my eyes on Devlin who was watching me and grinning. "Really, I feel like my old self. I think the worst is past. It's good you called; I'm heading to bed soon."

"Sar, it's only eight o'clock," Danial said curiously.

"Tell him you have company," Devlin whispered with a leer. "And you're being considerate of your guest's needs, going to bed early."

"What was that?" Danial said sharply. "I heard someone—"

"The TV," I said quickly, shooting Devlin a look to kill. "Really, don't worry about me. As for bed, I'll probably need to get up early to plow again, and I need my sleep."

"Has Theo called you?"

"No," I said coolly. "If he calls you, please tell him I'm fine. I'd rather not talk to him."

"All right," Danial said neutrally. "I'm very glad you are feeling better. Get some sleep."

"I love you," I said emotionally.

"I love you," he said tenderly. "Goodnight."

As I hung up, Devlin said, "You've never stopped loving him, have you?"

"No," I admitted, coming to sit beside him. "There were times I wished I didn't, but I never stopped, no."

"That is how real love goes," he said. "Do you really want to go to bed now?"

I made a face. "What I want is to avoid Theo. It's stupid really. He's not going to call me anyway, now he knows I know everything."

"Not that I'm on his side," Devlin said slowly. "But perhaps you don't know everything."

My eyes narrowed. "What do you mean?"

"You should be prepared for more to this story. I've known Theo through his actions for the better part of ten years, ever since he joined up with Danial. This behavior is unlike him."

"I agree," I retorted angrily. "But maybe you were as wrong about him as I was."

"Perhaps. In any case, I agree: you should not answer if he calls. Don't speak to him until you're face to face."

I'd been planning the same thing, but I didn't like being told to do it by someone else. "Then let's go to bed."

The phone abruptly rang, shattering the moment. I glared over at it, bit my lip, and remained where I was. After four rings, the answering machine picked up.

"Sar, how're you feeling?" Theo said hesitantly on the machine's speakerphone. "Are you there?"

"I'm here, ass," I said aloud, both angry and upset. "Where else would I be?"

"I talked to Danial," Theo went on. "He said you were better, but nothing else." There was a pause. "I just wanted to let you know I was okay. I'll see you at the Gathering on Saturday night."

"Good for you, Prick!" I shouted. "Don't put yourself out on my account!"

"I love you, and I'm sorry we...I'm sorry that I acted...I just wanted—" Click.

"Theo!" I shouted, bolting to the phone. I quickly picked up the receiver, but there was only a dial tone. He'd been cut off.

"So much for you not wanting to talk to him," Devlin said bitterly. "Why don't you call him back, if you're so desperate for him? I'll leave." He got up and headed for his leather clothes.

I went after him. "Wait, Dev. Look, I'm sorry."

"Sorry for what?" he said scathingly, slipping into his T-shirt.

"For loving him though he treated me so badly," I said grudgingly. "I want what you said to be true, for there to be a reason he did this. It hurts that he and I went through so much and it ends like this."

"You can go through a lot for someone, and have them not appreciate it," Devlin said pointedly. "Love isn't fair, it's cruel." He slid his jacket on.

"Sometimes it is fair," I said, taking his hand. "Come with me."

I led him into the bedroom. Going to my dresser, I got his choker out of Terian's box, and placed it in his palm. The emerald eyes of the bear winked in the light from the lamp.

"What do you mean to imply?" Devlin asked, raising his hand until the choker was between us.

"I'll wear it for you," I said, "until I leave on Friday. Will you promise me to take it off me when I have to go?"

He kissed me in a satisfied way and fastened it around my neck, the links sliding together with a soft clink. "By Friday, Sar, you'll most likely be able to take it off yourself," he whispered. "Anna could always remove hers as well, though we kept that a secret, between us."

He kissed me ardently. "I'm going to check the fire, Love. Do your nighttime routine, and I'll meet you in bed."

I let out the dogs, put them in their beds, did my cat count, and turned off the lights. Devlin was waiting for me in my bed, under the covers, looking like a dream come to life.

I stopped in the doorway to look at him. "We'll have to move downstairs, Dev. There'll be sunlight through those windows in the morning."

"We will, Sar," he said, patting the bed beside him. "But I wanted you here very much, years ago. I want to have you here in your bed, at least one time. Come here."

This had to do with Theo, with sticking it to him by Dev and I having sex in the bed that was once ours. Sure, it was petty. However, right about now being petty felt good. I pushed my robe off my shoulders. It landed in a pool at my feet. I stood naked before him, wearing just the choker.

"You're beautiful," he said softly.

"So are you," I replied huskily, and moved toward him. Soon I was beneath the covers, our bodies entwined, his lips on mine.

* * * *

The dogs were barking upstairs. Someone was pounding on the door.

That had to be Brian. Danial had believed me when I'd said I'd be up early. Ugh.

I looked over at Devlin. He was still asleep; admittedly exhausted from the two days he'd been awake before arriving at my door.

The doorbell rang, setting off a round of fresh barking from Ghost and Darkness.

Well, I had to get up anyway and feed everybody soon anyway. I got out of bed.

Devlin awoke when he felt me getting up. "What is it?" he rasped. He looked very tired, though amazingly, no less sexy.

"Brian or someone else is at the door," I said. "I've got to feed everyone anyway."

He sighed, got up out of bed, and shrugged his jeans on. "I'm going up there in case it's not Brian. If it is him, we need to talk." He went to his bike, pulling out an explosive bullets gun from the leather saddlebag. "Lead on."

I was not surprised he was armed, though this was the first time I'd seen him with a gun, ever. He handled it like a tool he was comfortable using, to my relief. I nodded.

He followed me upstairs to the dim woodstove room. As I got my robe and belted it around me, Devlin took up a position behind the door. Looking through the peephole, I saw it was Brian.

"Come in," I said, opening the door and giving him a smile.

Brian didn't reply, staring at me in shock. Flushing, I remembered I was wearing Devlin's choker, and that I had fresh fang marks on my neck from last night.

"Get in here, Brian," Devlin growled. "Now."

Brian came inside and I shut the door behind him.

"You said you wouldn't hurt her," Brian said neutrally.

"I have not hurt her," Dev said arrogantly, giving Brian a dark look. "She needs to be bitten, to feel fangs in her. There is no sense healing her, if I just have to open her again."

Brian looked upset, but didn't speak.

"Does she not look better than she has?" Devlin asked him seriously.

Brian looked me over. "She does," he said grudgingly. "But she smells different. There is the slightest taint of vampire to her now."

"She is part vampire now," Devlin said. "She needs me or Danial to keep her body in the state she is in. She is not turning."

Brian came close and scented me, breathing deep. After a few minutes, he moved back. "You're right. She doesn't smell like the other women you had sometimes at your home that were turning."

"Report to Danial that she is fine, that you saw her, that she was moving around more, and that she was not as tired as she had been."

Brian nodded, resigned. "There is going to be hell to pay when Theo returns," he said, his eyes on Devlin's. "He'll know what happened here, and he'll want your heart."

Devlin considered him a moment, unafraid. "He most likely will," he said finally "before all is said and done. He has only himself to blame. I was content to leave things as they were, but he and my brother almost killed her, and I'm not entrusting them with her health again."

He rounded on Brian, taking a step toward him. Brian took one back.

"Theo would not let her be with Danial. If he had, she would never have needed the drugs; she would not have been killing herself by inches to make sure his ego wasn't damaged. She would not have needed me! If I hadn't come to her and done what I did, Sar would have been dead before this week was out!"

"I'm glad she's better," Brian placated.

"That is all that should matter, not how it was done," Devlin said angrily. "I'll not let her die because Theo is thinking about what is best for him, or Danial is too afraid to do what needs to be done."

Brian was utterly quiet, looking at the ground.

"Leave!" Devlin said, baring his fangs.

Brian went immediately, without once looking up. His SUV started up, then faded away.

"Come back to bed, my dear," Devlin said tenderly, putting his arms around me. "You need more rest."

I gently removed them. "I need to take care of my pets first, it's feeding time."

"Do you want me to help you?" Devlin offered.

I shot him a shocked look.

"I have a cat myself, Sar," Devlin added. "I know how to care for cats."

My shock reached cataclysmic levels. "*You* have a pet?"

"Why are you so surprised?" he said curiously. "You must know that Danial had a cat once. Who do you think got him that one?"

"Not the same person who threatened to burn my home with my pets still inside."

"I was bluffing," Devlin said, irritated. "It was easy to see how attached you were to them."

"I don't believe you," I said sadly, moving away from him. "You meant it."

"I've burned many buildings in my life," he said darkly. "None ever had innocents inside, be they animal or human."

"Who decided if they were innocent?" I asked. "You?"

"Do not judge me by mortal laws," Devlin said angrily. "You were not there, and have no comprehension of what justice some of those burnings were."

"Did you ever burn an animal, a live one?"

"No," he answered. "I've received too many burns to mete out that punishment idly. But I've ordered the burnings of many vampires over the years."

I didn't reply.

"Sar, were any of your cats harmed?"

"No. I thought that they were lucky."

"Luck had nothing to do with it. My men know how I feel about cats."

"You do know that one of your men tried to shoot me that night, right?"

Dev was instantly enraged. "Who?" he growled.

"I don't know. I missed his heart the first time, but not the second."

"You were in no real danger," he assured with relief, hugging me tightly. "My men are all excellent shots. That guard would have grazed you, or shot the gun so you would drop it." He paused. "All of them fear my wrath and that of Lash too much to ignore a direct order."

I didn't reply.

"I'm sorry for what I did," he said, willing me to believe him. "I would take it back if I could. There is much I'd do differently with you if we had it to do over. Let me help you now."

What more could he do than this? He couldn't undo the past any more than I could.

"Sar?"

I let out a breath and managed a smile. "My house has too many windows, and not enough blinds, Dev. I can do what needs doing."

"Very well," he said, nodding. "I'll be waiting for you here."

I went to let out the dogs. When I came back through the house with the cat food, there was a new fire merrily burning in the woodstove. After seeing to the pet's needs, I sat down in a nearby chair, and watching the flames Devlin had created.

Could I trust him? Some of what he said was a lie. He didn't want me to think badly of him now, and he wanted to explain away what he could, so I didn't think of the past and turn from him. *Of what he'd said, what was lie and what was truth? What did he really want?*

What we had together right now wasn't real life. This was an affair, a fling with a deadline. When our time together was over, he most likely would go back to his life in Rio. He acted less afraid of Theo than he had last fall, even before he'd known of our marital troubles, but that could be just arrogance. Even though I was definitely under the influence of his blood he'd given to me, I knew enough of men to know it wasn't usually what they said, but what they didn't say that mattered. Devlin had made no mention of Oaths at all, or any kind of permanent arrangement, despite all his talk of love. He offered pleasure, unadorned and deliciously simple.

Did any of this ethical bullshit really matter? Whenever he bit me, I came for him immediately, whether or not he drank my blood when he did it. I still craved his touch just as much as I had the first time. He'd been right about me, and he'd risked his life to get to me in time. Even with his past actions, that counted hugely in his favor.

I sat there for ten minutes, fingering the choker at my neck, considering everything. Then, I said to hell with it all.

I'd done the best I could by Elle, Theo, and my other responsibilities. I wanted the man below waiting for me, the man who had saved me, the last one I'd ever expected to care for, the last one I'd ever expected to love me. I knew what he was capable of, what he was. And I was going to spend these days with him, because I'd been wanting him for so long it felt like forever.

This wasn't like it had been when he had come in yesterday and I couldn't help myself, or that day in the hotel room when he had forced me to stay with him. I was going to him now willingly, with full knowledge of what I was doing. I was going to take all he had to give me, and then ask him for more, because he was right, I couldn't get enough of him. And I'd had enough of waiting, just as he had.

Chapter Twelve

I descended the stairs. Dev was lying on his side in bed. As I came near, he opened his eyes, then his arms so I could crawl into them. We lay together holding each other, then drifted off into sleep.

I woke in the late afternoon. Dev was still holding me, deep asleep. Carefully untangling my fingers from his hair, I stretched and sighed.

God, I felt wonderful. My life was in freefall in an abyss, yet I felt alive, renewed, even hopeful. My eyes went to Devlin's still form, watching him breathe slowly.

I loved him.

The instant I thought it, I wanted to shake him, and tell him. Instead, I kept still, wondering if this love was really my emotion, or my being in thrall to him.

Dev's phone rang shrilly, making me start. Groggily, he reached over to answer it.

"Of course it's me," he said irritably. "I was sleeping. What is it, Lash?"

"Yes," he said with satisfaction, glancing over at me. Then his face grew grave. For several minutes he listened, no speaking.

"Yes," he said finally, cautious yet resigned. "If you say that's the best option, I believe it. Start things moving. Come tonight to Sar's and bring Titus with you. We'll discuss options. And please pick up a double order of roses I just ordered also, on your way here."

I smiled, pleased. For all of Dev's ruthlessness, he really was passionately romantic.

"See you in an hour then." Devlin hung up, and immediately placed another call, instructing whoever was on the other end to have a double order of fire and ice roses ready, that someone would be by to pick it up.

He tossed the phone to the nightstand, and sank back down into bed with a sigh.

"What are you planning?" I asked.

His brow knitted immediately. "Nothing that will endanger you," he said, propping himself up on one arm to turn his body towards me. "Tell me what you're worried about. There's a serious look in your eyes I haven't seen before."

I'm worried because I'm in love with you. Shit. How to answer? I thought furiously, and said nothing.

"Why did you delay upstairs, earlier today?" he said insistently, his eyes searching mine. "Did you reconsider coming down to me?"

"Yes," I admitted. "I thought about all the reasons I shouldn't."

"Yet you came. Why?"

"I wanted you too much not to. You were right about me, about what I needed. And I'm scared to death that I'm not coming back from that Vampire New Year's Eve Party."

Devlin hugged me, but didn't try to convince me all would be fine. His honesty scared me, but I appreciated that more than reassuring lies. I hugged him back, not speaking.

"Dusk has fallen," he said sometime later. "Do you want to go out tonight?"

"Why do you ask?"

"You're right that you may not return from that party, despite the efforts of many," Devlin said quietly. "If there was something that was important for you to do—"

He was offering me a last request. "Tomorrow, maybe," I said, shaken. "Tonight I just want to walk with you and my dogs, get some food, and then go back to bed." I turned to him. "But what do you want?" I added, caressing his face. "This is your time as much as it is mine."

"I want you to love me as I love you," he said, pulling me in for a kiss. "That is what I want most. That is all I want, right now."

This might be my last week alive. To hell with it. "You already have that."

Devlin sat bolt upright in bed. "If that's really true, tell me, Sar," he said anxiously, his eyes were molten with heat. "Say the words to me, so I can hear if you mean them."

"I've fallen for you, Dev. Despite you and me and everything that's happened between us, I think I love you."

He pulled me into his arms, and said:

"Thou art fairer than the evening's air,
Clad in the beauty of a thousand stars,
Brighter art thou than flaming Jupiter,
More lovely than the monarch of the sky
And none but thou shall be my paramour."

Her Secret

His phone began ringing again. Devlin grumbled, trying to reach for it and not let go of me. "Christopher Marlowe," he said to me, flipping open his phone. "What is it, Lash? Tell Titus he has to come, I need his help with something. The plans for later in the week can wait a few hours. See you."

He hung up and turned to me. "Come here, my paramour," he said intently. "I want to love you again."

I went into his arms eagerly. Dev began to kiss me slowly, touching me almost languidly. "We only have an hour," I teased. "You'd better hurry."

"You won't last a half hour, Sar," he said, reaching beneath the covers to touch me. I arched against him, gasping, as he sank his fangs in.

He was right. I didn't last five minutes.

* * * *

Devlin heard his men arrive just before the dogs began barking. He paused mid song, then said, "They just pulled up outside. I promise, I'll serenade you later, Love." He got out of bed, and put on his jeans and his shirt as I slipped into my robe.

"Should I dress?" I asked. "Am I supposed to meet them with you or stay here?"

"I want you to meet them," he said, caressing my cheek. "Please do get some clothes on. Your animals will need to be confined, as they are not going to like either Lash or Titus."

Hearing that, I wasn't sure I should let them in the house, but kept that to myself. Hurriedly, I brought the cats into the cellar, and put my dogs in the bedroom with a loud radio playing to an easy listening channel to calm them. Both had begun whining. It was apparent why; I could feel the evil out there. Demon blackness was weaving itself through the air, speeding my heart with nervousness.

Apprehensive, I quickly washed up in the bathroom, then put on some jeans and a long loose sweater. Conceitedly, I chose one with a scoop neck, so Dev's symbol was displayed. Then I brushed my hair, and fluffed it up as Tatiana had showed me so long ago.

There. I had the rosy glow of satisfying sex, but I didn't look disheveled as I had before. Meeting Devlin's closest friend for the first time, I wanted to look good no matter how scared I was.

I hurried out to find Devlin still alone, watching out the window. As I went to stand near him for a look, he slipped one arm around me.

There was a black Hummer, an H4, in my driveway. Two figures were coming towards me, both dressed in black. One was huge, towering almost, blackness pouring out of him. That had to be Titus, Terian's father. I shivered, but willed myself to ignore the evil crawling sensation on my skin. Hopefully, he was like his son. Terian hadn't inherited his goodness from his witch of a mother.

The other figure was small. That had to be Lash. After the way Brian had talked about Lash, I'd expected the Devil himself, complete with horns. This man looked innocuous.

Maybe I'd already bedded the Devil, and he was the one standing next to me.

As Lash and Titus came up to the door, Devlin let them in with one hand, his other arm still around me possessively.

Titus was easily seven feet tall. He was huge, muscular and his exposed skin shimmered a little. No, it was the air above his skin that was moving. Heat poured off him the way it came off hot pavement in the summer. He gave me a smile, revealing a mouthful of fangs like a shark. I didn't see any horns, but maybe they were hidden it his hair. It was about an inch long, black as pitch, and undulating from his heat.

"Pull in that blackness of yours, Titus," Devlin said mildly. "You'll scare Sar."

"If she scared easily, she wouldn't be with you," Titus replied, taking my hand. He kissed it, his lips hot. Abruptly, the blackness lessened considerably.

As well as the blackness, Titus had to be controlling his body temperature, too, or he would have burned me with his lips. I hadn't expected a full demon to be able to do that.

"It's interesting to meet you," he said, looking at me with crimson eyes. "I am surprised you aren't afraid of me."

"I'm good friends with a half-demon," I said, looking him over for resemblance. There was a little, in the curve of his jaw.

"Terian, yes," he replied slowly.

I wanted to tell him to contact Terian before it was too late. Instead, I bit my tongue and told myself it wasn't my place. "It's good to meet you, Titus."

Lash came before me, his eyes lowered. Oddly, his appearance was at odds with what I'd been told of him. He was dressed very warmly, in black polar fleece, a wool coat, and thick black wool pants. His exposed skin was a light tan color, and his hair was dark, cut above his shoulders in a shaggy style that was above his turtleneck. He had a scar down the left side of his face, a slash across one eye. Most of the blow had fallen on his cheekbone. It was jagged, making the amused smile he was giving me a grimace. There was a coiled bullwhip and a well-used survival knife on his belt.

Then he suddenly looked up, and our eyes met. With one look into them, I understood why Brian had been so afraid of him. For not being a large man,

Lash was scarier than Titus, more scary than Devlin or Danial at their worst, or even Theo when he was enraged. I was relieved that Devlin was by my side, that his arm was around me, and that this man wasn't my enemy.

Lash's eyes were flat, with no emotion in them at all. Snake eyes.

"Good to meet you," he said in a hissing voice that slid over me, as he took my hand. Instead of a kiss, Lash opened his mouth, and a forked tongue slid out to taste the air above my skin.

He wanted me to jerk back from him with a scream. Most women would have. But I'd held a lot of snakes in my life, and wasn't frightened. This was how snakes tasted new things.

I kept my hand steady in his. "Good to meet you, Lash."

He kept his tongue there, tasting me through the air, staring up at me with those flat eyes. I looked back at him evenly.

He nodded, then his tongue disappeared back into his mouth, and he let go of my hand. Though he didn't speak, I felt I'd passed some sort of test.

"So, which species are you?" I asked.

He gave me a smile, baring thin needle-like fangs, slightly curved back and a little longer that a vampire's. "You know what I am?" he hissed, surprised. "And you aren't afraid?"

"You're a weresnake. I haven't met one before."

"I'm impressed," he said, sounding anything but.

Just what I needed, another wise ass.

"Answer her," Devlin said mildly.

"Water moccasin," Lash said, something close to pride in his tone.

"Is your bite poisonous?" I asked warily.

"Only in reptile form," he hissed, tilting his head and giving me a considering look. Then he looked at Dev. "I like her. She's braver than I expected."

Dev gave him a proud look, then turned serious. "We need to talk. Come into the living room."

Lash and Titus followed us in, the latter producing an extra chair for himself from thin air. It groaned under his weight as he sat down. Devlin and I sat at one end of the couch, Lash at the other nearest Titus.

I deduced Lash enjoyed the heat Titus radiated. It was winter, and he was dressed very warmly. *Maybe he had cold blood?* Most snakes hibernated in winter...

"Excuse me," I said, getting up. I went into the other room and built up the fire so it was roaring. It wouldn't make a huge difference in the living room, but it would make some.

When I went back, the three of them were deep in discussion.

"It's doable, Dev," Lash said. "But I'm going to have to leave tonight with Titus to make it on time. Even with the two of us, we might not be able to do what needs doing."

"I know you, Lash. If anyone could do it, you can," Devlin said confidently.

Lash looked at me insolently. "If I'm risking my life, I want to taste her, Dev."

Devlin gave him a dark look.

"You've gone on and on for months now about how she tastes of summer. Years, actually. I want to know what summer tastes like. I want some of her blood, right from her vein."

With effort, I forced myself to remain where I was.

"She may not taste like summer to you," Devlin replied.

"I don't care, I want to know what she tastes like," Lash hissed audaciously. "I'll do what you're asking and never ask again for either her blood or to touch her, but that is non-negotiable."

"I feel the same," Titus agreed. "We may not come back from this. Besides, I am curious myself. I have never read in any of my tomes about blood tasting of summer."

Devlin looked at me hopefully. "Sar, will you agree?" he said, "I need to mark you anyway. This can be part of the process."

I nodded. "Danial was going to; we were just trying to find a way around the pain—"

"I can take away your pain, Sarelle," Titus said quickly, giving what I thought was supposed to be a reassuring look. "The easiest way is for Devlin to bite you as deeply as he did that first time, and then use a slow acting magical spell."

It was impossible for me to consider a mouth with that many teeth reassuring. "You can heal?" I replied, surprised.

Devlin ignored me, speaking to Titus, "What can we do to make the new mark I'll give her appear as old as the other scar she has from me?"

Titus came to my side, and turned my head to one side to examine the older scar, then to the other where Devlin's fresh fang marks were only partially scabbed over. "The new bite is far shallower, Dev," he said. "I can make it appear older, but they won't match. When the new one heals, there will only be a faint scar."

Devlin let out a breath that sounded like a growl. "These creatures will be looking for a chink in Sar's armor, any excuse that they can get to share her amongst themselves. We need to make the marks look identical, both in depth and in age. There needs to be no doubt that Sar is Oathed and has been for some time."

"It will be done," Titus said, then focused on me. "As to your question, Sarelle, it wasn't easy for me to learn healing, being what I am. Alerian taught me what she knew, all of it. It's a process. Every year, I learn a tiny bit more."

"I'm sorry for my part in what happened," I said, touching his hand.

Titus looked uncomfortable, and withdrew his hand from mine quickly. "She attacked Terian. He defended himself, and you defended him. I loved her, but I can't blame anyone but her for what happened." He got to his feet. "I'll get what I need from the Hummer," he said. "Prepare her." He left me alone with Devlin and Lash.

I looked uncertainly at Devlin. "There was talk of faking Danial and I being Oathed—"

"Who thought that shit up, Wondercat?" Lash hissed sarcastically.

"Danial should have known better than to try and fake it," Devlin said, irritated. "Any vampire in that room Saturday guesses that you don't truly belong to Danial, you're up for grabs."

Irritated at Lash's comment, I retorted "We weren't going to fake the marks. Danial and I decided to do it. As I said before, I was worried about—"

"Be that as it may, Danial isn't here and I am," Devlin replied. "And you're going to give me an Oath of sorts, too."

I blinked my eyes. Had I imagined that last sentence?

"Now, will you share your blood with them?" Devlin asked.

"Will it hurt to?" I said hesitantly. "Do I have enough, I mean, after what you took?"

"They are not going to drink your blood as I do; they just want a taste. You should be fine."

Lash gave me a hungry look. "Don't worry. I'll be gentle."

My flesh crawled at the sexual implication he'd wanted me to hear. I looked away from him.

"Lash," Devlin warned.

Devlin hadn't risked all he had in the last few days to let his friend and his demon drain me now. "Yes, it's fine, Dev. But no biting, unless it's you."

Lash looked amused, and let out a snort.

"It will only be me," Dev assured. "I'll be right here, Love. Now lay back onto me."

I reclined back against him and he put his arms around me loosely. Carefully, he sank his fangs into my scabbed bite. I moved involuntarily, even though I tried to keep myself still, arching my back in his arms as they tightened around me. Just feeling him penetrate me gave me something akin to a small orgasm. My sigh of pleasure was loud in my ears, loud enough for me to flush slightly.

Blood rose up in the wounds. Devlin withdrew his fangs and motioned to Lash. "Now."

Lash went to his knees on the floor beside the couch and leaned over me, bringing his lips to my throat as his hand gripped my neck. I shivered, my heart hammering.

Devlin kissed the other side of my neck. "I'm here, Love. Everything will be fine. Lash won't hurt you. Just hold still."

Lash's mouth slid over the wounds left by Devlin's fangs. I felt slender fangs penetrate me, but just barely. Making a tight seal over my wound with his mouth, he began sucking gently at my neck and swallowing. Other than that, he made no other noise at all. His hand was not slimy, clammy, or scaly, it felt normal, smooth and warm, just a touch colder than a human's would have been.

Dev kissed me again. "Everything is fine, Sar. I have you."

Abruptly, it was over. Lash carefully withdrew his fangs and mouth, then sat back from me on his haunches. He licked his lips, his forked tongue vibrating slightly. His eyes were thoughtful. "She doesn't taste like summer to me."

"What do I taste like to you?" I said grumpily.

"You taste warm and good and alive, but otherwise normal."

I snorted. "That's the first time in a while I've been called normal."

Lash looked surprised, then smiled a little. "That's because of your friends." He got to his feet, then sat back on the end of the couch, still licking his lips with his forked tongue.

Titus came back in and kneeled beside Devlin. "Remain calm. I'm not going to bite you," he said seriously. "I will taste your blood when I heal you, after Devlin bites you."

That meant I'd likely come in front of them when Dev bit into me. I shut my eyes, embarrassed just at the thought. "How long will it take?"

"Devlin has only to sink his fangs in, and then take them out. It will be painful for a half second, until he withdraws. Then I'll begin healing the bite and taking the pain away."

I opened my eyes and took a deep breath. "Okay. I'm ready. Do it."

Titus got a bunch of powders from a leather satchel, and stirred them together with his finger. The mixture took on an ice blue color. He held his wrist to Devlin. Devlin took it, opening a shallow cut with one fang and a shake of his head. Titus added one drop of blood to the mixture. It began to glow, the color changing until it was a smoky gray color, pulsating faintly.

"Devlin," Titus intoned.

Devlin took tight hold of me, baring his fangs and positioning himself, then tilting my neck to the side. He looked to Titus.

Titus nodded to him. "Now."

Devlin sank his fangs all the way in, biting me as deeply as he could. The rush of pleasure hit me like a freight train and I began to climax, drawing in a deep shaking breath to cry out my joy. Intense pain suddenly hit me. I screamed, my muscles tensing involuntarily as I jerked back, trying to get away. A second later, Dev withdrew and Titus began smoothing some of the glowing mixture over the bite. The pain eased immediately. I relaxed limply back into Devlin's arms.

"It will take some time for this to heal," Titus said, applying a little more mixture. "Hold still now." He dipped his head, his hot lips sliding over my skin as he licked my spilled blood.

"What does she taste like to you?" Devlin asked curiously. "Lash said he couldn't taste the sweetness I can."

Titus sat back on his knees, studying me. "She tastes of me," he said, incredulous.

"What?" Devlin and I both said together.

Titus ran his tongue across his lips. "She tastes of demon."

Chapter Thirteen

"Sar is part demon?" Devlin said, shocked. "That can't be. I know the taste of demon blood. There is no taint to her."

"There has to be," Titus said, still savoring the taste of my blood. "I can taste it in her."

"I cannot, which I find odd. It must be only a slight taint," Devlin mused. "How and when did it happen?"

"When Terian and Danial fought years ago, Danial cut Terian," I supplied. "After Danial was safe, and Terian had gone, I went to get the knife. I tried to clean it off, but the blood seemed to stick to my hands. I had to rub really hard to get it off."

"You rubbed it into your skin," Titus said, glancing at Devlin.

"That's what Terian said when I told him," I continued. "He said that my skin absorbed some of his blood, altering me."

"You were resistant to the vampire virus before, and this made you more resistant," Titus explained. "It strengthened your natural immunity. This is probably why you were able to carry the dhamphir to term. It's also likely why you survived your miscarriage."

Devlin kissed my neck again. "Perhaps that is why you taste of summer," he whispered into my ear. "I never had your blood before you were exposed. If I had, I'd guess the taste would have been lighter and less heady, closer to spring."

Closer to Anna's, you mean. "Maybe."

Titus checked my bite, then wiped it clear of luminous material. Taking a small mirror from my wall, he held it up so I could see Dev's bite. It was a twin now for the mark on the other side of my neck. Logical; it had been made by the same pair of fangs.

"Will this one stay?" I asked him. "Danial marked me two years ago like this. The scars healed over the years."

"I can't say," Titus said. "Devlin?'

Devlin shrugged. "I can't say either. I marked Anna before she was as you are now. Her scars never faded, as your older one from me won't. But the new one might with time." He gave me a grin. "Don't worry, Love. I'll be around enough to sink myself into you anytime you need me to." He turned my head up and back towards him, then kissed me passionately.

Maddened with sudden desire, I ran my hand back through his hair to hold his lips on mine.

"We'd better get moving," Titus rumbled uncomfortably, rising from his knees to stand beside the couch. "There is a lot to do and not much time."

"You are going to have to kick Lash," Devlin said, breaking the kiss. "Or go it alone. The warmth of you and Sar's fire put him to sleep."

Lash lay unmoving in the corner of the couch, his head on his arms, facing the wall.

"You kick him," Titus grumbled. "You know how he gets in winter, especially when he gets this comfortable."

"He must be exhausted," I said sympathetically. "Why not just nudge him or put your hand on his shoulder and shake him?"

Dev nibbled my shoulder gently. "He'll bite," he stated. "It's instinct."

Jesus. I moved back from Lash, crowding close to Dev.

"He hates winter and cold," Devlin elaborated. "Right now, he's warm and content, probably wishing we were back in Rio. He's not going to like being woken up, especially to have to go back out in the cold."

"Can't you say his name to wake him, then?"

"He'll strike then possibly, too," Titus rumbled. "Either with his knife or his whip."

We all stayed where we were, unmoving, for several minutes. Lash kept sleeping.

"Grab the poker from the wood stove," Devlin said finally. "I'll grab him, when he strikes. Sar, move over behind me. I want you out of striking distance."

Titus got the poker as Devlin maneuvered his body between mine and Lash's. Then Devlin nodded at Titus. From a safe distance, Titus gave Lash a sharp jab in the back. Utterly silent, Lash erupted, eyes shut and fangs spread wide, striking in the direction of Titus. Devlin darted forward and grabbed him gently at the neck, holding him back.

"Lash!" Devlin said loudly.

Lash blinked his eyes, then shoved Devlin's arm away. He shrugged his clothes back into place, more from irritation then that he was disheveled. His forked tongue came out vibrating madly as he hissed, baring his fangs. Angrily, he turned to Devlin.

"Fuck, Dev, couldn't you have gone and had sex with Sar again and let me sleep?"

I blushed, not knowing what to say. Lash continued bitching a blue streak.

"I've been up all day and all last night and the day before, since we got back! Hayden's a shitpile—"

Dev cast a worried look at Titus.

"There's a lot still to do, and most of it is inside work," he rumbled. "We have trees to clear from that massive storm that hit in early November."

That storm had flattened one of my trees too, causing a power outage. Theo and I had lit candles. We had...I shut down the memory, then buried it beneath a sea of images of myself and Devlin.

Lash was still bitching. "Don't fucking say 'trees to clear' like it's a pile of twigs, Demon. We have at least three large trees blocking the back supply road. They need to be sawn up and moved out before any supplies are delivered from the lumberyard."

"Leave them," Devlin said firmly, putting his hand on Lash's shoulder. "We've all got more important things to do. Titus can teleport any lumber directly from the truck inside the house, if it comes to that. I need you en route as soon as possible."

Lash looked at him, then nodded once. Without a word, he got up, and headed for the door, Titus and Devlin following. Curious, I followed.

Titus went out first, after a small smile of farewell. Lash stood at the door, as if waiting for something.

Make an effort to be a good hostess. "Do you want an extra blanket?" I offered.

Lash looked at me, his flat eyes concealing if he was amused or irritated. "Titus will keep the Hummer warm enough. At least I'm not in Europe. Russian winters are the worst." He turned to Devlin. "Why can't you ask me for simple shit?"

"Thanks again for doing this, Lash," Devlin said, clasping Lash on the arm.

Surprisingly, Lash did the same to Devlin. "It's about time that you're finally doing something to regain your power, Dev," he replied, grinning widely. "I was getting tired of being a second-class citizen." His grin faded. "South America was nice and warm, but it's not home."

He stepped back as Devlin released him, then faced me. For a moment he stared, then he moved his jaws, the lower one unhinging as he bared one fang at me in a wide lopsided smile. "Thanks for the blood."

"What exactly are you doing for Dev?" I asked, repressing a shiver.

Lash's eyes flicked to Devlin, then he turned to leave.

I reached out and touched his back. "Wait, I—"

He turned so fast I jumped backwards. Devlin caught me.

"Don't ever touch me, Sar," Lash hissed at me. "Not ever."

He came toward me, moving his head and shoulders from side to side, his tongue flicking until I was backed up against Devlin's chest and couldn't go any farther.

"You were anyone else, I'd backhand you," he hissed.

Asshole. "I gave you my blood," I said angrily. "Answer the question. We're on the same side."

"Are we?" Lash hissed menacingly.

"Past is past," Devlin interjected. "She is Oathing to me, Lash. That puts her on our team. Answer her."

I expected an apology. Instead, Lash's flat eyes bored into mine, until I was the one who looked away. "We're trying to protect you from those who'd like to make you little more than a brood mare," he hissed. "That is all you need to know." He grasped my chin. "Anything else you want to say?"

"Good luck," I said quietly. "Godspeed."

"Demon speed, you mean," he said sarcastically. "God has no place in this." He turned from me and walked outside.

Devlin gently moved me aside, and went after him. I stayed in the doorway, waiting.

Together, they walked to the SUV, then Lash got in the Hummer. A few seconds later, he handed something to Devlin through the SUV window, and then the window went back up quickly. Dev hit the side of the vehicle lightly once as it left, its headlights disappearing around the turn of the driveway.

Relieved the visit was over, I reached up and touched the newer scar.

"It looks as it should," Devlin commented, coming back inside, a duffel bag slung over one shoulder. "Very nicely done, if I do say so myself." He handed me two dozen beautifully wrapped fire and ice roses.

I took them with a smile. "Thank you. You didn't have to, you know."

"I enjoyed sending you flowers from afar, but I prefer to give them to you myself, Love," Dev said casually, walking to the basement door. "Come below when you've seen to the pets."

"I'll be a while," I answered haltingly. "I'd like to shower first."

"Sounds like a plan," Devlin purred temptingly. "I'll be back shortly." He gave me a smoky look, then descended the stairs.

Though my loins had me longing to follow, I shook off my desire and quickly tidied up the kitchen and living room. Although three beings had fed on me here, there were no blood spatters visible. Relieved, I settled the pets for the night, including giving the dogs a couple bribery Cheweez each for patience and understanding, then quickly stuck the flowers into two vases, leaving them on the bedroom dresser.

Devlin hadn't returned. Instead of starting the shower, I decided to make the most of his absence. He'd marked me tonight and I wanted to celebrate it.

I went to the linen closet and got the satin sheets that Theo had hated. Vindictively, I put them on the bed upstairs, then pushed open the closet door to survey my lingerie choices. My eyes went first to the matching slip.

No, I'd worn that for Theo. I yanked it off the hanger and stuffed it into the garbage.

As the minutes stretched, it became apparent that Theo aside, I didn't have anything that hadn't either come from Danial, or that I hadn't worn for him in the time we'd been together. This wasn't a night for recycling outfits. I wanted something that was Devlin's alone, something he didn't have to share...*Yes!*

I went to the spare closet, cursing as I shoved boxes of books out of the way. Opening the door, I pushed my old prom gown and my wedding dress aside, and pulled out a protective bag way at the back. Quickly, I brought it into the bedroom and unwrapped it.

I'd worn this long ivory slip gown only once: on my wedding night for Brennan, years ago. The top of the bodice was silk with satin and lace inlay, beads and sequins all down the front in a V-pattern. The lightly gathered sheer skirt scalloped on both sides like an upside down tulip. I'd felt beautiful once wearing this. It would be perfect if it still fit.

"Sar," Devlin called from downstairs. "Come down, please."

Curious, I hung the gown on the back of the door, grabbed one vase of roses, and went downstairs. Dev had just finished making up the large bed with new sumptuous sheets. Instead of the expected black, they were a silvery gray color. I put the vase of flowers on the nightstand, and helped him finish putting the comforter in position.

"These are beautiful. I'll take the old ones upstairs and wash them. Do you have any clothes you want me to wash?"

Devlin looked at me in surprise. "No. They weren't really dirty; I just prefer my own."

He hadn't commented on my odd need to plow; I wouldn't comment on him needing his "security" sheets. I nodded assent.

"Are you hungry?" he asked.

"What?"

"Aren't you hungry?" he repeated, concerned. "I'd expect you would be."

"Yes, but I really want a shower first."

"Shall we go take one then, Love?" He offered me his hand.

I took it, following him upstairs with the used sheets under my other arm. "We can use the guest bathroom. The master bathroom's too small for more than one person."

"You can tell I don't live here," Devlin said with a grin. "We'll have to enlarge it. No one should shower alone."

I cast him a look, then rolled my eyes. "You can start the shower. I'll be back." I carried the clothes into the laundry room, embarrassed that I didn't have a shower for two in the master bathroom. Until now, it hadn't ever been a problem. The Jacuzzi tub took up most of the master bathroom. Theo hadn't minded…

Angrily, I made myself put him out of my mind. I was not on his mind, and it was stupid to waste time thinking about a man who was cheating on me, no matter that technically I was cheating on him now, too. This was a time to enjoy myself and to hell with the consequences.

I returned to the bathroom, then Devlin and I stepped into the running water. Devlin had adjusted the water temperature so it was almost too hot. The heat was just that edge of too much, and more than enough. It felt delicious pouring down on us, as we stood holding each other in its spray.

"Does this warmth feel good to you, Sar?" Devlin said softly, sliding his hands over my body. His skin was much warmer, though not as warm as the water.

"It feels better than good. It feels better than almost anything," I said, closing my eyes to luxuriate in the feeling. "Just feeling the sensation is completely satisfying."

He laughed in a rich low way as he brought his hands up from my waist over my breasts to cross over my chest, pulling me tight against him. "That is how you feel to me, Love," he purred, kissing the side of my neck gently. "Being in you is better than almost anything."

I leaned into him and took a long shuddering breath. There was the slight pressure of Dev's fangs as he nibbled my neck, then soft kisses. I closed my eyes, wanting nothing more than to be with him like this forever, to never not feel the press of his skin on mine. We'd had sex many times in the past day and a half, yet my longing for him only seemed to increase.

"I want you, too, Love," he whispered. "Regrettably, that must wait for now. Would you please hand me the shampoo?"

Startled, I put some in my hair and then handed it to him. We both scrubbed ourselves with soap quickly, then rinsed off,

He finished much faster than I. "Take your time with your lovely hair." Devlin stepped out, giving me a quick kiss. "I'll be right here."

I finished washing and conditioning my hair, then went out after him. He was standing near the sink, having finished shaving.

"Better?" he asked, glancing over at me.

"If you mean me, I feel better now I'm clean, yes. If you mean you, I told you before I don't care if you shave or not."

"I've been told I'm more handsome cleanly shaven." He smiled ruefully. "But actually, I meant you."

Something made me think Anna had preferred him that way. "You couldn't be more handsome," I said derisively. "How could you worry I would find you anything but to die for?"

He pulled me to him, and turned me to the mirror. "Look at yourself," he breathed in my ear. "You are to die for."

I looked into the mirror, amazed. I was no longer the ghost I'd been the last two months. My skin was pale, but my cheeks were flushed. My eyes were bright, the green of them standing out in the bathroom light. My lips were a dark red-pink. My skin shone softly, with just the edge of the luminosity of Devlin's. His choker glittered in the light at my throat, the emeralds shining. Even with the new scars that now adorned my neck, I was beyond the picture of health: I was supernaturally striking.

"You are breathtaking, Sarelle," he said with absolute delight.

"Call me Sar," I purred, then kissed him passionately.

Kissing me ardently back, Devlin dropped his razor into the sink, and lifted me onto the bathroom sink, maneuvering between my thighs as he began to slide his hands lower.

I pushed him back gently. "Wait."

He pulled back from me. "What?" he asked, worried.

"Did you mean what you told your friends about getting an Oath from me?" *Would he deny he'd said it? Had it just been to make Lash behave?*

"Of course, or I'd not have said it," Devlin replied, looking in my eyes. "I want you to make me a promise."

I looked away from him uneasily, and eased off the bathroom sink, gathering up my clothes and his. "Then we need to talk. I need to dry off, and—"

"As do I," Devlin said curtly. He pushed me out the door, and shut it abruptly behind me.

In a daze, I went into my bathroom. After applying some Victoria's Secret lotion, conditioning my hair, and dressing in polar fleece, I emerged to find Devlin waiting for me on the satin sheets, wearing only the guest robe from the bathroom.

I let my eyes linger on him. "You're going to have to settle for me smelling sexy. It's too cold to be walking around in lingerie."

"I'll keep you warm," he said with a smile. He slid his hands over the comforter. "This was a nice surprise. I didn't take you for the kind of person who had satin sheets, Sar."

"Am I too rustic?" I said sarcastically.

He grabbed me and pulled me down to sit by him. "Not for me," he said throatily. He began to kiss me again, then moved to push me onto my back.

Resisting my urge to strip off my clothes for another round of Paradise, I pushed him back. "Wait. Listen, Dev, I can't promise myself to you. I'm already married to Theo. Despite he's a jackass, I can't jump into whatever it is you want with me until I deal with that."

Devlin leaned back, a considering look on his face.

"I love you, and I'm tired of resisting how I feel. But I can't promise you anything until I talk to him."

"You don't owe him anything," Devlin said casually. "I hope you realize that."

My eyes narrowed. "He is my husband, and I took my vows seriously. I owe him a chance to explain himself."

"When I told you that you didn't know the whole story, I didn't mean that Theo had anything to explain. He loves this other woman. He's abandoned you twice now in her favor."

That stung. "I'm not saying I'll take him back. I'm saying I'm on the rebound, and this is probably the worst time to get seriously involved with someone else. I don't want to hurt you." *And I'm not sure you're over Anna, even if it has been two hundred years.*

"I'm not afraid you'll call me by his name," Devlin said sarcastically, narrowing his golden eyes.

But what if you call me by hers? "I just want to be honest with you. I want to make sure you know where things stand. I should have said this to you before, and I'm sorry I didn't."

"Sar, no matter what else happens, Theo is going to know when he returns that you and I are in love. He'll also have to accept you having a vampire lover. All I need to know from you is whether you'll want Theo in your bed or not."

I gaped at him. "What? You said you wanted a promise from me."

"That won't affect Theo's affection for you if he thinks this is an Oath you took a long time ago, back when he was gone. I can work towards that end, if you want me to."

"I don't see how you think you can manage this."

"Perhaps you would if you let me finish a sentence or two," he said in mild annoyance.

I flushed. "Go ahead."

"Sar, I don't want Danial to cover this up. I don't care anymore if Theo knows. In fact, I want him to! I don't want to hide anymore what I feel for you or for you to hide what you feel for me. We have crossed a bridge, and we're not going back, we are going to burn it behind us. You are going to have to take a vampire lover, be it Danial or me. Theo will have to accept it or let you go."

"He'll let me go," I said sadly. "He couldn't handle it last fall and that was only for a weekend. This is for the rest of my life." Shock suddenly hit me. "You don't want my Oath to be just to you?" I added in disbelief.

"No," Devlin replied, amused. "I don't even want you to swear you'll love me for all time." The amusement left his face. "I want you to swear to me tonight that you'll never take another vampire lover unless Danial and I are both dead."

"That is morbid and disturbing."

"You'll understand better with time," Devlin said sadly. "Theo is not immortal. You may well live to see him die, Sar. I don't begrudge you whatever happiness you find in his arms in the years he has left." He paused. "Danial or I are not truly immortal either, despite being vampire. You'll need another vampire to sustain you, should something happen to us."

"Why are you talking about your death, about Danial's death?" I said, upset. "The Oath I took to Danial was nothing like this."

"Yes, and yours to him lasted how long?' Devlin said sarcastically.

"I understand you're being realistic," I said slowly. "But that doesn't make it less upsetting."

"Let's come back to this later," Devlin said, rising. He offered me his hand. "You said you were hungry, and I want to make sure you eat. There will be time tonight to discuss this further."

I took his hand. "What about you? Despite your past cracks about my being a poor hostess, there's likely not enough of my blood left to offer you any more of it tonight."

"You are endearing," Devlin said, pushing a strand of my hair back from my face. "Tomorrow will be soon enough, Love. Come." He took my hand and led me into the kitchen.

I quickly made and devoured a sandwich with chips, then made another one, and ate that, too. Next was ice cream, chocolate, and some M&Ms. Happily full at last, I stretched out on the couch, satiated.

"I'm glad your appetite's returned," Dev said, watching me with a smile. "I remembered your desire for food from the hotel, and it seemed to me that if you were feeling normal, you should be eating a lot more that you did yesterday."

What was he saying exactly? I let it slide. "It's good to be hungry again."

Devlin picked me up, carrying me to the bedroom to lay me on the satin sheets. "There are many types of hunger, Sar." He kissed me slowly, then whispered, "Some can never truly be sated."

I moved to pull him atop me, and the phone promptly rang. "Damn it."

Devlin sat up and leaned over to look at the phone. "It's Danial." He handed me the receiver.

I took it. "Hi, Danial."

"Sar, where were you today?" he exclaimed, worried.

Shit, I hadn't heard the phone ring. "I've been here all day."

"Terian called and got no answer. He almost teleported to your house, but didn't want to leave Theoron alone."

That would have been a bombshell. "Why didn't he leave a message?" I said, getting angry. "There was none on the machine. He must have called when I was in the shower."

"Do not get all riled up. He is just worried and nervous. We all are."

"Look, I'm sorry for worrying you. Next time, tell him to just leave a message."

"What have you been doing today?"

Getting marked. Having a weresnake drink my blood. Having a former denizen of Hell tell me that I'm part demon. Having sex with your brother. Thinking about having sex with you.

"Doing laundry, cleaning, napping, and walking the dogs," I answered.

"I will see you on Friday. I'll be coming back early. I'd like to make a plan now for marking you, if you're amenable."

"Theo called you and gave you permission?" I asked scathingly.

There was silence.

"You wouldn't have said all this if he hadn't," I persisted. "What else did he say?"

"He told me to mark you, that he thought it was best for you."

Theo had fought too long against me being with Danial to give in unless he was letting me go. This wasn't Theo being understanding. It was the way he cut himself loose.

"Sar, I—

"Come to me Friday night," I said abruptly. "My house. I'll be waiting."

"I'll be there, Sar," Danial said sadly. "I'm sorry."

"Danial, don't be sad about this. Theo made his decision. He has to do what is right for him."

"You sound very understanding," Danial said suspiciously. "Too understanding. What is going on that you are not angry?"

"Because I'm getting the better deal." That was true: now that I didn't have to worry about being turned, the thought of being with Danial again was intoxicating.

"We were here several months ago," Danial said angrily. "Don't say we'll be together if you don't mean it. I'm tired of getting my hopes dashed—"

"This isn't going to end in any way but us together," I said happily. "Come to me Friday night. If you want to send someone to watch the animals, I'll come to you—"

"No, I will come to you. I have many memories of you in those first months we were together and of that summer we spent with Elle at your home. If I'm later than usual, I'll use my key."

"I'll see you Friday," I said sexily. "I love you."

"I love you, too," he said eagerly. "And I'm going to have you as soon as I am there with you, Darling, so be ready." Click.

I clumsily hung up the receiver, excited and filled to the brim with adrenaline rush.

"He's got it bad for you," Devlin said in my ear.

I let out a yelp. "You were listening?"

"I wanted to hear what my brother had to say," Devlin said. "I'm glad you still love him. It will be safer for you if you have more than one source of what you need. That is why I proposed including him in your Oath to me."

I couldn't believe what I was hearing. "Devlin, is this really done? I have never heard of two men, much less two vampires being willing to share one woman. Someone always gets hurt."

"That might be true if Danial and I were human, but we aren't. There will always need to be other women for us."

The way he'd said it indicated the other women might not just be for blood. I took a deep breath. "If I do what you're asking, I know Danial will be faithful to me. I need to know if you'll take other lovers, Dev. Answer me, and be honest."

"Would you be angry if I did?" he asked, gazing at me with his melting gold eyes.

This all seemed so sordid suddenly. "I'd be upset, of course. I don't like to think of you with someone else. But if I'm going to have two men, and you're only going to have one woman between you—"

"So you want to let me have another woman, to be fair?" Devlin supplied.

I blushed furiously. "It's unfair not to agree to that, but I'd ask that you limited...yourself...um..." I couldn't get the words out, my tongue tripping over itself.

Devlin chuckled. "I've had over fifty women since that day in the hotel with you, Love. None of them looked at me as you did. None of them said they loved my eyes."

I was floored into silence, then disgusted. Then I was very, very glad he couldn't give me any diseases, being with all those other women.

"I can see I should not have mentioned a number," Dev said ruefully. "Forget them, please, My Dear One. They didn't matter to me, not like you do."

I didn't reply, trying to get my mind around the number fifty. *Was that more than one a night? He hadn't said how many times he'd had each woman...nauseating...*

"Sar, look at me."

"It's hard to."

He took my hand in his. "What I tried to make you understand was that no matter how much I tried to forget being with you, I couldn't. I haven't loved anyone in a long time. If you'll give me your promise, I won't be with anyone else but you. I won't swear that to you forever, but I'll swear it for the next decade, provided you swear not to deny me your favors."

I nodded, still in shock.

"Let's adjourn this conversation for tonight. The night in fact is drawing to its close, and we're both exhausted. I will take your Oath tomorrow, after we've both had a chance to rest." Devlin offered me his hand. "Come."

I didn't move.

Devlin took me in his arms. "I love you, Sar. No one else. There is no other woman who I'd have risked so much for." He kissed me tenderly. "There is no one for you to be jealous of."

He had risked a hell of a lot coming back here. "I'm just worried," I said in a small voice.

His brow creased as he looked down at me. "About what?"

"That this isn't real," I admitted hesitantly. "That I'm going to wake up and find out this is all a dream, that I'm still sick."

"It's not a dream," he reassured. "I'm real and my feelings for you are real. Now come to bed and rest."

"No. When you came to me, you said you had plans for you and I. I'm not tired." I twined my arms around his neck. "What was your fantasy?"

Dev smiled recklessly. "Feel like going for a bike ride?"

"Sure, but what do I wear? I don't have leather gear like you."

"Ah, but you do, Sar," he said, grabbing my hand and leading me down to his motorcycle. He reached into the saddlebags on the back, and pulled me out some black leather pants. "These should fit. They're the same size as your jeans."

"How did you know that?" I said, taking them from him and glancing at the tag. Sure enough, they were the right size.

"I looked when I sent your laundry down to get washed in the hotel."

Good thing I hadn't gained any weight. I'd have been royally embarrassed when they didn't fit. "What about a helmet?"

"You can wear mine. Being night, I won't need it."

Trepidation hit me. It was going to be freezing cold riding on the back of a bike at night in the middle of winter. I'd always liked motorcycles, but I'd never ridden on one before.

"I'd put on a heavy jacket, if I were you. Hurry, the moon is setting."

His excitement and surety swayed me. "Sure," I said, giving him a smile. "Let me get these on and grab my jacket."

"I'll come with you. My clothes should be dry by now."

After dressing in leather, and also for me, multiple layers of polar fleece, we headed back downstairs. Devlin climbed astride the bike, and began checking it over. "Nice boots."

"Thanks," I replied, slipping on the bike behind him, my feet clad in the high boots he'd given me. "I told you I liked them."

"So you did." He handed me the helmet.

I buckled it on. "All set."

"Hold on to me tightly. You won't hurt me, and I'd rather you squeezed me than fell off."

"Will do." I hit the opener, slipping my arms around his waist as Devlin kick-started the bike. It roared to life with a throaty growl and he backed it out slowly into the cold December night. I hit the garage door opener again. The door slid closed as Devlin slowly drove in a half circle and then out and down my driveway.

I hadn't been outside at night for a long time. Then I'd been too cold, but the night was exhilarating. The full moon was shining down, lighting up everything around us.

As we got to the end of the driveway, Dev put his legs down for a moment, checking both ways. "Remember, hold on."

I renewed my grip on him, then he gunned the throttle, and we drove into the night.

The words I could use to describe what I felt riding with him wouldn't do it justice. The moon seemed to follow us. The night was alive, the air crystal clear. All the stars were out above us, and they shone down so we alone could see them. The strength of Devlin's body in front of me eased my fear, and blocked most of the wind. He was a little too tall for me to look over his shoulder easily in the bulky helmet.

We rode for about ten minutes, mostly on back roads. Everything seemed so animated. The sound of the engine growling as the bike raced through the night, the yellow markers in the road speeding by one by one. The cold air rushing past us, the moon above shining down. The feel of his hair whipping back in the wind, sliding over my helmet. I breathed it all in, wanting never to let it go. The only overwhelming feeling was to spend forever in this moment, for it never to end.

Devlin slowed, bringing the bike to a stop, and then turned to me. He lifted me from behind him to sit over the front of the motorcycle, its engine still vibrating loudly. He unbuckled my helmet, setting it on the back of the bike. Then his hand slid into my hair, bringing my lips to his in a hard kiss that took my breath away.

His lips were like ice. Danial had told me often how easily vampires lost heat. It had cost Dev a lot to ride without a helmet tonight, and a lot more to ride from his house to mine by bike in the middle of winter. I pulled him closer and took off my gloves, putting my hands on his face to give him some of my warmth.

After a few seconds, he broke the kiss, pulling back from me. "As much as I wanted this, we are going to have to head back, Love. The night is too cold, and the colder I get, the less control I have of the bike. Your safety isn't worth the thrill of being here like this with you, as much as I like the warmth of your caress."

"When we get home, I'll warm you up," I promised, moving again in back of him, putting my helmet on, and clasping him around the waist.

"Sounds good." Devlin gunned the engine and we roared back into the night.

The trip home took only minutes, but I'd gotten chilled by Devlin's icy kiss. By the time we arrived home, I was glad the ride was over.

Soon, we were in front of my wood stove, taking off our clothes and holding each other under a polar fleece blanket. As soon as he gathered me into his arms, I let out a slight yelp, trying not to flinch away from his icy skin.

"Are you going to warm me, as you promised?" he teased.

I rubbed his skin as he had rubbed mine yesterday. Between the fire and my warmth, Dev slowly got warmed again.

"Feel better?" I said, kissing him. "Are you warm enough?"

"I told you where I feel best, Love," he whispered in my ear. "Invite me in."

"Come in," I whispered, as he lay me down beneath him. "Come inside and be warm."

* * * *

A little before dawn, our fire dwindled to the point that the room cooled, waking me. I let Devlin sleep as I fed my pets, built up the fire, then awakened him. "We'd better go downstairs."

"You're the kind of woman who makes me forget it's dawn," Devlin said self-depreciatingly, standing up and taking my hand. "Let's go."

The roses near the bed downstairs had begun to open. The red and white petals were like a work of art, perfect and lush with beauty and life. "I'm so glad these opened, Dev," I said, touching the petals happily. "I've had a lot of roses in my life that never did. They were pretty, but they died too soon."

Devlin slipped his arm around my shoulders. "Roses are never so beautiful as when they finally open their petals. It's only then that you see how beautiful they can be, the whole of the flower, not just the bud."

Devlin ran his hands up my shoulders to pull my hair up and back, letting some of it fall though his hands as he began kissing the back of my neck. "The same is true of women, Sar," he added softly, pressing gently on my skin with his fangs. "Especially you."

Chapter Fourteen

I awoke midmorning to the sound of the phone ringing faintly.

Damn it. I hurried from bed, running into the adjoining room. "Hello?"

"Sar?" Terian said oddly.

"Of course. What's wrong?"

"I need to talk to you, Sar. It can't wait."

Not now, damn it. I kicked myself for answering, and not letting the machine take a message. "Give me a couple hours to shower and dress, and—"

"No, I'll come get you now," Terian interrupted. "Teleporting will take only a second—"

"No!" I yelled, panicked. "I just got up. I'm not dressed!"

"Five minutes then," Terian said. "I'll be at the front door."

God damn it! "Ten. I'll meet you outside, on the deck."

"Okay."

I hung up the phone and ran upstairs, swearing loudly. I dressed in my highest-necked turtleneck, slipped on some jeans, and was trying to put on two pairs of socks at once, still swearing, when Devlin came up the stairs in his jeans.

"Why did you come up here? Why are you dressing?"

"Terian's going to show up in five. He said it couldn't wait."

"Now? Shit!" he said loudly. "What the hell does he want?"

"Whatever it is, I'll talk to him, and get back to you as soon as I can, hopefully by noon."

"Fine," he replied. "Take your cell and call me if there's a problem."

I nodded, not wanting to remind him he was 0-1 with Terian. But my expression gave my thoughts away.

"I'd send Lash for you," Devlin supplied, annoyed. "He's the best there is, Sar. Terian wouldn't be a problem for him, trust me."

"Terian's a pain right now for us, but you're talking about killing him," I

181

reminded him. "I'm not appreciative, Dev."

"I'm just defensive of you," he replied, putting his hands up. "I worry that he said this couldn't wait."

"Me, too," I said, tying my boots. "I'll call if I need you, trust me."

"When do you think you'll be back?"

"No idea," I said. "Maybe a few minutes, maybe noon."

"Noon?" he said, annoyed.

"Sooner, if I can. That's the absolute latest."

He made unsatisfied sounds, but hugged me. "I'll be downstairs. Come down when you get home." He went back to the cellar.

I went outside. Terian appeared a minute later. He grabbed my hand and suddenly we were in Danial's great room. He stepped away and faced me. "I had to talk to you."

"Did something happen to Danial?" I asked, suddenly scared.

"No. He's fine. But I think that I gave you and him bad advice."

No, really? "What do you mean?" I said carefully.

"I mean it's possible that you weren't turning at all. You were with Danial for years, and you didn't turn. That's never happened, as far as I know."

Except with Anna and Devlin. "I'm resistant to the vampire virus."

"I think being exposed to my blood changed you, made you more resistant. But I can't tell for sure without a sample of your blood."

If he looked at my blood now, it would be teeming with virus. "It's okay, Terian. I'm feeling better."

"Danial told me you're cooling down. That's a bad sign, a sign of either death or transformation." Terian clasped my wrist. "I just need a small sample—"

I jerked my hand away. "No. I've been poked and prodded enough these last months. I don't need you to prove what I already know."

"You're stronger," Terian said, his defeated and desperate look becoming suspicious. "I'm glad, but we need to know why you're better, Sar. You may relapse."

"No, I won't," I retorted fiercely. "Now that I don't have Theo telling me what to do and what not to do. Danial and I will be together, like we should have been months ago."

"Danial's in LA," Terian said anxiously. "Waiting for you. I told him I suspected that my blood had altered your resistance to the vampire virus, possibly making you dependent on regular infusions of the virus into your system to survive. Maybe having Theoron had something to do with it too. I'm not sure. In any case, he wants to see you immediately. He said he could sense if you were mortally ill from your heartbeat and temperature." He reached for my hand.

If I went to Danial now, he would know instantly my turtleneck was hiding something. If he saw the choker on my neck, he'd know it was Devlin's. Something deep inside told me that would screw up Devlin's plan royally, whatever it was. I evaded Terian, putting distance between us.

"I'll drag you to him if I have to," Terian said angrily, moving toward me. "Stay there, or else. You can't move faster than I can teleport."

"Terian, take a good long look at me," I said emphatically. "Now."

Shock etched his face. "You're better. You look...you're better."

I couldn't guess how he missed my luminous skin. Maybe it was the strong light we were standing under, and that I'd chosen to wear a dark pink top over a white turtleneck. Black would have made my skin much more obvious. "I'm recovering, no thanks to Camlyn. I felt awful these past few weeks, but I turned the bend finally." I paused and forced a smile. "Please tell Danial I'm looking forward to Friday." I turned from him, and headed upstairs, hoping he'd leave if he thought I was headed to work.

"Sar, there is something odd about you," Terian said slowly. "Something's off."

I didn't stop or turn. "Tears, leave it."

"You aren't just better, you're almost overconfident—"

I had a few seconds to take control of the conversation and refocus him before Terian teleported up here to grab hold of me and discovered my secret. "Has Theo called and told you how happy Tasha's making him?" I said bitterly. "He called me to apologize. Wasn't that thoughtful of him?"

"He's being a jerk," Terian growled, blackness spiraling upwards from him in cold nerve-wracking waves. "I've told him so. We aren't speaking." He paused. "For what it's worth, I think he's making the biggest mistake of his life."

Refocusing complete. "We'll probably split up when he gets back. It's just as well, because I made a huge mistake marrying him. Now if you're done, I'm going to get a little work in before you take me back."

"Fine, but don't leave the grounds. I'll go tell Danial you're better." He disappeared.

Relieved at the close call, I sank into Danial's chair and turned on the computer. Since I was here anyway, I might as well check over the new emails.

After looking through them, I called a few potential clients and explained we were closed until the end of January and booked up until February. All wanted to wait for him, so I booked them for appointments with Danial in March. There were also a couple nice emails thanking him, which I printed out and left on his desk with my usual happy face drawn on top. Lastly, there was one asking for revenge that I sent onto Devlin with a number and question mark, wondering if he'd checked his email from his phone or if Lash was checking email while Dev was at my house.

There was also a poem from Devlin, with no author cited:

I miss you in the evening, dear, when daylight fades away.
I miss the sheltering arms of you to rest me from the day.
I try to think I see you yet there where the firelight gleams.
Weary at last, I sleep, and still I miss you in my dreams.

I hit reply, thought a moment, and wrote back:

I have been with you beneath the stars
I have lain in your strong arms by day
I have seen you where the firelight gleams,
I love you deeply, come what may
And I will feel you again within me
before our time together slips away.

That was pretty good for just off the top of my head. I hit send, and turned off the computer.

It was about ten a.m. I had time to see Theoron and Elle quick, if they were here. Though I went to each of their rooms, neither of them were there.

I walked back to the great room, debating what to do. The kids had to be with Cia. If I went to the werefox compound, the foxes would scent vampire on me for sure, as Brian had. They would also be suspicious of the turtleneck. It was better not to risk it. Every moment I stayed here increased the odds of someone discovering the means of my newfound health. I needed to get out of there as soon as possible.

I sat down, anxious. What if Danial wanted to see me for himself? What if Terian reappeared and wanted to talk further? I had to get out of here. I wanted to be with Devlin. I wanted to be with him now…

Suddenly, I was back in bed with him. I let out a startled scream. Devlin's eyes flew open and he let out a yell, shoving backwards from me. "What the hell? How'd you get here?"

"I teleported myself," I said slowly, not believing the words. "Titus was right about there being demon in me. Terian was right, I can teleport."

"But it didn't work that day you tried it," Devlin said, curious. "You haven't had any demon blood. That drop of Titus's in the potion wouldn't have caused this."

"It was my being on the drugs," I answered. "Terian said I had to want to be somewhere, to imagine it. I couldn't want anything much on them."

Devlin touched me gently, slipping his hands down over my arms. "But you wanted to be back with me?"

I nodded, still in shock.

"What did Terian want?" Devlin asked.

"Shit!" I swore, getting up from bed. "I have to call him, and tell him I'm home. I don't want him showing up looking for me." I went upstairs and called Terian's cell. "Terian?"

"Sar, what is it?" he said, worried.

"I teleported myself home," I said quickly. "You were right, I have the power. I just wanted to let you know, so you wouldn't worry."

"Sar, this is amazing. I've got to have a sample of your blood to test—"

"No samples, Terian. I'm tired, I'm dirty from ending up sprawled on the floor, and I'm going to go shower. You saw I'm fine. Leave me alone, unless it's an emergency."

"Okay," he said, offended.

"Good-bye," I said, and hung up.

"What sample? What did he want?" Devlin said, standing in the darkness of the stairway. "What was so urgent?"

"You can come up. The blinds in here are still closed." I sighed, and sank into the nearest chair. "He wanted to take me to Danial, because he'd heard I was cooler and he was worried I was dying. Some of what he said sounded like he suspected I might have been changed by having Theoron. Mostly, he wanted a sample of my blood, which I didn't give him."

"Good. That's for me," Devlin teased. "He saw you were better. Does he suspect why?"

"He's suspicious, though I distracted him for now. He didn't see the choker."

"Good," Devlin said, relieved.

"Why are you relieved?" I said sharply. "You tell me you want my Oath, yet you don't want anyone to know?"

He came up and put his hand on my arm. "I need you to trust me. Besides, until I know if you want Theo in the Oath, too, we can't let anyone know."

"Now we're up to three men?" I said sarcastically.

"Hush," he said, pulling me close. "If he was going to leave you, Sar, would he not have taken Elle, and just left? Why come back at all, if he wanted to be with her? It's obvious you still love him. I would rather include him now than have to re-Oath you later if you kiss and make up."

"We aren't making up," I said decisively. "Maybe he did love me once, but you're right that he loves her more."

"Then he is a fool, and you are well rid of him," Devlin said, hugging me. "Now come back to bed. Tonight we have much to do."

* * * *

Devlin woke me at dusk. "We have to hurry. Get dressed."

"What do you mean?" I asked, yawning. "Sure this is our last night, but—"

"I mean go now and get dressed, Sar. I'll meet you at the front door."

"The dogs—"

"Let them out, and get moving! We'll walk them when we return." His eyes were cruel and masterful, that of the old Devlin who expected to hear "yes" to every command.

I got moving, dressing fast, and letting the dogs out. "Are we taking the motorcycle?" I asked, letting the dogs back in.

"We'll need to take your truck, the journey is too far," Devlin said on his way up the cellar stairs. "Where are the keys?"

I tossed him the keys from the counter. He caught them, striding fast to the door. We hastened to the garage. He got behind the wheel, and peeled out, before I had time to get my seat belt on.

"What is the rush?" I said, annoyed.

"There is something that needs to be done tonight, Sar. I am not sure how long it will take. The minutes we have together are slipping away faster and faster."

We drove south, Devlin remaining edgy. An hour later, we pulled up at a wooden building that had seen better days. With no light but the truck's headlamps, it was hard to tell if this was a house. All that was visible was rusting cars on the front lawn, surrounded by brambles. The road we were on was little more than mud and gravel, the surrounding area overgrown fields and dark forest.

Devlin got out. "Hurry."

"Is this place deserted?" I asked, getting out of the truck. "There are no lights."

"He likes the dark," Devlin said, going to the door and knocking loudly.

The porch light came on immediately. A huge bearded man opened the inner door, dressed in a clean Harley T-shirt and black jeans. He looked mean, but the moment he saw Devlin a smile split his face. "Dev, my man, how the hell are you?" he said, extending his hand.

"Great, Cleave," Devlin said, flashing a radiant smile, and shaking Cleave's hand.

Cleave noticed me. "Nice piece, Dev," he said, looking me up and down.

"She's more than a piece, Cleave," Devlin said sharply. "That's why we're here."

"You want the regular?" Cleave said with a grin.

"No," Devlin said intriguingly. "Something different."

Cleave's eyebrows shot up, and he opened the door wide so we could get past him. "Come on in and have a seat." He closed and locked it behind us, then led us into what I guessed was both his place of business and his house. I expected it to be filthy, to have beer cans or sex magazines interspersed with dirty dishes. Instead, everything was moderately clean, only one Penthouse magazine lying across the chair.

We must have interrupted the night's reading agenda.

Cleave moved easily with the grace of someone who exercised regularly, despite the outside of his house. Once we'd been seated, he turned to Dev, putting his hands together.

"What did you have in mind?"

"This," Devlin said, pulling me into his lap, and showing Cleave my choker pendant.

"Take it off her. I'll need to see it better, especially to sketch a drawing for size."

Devlin undid the choker and handed it to him.

"You want the bear to have red eyes or another color?"

Devlin considered that for a moment. "Red," he said finally.

"I'll need to enlarge it to at least double the size of the pendant," Cleave said. "Or you won't have much more than an outline of the bear."

"Make it as small as you can and still be detailed," Devlin answered. "It must be obvious that it's the exact same symbol."

"Sure," Cleave said. "I've got small needles."

I turned to Devlin. "Isn't the choker enough?"

Cleave got up hurriedly, the choker in his hand. "I'll be back in a bit, when I have a sketch for you to approve. Then we can get started."

"How long will it take?" Devlin asked.

"Thirty minutes to sketch and then an hour or thereabouts to apply the ink," Cleave said. "If you want more color than just red, white, and black, it will take longer."

"Just those colors."

"If I rush, it won't be as good, you know that."

"I know," Devlin said, nodding. "Take your time."

"You didn't answer me," I said angrily.

"Be back," Cleave said and left.

I turned to Dev, still on his lap. "You could have asked, you know."

"But I'm not asking," he said devilishly. "Rings can be taken off. Marks can be healed with time and magic. Oaths can be broken. I want something more lasting."

"A tattoo of your symbol."

"I want to be under your skin, Sar. And I want you never, ever, to be able to get me out."

His words made me shiver. "Tattoos can be removed."

Devlin reached out and tilted my face, so his molten gold eyes met mine. "Ordinary tattoos can be removed with surgery. Cleave's specialty is tattooing supernatural beings, those that heal almost anything. He has done this for me before, and he knows what to do. Even with your new physiology, it will be difficult to remove this one, if not impossible."

"Did you mark the women you turned this way?" I said angrily.

"A chosen few, over the years," Devlin answered. "But just with a "D," never with my personal symbol."

"What if I say no?"

"Then I'll bite you and drink until you lose consciousness again, and he'll do it while you're out," Devlin replied. "I want this very much, Sar. Please give your assent."

As much as I was annoyed with his pushiness, I liked very much that he wanted me to wear his symbol permanently, not just as a neck decoration. "Will it hurt?"

"There will be some mild pain, but not much. And you will bleed slightly, also."

"Where is he going to put it?" I asked apprehensively.

"Where do you want my symbol to be?" he said, giving me a sexy smile.

"I can tell you where I want it not to be," I said heatedly.

He laughed. "On your hip is fine, Sar," he said, patting me there gently. "It will hurt less there, anyway."

"Are you going to get one?" I asked.

"No," Devlin said gently. "But I will look into a ring for my left hand. Will that suffice?"

I felt a rush of feeling for him. "Yes, if you'll wear it."

"Why would I get one and not wear it?" Devlin said angrily. "I tell you something meaningful, and instead of happiness, you give me sarcasm."

"I'm sorry," I said quickly. "I didn't mean it like it sounded."

Devlin didn't reply.

We sat in silence for a minute or two. I broke first. "Look, I'm sorry. Don't be angry, please."

"I'm not angry with you, Love, just on edge. What do you want to talk about?" Devlin said, leaning back on the couch and giving me a bemused glance.

"Tell me about yourself. I know very little about you." *That was good, anyway.* "I do love you, but that is for what you've done for me, been to me, since I had Theoron, and for what you've done for Danial—"

"What do you mean?"

"You protected him down through the years, didn't you? You were hard on him because of Anna, but you kept him from being harmed. Danial can be tough, but he's not ruthless enough to have lasted four hundred years without someone watching out for him."

"You are astute for a woman," Dev said with a tiny bit of respect. "Yes, that's true."

I glared at him. "I'll pretend you didn't say that. The dark ages are over."

"Alas, they are," Devlin said with a mock sigh. "But I remember them with nostalgia."

"You're not that old, Dev. But please tell me of your past, if you would."

He caressed me gently. "Of course. What do you want to know?"

"Tell me what really happened with Anna. I was told by Theo that Danial seduced her and you never forgave him. That ever afterward, you tried to seduce anyone he loved."

"That is all true," Devlin said coolly. "And that's it, in a nutshell. What details are you looking for; how I found out about them?"

"No," I replied, blushing. "But you wouldn't share her with Danial, yet you want to share me. What changed your mind?"

"You want assurance I don't love you less than she," Devlin said. "Be assured I do not."

"Tell me what happened."

He took a breath and began. "Simply put, we loved the same woman. She'd sworn herself to me and Danial was jealous, so he seduced her. I found them together. We fought, and I almost killed him. We didn't speak for a decade, until after I had become Ruler, and she had died. I've been taking my revenge on him ever since."

"I'm sorry for you both," I said softly.

"I was angry for a long time, Sar. I'd never met a woman like Anna. Losing her was like losing all I had left that meant anything to me. I was filled with rage at the unfairness of having eternity and not having the person I wanted most of all to share it with. I channeled all of my anger and hate into becoming Ruler."

"Once you had, why not make up? Danial was the only family you had left. And there must have been many women you tried to ease your loneliness. Why not be comforted?"

"Danial did not want to make up, and neither did I; we were both too angry." He held me close. "There were always women, but I didn't want to be loved or have anyone look at me with affection or tenderness. I didn't want to love anyone ever again. I found my pleasures in other ways, some of them cruel. As the years passed, then centuries, I let other women into my heart, even loved some of them a little. But no matter my precautions, eventually they all turned. After they changed, we separated. A great part of sex for me is the blood exchange, Sar. And vampire blood is bitter." He sighed miserably. "But most of all they weren't her, none of them."

Unbidden thoughts rose in my mind that I wasn't her, either. Doubt filled me that Devlin would care about me at all, if not for my blood. More heart wrenching was wondering if he would have come back to save me if I hadn't reminded him of his lost love. I kept silent.

Devlin paused for a few moments, then said, "And the sunlight clasps the earth, and the moonbeams kiss the sea. What are all these kissings worth if thou kiss not me?"

I drew his lips to mine gently, and gave him a light kiss. "I will always want to kiss you."

"I hope so," he said, hugging me. "That was Shelly."

"For being brothers, why are you and Danial so different?" I asked.

"We are not so different, save in sexual desire," Devlin replied, then let out a wicked laugh.

"Your views are different from Danial's," I amended firmly. "He devotes his life to his business, and you devoted yours to Ruling. I remember your words to Danial on my behalf. Although you used the law for your own ends, you took your position seriously. At least, you made me believe you did."

"I always did," Devlin replied, nodding. "Those in power have a responsibility to those under them not to abuse that power. Tyrants get overthrown."

"We talked once about what you'd do if you were facing an attack. You said you'd kill a few innocents to save the lives of many. Danial said he'd leave instead."

"What did he say, exactly?"

"He said he would do what the woman he loved wanted, that fighting over a piece of ground was not worth dying for, that people always died in wars and you couldn't save them."

"Sounds like him," Devlin said, rolling his eyes. "Ever the pessimist."

"Not to me," I said, looking at him carefully. "To me, it sounds like you.

What I might have expected you to say. And your answer was more what I expected him to say."

Devlin looked at me for a long moment. "Perhaps you don't know either of us that well."

"Perhaps I don't know you," I said quietly. "But I want to."

He sighed. "There are reasons for his answer." He paused for a long moment. "Did you never wonder why being brothers, we look so different; why I'm fair, and he's dark? Why our bodies you have come to know so well are markedly different in some ways?"

I had never thought about it, but now that I did, it all came together instantly. God, I should have figured it out years ago. "You aren't full blood brothers."

He nodded. "We are half-brothers, Sar. Danial had a different mother than I."

"You're older."

"Yes. When I was changed, I was thirty-five to Danial's thirty—"

"He told me he was changed at thirty-five!" I exclaimed, shocked. "He wasn't?"

Dev laughed. "He so wanted to be like me. No, he was younger." He paused. "We have different backgrounds because of having different mothers. All our mortal lives, we were separated by class." He turned sad. "I was the legitimate heir, the spitting image of my father. I was trained from birth to rule men, to study strategy and tactics, and to learn the finer arts, like music, reading and writing. My father had no title, but he was the liege lord's strategist. He taught me all he knew, including how to seduce women, and I took my first one when I was sixteen, much as I took you that first time we were together."

"Danial's mother was not only the most beautiful woman in her village, but also the most comely within the territory. She had the misfortune to be both beautiful and poor. She was only sixteen when she caught my father's eye. He took her as his mistress almost immediately, despite her objections. Danial looks much like her, with her dark hair and eyes, though he has the same general build as I do, from our father."

"Danial had none of my training, Sar, none of my education. Despite that my father supported him and his mother, he didn't have an easy time of it. He knew who his father was, as did everyone, but my father would not acknowledge him publicly. Despite my father's objections, when he was five, I took him under my wing and taught him what I could. My father frowned upon our relationship. He thought only of what Danial was to him, not what he could become someday."

"God, how awful. No wonder Danial is the way he is." I wiped my filling eyes. "He always declined to answer my questions about his parents and his past, saying he didn't want to remember. He even did that with his birthday." I wiped again at my leaking eyes.

"Don't cry," Devlin said gently, putting his arms around me. "He's a happy father now, and soon to be Oathed again. Danial needs your love, not your pity."

"Can you fill in more of the blanks for me?" I asked.

Devlin nodded. "If I know the answers."

"Why didn't your father accept him? I understand class hierarchy, but when it comes to sons, didn't—?"

"Because of his eyes," Devlin said sadly. "My father had other children out of wedlock. The ones with gold-colored eyes he did acknowledge. Danial had the misfortune not to inherit my father's favorite attribute." He squeezed my hand. "There is no more to say about it other than that was unfair and evil."

Hopefully, Dev's dad was roasting in hell. "I know the story of how you were attacked. If you were a higher class than Danial was, how did you both end up doing guard duty together?"

"The prisoner was a visiting Duke's son, accused of rape and murder. He'd been found with the body of my father's favorite maid, the knife still in his hand. In those times, an upper-class man harming a lower-class woman was common, and usually unpunished. But my father was annoyed with the loss of one of his choice conquests, and he asked that I go to give account, to make sure the man was punished. He put me in charge of the group."

"Were you Captain of the Guard, or something?"

Devlin rolled his eyes. "You say that as if I had been having fun playacting. Believe me, overseeing guard duty was deadly serious in those days."

"I'm sorry. Go on."

"I didn't have a title, other than what could be loosely translated into "The Leader," Devlin said with a smile. "It was just another rung on the ladder on my way to the top."

"What happened to the murdering asshole?"

"When we were attacked, he was killed." Devlin's tone turned full of hurt and bitterness. "Danial went back, as you know. I knew that there was nothing for me back there, that my father would never accept what I had become. I learned later that my father had been hung. The Duke suspected my father had planned the attack to cover the nobleman's murder, that he'd had me kill him in revenge. As for my mother, she married another man to save herself from ruin."

"Did you have a wife, or someone you cared for?"

"No, I had never been married," Devlin said, shooting me an uneasy look.

"I had several lovers at that time, but no one I loved. I'd wanted the woman Danial married for myself, but I had known that I couldn't have her as he could, as she was below my station. My father wanted a good match with a family that would pay a large dowry. As it was, it was good I was turned, as my father planned to choose a wife for me in the coming summer. And then I would not be with you now."

"So you never married Anna?"

"No," Devlin admitted, clearly upset. "She wanted to. I Oathed her instead, believing she was safer." He paused. "I should have. She would have been so happy."

I wiped away a single tear that had traced its way down his cheek. "I'm sorry, Dev. I don't mean to pry."

"I don't mind telling you, Sar," he said, his tone rough with emotion. "It's just that no one has asked me about my human life before, not even Anna."

Cleave came out and showed a slip of paper to Devlin. "Any corrections?"

I looked at the drawing in Devlin's hands. Cleave was a good artist. His drawing depicted a stalking grizzly with red eyes, snarling, its paw ready to strike. It was twice the size of the pendant on the choker.

"Very nice," Devlin said. "Put it on her left hip."

Cleave led me in to a brightly lit adjoining room, and had me sit in what resembled a dentists' chair. I blinked, trying to let my eyes adjust.

"Pull down your jeans on that side a little," he asked as he laid out needle tips in plastic packaging and mixed up the inks. "That will be enough."

I pulled them down and leaned on my right side. Cleave used the paper to transfer the image to my hip, as Devlin pulled up a chair to watch.

Cleave was a professional. First, he did the outline, then the details, and then he filled in the rest. The entire process took about an hour. As Devlin had said, there was some pain and blood, but not much. The overall sensation was as if someone was lightly sanding my skin. Occasionally there was a sharper poke, especially when he did the eyes and the bear's fangs. We didn't talk, as the noise from the needle gun was constant and loud enough to make conversation difficult. As I watched, the bear slowly appeared on my skin.

Cleave got up. "You're all set."

Dev's bear snarled on my hip. It seemed to move as I moved. I ran my hands over it lightly, the skin red, raised, and sore to the touch. "It looks like I could wipe it off."

"Guaranteed not to," Cleave assured me. "You need any touch ups, you just come back with Dev."

Dev had gotten his wish. "Thanks."

"Enjoy," Cleave said, giving us a smile. "You want salve?"

"Just a little," Devlin replied. "For tonight, if it bothers her."

"Here." Cleave handed me a tiny jar which I put it in my purse.

"You want payment now or later?" Devlin said.

"Now is good," Cleave replied.

Devlin handed him three hundred dollars from his back pocket. "Enough?"

Cleave took it, nodding. "Always good doing business with you, Dev." They clasped hands. "Have a safe trip back, and like I said, come back if you need a touch up."

"Thank you," I said, giving him a smile.

"Sure thing, Honey," he said, winking at me.

He stood in the doorway as we got in the truck, and Devlin started it. "Stop back in when you have more time!" Cleave shouted, waving.

Devlin waved back, then sped off toward home. I sat back in the truck seat, considering the ramifications of this latest development. Almost at once, Devlin turned on the radio, tuning it to a classic rock station. Aerosmith engulfed us. I gave him a surprised look.

He caught it. "What?"

"I figured you for, um, lighter music. Maybe classical."

"I like most music, Sar," Dev said, smirking. "What I listen to depends on my mood." He turned the volume all the way up, until the music was blasting. "Let's make some noise."

The whole way back, we shouted and sang along with the radio. While I knew some of the songs, Dev knew all of them. Despite his boisterous mood, he acted calmer now, as if by tattooing me he'd won a decisive battle. He glanced at me sporadically, satisfied.

"Why did you want this so much?" I finally asked.

"I wanted you to be mine," he said, pleased. "And very shortly, you will be."

Uneasy at his certainty, I looked away and didn't reply.

As soon as we arrived at my house, Ghost and Darkness began whining, their tails wagging frantically.

"They need to be walked," I said quickly, hoping to buy time. "Will you come with me?"

Devlin offered me his hand. "Yes, but let us go now. The rest of this night is for you and me."

We began walking. Though the night was clear and beautiful, I was focused only on Devlin, trying to determine what he was planning for me.

"You're unusually quiet," he said, stopping and facing me. "Why?"

"I was wondering why you've never asked me about myself," I said shyly.

"I know all of you I need to in this moment," he said, pulling me into his embrace. "There will be much time to discover your quirks in our future, those that I don't already know, of course."

"I'm not quirky," I protested.

"You most certainly are," he said lovingly. "But that is good, as it makes you interesting, Love."

You are, too, but it makes you scary. "What exactly am I to promise you tonight?"

Devlin began walking again, his arm around me. "As I told you, I want you to promise that my brother or I will be the only vampires you'll have as lovers, and that you won't share your blood with anyone else. If you want to be with Theo, that is understood. He has prior claim to you. But no one else, especially no other vampires, not under any circumstances."

"That's all?"

"No. If you remain his lover, Theo is never again to hurt you."

I stopped and looked at him in confusion. "Theo never hurt me, Dev."

He faced me, suddenly angry. "I saw the bruises on you the day I came to return Theo's shirt. I smelled your blood where he had hurt you inside. That will not ever happen again."

"I gave him permission for that," I said defiantly. "I wanted him to not hold back with me."

"You are not a woman who enjoys pain," Dev said bluntly. "What he did to you had to hurt a good deal. He's not going to do that again, ever."

"Dev, under normal circumstances, getting bitten hurts me. Are you going to stop biting me when it becomes painful again?"

Devlin's eyes tinged red. "It's not the same. I can heal you afterwards, and take the pain away. He cannot."

I folded my arms across my chest. "Isn't that my decision? I thought you didn't begrudge me any pleasure I found in his arms?"

Devlin grabbed me roughly. "Sar, that is how it's going to be. Accept it."

"Or what?" I said, jerking away from him.

He yanked me back into his arms, threw me over his shoulder, and began striding back to the house.

"Put me down!" I commanded shrilly. "Right now! I mean it!"

"Shut up!" he snarled back.

The dogs thought this was some sort of new game, leaping and jumping around him as he walked. After shooing them inside, he brought me into my bedroom. In one swift motion, he slid me off his shoulder and onto the bed. I landed on my newly tattooed hip, letting out a yelp. Devlin glared down at me, his eyes tinged red.

"Ah, here is the Dev I remember," I said nastily, then got up from the side of the bed. As I went for the door, he grabbed me by the throat.

"Let me go, Dev," I spat. "You don't own me!"

He squeezed his hand slightly, cutting off my ranting. "I do own you, Sar. And if you keep pushing it, I'll show you just what it means to be owned by me."

A shiver of fear went down my spine at his cruel tone. Afraid, I relaxed in his grip and stopped fighting.

Devlin relaxed his grip, then let go. "Sit back down."

I eased back on the bed, watching him warily.

"The time of dreaming Dreams is over. As lover to lover, Sweetheart, I come." Devlin paused, his eyes boring into me.

"Who is the author?" I asked.

"Sar, I want your Oath and I want it tonight. And I will have it, however I must draw it from your lips."

"I said I would give it to you—"

"You actually didn't." He bared his fangs. "But you will give it to me now. Repeat after me—"

"No," I interrupted. "I wanted to look a certain way. I need to change clothes."

"Change then," he said, widening his arms in a permissive gesture. "I'll wait here for you. You have five minutes."

"Leave the room, please," I replied, expecting a fight. "And I'll take whatever time I need. You want this to mean anything to me, don't force me."

Devlin's eyes narrowed, but he nodded. "You're right. My apologies, Love." He kissed me gently on the cheek. "I'll be outside the door. Call when you're ready."

As soon as he left, I got up immediately, went into my bathroom, and looked in the mirror. What in hell was I thinking, doing this? He was the same person he had always been. Did it matter he had reasons for being the way he was? The violence and sadism in him was still there, no matter that he covered it with soft words and kisses now. It was only a matter of time before he showed his true colors again.

Did I want him? That was a resounding yes.

Did I trust him? To a point.

Was I going through with this?

I looked into the mirror at my reflection, considering everything.

He'd saved me all those times before. He'd risked his life to save mine, even if he had enjoyed himself doing it. He'd given me a mark to wear without the usual painful cost. Now he'd sent Lash and Titus on some mission, saying he'd done it to protect me.

I closed my eyes. Be logical, Sar. Put aside all the romance, the sweet words, and the dashing deeds in your defense. Grab what's left of your reason out from under Dev's thrall, and think.

There was no way to know how much of his love for me was just longing for his Annabelle resurrected, or what the future he imagined for us would be like. Only time would tell.

Dev wasn't asking for all of me, just a part of me. I was getting something in exchange for being Oathed to him, namely his best efforts to protect me. That might make the difference between people I loved living or dying, including me, if I got him and his men to fight with us.

I looked into the mirror, and took a deep breath. Was I going to do this?

If he agreed to throw in his lot with Danial, yes.

As he had so many times before, Dev had gotten just what he wanted. This time, it was me.

Chapter Fifteen

I took off my clothes and slipped into the pale ivory beaded nightgown. It still fit; the bodice tight over my breasts, the thin straps almost superfluous. It looked as good as it had years ago on me. I fluffed up my hair, put on a touch of lipstick and then rubbed it off. What was the point?

Resigned, I picked it back up and reapplied it. The point was I needed Devlin to agree to my terms. Anything that might help that end, I had to do...

Instantly, an idea sprang to mind. I went quickly to the bookshelf near the bed, scanning titles.

"Sar," Devlin called from outside the door. "I'm coming in."

I hastily grabbed a book of poems, and retreated to the bathroom. "Come in and get comfortable. I'll be a few more minutes."

I heard him come in, then the noise of him shedding his clothes. Hurriedly, I used the book index, looking for an appropriate poem.

"Come out," Devlin called sexily. "Your lover aches for you."

I took a deep breath, and went out to him. He was waiting in bed, his clothes folded neatly on the dresser.

He beckoned to me. I walked to the foot of the bed, faced him, and began to speak.

"Is your heart an ocean so strong and deep I may launch my all on its tide?

A loving woman finds heaven or hell on the day she is made a bride.

I require all things that are grand and true, all things that a man should be

If you give this all, I would stake my life to be all you demand of me."

"From a Woman's Question," Devlin said, studying me. "I know the poem well."

"Will you answer the question?" I asked seriously.

He considered me for a few heartbeats. "You have my all, Sarelle," he said finally. "That I promise you. To do whatever it takes, whatever is necessary." He held out his hands. "Come."

I sat down beside him on the bed.

"Repeat after me," he said, holding my gaze. "I, Sarelle O'Connor, promise you, Devlin Dalcon, and your brother, Danial Racklan, that I shall be yours and no other vampire's, under pain of death, until life should leave me, or both of you should perish."

I repeated what he had said.

"I shall share myself with no other, save my current husband, Theo O'Connor, under pain of death."

I repeated that as well.

"I give you my love and authority over me, understanding that I am given in return your love, your protection, and your life's blood, that is now my life's blood."

I repeated his words, wondering how much more was still to come.

"So I swear, this day of December 29, 2012."

Relieved, I repeated that.

"I, Devlin Dalcon, accept your Oath, Sarelle O'Connor, both on behalf of myself and on behalf of my brother, Danial Racklan." He said the words slowly with pleasure, savoring each one. "I pledge you my love, and that of my brother's, to protect you to the best of my ability, and to never deny you what you need—" Suddenly, he grabbed hold of me fiercely. "It is done," he whispered. "You're mine."

I didn't answer, trembling.

Devlin held me close, then began to speak:

"I need so much the quiet of your love after the day's loud strife

I need your calm all other things above after the stress of life

I crave the haven that in your dear heart lies after all toil is done.

I need the star shine of your heavenly eyes after the day's great sun."

"Towne's Nightfall," he added, kissing my forehead. He pushed me back gently onto the sheets, and held himself above me, looking down into my eyes intensely. "I'm going to take you now, Sarelle. We need to consummate the Oath, both with our bodies and with our blood."

I looked up at him apprehensively.

Devlin's golden eyes softened. "Relax, Love. You are my Oathed One. You have nothing to fear from me ever again."

He began kissing me. Soon, I relaxed under his deft ministrations and embraced him fully, moving involuntarily under his hands, my skin hypersensitive to his kisses. Devlin parted my legs and began sliding inside inch by delicious inch. I arched up against him, trying to hurry him, but he would not be hurried. He held me still beneath him, even as I let out little whimpers, contracting my muscles, trying to get him into me.

"I love how much you want me, Sar," he said heatedly. "I love that you let it show to me and don't try to hold it inside, as you did before."

At long last, Devlin eased the last of himself inside, then gave a soft groan of contentment. Slowly, he lay his upper body down on mine, still keeping most of his weight on his arms, and began kissing me, running his fangs over me, kissing my neck, my breasts, my face. My lust for him crashed over me, and I writhed beneath him, grasping his hips.

Devlin let his weight down, pinning me to the bed. "No, Love. You will wait until I say, unbearable as that will quickly come to feel." He began to kiss me again.

My tension and desire mounted with every second, my heart beating furiously. "Please," I moaned eagerly. "Please, I'm ready."

He took my face in his hands. "I know you are, Love, but I'm not. Wait for me." He kissed me deeply, cutting off my reply.

Maddened, I focused all my concentration to contract my inner muscles, squeezing the length of him tightly. Devlin's head went back with a jerk, a tremor going through him. He lowered his eyes so they were an inch from mine. They were melting gold, bursting with desire and need. He gave me a slow smile, and began to move. I let out a long moan, awash in the blissful sensation.

"You are never more beautiful, Sar, then when you are as you are now, open to me completely," he whispered. "When we are joined together, as we were always meant to be."

Dev stroked me over and over, slowly, unhurried, his kisses gaining heat and passion. His breaths came fast, soft cries of pleasure escaping his lips every time he sheathed himself. I was wild beneath him, my hands caressing his slick flesh, my kisses covering all of his skin within reach. The impending orgasm built and built, until we were both shaking slightly with the strain.

Abruptly I gasped, "Please, Dev, now. Now!"

Devlin let go of his control with a snarl, pulling my hips tight against him, and began thrusting fast. In a second, I was there, orgasming harder than I ever had before in my life, screaming his name with all the air in my lungs. "Dev! Dev! Dev!"

His shout was as it had been that day months ago in the hotel. It was loud enough to shake the room as it tore out of him, as if it was tearing out his heart. "Saaaaaarrr!"

Devlin held me tightly, his hips still shuddering against mine as he shouted my name over and over. Several minutes later, he stopped spasming, then hugged me tightly.

"I love you," he whispered. He carefully withdrew his softening penis, then wrapped me in his arms.

"I love you, too, Oathed One," I whispered, closing my eyes as I hugged him, contented.

Though I meant just to doze, I quickly dropped off to sleep. Sometime later, Devlin awakened me with a kiss.

"Sar, how do you feel?"

"Wonderful," I said languidly, stretching. Every muscle I had ached, but it was the good ache that a woman feels after she has been well loved. "That was incredible."

"Yes, it was," he said, deeply satisfied. "But one thing still remains."

"I don't want to drink your blood," I said, trying to be as nice as possible about it.

He laughed, touching my face with his hand. "You don't have to, Sar. We have shared enough these past few days that it isn't necessary, though that is what is usually done. I've given you my blood to heal you, and you have given me yours, both for pleasure and to sustain me. The Oath is satisfied."

"I have to ask something," I said, curious. "Danial never asked me to drink his blood. If that is what is done during Oathing, why didn't he ask me?"

"He was new at it," Devlin said, unruffled. "He had never Oathed anyone before you, Sar. Also, he didn't want to hurt you, and he probably thought his blood was dangerous to you back then, as it might well have been. He may have been unsure about what amount to give you or even how to give it to you. Any vampire who has taken blood from a donor and then healed them with their own blood has done enough to validate the blood exchange asked for in Oathing. I merely mention it to you out of formality."

"How is it usually done then?"

"Usually, the vampire, be it man or woman, opens a cut or has their intended do it, and then the intended kisses the wound. Or, the vampire will taste their intended in a long kiss, then open a wound themselves, and give their intended one their blood in that kiss, much how I shared my blood with you that night we met." He gave me a pleased smile. "As I said, that part of the Oath is well satisfied."

I hadn't liked him doing it then, but oddly I remembered that the taste of his blood had reminded me of maple sugar. And Devlin had liked it very much. "Do it again."

Devlin glanced over, startled and clearly excited. "You want me to taste you?"

"That night, I was scared," I admitted. "Too scared to remember much except it hurt."

"You're right that if I do it now there will be no pain," Devlin answered.

"Are you sure you want to? It is more a symbolic gesture than anything else. It has no lasting effects, at least that I know of." He kissed me softly again on my forehead. "Not five minutes ago, you just said you didn't want to drink blood, Love."

"I want to taste yours," I said deliberately. "As your Oathed One, it's my right."

Devlin lowered his eyes, his smile widening. "Then sit up, Love. Your wish is my command."

We both sat up. He took my face in his hands. "Tell me if it hurts, and I'll stop."

I nodded.

Devlin brought my lips to his. After a few seconds, I felt one fang slice my tongue. There was no pain. Devlin began to kiss me harder, his tongue delving into my mouth as he swallowed. Languid pleasure washed over me. I kissed him back harder, thrusting my tongue into his mouth. He suckled it gently, then let it go, drawing back slightly, our lips parting. Within a moment, he kissed me again, his mouth opening on mine. Again, I tasted sweet maple sugar with a faint undercurrent of copper. I kissed him eagerly, licking the inside of his mouth. Devlin let me, emitting soft groans of pleasure. Gently, he pushed me away.

"God, that was wonderful," he sighed, sprawling back on the bed.

"Why do you like it?" I asked curiously. "I get that you're a vampire and you drink blood, but why the sexual aspect to it?"

"I'm a man of many desires," Devlin said wantonly, smirking. "You must have a favorite food? Name it."

"Several. Chocolate in all its forms, pizza, French fries, hamburgers, eel—"

"Are these in order?" he said, laughing richly.

"The first one is," I said, laughing.

"Imagine the rush you get, the intense pleasure just tasting the chocolate, the joy you feel as it melts in your mouth and you consume it. I feel that same joy."

"With my blood?"

"With most blood," Devlin amended. He kissed my hand. "Yours is a hundred times more intensely flavored. My only lament is that tonight will be my last taste for some time."

Panic flooded me. "Won't you be leaving on Friday night? Why will the last time be tonight?"

"Danial is coming back Friday, which is tomorrow night. He will be here right after nightfall, perhaps sooner. You need time alone together, both to celebrate your love with him, and to cement your final plan for the Gathering."

Ask him now. "Please come with us," I begged, clasping his hand in both of mine. "You said Lash is the best—"

Devlin grasped my hands in his. "I'll do you more good by not being there. You are better off making plans with Danial, and letting me fight this war from a different front."

I broke down crying, devastated. Devlin hugged me close, but didn't say anything.

"I need you," I sniffled. "Danial needs you. I'm scared to death of what's going to happen to Theoron."

"Terian will watch him like a hawk," Devlin said soothingly. "He will be the safest person at that party. It's Danial and you who must be watchful. Do as he says, Sar. And you must also do as I tell you."

I wiped my eyes. "Tell me your plan. I can face this if I know it, Dev. I'm terrified."

"I'd tell you if I could," Devlin said, serious. "But you must know nothing of it for it to work—"

I gripped the choker with both hands, and yanked hard, letting out an anguished cry. "Take this damned thing off! You don't love me!"

Lightning fast, Devlin grabbed my hands, pulling them away. "Stop, you fool, or you'll cut your flesh." He hugged me close. "If I feared for your safety, I'd not let you go. The worst that can befall you is that you're taken hostage against your will. If that happens, I will send Lash for you. He has never failed me."

"He hates me," I sobbed. "I tried to be nice and he hated me."

"He doesn't hate you," Devlin said, clearly uncomfortable. "He's just having trouble adjusting. In any case, he never lets his emotions interfere with his job."

"I'm scared," I whispered. "They're going to kill Danial. He thinks so, too."

"I know one who will likely try," Devlin said, vengeful. "But you leave that to me, Love. As I promised you, I'll do all that I can."

I moved away from him, wrapping blankets around me. "When are you leaving?"

"I have to get back early tomorrow morning to Hayden."

"Did they succeed?" I asked hollowly.

"Yes. Lash called this morning." He turned regretful. "I would have loved seeing the look on Danial's face when he learns you're his again. It is going to be something to see." He kissed my hand fondly. "You will have to tell me of it later."

"There won't be a later," I said darkly.

Devlin turned me to face him, then hugged me. "Yes there will. Come, get dressed. We are going out to celebrate."

"It's got to be eight at night at least. Besides, I don't feel like celebrating."

"I do," Devlin said pointedly, getting up. "Worrying and sulking is a waste of your time, particularly if you believe you have not much left. Dress, and let me take you out."

I got out of bed, and began to put on clothes, not answering.

"Sar, I have to feed," Devlin continued. "I can't take any more from you tonight, save that little taste later, or Danial will not be able to drink from you tomorrow. Also, there may be some kind of public display Saturday you need to do with him. You need me not to feed from you, especially not the amount I need to take." He turned me to face him slowly. "I could go alone, but a large meal would do both your body and your mind good." He embraced me again. "And we have never been out together before. Please, come celebrate with me."

I pushed him away and finished dressing. Still silent, I hung up my ivory gown. It was remarkably smooth for all my time in it.

"Wear it for him," Devlin whispered sadly. "I want him to have a night as enjoyable as ours was, at least at the beginning."

Upset, I clasped his hand. "I'll go with you. Get dressed, and meet me in five."

Devlin left. I washed up, then put on some makeup and fluffed my hair. When I emerged, Devlin was dressed, and had just given the dogs some treats they were gnawing.

"Ready?" he asked.

I nodded, then tossed him the keys. "You drive."

* * * *

"They have fries, hamburgers, and chocolate here, not to mention wine," Devlin said, parking the car at a popular chain restaurant.

"This is good," I said, nodding. "I'm hungrier than I thought."

The night was a slow one. Within minutes, we were in a booth, sipping the best red on the wine list and perusing the menu.

Devlin put down his glass, and leaned across the table. "Sar, I am leaving now. I'll try to be back in a half hour or so. Order whatever you want to, and eat without me."

Panic filled me. "What should I do if a—" I cut off as a waitress passed close by.

"You will be able to resist," Devlin replied, squeezing my hand. "And they will not be drawn to you, should one see you. All danger of uncontrollable behavior is over. You are safe here with so many eyes watching you." He kissed me once more, then got up and left. He hurried to the truck, started it, then drove off.

The waitress came back, noticed Devlin gone, and gave me a sad look. Ignoring her misplaced pity, I gleefully said, "Salad for an appetizer, and then some fries and a rare colossal sized hamburger, then some Tiramisu for dessert."

When she'd gone, I called Danial. He answered on the first ring.

"Sar, I was about to call you. Are you still well?"

Say as little as possible, or he'll know something's up. "Yes."

"I'm getting done early out here. I should be to you by six tomorrow. I need to take Elle to your parents' home tomorrow, but that will only delay me a short while."

"Danial, I'll take her," I offered. "Now I'm better, I'd like to spend some time with her before we leave Saturday."

"We are leaving for Canada on Friday around midnight," Danial said primly. "Theo wants us there before Saturday, remember, so he can take that entire day to check out the hotel, and the Gathering place?"

"Sorry, I forgot. What should I bring to wear?"

"Tatiana has made you a dress, and she has accessories for it as well. You need only pack whatever else you need for the journey."

Time for the big question. "What are the hotel arrangements?"

"As when we have traveled before, Sar: a two bedroom suite."

"What did Theo say, Danial? Have you talked to him?"

"He asked that he be allowed to sleep on the sofa outside. He said that you could take his room, that he could guard us both better that way anyway."

"He can have his room. I'll be in yours. I was really asking about his plans."

"He said only what I just told you—"

Stymied again. Shit, why did I care? I told myself I didn't care.

"—what I want to know is where you are. You're calling from your cell phone."

There was fear, but also delight. Yet suddenly blurting that we were Oathed again via phone was not how I imagined breaking the news to him. I wanted to be face to face. "I'm out."

"Out where? With who?"

"I'm with no one right now," I said honestly. Devlin still hadn't returned. "Trust me."

"I do trust you. Now tell me where you are and who you're with."

"I'm at a restaurant waiting for food in a booth, alone."

"I know who is with you," he said menacingly. "What have you done—!"

"Danial, I love you and I'll see you tomorrow," I said, and hung up. Quickly turning off my cell, I put it in my purse. Danial would call back immediately, so it was better he got voice mail.

The waitress brought my food. I began devouring it, relishing how good the fatty food tasted. I was just finishing my fries when Devlin appeared. He was almost glowing, his stubble again present.

"Hey," he said, kissing me quickly on the cheek and sitting down. "How was your food?"

"Good," I said, giving him an appreciative look. "I take it you're full, too?"

"Yes," he said, sipping his wine. "I was starving. Do you need more wine?"

I was halfway through my second glass. "No." I wanted to ask him if he'd killed the person he'd bitten, but remained quiet.

His phone rang. He checked the caller ID, then shot me a grin.

"Danial?"

He nodded. The phone continued to ring.

"Should I answer, Sar?" Devlin said teasingly. "Or should I let him wonder why I don't?"

He was enjoying this way too much. "I called him, so he wouldn't worry when I didn't answer at home. He suspects you are with me, Dev," I said, drinking the last of my wine. "I told him I was out eating alone at a restaurant, and he still knew."

"If I were him, I would have suspicions by now, too," he said jovially. He picked up the phone. "Danial, how good to hear from you."

"Yes, I'm with her," Devlin said, shooting me delighted look.

"Yes," he answered, deeply satisfied.

"Yes," he repeated with even more satisfaction.

"Since Tuesday," he said, enough relish dripping from his words that some spattered on the table. Instantly, I heard Danial shouting at him as he held the phone away from his ear.

Devlin cut him off, his voice velvety. "Listen before your jealousy overloads your mouth. She was dying. All your lofty plans would have been for nothing. You owe me a thank you, Brother."

"You're welcome," Devlin continued. "Best of all, not only is the marking all done for you, but you're Oathed again."

There was a pause, then Devlin became irritated. "I'm not lying," he said, miffed. "Sar can tell you herself." He handed me the phone.

"Hello—?"

"Is it true?" Danial shouted. "Did you swear to me or only to him?" His tone was tumultuous: tears, anger, hope, jealousy and love all mixed together.

"I swore to both of you. He accepted on your behalf."

"You will tell me everything, all of it on Friday," Danial said furiously. "You will not leave out one Goddamn detail, is that understood?"

"Of course," I said, irked. "I planned to tell you, Danial, but I wanted it to be in person where we could do more afterwards than me telling you more words over a phone."

Danial let out a loud stream of swear words, most of which I'd never heard him utter before. I held the phone away from my ear, grimacing.

Devlin took it back. "Restrain your frustration. Remember, you are Oathed." He hung up, then shot me a wide grin. "Well, that went well."

"You are incorrigible," I said, smiling.

The waitress brought my tiramisu. As I devoured that, Devlin finished his wine, then paid the bill, asking the waitress to seal the bottle for us to take along.

On the road home, we passed a small bar on the outskirts of town. The parking lot was half-full, a live rock band inside singing loudly. "Want to go in?" Devlin said, giving me a daring smile.

"Okay," I said, taking his offered hand.

The place was a dive, but the music was great. Devlin and I went to stand with the throng at the front of the stage, swaying to the beat. It had been a long time since I'd seen a live band in a bar. It was larger than life, the loud music engulfing us, the energy of the people around us intoxicating.

"Like it?" Devlin said in my ear.

"Yes!" I said loudly, trying to make him hear me. He laughed, though I felt the vibration of it through my back more than heard it.

"Devlin?" a voice called questioningly.

We both turned. An African American man was making his way through the crowd to us. He looked about twenty or so, well dressed for his surroundings.

"Stay silent, no matter what," Devlin said quickly to me. He moved away toward the man. I watched worriedly, understanding he'd both recognized the man and expected trouble. They met about ten yards away, just close enough for me to make out their loud words under the music.

"Devlin," the man said again in surprise, his manner friendly. "What are *you* doing here? I heard you were in Europe. Are you going to the Gathering?"

"I'm trying to get laid," Devlin said, glancing over at me pointedly.

I looked at the floor, appalled, pretending to be oblivious.

"She's cute," the man replied. "Does she do doubles? I could go for a double team tonight."

It was all I could do not to reach into my pocket and wrap the choker around my neck. I forced my eyes to remain on the ground, even as my face turned scarlet.

Devlin said something else, and then they both laughed. Looking up casually, I saw a quick flash of fangs. Scary as that was, it was also a relief: Devlin had been adamant about barring me from other vampires.

"No," Devlin replied. "I'm not sharing her with you, Nate. Get your own; there are plenty here."

"Why not?" Nate persisted, annoyed. "We've done it before—"

"Because I want to drain her during," Devlin said, giving Nate a cool smile. "You know well how good it feels, how they jerk at the end. When they finally realize what's happening, and they are trying to get away, but no longer have the strength. This one loves vampires." He bared his fangs slightly. "She's in for a big surprise with the real thing."

My dinner shifted in my stomach. I swallowed, trying not to throw up.

"Have a good time," Nate said regretfully. "Shoot me an email later and tell me how long she lasted." He gave me one last hungry glance. "See you around, Dev." He turned and began making his way back though the crowd.

Devlin came over and put his arms round me. "I apologize deeply for that," he said quietly in my ear. "Nate was the last person I expected here. He Rules Tennessee. He's en route to the Gathering."

The vampire that Leri had threatened to take me to. Shiver. "We should have put the choker back on me," I whispered back angrily. "Then I would have been safe meeting him."

"That was not an option," Devlin replied. "Everyone needs to think you belong to Danial, not to me. No one can see you in my choker."

"Then why give it to me?" I yelled angrily. "Why get my Oath?"

Devlin scanned the crowd. "We can't risk talking about this here. Come."

I refused to budge. "I'm not leaving."

Devlin picked me up in a smooth motion, then strode with me to the exit. He set me down by the car, still fuming.

"Get in, or I'll throw you in," he said angrily. "We don't have time for your tantrum."

I curled myself into a corner of the truck cab, and stayed there all the way home. I couldn't get the words Devlin had uttered to Nate out of my head. He had killed a woman as he had her and savored it like the wine we'd drunk tonight. How could I let someone touch me who had enjoyed such a loathsome act?

When we arrived home, I went inside quickly. After checking on the dogs,

I went into the bedroom and took a long shower. No matter how I scrubbed, I still felt unclean. Tiredly, I put some salve on my mostly healed tattoo, dressed in pajamas, and went to face Devlin. To my surprise, he was nowhere to be found, though his bike and leather clothes were still in the basement.

He had to be outside walking. Maybe he'd left in my truck. Either way, I was too exhausted to care. I checked on the cats, let the dogs out and in, and then went to my bed, setting the alarm for dawn so I wouldn't forget to feed my pets in the morning.

I awoke an hour later, when someone slid into bed next to me.

"Dev?" I said softly.

"Yes, it's me," he said, sliding his fingers down my arm. "I wanted to give you some time alone."

"I don't need time alone," I retorted. "I need to know what your plans are for me."

"What you want is an assurance I'm not going to drain you during lovemaking," he said, annoyed. "I thought Oathing would have settled that."

"You've done it before," I said accusingly. "You enjoyed it, too."

He was quiet for a moment, his hand on my arm still. "I have done it before," Devlin said grudgingly. "What I said to Nate is true: it feels exceptionally good while it lasts. But it makes you feel disgusting afterwards, to know that a woman trusted you enough to let you inside her and then to take her life along with her body. I had a taste for that once, but that was decades ago. Nate is younger. This is just a phase he's going through."

"These are people's lives," I said, appalled. "I understand vampires need blood, but they don't need to kill for it."

He turned me toward him, embracing me. "Nate likes to do that. He does it on a regular basis. Tennessee has a high murder rate for a reason. He has to get rid of the bodies with no one the wiser."

Leri hadn't threatened me idly. Something to remember. "Then he's a monster and a serial killer."

"He is," Devlin agreed. "But you're really accusing me of the same. My answer is that I am a killer, Sarelle. I freely admit it. I revel in both killing and lovemaking, but I don't mix the two. It is enough to take a woman's blood and her body. It's wrong to take her life as well, when she's given herself freely and utterly."

"Did you kill someone earlier tonight?"

"Yes," Devlin replied. "It was either drain someone or leave you sitting in that restaurant alone until it closed. Rest assured that I picked a deserving candidate."

I didn't reply.

"Sar, I'll have to leave in a few hours. I want to make love."

I didn't reply.

"Don't deny me, Sar," he said, kissing my face. "Not when you know I love you."

"I can't understand how I could love or want someone who scares me as much as you do," I whispered. "Sometimes you horrify me, Dev."

"I'm sorry," he said softly, as he kissed down my neck. "I don't mean to. I'm not as gentle as Danial is, I don't have his patience. Mine has always been a darker temperament. I have a taste for violence, and I can be cruel. My patience is easily lost, and I say whatever I am feeling, strike out in anger before thinking."

"Then you understand why I fear you."

"Know that whatever I might say or do, I won't ever cross the line and strike you." He touched my cheekbone, then gently kissed the tiny scar that remained there from Danial's ring. "The only scars you'll have from me are the ones you wear now willingly."

"I believe you," I said softly. "You've never hurt me purposely, in spite of your threats."

He took the choker off the bedside table, then fastened it around my neck. "We are going to have a good life," he whispered. "That is my plan for us, Love. And I'm going to do my damnedest to make it come true."

I didn't believe that, but made no reply.

"Tell me you love me," Devlin said tenderly.

"I do love you. But I'm afraid of how this is going to end."

"We are not at the end, only a new beginning," he corrected gently. "I love you, Sar, with everything that I am."

"Then promise me that you'll never lie to me," I said, watching him carefully.

He didn't hesitate. "I won't ever lie to you again."

"Then love me again, please. Bite me gently, and take what you need. Sing to me. Most of all, afterwards, hold me and tell me I'm safe, that you won't let anything happen to me."

Devlin did all those things with the grace and sensuality that was his and his alone. When he told me I was safe, that he wouldn't let anyone hurt me, I believed him.

We moved to the basement at about five a.m. Dawn came before I was ready for it, and I clung to him, afraid to go back to sleep, and miss these last moments with him. He stayed until eight, holding me tightly, neither of us sleeping. Then he got up, and dressed in his black leather. I followed him to his Harley in my robe, watching him as he checked over his bike.

"Do you need gas? I have an extra five gallons in the garage."

"It will save me a stop," he said with a tired smile. "I'm riding on fumes now."

"Red can," I said, biting my lip. "Yellow is the diesel. Password is 'lions'."

He nodded. "Come to me, Love," he said, holding out his arms.

I came to him, and he hugged me, his leather creaking. Then he took off my choker, and handed it to me. "Put it on yourself."

I held it to my neck, willed the ends together, and felt the magic-laden metal fasten.

"Good. Wear my choker with you to the Gathering under your clothes. Do not let anyone see it until then, save Danial."

"How?"

"Wrap it around your ankle twice. It will stretch a little, if you ask it to."

I remembered Elle's necklace, how I'd wondered if it had grown with her, and nodded.

"Be strong, Sar. No matter what happens, remember, you are far too valuable to any vampire there for them to harm you. Stay with Danial and Theo at all times. They will keep you safe." He embraced me. "Tell me again that you love my eyes."

"I love them," I said simply. "The purest gold is a poor shadow of them."

"I will see you as soon as I can," he said, then leaned in to me, his hand gripping my robe in his leather glove. He kissed me lingeringly, slowly. "My love goes with you, Oathed One," he said, pulling back reluctantly. "Take care."

I backed away as he kick started his bike, sliding on his helmet. As he backed out of the garage, he held up a gloved hand in farewell. I blew him a lone kiss. He did a half circle, and roared off down the driveway.

As I shut the garage, reality kicked me in the ass. There was a hell of a lot to finish today before Danial arrived.

The next hour was a flurry of activity. I cleaned the woodstove, dumped the ashes, then started a fire. Quickly, I stripped the upstairs bed, readying it for the werefoxes, and did laundry. After feeding the pets and myself and tidying up the house, I called Danial's looking for Elle.

She came to the phone a few seconds later and shouted into it, "Mom! Dad says you're better!"

I winced, my ears ringing. "Yes, I'm better. Do you feel like a little shopping trip?"

"Yes!" she said excitedly. "What time should I be ready?"

I glanced at the clock. "How's noon? Make sure you are packed for at least a few days, as I'll be dropping you off at your grandparents' right after."

"Dad said to pack for a week," she said in a hushed voice. "He sat me down and explained everything. He said it would be dangerous, but that he would make sure you were safe."

Damn it, Danial. You had no right to promise her that. "He's going to do his best, as will your father," I said, trying to sound certain.

Elle went silent.

"Elle, what is it?"

She didn't answer.

Damn you, Theo. "Elle, I'll see you later, okay? I'll bring you some cookies I baked."

"Bye, Mom," she said flatly, then hung up.

I thought about calling Theo and asking him what he'd told her. But what was the point? I'd find all that out soon enough.

Angered, I put the phone back in its cradle and went back to work, bringing up a full rack of wood. Afterwards my muscles ached, having grown unused to heavy lifting. But they would grow strong again, provided I lived that long…

I closed down that morbid thought, and renewed my efforts. Within an hour, the house was clean, all the laundry was done and put away, and I was in the shower. When I emerged, it was quarter to twelve.

I'd never make it in time to Elle via driving. I might as well try to teleport.

I got dressed, coiled up my wet hair, grabbed my purse, and concentrated hard on the great room at Danial's home. The next moment, I was standing in snow to my knees on Danial's lawn.

My sneakers wet, I gingerly walked out of the snow, and onto the shoveled path. *Oh well. I'd get better with practice, right?*

Elle opened the door. "Mom, where did you come from? I didn't hear a car."

"I can teleport, but I'm just learning," I said proudly. "I'll have to practice."

Elle gave me a look of awe, handing me her bag. "Can you teleport us to the mall?"

"Remember, you aren't to tell your grandparents anything but that Danial, Theo, and I are attending a convention." I hefted the bag with difficulty. "What do you have in here, rocks?"

"No, I—"

"Sar?" Terian called from inside the house. "Elle?"

I grabbed Elle's hand, and concentrated hard, desperately imagining the mall parking lot.

Chapter Sixteen

We arrived instantly halfway up one car aisle. The sky was clear, the sun shining brightly.

"Pretty good," Elle said, letting my hand go. "We didn't get hit."

"Thanks for your faith," I said grumpily. "Come on, we don't have more than a few hours. Let's make the most of them."

* * * *

Over our dessert at lunch, she dropped the bombshell.

"Mom, Dad explained to me that you needed Uncle Devlin to make you better. He said that you had Oathed to him again, and to Devlin, too."

Part of me was annoyed at not getting to announce my own news, and the other was pleased that Danial had smoothed the way yet again. "How do you feel about that?"

"I'm worried," she said hesitantly. "Dad said that you weren't cured. That you would need his help and Devlin's for the rest of your life."

"That's true, Elle," I said carefully. Having no idea how much Danial had told her, it was safer not to elaborate.

She looked at me out of the corner of her eye. "Will you come back and live with us?" she said hesitantly. "Dad misses you. I see it in his eyes sometimes when he's alone."

"Elle, there's a lot that I have to work out first. Theo—"

Elle slammed down her spoon. "I hate him! He left you when you were sick! He's jealous of Dad. I used to smell it on him."

The diners nearest us were staring at us.

"Elle—"

"I want him to stay with her, and I don't want to go live with him!" she screeched.

The manager was coming toward us. We had to get out of here.

"Elle, let's go. We can talk about this outside the restaurant."

After quickly throwing down some cash, I walked out with Elle, and sat on a wooden bench. "What did Theo tell you about why he left?" I asked.

"I know about that other woman," she replied, her tone livid. "He called me that night after he left, apologizing about what happened. He said he was coming back. Then he showed up this morning with that woman—"

"She's here?" I said weakly.

"She's at the fox compound," Elle said scathingly. "He introduced us and I growled at her. She got scared and he got angry."

"Next time be polite," I admonished her. "No matter how bad his behavior, yours should always be good, Elle. Danial would tell you this, if he were here. Come on," I added, offering her my hand. "We need to get you to Grandma's house."

* * * *

After dropping Elle off at my parents' house, I headed home.

The moment I'd seen my mom, I desperately wanted to go inside and spend one last golden hour with my parents, to hear the same stories I'd heard so many times before that I knew them by heart. But it was too risky and there wasn't time. I had too much to do as it was.

After packing an overnight bag, and putting Devlin's choker on my ankle, I took Ghost and Darkness for an hour walk. Unlike my usual purposeful foray, I let them smell everything they wanted to, hunt for mice, and dig in the earth, flinging mud everywhere. By the time we got home, they were filthy but happy.

I cleaned their feet, cut their nails, and then brushed them as they writhed in happiness, wriggling all over. Then I gave them some lunch meat, parceling out a few pieces. After that, I handed them each two Cheweez. "You are the best dogs ever," I said emotionally. "I love you both very much."

I left them chewing, sat down in front of the wood stove, and pulled Jessica into my lap. We hadn't sat here in a long time. When I'd been sick, the floor had been too cold, despite the fire. I stroked his coat repeatedly, murmuring "Little sweet cat laying there." Soon he was a limp warm dishrag in my arms, purring softly. As he dropped off to sleep, Cavity came over. I moved Jess over so there was room enough for him, then lifted him onto my lap, too. "You're a monster cat," I said lovingly, petting him. "You're my monster cat, Cavity."

I sat there for an hour holding them, then reluctantly moved them and got up. After building up the fire, I let the dogs out one last time, and then taped a note on the front door that said "Downstairs." Going into the bedroom, I changed back into the clean ivory gown, fastened Danial's choker around my neck, and went below into the basement to wait.

It wasn't long before the dogs barked upstairs, then the front door opened. Their barks became happy whining, then their feet moved away. A second later, Danial descended the cellar stairs calling, "Sar?"

"In here." I stood for him on the floor at the bottom of the bed, waiting.

He opened the door, glancing at the cracked frame. Then his eyes found me.

I opened my arms to him. "Come to me."

He crossed in two strides, then grabbed me roughly, kissing me hungrily. I put my arms around him, pressing my body to his. He threw off his jacket, pulled off his pants, and then stripped my gown over my head and tossed it aside. Then he pushed me backwards. I went sprawling on the bed, my eyes wide.

Danial unbuttoned his shirt. "Down on your knees, Oathed One."

I gaped at him. He finished undressing, then glared at me with red eyes. Suddenly afraid, I got up from the bed and ran towards the door. Before I could open the door, Danial grabbed me by the back of my neck. I went still and let out a whimper.

"I told you to get on your knees. Get back on the bed, now."

I did as he asked. Danial took up a position behind me. His erection brushed my backside, then teased me, the tip just outside my vagina. I pushed back hard. Danial clenched his muscles, our combined actions thrusting him deeply into me. My head went back as I let out an eager moan. He groaned loudly, pulling my lower body back hard against his, one hand on my hip to move me, the other reaching up to massage my breasts as he kissed my neck.

He leaned forward, bearing me down onto the bed with his weight, moving fast, grunting with effort and need. Then it was over, as Danial came, his spasms frantic. He moved off me, breathing hard. I moved to face him, apprehensive.

"Why," he growled. "Tell me why."

"Why what?" I ventured.

Danial moved supernaturally fast, grabbing hold of me, his eyes tinged red.

"I gave you everything I had to give. I did everything you asked of me, and more. I listened to you when you needed me to, held you when you wept, covered up what happened between you and Devlin. I cared for our child, when you abandoned him and me to be with Theo. I let you go when you asked me to, and came to you when you asked me to."

He shook me furiously, making me cry out in fear. "Stop it!"

"You knew that I wanted you to swear to me! You knew I'd have done anything to have you promise to be mine! After all the shit you and I have been through, how could you give your Oath to Devlin after being with him only a few days?"

"Dev didn't give me much of a choice." I touched his hands gently, easing them off me. Danial shook with fury under my fingers. "In any case, we needed his help. Everything was falling apart, no matter how you and I were trying to hold things together." I clasped his hand. "But we have a good chance now. I'm marked, we're Oathed, and I'm strong enough now to stand with you tomorrow to face the other Rulers without worrying about losing control."

Danial hugged me tightly, as if we'd been separated decades instead of days. "I'm sorry I frightened you, Darling. Forgive me."

"I'm sorry you found out about everything like you did," I replied, hugging him back. "And I have more to tell you. Devlin has some plan he is orchestrating. Lash said—"

"You met Lash?" Danial said in shock. "I thought I scented snake upstairs—"

"He came here to talk strategy with Devlin. Titus was with him. I didn't overhear any details. All I know was that Lash succeeded in whatever his mission was."

"Interesting. When did Devlin leave?"

"Dev left early this morning."

"This morning?" Danial said, doing a double take.

"Yes, he was riding his Harley dressed in leather. We went for a ride one night. It was cold."

"He knows better than that," Danial grumbled. "It's too cold this time of year. We lose heat too quickly." He held me tight in his arms, stroking my hair. "I'm sorry again for my anger."

"Good," I said approvingly. "As Devlin said, this is a time for celebration."

"What of Theo?" Danial said, his eyes searching mine. "Have you spoken to him?"

"No," I said, angry instantly. "Elle let slip that he had asked her to come and live with him and Tasha. I think it's safe to say he hasn't come back to try to work things out with me."

"Over my dead body," Danial growled. "She is more my daughter than his. She is more your daughter than any other woman's." He looked at me. "My question to you is can you handle seeing him if he decides to continue working for me?"

"That depends on if I have to see his jailbait."

"I don't want to see her either, so don't worry about it," Danial said disdainfully. "But we have more important things to talk about. I hadn't known Theo offered Elle another home. What did she seem to think of his offer?"

I snuggled against him. "You don't have to worry. Elle refused. Theo said he would let her stay with you."

"That's good," Danial said, relieved. "I do not want to fight with Theo if it can be avoided. We have enough problems."

"What is the plan, by the way?" I said, kissing him gently on his neck.

"Terian will pick us up here at eleven. We'll get to the airport by midnight, and should arrive in Toronto by one or one thirty. We'll order room service for you and Theoron, while Theo, Terian, and I plan strategy for various scenarios. After, we'll sleep the day away, showing up promptly at seven for the Gathering."

"I'm afraid," I whispered.

"So am I," he said heavily, hugging me tight. "So am I."

* * * *

Close to ten, we got up and began dressing.

"Do you need me to put on your choker?" Danial asked, buttoning his shirt.

"I'm not sure," I answered. "Devlin's will open for me, but—"

"I should have suspected, after seeing your hip," Danial answered. "That was one of the items you hid in my safe, wasn't it?"

"Yes," I admitted. "I knew you'd destroy it if you knew."

"My jealousy is over," Danial assured me, his smile easy.

"I spoke to Dev about this," I began hesitantly. "He said he was fine with this arrangement, too. But agreeing to it and living it are two different things."

"I'm happy with the arrangement," Danial assured.

I put my finger to his lips. "Are you sure? Because for all you and he say that, you both seem to need to possess what it yours utterly. And sharing means recognizing another had a right to what you call your own."

"Sar, we are men, and men never willingly share, if they think there is even a chance they will not have to. That said, Dev was good enough to include me, when he could have cut me out. I'll not cause a rift over including him, especially as you say you love him now." He fastened the choker about my neck. "I want you to be happy."

"I'll be happy to make it back home alive," I said with a ghost of a smile. "Even with all of our preparations, I'm worried. My sense of foreboding increases with every passing minute."

"No despair," Danial said sternly. "Come, I hear Terian in the driveway."

* * * *

When we arrived in Canada, Theo was on the macadam waiting. He smiled when he saw me. I gave him one in return before I remembered myself, and looked away.

The trip to the hotel was a somber affair, Theo relating to Danial the layout of the hotel and Gathering room.

The hotel itself was gorgeous. As expected, it was grandiose, with a huge waterfall in the open-air lobby and real trees. As Danial checked us in, Theoron wriggled in my arms, eager to explore, his fangs distended in his excitement.

Danial returned, touching Theoron gently on his head. "I have to feed. I will be up as soon as I do. Ebediah has provided food for all the attendees. Order some room service, and wait there for me."

I nodded to him, expecting him to nod back to me. Instead, he grasped the front of my coat, and pulled me in for a rough kiss. Shocked, I kissed him back, figuring he had done it for someone watching.

"Keep alert," he said. "Trust no one."

"Let's go," Theo said roughly, clearly jealous, then strode off. I, Theoron, and Brian followed, Terian heading off with Danial.

I'd just unpacked in one of the rooms when there was a knock at the door.

"Sar, can I come in?" Theo asked.

I wanted to scream at him. I wanted to fall into his arms and admit everything I had done and beg his forgiveness. I wanted to tell him that there was no point being nice to me, because it was over, and he was probably better off without me. "Come in."

He came in, shut the door, then faced me. "You look like your old self."

"I am," I said evenly. "You on the other hand are someone I don't know."

"I'm sorry for how I acted," he said tentatively. "I never meant to hurt you."

I sat down on the bed, and burst into tears. Theo sat beside me, then put his arms around me.

His embrace was too familiar, so much that the act put me from sadness into hysterics. I gasped for breath, tears pouring down my face, furious at myself for not handling this calmly. I'd wanted to denounce him, to tell him to do whatever he wanted with Tasha because he and I were through. Instead, I was going to pieces.

I bit my lip as hard as I could. The pain let me get a clumsy hold on myself.

Pulling free of him, I went to the bathroom, wiped my eyes, and washed my face. "After this is over, you're moving out, right?"

In the mirror's reflection, Theo ran his fingers through his hair, but said nothing.

"Theo, don't make this harder for me than it is already," I said angrily. "Just tell me the truth."

He met my eyes and looked away.

I lost it. "Just tell me you love her and not me and you're leaving!" I shouted at him, my chest heaving. "Just say it!"

Theo swallowed hard. "I love her. I'm moving out, as soon as this is over."

I'd known it, but hearing him say it still hurt. "Get out," I said, turning from him.

He crossed the room and grabbed a hold of me. "Sar—"

"No!" I screamed at him. "I am not going to listen to another word from you. Brian!"

Theo released me, as Brian opened the door. "I'm here, Sarelle."

"I didn't plan this," Theo said. "I just went to help her escape. I'm sorry how this worked out—" He grabbed my arm.

I sank my teeth into the back of his hand. With a growl, Theo released me.

"Theo, you should leave," Brian said firmly.

"Get out," I said in a raw voice. "I never want to see you again."

"You will see me again," Theo retorted, rubbing his healing hand. "I'm not leaving Elle, and she won't leave Danial. Tasha and I will be staying at Danial's in the werecompound until we can find a place of our own. I'll be working the night shift, so you and I can avoid each other days. But I'm not going to disappear out of Elle's life. You're going to have to deal with that."

"Fine," I spat at him. "Just get out."

"Sar, I'm sorry—"

"Fuck you and fuck your being sorry!" I yelled. "And one more thing," I added, my tone sandpaper. "Don't ever call me Sar again."

Chapter Seventeen

Theo nodded angrily, then turned and left, slamming the door behind him.

"I'll be outside if you should need me," Brian said formally.

"We'll be fine," Danial said, moving past him into the room. "Don't disturb us until morning."

Brian nodded, then shut the door.

"I hope you've not taught our son a new word in your anger," Danial said mildly, picking up Theoron.

"I'm sorry." I sank down onto the bed. "I just never expected to have him bring her back with him. I'd be handling this a lot better if he wasn't stuffing her down my throat."

"Do you want something to eat tonight?"

"No," I said tiredly. "Can you take care of Theoron?"

"He's almost asleep already," Danial said, laying down Theoron beside us. He put his other arm around me. "It's you I'm worried about."

I didn't answer, my thoughts in turmoil. Sometime later, soothed by his touch, I slept.

* * * *

After some calorie-laden room service at noon, I dressed in casual clothes, and played with Theoron. When he tired around four, the both of us took a long nap. Brian woke us close to ten.

"Danial said for you to start getting ready. He's not sure what time you'll be asked to come to the Gathering room."

"Is everyone else set to go?" I asked sleepily.

"Danial is feeding again, with Theo nearby. Terian is outside the door. Danial feared a possible attack, as it's known you and Theoron are here without him."

Unnerved, I grabbed a robe, and got up. "Can you order me some French fries?"

"Of course," Brian said. "Anything else?"

"Steak for Theoron, just a small one." I stifled another yawn. "I'd like some wine, but it's better if I don't."

"Yes," Brian agreed. He closed the door, then opened it.

I whipped around. "What is it?"

"Be careful," he said gravely.

"I am being careful," I said, looking steadily at him.

"You are in over your head, and you don't even see the water."

"I did the best I could under the circumstances," I said bitingly. "There wasn't another choice."

"Wasn't there?"

"You sound like Lash," I said, liking the way the name made Brian shrink back in fear. "This is no more your business than it is his. Keep your mind on your job, and tell me when the food gets here."

Brian nodded, then shut the door.

* * * *

I'd no sooner finished showering than Danial returned.

"Did you eat?"

"Yes," I answered, taking out the dress. "God, this thing's elaborate. You'll have to zip me up."

The dress was deep burgundy with lace trim of old ivory, and so fancy that it was almost a ball gown, pearl beading all over the bodice, down the arms and even on the skirt. There was a poofy skirt to go under it, making me bell shaped. The matching shoes at least were low heels.

Danial put on a matching colored shirt of burgundy, his black leather pants and his high boots. After buckling on a rapier, he zipped me up.

"You look lovely," he said appreciatively. "Please dress Theoron, and come out when you are done." He gave me a kiss, then left.

I wound up my wet hair and got to work on Theoron. After dressing him in a tiny replica of Danial's outfit, complete with leather boots, I put on my fox head earrings, slipped on my shoes, fluffed up my hair with magic, and then slipped on the burgundy headpiece encrusted with pearl beading. After putting on some light makeup, and dousing my hair with hairspray, I glanced in the mirror.

"Hello, Christmas Extravaganza Barbie. Ugh."

I gathered up Theoron and his bag of supplies, and went out the door. Terian was there waiting, glowering.

"What is your problem?" I said, irritated. "Just say it."

"Danial wasn't the one who made you better, Sar. It was Devlin, wasn't it?"

His assumption wasn't a huge surprise. Dev was the only other vampire who was ever around me. Danial didn't have any vampire friends, just allies I'd met at parties. "So what if it was?" I said harshly. "I'm glad not to be dead."

"How could you let him touch you after what he did to you before?"

My eyes narrowed, looking into his red ones. "I loved what he did to me, Terian. My only regret was I waited so long to let him have me."

"It wasn't you, Sar, it was just your body needing the virus—"

"I feel nothing but love and lust for him. It was longing to be back in his arms that showed me I could teleport."

Blackness curled out of Terian. "You make me sick. No wonder Theo's leaving you."

"I am who I am," I retorted. "At least I don't hide my nature, pretend I'm someone else."

"What do you mean?" he said angrily, his eyes bleeding to full red in an instant.

"I mean enough of the crap about how this job isn't you and how you hate killing. I've seen your face, Terian. You enjoy it as much as Theo does. It's in your nature, and you might as well accept it."

"I'll never accept it," he growled low. "I don't want to hurt anyone."

"You do," I said gleefully. "You can't help yourself, being what you are. What has taking the high road ever gotten you, Tears? You're doomed to evil and you might as well face it."

"I can't believe you said that," Terian replied, hurt. He left the room.

As soon as he'd gone, I kicked myself for saying what I had. *I hadn't meant it…*

Brian opened the door. "We're ready when you are, Sarelle."

I left the room, joining the group in the hallway and walking downstairs. Danial, Theoron, and I were all in burgundy, with Theo, Terian, and Brian all in black. I didn't understand the significance of the colors, but didn't ask.

When we reached the main floor, we entered the main conference room. The sign said it would seat three hundred, and it appeared at least two hundred people were there already. As we entered, those inside parted like a wave to let us through, watching us with interest.

"We're up there," Danial said, pointing to a raised dais with several luxurious chairs. One was clearly a throne of some kind, and two smaller chairs were beside of it. We ascended the dais and sat in the chairs, me holding Theoron. Theo, Terian, and Brian took up positions around us.

"What are we supposed to do now?" I whispered.

"Sit here and be looked at, mostly," Danial said. "Prepare yourself for not only a tiring evening, but a boring one, too." He flashed one of his fake smiles to the surrounding crowd. "Ebediah should be here soon to take his throne. He is the Vampire Ruler for Canada."

"Is he mean?" I whispered.

"He's old," Danial whispered back. "Like Samuel. He's not mean, but he's exacting."

I was thinking about what that meant when I looked down and saw I was still wearing my wedding rings. Angrily, I took them off and handed them to Danial, who put them in his pocket. I glanced at Theo discreetly, wanting to see if he'd also taken his off. To my surprise, he hadn't.

I pondered that for the next half hour, as more people arrived. Though many people mingled in groups on the floor, no one approached us. Whether that was because of our guards or out of respect, I wasn't sure. The only thing I was sure of was that I was getting tired of being stared at.

A lone figure approached us. "Sarelle, Danial," Samuel said politely.

"Hello," I said, extending my hand.

He kissed it. "You look lovely as ever." He shook Danial's hand too, but his eyes were all for Theoron. "May I hold him?" he asked eagerly.

"No one may hold him, save Sarelle, I or Terian," Danial said politely. "But everyone may look at him, and we will feed him later, so everyone can see his dual nature."

"Is it true he can walk in the sun?" Samuel said in a hushed voice.

"He can't walk yet," I said with a smile, "But yes, he can sit in the sun, and we're working on walking."

"He can eat food, other than blood?" Samuel said intently.

"Yes," I said, rummaging in Theoron's bag. "I brought some ice cream with us to feed him. That's one of his favorites."

"This is a miracle." He took my hand again, and slowly sank to one knee. "My Lady, I don't have words to say what this means that you have shown us this is possible. Know that no one here wishes you or your child harm."

He'd left off Danial, and it hadn't been a slip. I pulled my hand out of his.

Danial got to his feet. "Samuel, where is Ebediah? He should be here by now."

"He asked me yesterday to open the festivities for him," Samuel said smoothly. "He had a last minute problem he needed to take care of, some nasty murder in Quebec. Excuse me."

He turned to the crowd. "Attention, everyone! I have been asked to start the evening festivities. I ask you all to be polite and courteous to our guests of honor, Danial Racklan, Ruler of the Common States, his Oathed One, Sarelle

Racklan, and their blessed gift of a son, Theoron Racklan—"

My skin crawled. I gripped Danial's hand tightly. He gave my hand a squeeze.

"—everyone may come and see the child, but no one is to attempt to touch him. Any attempts will be dealt with harshly, immediately. Please enjoy yourselves." Samuel motioned and the small orchestra to the side of the dais began to play as the first curious vampires came forward.

Everything went well at first. Despite Samuel's speech, everyone asked to touch him, and were irritated when we refused. Theoron behaved well, though he was as bored as we were and wanted the ice cream. Finally, I gave in and gave him some. Everyone watched that event like the finale of a favorite TV series, their fixated attention and complete silence unnerving.

Shortly after, I met two of the notable Rulers that Danial had spoken of, Zane and Perseus, as well as many lesser vampires with titles from around the world. All of them were courteous, but their polite and flowery words were devoid of everything except their interest in Theoron and I. Surprisingly, Zane was not what I expected, being not African American, but instead Asian, though his smaller size did not make me any less afraid of him. He was the first to push the envelope, when he refused to release my hand after kissing it, and Danial had to ask him to release me. His dark eyes were full of malice, even as he did so.

The worst was Perseus, who I somehow expected to be nice, perhaps because of his namesake. He was Mediterranean in looks, perhaps an actual Greek by birth, the oldest next to Ebediah and Samuel, according to Danial. He said no pleasantries after kissing my hand, and introducing himself. Instead, he shifted his eyes to Danial and began talking as if no one else was there.

"Danial, you can say what you like, but I know that you have no claim on Sarelle."

"You see the marks on her," Danial said calmly, meeting Perseus's eyes with his own.

"At least one was made by your brother," Perseus said coldly. "And the only Oath I know that she has taken is to your werecougar there." He glanced at Theo, who growled. "Marriage is a human custom, Danial; it is no barrier to such as us."

Theo growled louder.

"I have an Oath from her," Danial said, narrowing his reddening eyes.

"You did years ago, but you rescinded it," Perseus said scathingly. "Manir told that to me months ago, in exchange for some information I gave him. He said he had tortured one of your weres for it."

I closed my eyes at the horror of it. He was talking about Suri. Theo was snarling now openly, Terian's blackness seeping into me from where he stood at my back.

Danial stood up slowly, his eyes bleeding to solid red. "Perseus, I have her Oath. You do not need to believe my words for that to be true. Now get out of here, before I ask Samuel to escort you out."

Perseus said nothing, only bared his fangs, and left, moving away from us, Zane beside him. Danial sat back down.

Theoron grew antsy before too much time had passed, his usual easygoing mood turning irritable. Samuel used that opportunity to bring out a young woman, who he presented to Theoron. "Drink your fill, little Prince."

Theoron looked at me, bewildered.

Danial stood. "Samuel, in my son's best interests, please demonstrate he has nothing to fear."

"Not afraid," Theoron whispered to me. "Why—"

"Shh," I said.

Samuel drank from the woman, then faced us, proffering her bloodied wrist. Before I could react, Theoron lunged, sinking his fangs into her wrist with a growl. She let out a shriek, and tried to pull back. Samuel stopped her, keeping her wrist immobile as Theoron ravaged it. She began to cry.

"Enough," Danial commanded, grabbing Theoron and prying him off the woman. Samuel nodded, then led the frightened, sobbing woman away, passing her off to one of his guards. As I cleaned up Theoron's face with a wet nap, his fangs receded, becoming their normal human size. No one else had spoken, but the energy level of the room had risen exponentially.

It was time to leave. I turned to Danial. "Why don't you have Terian teleport—?"

"Shit," Brian said under his breath. "Look who just walked in."

Chapter Eighteen

Devlin stood at the entrance to the room, dressed in black finery, complete with a long cape, and as always, his high leather boots. He was breathtaking, shining like the moon itself. He was scanning the room, Titus beside him.

I had the sudden urge to run to him, got partway up, then sank back down in the chair very, very slowly. Giving anything away in front of so many people would be stupid and dangerous. What was he doing here? Did his presence mean his plan had failed?

I needed to talk to Danial alone. "Danial, let's dance."

Danial nodded, and took my hand. "Come."

I handed Theoron to Terian. He took him, giving me a cool glance. Danial led me to the dance floor. Slowly, we swept from one end of the dance floor to the other.

"I didn't expect him," I said pointedly, hoping he knew who I meant.

Danial nodded. "I'm surprised, too. I hope he behaves. We don't need a scene with him and Theo, tonight of all nights."

"There won't be any scene," I said with finality. "Theo and I are done."

"Then why is he still wearing the ring?" Danial replied. "I'm sure she requested he take it off."

"I can't imagine—"

Then there was a tap on Danial's shoulder. Devlin stood there.

"Speak of the Devil," Danial said darkly, glaring at Devlin pointedly.

Devlin's golden eyes were all for me. "Can I take her from you?" he said seductively, glancing to Danial meaningfully.

"No," Danial replied just as meaningfully. "Wait your turn, Dalcon."

"Fine, Racklan," Devlin grinned. "I'll expect you to give her to me when the song ends." He stepped away to watch us from the edge of the dance floor, Titus beside him.

"What should I do?" I said worriedly. "I think his plan fell through. He was adamant that no one know about us."

"The most he'll do is get you out of here via Titus. He may be expecting an imminent attack. Follow his lead." The song ended, and Danial kissed my hand, then handed it to Devlin, who'd come up beside us. "One song," Danial said in a warning tone.

"I'll only need one," Devlin said arrogantly. My stomach twisted as he led me to the middle of the dance floor.

"There's no music," I hissed at him. "What are you doing, Dev?"

"Wait and see," he said with a wide smile, walking a little way off.

I turned from him, and began walking away. Abruptly, the orchestra started playing, and Devlin began to sing.

I turned back to him in utter horror, crimson from head to toe. There was no imminent attack. They were playing "Point of No Return" from Andrew Lloyd Webber's play, Phantom of the Opera.

"You've already succumbed to me, drop your defenses, completely succumb to me," Devlin sang, slowly stalking toward me.

I couldn't move. I couldn't think. I stood there, transfixed like a deer in headlights.

"Past all thought of 'if' or 'when,' no use resisting…"

I turned from him, looking for Danial. He was watching angrily, but only nodded to me. Devlin stopped singing, but the music went on. I took a deep breath and looked away from him, beginning to sing. My voice was clear and strong. All those lessons with Devlin had paid off.

"You have brought me to that moment where words run dry," I sang, looking at the ceiling as I tried to stop flushing. As the duet continued, I calmed, until at the last stanza I faced him confidently. "When will the flames at last consume us?"

Devlin's eyes were liquid gold, lust pouring off his body like water. As our voices joined, he pulled me close. "The bridge is crossed, so stand and watch it burn. We've passed the point of no return."

My heart was beating fast, his heart beating just as fast behind me. I trembled in his grip, remembering how he had felt just hours ago, what we had done together. The sweet smell of him was heady, intoxicating.

The orchestra began again softly.

Oh, shit…

"Say you'll share with me one love, one lifetime. Save me, lead me from my solitude," Devlin's melodious voice echoed in the silent room for everyone to hear. "Say you want me with you here beside you," he sang, turning me to look in my eyes. "Anywhere you go, let me go too. Sarelle, that's all I ask of you," he sang, a smile forming on his face as he finished. The orchestra stopped abruptly, and there was utter silence.

I looked at him standing there, so clearly pleased with himself, like the cat that ate the cream, and anger roared through me. With vengeful eyes, I took a deep breath and sang, "Pitiful creature of darkness, what kind of life have you known?"

His eyes went wide with shock, and it pleased me utterly, that he knew what was coming, and had no power, none at all, to stop me.

"God give me courage to show you, you are not alone." Grasping my courage with angry hands, I kissed Devlin with ravenous hunger. I drew back, a triumphant smile on my lips.

Devlin's eyes were melting pools of fire, and he was no longer smiling.

Danial's voice rang out. "Bravo! Bravo!" He was walking toward us quickly, and clapping loudly. Others followed his lead after a few seconds.

"Your performance was as wonderful as we planned," Danial lied smoothly. "My thanks again to you for your help in teaching my Oathed One to sing."

"The pleasure was all mine," Devlin said seductively.

"We must be going," Danial said, motioning to Terian, Theo and Brian. "It was—"

"Go?" A voice repeated in sarcasm. "You can go, if you wish." Perseus appeared at the crowd's edge. "Your son may also. But Sarelle is staying here."

Theo growled, and Terian put his hand on his gun.

"Come now," Samuel said, taking a stance beside Perseus. "We don't need to upset anyone."

"Yes," Zane said, coming to stand on Perseus's other side. "Perhaps we do."

Danial faced them. "Is there some problem?" he said almost casually. "We have been more than generous with our time—"

"Yes," Perseus said curtly. "We have seen the miracle you have worked with Sarelle, this child that is half human and half vampire. We knew that she could no longer have children. Because of that, we were content for her to live out her life as she saw fit."

Damn Stephen and his medical papers.

"We know now that she can again bear children. We do not intend to let her waste herself with a were."

Theo snarled at that insult. Both Terian and he took aim. Danial had not moved.

"It's not your business," I said loudly. "Who I'm with is my choice."

"You are Oathed to Danial, Sarelle," Samuel said, giving me a narrow look. "It is his choice, not yours."

Danial stepped in front of me protectively. "You are right, she is mine, Samuel, and I alone decide what is best for her. She has given me a child, made the impossible a reality I can touch and love. If I choose to let her have another man's child, or to have no more children, it is my choice and mine only. You have no say in it!"

"Danial," Samuel said cajolingly. "We need to have Sarelle try again, this time with a different vampire and to document everything. We need to know how it was done, why it worked with her where for hundreds of years it has failed. We need to know if it can work with a different vampire as the father."

This was worse than a nightmare. "You swore no harm would come to me," I said harshly. "How dare you stand there and tell me to break my Oath?"

"Danial will see the light to amend your Oath, I'm sure," Perseus said, matter of fact. "And so will you," Zane said with a suggestive smile in his dark eyes, "When you are beneath me."

I was shocked into silence, flushing.

"You three stand against me," Danial said calmly. "What say you, Michael?"

Michael, whom I had not met before, came forward calmly. He looked ordinary enough, with light brown hair and eyes, and a full beard. From him I got none of the excitement that seemed to surround all the other vampires here.

"I am here only because my position demands it," he said softly, his words clipped with some unfamiliar accent. "I have no interest in making my own dhamphir with her, if it is even possible to do a second time, which I truly don't believe." Michael looked disdainfully at Zane, Perseus and Samuel. "I abstain from the proceedings." He turned, and went back to whatever section of the room he had come from.

Zane, Perseus, and Samuel stood unmoving in a wall before Danial.

"I will not agree to this," Danial said, forcefully breaking the silence. "You have no right under our laws to take Sarelle from me, or force us to accept another man in our bed, one I do not authorize or invite, one which Sarelle refuses!"

"This child has changed the laws," Zane said in a low tone. "How can you be so selfish, to keep this gift for yourself alone?"

"She is only a human," Perseus said, eyeing me coldly. "Her wishes are not paramount."

"Stop," Samuel said, glaring at Perseus. "Sar, no one will harm you, and you may have anything you want, anything at all, if you do this for us. All we are asking for is a year of your life, maybe less. You want to be with Danial, fine, go back to him when it is done. You want your werecougar waiting for you when you return, it will be done. But you must do this for us."

"How dare you!" Danial shouted. "I am her Oathed One, and a Ruler of a country in my own right! The law is on my side, and even if it was not, I'd not let anyone touch one hair on her head without my permission. If one of you three tries to, you are dead!"

There was absolute silence. No one moved.

Samuel fixed Danial with a steely glare. "You do not have the power to stop us, Danial. And if you do not concede her, you will be the one who is dead."

Samuel looked at me, raw desire for what I could give him in his eyes. I braced for attack, my arms tightening around Theoron, who began to wail.

"You are forgetting Ebediah," a melodious voice said. "He has a say, as Canada's Ruler."

Devlin walked up, and stood directly in front of Samuel, a serene smile on his face.

"He is not here—" Samuel said, glancing over at him.

"Nor will he be!" Devlin said loudly, smirking. Samuel's mouth dropped open, but no words came out.

"You bastard," Perseus said, his eyes widening. "You'll burn for this!"

"You're bluffing, you has-been," Zane said, sneering. He took a step toward Devlin.

"Ah, now, you need to learn respect for your elders," Devlin said and shoved him. His blow sent Zane all the way across the room to crash into the wall. He stayed there, stunned, some of his bones clearly broken.

"You drained him," Samuel said, aghast. "You drained Ebediah."

"Him, and his lover," Devlin said, still grinning. "They were almost the same age."

Titus came up beside Danial, a ball of that glowing blue fire in each hand. Blackness engulfed me suddenly, as Theoron's wail became a scream of terror. A whip cracked unexpectedly, the crowd scrambling to get out of its path. Lash walked up to stand beside us, drawing his knife with his left hand.

I gaped at him. Where the hell was his gun? We faced vampires...

"You do not have enough power, even with what you stole from Ebediah and Sola," Perseus said through clenched teeth. "Not even you and Danial combined are a match for the three of us, especially with so few guards—"

Lash struck with his whip, making Perseus's guard at his side flinch backward, barely evading the whistling leather.

"You may be number one, but that doesn't mean much," Perseus said, baring his fangs at Lash. "I have fifty guards here, some of them flanking you as we speak—"

Lash turned in a smooth motion and threw his knife. It hit a large man square in the chest. He began shrieking, black blood pouring from the wound, then collapsed.

"Anyone else?" Lash hissed in the dead quiet. He went to the twitching body, then pulled out the knife. The body began to collapse in on itself, eerie blue flames slowly eating it from within. The crowd moved back quickly, leaving Perseus and Samuel standing alone before us.

"Do you want a war, Samuel?" Devlin said, his words a caress. "It's true you may take her if you attack in mass. But you know me. You know that won't be the end of it!" He grew louder. "I'll be your enemy forever after! And I have so many other ways to get to you and more especially, those you love! Such as your sweet Olivia, back in Madrid? Or gentle Gwendolyn, or Beatrice? You want me to visit one of them some night, when she is alone, Samuel? Ah, the things I could do to her in just one night! And after, she would never be the same—"

"Enough!" Samuel shouted, his face white. "What do you propose, Devlin?"

"I lay claim to Sarelle," Devlin said, taking my hand. "I'll not share her with you!"

"You who've bedded countless women," Zane said painfully, as he walked to rejoin Samuel. "What concern is this of yours?"

"I am making it my concern," Devlin replied. "Though everyone else here cowers at your feet, I will not stand by and see evil done to innocents in my home domain." He glanced at me, then back to Samuel. "Someone must. It's time I was that someone again."

"You have no claim on her," Perseus said scathingly. "Probably no more claim than your brother has."

"I have drunk her blood, I have marked her, and I have lain with her," Devlin said, his voice echoing loudly. "I have more claim than any other vampire here, save Danial. Sarelle took an Oath to me as well. You would have her break that, by taking a vampire lover other than my brother and I. The Oath she took excludes all others, save us two."

There was a collective gasp, then muted conversations began all over the room.

"Sarelle, if what he says is true, say it now," Samuel said.

"It is true," I said defiantly.

"Is it true?" Samuel repeated.

"Yes," an aged voice said flatly from behind him. "She speaks the truth, and so does he."

"I will not be robbed of my prize—" Perseus snarled.

"I am not going to break the law," Samuel said, turning on him. "I recognize his claim."

"If she is Oathed to him, where is her choker with his symbol?" Perseus said, his eyes livid. "To be truly Oathed, she must always be wearing it while in the presence of other vampires—"

"Sarelle," Devlin said softly, glancing over at me. I stepped forward, and raised the hem of my dress, revealing his choker at my ankle. The emerald eyes of the bear sparkled in the light.

Samuel gritted his teeth, then let out a breath. "We recognize your right to Sarelle, Devlin. You may try to have a child with her, and we will not interfere. You have one year."

"Then someone else will try," Perseus added.

"No one else will try with Sar, ever, save me and my brother, unless we give permission for it," Devlin retorted, his eyes completely red. "You will agree to that, here and now. There will be no breaking of the law, or amending it either."

"If we do not agree?" Samuel said, his eyes full red.

"Then it will be war, and though you may bring us down, we will destroy you as well," Devlin declared. "I swear it!"

"It will be war," Perseus said, not backing down. "She is the only one who can—"

"No, she is not," Devlin said. There was another collective gasp.

"The key to her success is her resistance to the vampire virus that lives in our bodies," Devlin continued loudly. "She is not the only one, though women like her are rare. I know this as I knew a woman centuries ago, Anna, who was like Sarelle is. This resistance can be determined by her blood, which will taste unusually sweet. I call it the taste of spring. Find such a woman, and expose her to demon blood. When her blood turns even richer, matures from spring to summer, then she will be ready to bring forth a dhamphir."

Conversations again started, some of them loud and excited.

"How do you know all this?" Samuel said, amazed.

"I have a brain," Devlin said scathingly. "I can reason that this is the way, from what I have seen and what I know was done. Other women must exist; it is only a question of who will find them first—"

"I know of a woman, my Lords!" a voice cried out loudly, over the others. "My Harriet is such a woman."

Perseus turned immediately toward the voice, and strode off toward the crowd, Samuel and Zane following.

"Well, that went well," Devlin said, turning to Danial.

"How the hell did you kill Ebediah?" Danial said, incredulous.

Devlin ignored him and came over to me. "Miss me?" he said teasingly. "I have missed you, Love."

Theo growled, his eyes light yellow.

"Upstairs to my rooms," Danial said. "We can talk better there."

Chapter Nineteen

Devlin and Danial strode into the hotel room, talking loudly. I followed them with Theoron. Brian, wanting no part of this, stayed outside with Terian.

"Why didn't you tell me you had taken Ebediah's blood? Why didn't you tell us what you were planning?" Danial asked angrily.

"I knew what was going to happen here, and I knew I had to be powerful, knew that I had to be strong enough to protect Sar. You weren't going to do it," Devlin said sarcastically. "I'd be surprised if our secret isn't out now, Brother." He chuckled. "That or they'll think you're bi."

"Very funny," Danial said angrily. "Our kinship's not a concern, or less of one anyway. It was bound to come out before long with all the attention we've been getting."

"On the contrary, it's a shared weakness," Devlin cautioned. "What is Theo's position? Is he leaving your employ or not?"

"I'd like him left alone," Danial said with a grimace. "He's staying; I'm not sure for how long."

"We have the advantage, but it's only momentary," Devlin cautioned. "We need to decide on a plan—"

The door burst open, and Theo came in, his eyes light yellow slits. He walked up to Devlin and punched him in the jaw, knocking him to the floor.

Devlin picked himself up. He grinned at Theo, baring his fangs. "Theo," he said evilly. "Come to thank me for saving your life?"

"So you were Sar's lover," Theo growled, still glaring at Devlin. "I'm surprised Danial shared her with you, but I know that he liked to share women with you sometimes in the past. I'm surprised she let you touch her." He gave a bitter smile. "I'm not sure how you fooled them into thinking she'd ever promise herself to you. That must've been your demon's spell."

Theo clearly thought Devlin had been my lover sometime in the years he'd been separated from me. I resisted the urge to correct him.

"This explains a lot," Theo continued. "Why you brought her flowers sometimes, why you took those bullets for her, and why you went to save her that night she was taken." He smiled sarcastically. "You must have been pissed off when she and Danial split up and she married me. So much for your being irresistible."

"I Oathed to Dev a few days ago," I said scathingly. "As for us being lovers, that's been going on a while. My only regret is that I didn't say yes from the first."

Devlin glanced at me in surprise. Danial rubbed his forehead in irritation.

"You slut," Theo shouted, rounding on me. "I suppose all those Saturdays at Danial's were really orgies—!"

"That did not happen, Cougar," Devlin said coldly. "Sar has been sick, no thanks to you. Now that she's well, she'll be moving on with her life." He took my hand. "Go back to your child lover, where you belong."

Theo glared at me. "He tried to kill you and you're letting him fuck you."

Devlin's patience snapped. "She came for me all night, Theo," he said silkily. "We've been having quite a time while you've been away. Don't you think that her eyes as she climaxes are the most beautiful green you've ever seen?"

Theo turned in a murderous rage, screamed once, and launched himself at Devlin. Devlin caught Theo easily, and held him, his fingers like a vise around Theo's neck, holding him off the ground. Theo thrashed and roared, but couldn't get free.

Devlin bared his fangs, his eyes almost glowing. "Theo, you have many failings I could call to your attention. But the best is what you just heard; that if Sar could go back, she'd have started with me instead of you. You must be truly awful."

"Fuck you," Theo growled, his eyes yellow.

"Don't fuck with me, Theo," Devlin said, his eyes turning from gold back to reddish gold. "You'll end up dead. You exist on my good graces, as you always have."

"I should have killed you there on the great room floor, years ago," Theo snarled.

"You've never been too bright," Devlin said, nodding. He threw Theo to the ground. "Now get out, or face not only my wrath, but Lash's."

Theo got to his feet, shot me an angry glance, then left.

"He'll be gone before the week is out," Danial said sadly. "You've humiliated him."

"I'm sorry," Devlin said quietly. "He pissed me off."

"He pissed me off, too," I said regretfully. "I should've stayed quiet."

"What's done is done," Devlin said, hugging me. "I'm glad of your decisiveness, Love. I've never liked dealing with Theo. This will make things easier."

"It will," I agreed. "You're right; we should make some kind of plan. The Rulers are going to expect a child sometime in the coming year. We need to come up with something to tell them—"

"We don't have to worry about that," Devlin said. "We'll have a child by then to show off ourselves."

I gaped at him, my face whitening. "What?"

"As for a plan, I have one," Devlin continued. "I've much to do here, both in building up some provincial Rulers I can trust, and figuring out Ebediah's governing system. That will keep me very occupied until late Spring. Danial, you'll also be busy getting Solutions, Inc. back on track, not to mention hiring a replacement for Theo—"

Danial nodded.

"—Sar can spend some time with you and some time at Hayden with me. Now that she can teleport, there's not so much worry about her needing to be guarded. Still, we should have at least two guards with her at all times—"

"I didn't say yes," I said loudly, backing away from both of them with Theoron in my arms. "I didn't say yes to another dhamphir."

Devlin crossed to me. "You've heard my proposal. What do you say?"

"I don't want to be clawed up again, Devlin," I said with trepidation. "Another dhamphir baby might kill me."

"Sar, if there is any danger to you, we'll abort the child," Devlin said flatly. "I'll not risk your life, even to have a child of my own. I promise you that."

I didn't reply.

"Will you try with me?" Devlin said, both hopeful and fearful.

"Do I have a choice?" I said with a ghost of a smile.

"You always have a choice with me," Devlin replied, his eyes on me. "Truthfully, I wish you had more of one. But I realistically know that if you had more of a choice, you would not even consider this."

"That day, when I asked you what you wanted of me—"

"Yes," he replied. "I told you the truth, Sar, as I said I did."

"Remember, she is Oathed to both of us," Danial said warily. "There is going to be time in her life for me as well as you."

"Stay your jealousy, brother," Devlin said, rolling his eyes. "It is your symbol around her neck, not mine. It was you in her bed, not me, your child she holds in her arms. I wanted her to come to me then, but she stayed with you. I am the one who has been jealous all this time."

Danial gave me a satisfied look, but didn't reply.

I faced Devlin, realization dawning. "You planned this all. Everything from my rescue from Alphonse to Oathing me."

"Of course," Devlin said arrogantly. "Rescues work best when they are planned, Love. Samuel's plan was obvious. Getting into position where I could use the law to entrap him was the hardest."

"What about me?" I said, my eyes filling. "How much of this is you getting what you want, and now much is really you loving me?"

I expected denials or vows of love, and got neither. Devlin exploded with anger. "Damn you! How can you say that, think that, after all I've done for you?"

"You asked me once if I knew what you were capable of. I know well, Dev. Anyone who could pull off what you did tonight could easily do it. This worked out too neatly—"

"It was not neat," Devlin said coldly. "This has been bloody, and above all, highly costly. Do you know how many men I lost taking Ebediah? I needed to have him taken alive, Sar, unharmed, so I could take his blood. I sent my ten best men with Lash and Titus, and only three returned. They'll live, but only because they're were, and Titus healed the worst wounds. The others are dead. Some had been with me their entire adult lives." His eyes bored into mine. "It's true that I wanted to be a Vampire Ruler again, but by taking Ebediah's place, I now have to deal with all of the problems of being Master of a territory again. Between that and repairing Hayden—"

"What is wrong at Hayden?" Danial interrupted. "Titus and Leri were supposed to be staying there—"

"Staying there and fighting," Devlin spat out. "Mostly it was Leri, or at least that's what Titus says. In any case, a roomful of my favorite crystal and glass sculptures are shards, along with most of the furnishings, not to mention structural repairs. There are also several trees down—"

"You have Ebediah's men now," Danial said, coming to put his hand on his brother's shoulder. "His bears should be of help."

"True," Devlin said with a faint smile. "What's left of them, anyway."

"I'm sorry," I said hesitantly. "I didn't know about your men."

"All is not troubles, and problems," Danial said gently. He gave Devlin's shoulder a squeeze, then turned away, taking Theoron into the other room. "Sar has agreed, Dev."

Devlin blinked. "She said nothing."

"I know her," Danial said from the other room. "She didn't have to say the words."

Devlin hugged me tightly. "Is he right?"

"He's right," I whispered back.

"Then stop taking the pill tonight," Devlin commanded. "There is no need for you to be on it now."

"I haven't all week," I said, blushing. "Not since I found out about Tasha."

Devlin groaned. "I'd give so much to go with you and Danial this evening. But there's no way. I'm host of this Gathering, for whatever that's worth. Also the worst of Ebediah's tangled affairs will have to be settled before returning home."

"You know where I live," I said, giving him a wan smile. "Call me."

"I'll be with you as soon as I can," he promised.

"I'll be waiting." I leaned up to kiss him.

I intended a gentle kiss, full of good things to come. Instead, Devlin kissed me as if this was the last kiss we would ever share, and he wanted me to know in no uncertain terms everything he felt for me. It was lust, love, longing, passion, and complete abandonment to sensation, everything we were, and had been to each other, all in a single kiss.

Devlin broke the kiss, looked down into my eyes, and smiled, pleased. "Your eyes are so dark, Sar. Dark and deep as an untouched, ancient forest."

I gave him a wide smile back. "If you had any more heat in yours, Dev, I'd be ashes where I stood."

"Sar, we have got to go, or we won't make it back before dawn," Danial said, poking his head out from our bedroom. "We have five minutes to dress, and pack. Dev, you should leave."

"I could help you change," Devlin purred, his hands sliding over my dress to unzip the back.

"No way," I said, slapping his hand away. "Or I'll never be ready in five minutes." I went into my bedroom, where Danial helped me out of the dress.

"Why do you get to be in there and I'm out here?" Devlin called playfully through the door.

"Because I can be trusted not to take advantage," Danial said, just as playfully.

I slipped into some jeans and a pullover sweatshirt, grabbed my bags and Theoron, and followed Danial out to Devlin.

He took one look at me, and shook his head. "You are mine now, not Danial's, so far as every vampire is concerned. Take off his symbol, and put mine where it belongs."

Danial nodded. "He is right, Sar. Exchange them."

I undid my choker with Danial's symbol, and put it around my right ankle. Then I undid the choker of Devlin's, and fastened it around my neck.

"Good," Devlin said, gratified. "Go, Love," he said, hugging me one last time. "I'll see you in a week at most, a few days if possible."

* * * *

Hours later, we disembarked back in America. As we were walking toward Aran and the waiting Expedition, Danial grasped my arm. "Brian, Terian, go on to the SUV."

With one last glower at me, Terian left holding Theoron, Brian following.

"Are you sorry, now that you've had time to think?" Danial asked.

"This ended the best way it could have, considering what they wanted of me, and what they would have done to get it."

"But you are the one who will pay the price, Sar," Danial said. "You hadn't expressed interest in more children, at least to me."

"I don't know what I want," I said absently. "Everything's changed in this last week. I've changed."

"Nothing that's happened changes that you are the woman I love and the mother of my child," he said, drawing me into his arms. "You are still Sar."

I hugged him, but didn't reply.

He let me go. "Terian will teleport us, while Aran takes you home. Take a few days off, Sarelle. You are right, you need some time."

* * * *

Aran didn't speak until he'd pulled into my driveway. "You're wearing Devlin's symbol, but Danial's not upset. Is it true you're Oathed to them both?"

"Yes," I said, fingering the tiny bear pendant.

"Cia and I scented him in your house," Aran said, blushing slightly. "We'd hoped it was by your invitation."

"It was," I assured him. "Thanks for watching over my pets."

"Theo is my friend," he said suddenly. "Or he was, until this woman showed up yesterday."

I explained Theo's dalliance with Aspen and Tasha, then got out. "We were wrong about him."

"Then it's better he's leaving," Aran said with regret. "I can't take orders from someone I don't respect. See you."

"See you."

He honked once, the sound echoing in the early dawn, then drove off.

My pets steamrolled me as soon as I opened the door. After forcing myself to feed everyone, I ate some cereal, watching the sunrise. The sun was just coming up over the trees then, trying to burn off the fog that was rising from the creek near the road. It would have been pretty if I hadn't felt so bad.

Despondent, I locked up, then went downstairs. Undressing, I got into bed and tried unsuccessfully to sleep.

What would happen now? I didn't want to bear Devlin's child, even though I loved him. But what choice did I have? What would the living arrangements really be in the weeks to come? Worst of all how long would it be until Theo arrived to get his things, Tasha in tow?

I lay there a long time before sleep came.

Chapter Twenty

Theo was walking toward me, trying to tell me something. We were back in Casper. I walked closer to him, but I couldn't make out what he was saying. Then he suddenly turned, and began running. I ran after him, chasing down the street to the corner.

"Theo!" I shouted.

He didn't turn, didn't stop, and as he crossed the street, a car ran him down.

"Theo!" I ran to his side. He was trying to speak, but he was covered in blood. He reached for me, and then slumped, his head lolling back as his eyes glazed.

"Theo!"

"Wake up!" Someone shook me hard. "Wake up, Sar."

I blinked my eyes. My heart was beating fast. I was covered in nervous sweat. And Theo was here, very much alive, holding me in his arms.

The first tears slid down my face as I struggled in his grip. "Let me go."

"You're okay," he soothed. "It was a nightmare."

"You were dead," I got out, rattled.

"Shh," he said softly. "I'm right here, alive and well. God, I thought you were in trouble. I broke the front door down getting in."

Anguish hit me. Theo was here for his stuff. I pushed him away, aware of my nudity. "I'm sorry."

He put his gun away, then handed me a robe. "So what did me in?"

I fastened it around me. "A car."

"A car wouldn't kill me. Maybe a tractor trailer—"

"Stop being morbid," I said angrily. "It's not funny. I was terrified."

"It's good to know I meant something to you," he said gruffly, his eyes narrowing. "At least enough that you'd cry over me if I died."

"Stop," I said, looking away. "I don't want to fight with you."

241

He sighed. "I don't want to fight either, Sar...elle," he finished quickly. "I'm just here for my things."

"Give me a minute to put some clothes on."

* * * *

Within the space of an hour, Theo packed all of his things in his truck. While he did, I stood and watched, unsure of what else to do.

"That's everything," he said, coming over and handing me his key. "I'm sorry for how things happened. I didn't want this to end this way."

"I'm sorry, too," I replied with tears in my eyes. "I didn't want us to end."

He pulled me roughly into his arms, holding me tight. "Sar, I love you. It's killing me to do this—"

"Then don't do it!" I cried out. "Don't leave! No one is making you—!"

"Sar, I have to—"

"You don't have to," I said bitterly. "You are choosing to, because that's easier than sharing me."

Theo drew back from me and went to the door, pausing. "I don't have to share Tasha with anyone. Take care of yourself."

As the sound of his tires receded, I began to sob, my tight hold on my anguish dissolving completely. This was it. We were over.

About the Author

Tara Fox Hall's writing credits include nonfiction, horror, suspense, action-adventure, erotica, and contemporary and historical paranormal romance. She is the author of the paranormal action-adventure *Lash* series and the vampire romantic suspense *Promise Me* series. Tara divides her free time unequally between writing novels and short stories, chainsawing firewood, caring for stray animals, sewing cat and dog beds for donation to animal shelters, and target practice.

Other works by the author with Melange Books, LLC

Return To Me
Surrender to Me
The Origin of Fear in Spellbound 2011 Anthology
Night Music in Midnight Thirsts II Anthology
Partners in Midnight Thirsts II Anthology
Kink in Wicked Christmas Wishes Anthology
The Oath in Wicked Christmas Wishes Anthology
Bedtime Shadows Anthology
Make Me Behave Anthology
Latham's Landing, An Anthology

The Promise Me Series
Promise Me, Book 1
Broken Promise, Book 2
Taken in the Night, Book 3
Taken for his Own, Book 4
Promise Me Anthology, Book 4.5
Immortal Confessions, Book 5

Coming Soon
Point of No Return, Book 7 of the Promise Me Series